ISBN 978-0-578-56749-5

A.S.GUINN

Notes

A.S.GUINN

ETERNAL KNIGHTS OF EDEN II

Notes

ETERNAL KNIGHTS OF EDEN

ANGELS FALL

CHAPTER 1

THE STORY CONTINUES

[The forests of the Alliance of Pandora. Present Day]

The Nekomata named Nyuralisiania dives and dashes through the brush on the forest floor as tree bark explodes all around her. She hunkers down silently in the underbrush, trying to get eyes on her attacker.

Six months ago, Nyu returned to the forests of her birth when she had gotten wind of trouble brewing in the west. Not long after the Elmeri declared a biohazardous disaster to be averted, unusually high numbers of corrupted beasts began appearing in Pandora.

This is not normally be considered unusual, but they are appearing much further north than normal. After receiving a letter from her cousin (one of the only people in her homeland who would speak to her after her mother left the country) describing the anomaly, Nyu decided to return to her homeland for the first time in many years.

Now she is in her current predicament. As she peers through the brush, hunter's instinct telling her to stay low and still, she catches sight of her attacker.

A Nekonoshini Queen.

Nyu observes her quarry carefully and notices that she doesn't look quite right. She is larger than she should be, and her features seem distorted. Nyu doesn't have much if any experience on the subject, but if she had to guess, this would be a corrupted beast.

The big cat's lightning magic was also substantially more powerful than normal. Nyu had dealt with a handful of Nekoshin in her time as a hunter, but she had never met one that could cast powerful magic in quick succession like the one before her. She momentarily deliberates attempting to flee, but then she reasons that outrunning this native beast is unlikely. Her only remaining option is to fight.

In front of her, the Nekoshin Queen slowly prowls in a circle, sensing her prey remains nearby. Nyu patiently waits until the cat's back is turned, and jumps up, casting a wind-blade through the air as she jumps up and lunges forward.

The spiritual wind-blade attack screams past the Nekoshin and slices through a tree. The oversized cat turns to the falling tree, distracted momentarily from its prey.

As the Nekoshin is distracted by the splintered tree, Nyu simultaneously buries her bladed-spear deep in the Nekoshin's side, channeling a wind-burst through her spear on impact.

It is at this moment that Nyu realizes she had misjudged this cat's size. A normal Nekoshin Queen is around eight feet long nose-to-rump and five feet at the shoulder, with variable tail lengths depending on sub-species. She had thought this queen was only slightly bigger than normal.

She now realizes she was wrong.

This corrupted queen was twelve feet nose-to-rump, and at least six and a half feet tall. She was massive.

Nyu's attack successfully blows a small chunk of flesh from the side of the great cat, but as it slowly turns its head and glares back at her, she realizes she is in desperately over her head.

Nyu pulls her blade out and delivers a quick series of rapid slashes before backflipping away. She moves just in time.

The great cat delivers a massive swipe with a paw the size of a small child, and claws like small swords. The claws miss Nyu by less than an inch.

She is not so lucky with the lightning bleed-off. She feels a surge of energy pulse through her body, locking her up for a moment and making her land flat on her face.

She twitches a couple of times, stunned by the shock and subsequent impact on the forest floor. She opens her eyes and rolls to the side just in time to avoid a heavy paw coming down on top of her.

She finds herself underneath the Nekoshin Queen, and instinctively attempts to thrust her spear from underneath. The Queen is too close to get an effective hit, but she manages to cut her enough to rear her head back.

Nyu sees her opportunity and rolls back, kicking the cat in the raised chin as hard as she can manage. The impact causes her to take several heavy steps back, giving Nyu a clean shot. She thrusts her spear forward, burying it deep in the cat's neck. A wind-strike burst leaves a severe wound where she stabbed the great beast.

Nyu's mistake was assuming the beast would go down. The Nekoshin Queen recovers from this attack almost instantly. She lowers her head, dislodging the spear, and roars in Nyu's face, hitting her with over one-million volts of lightning in the process.

Nyu is picked up from the ground and hurled twelve feet away into the side of a tree. Her eyes bulge as the wind is knocked from her lungs and she feels ribs crack. When she hits the ground, she struggles to remember how to breathe for a moment. Her muscles are not responding from the lightning attack.

She feels the heavy paws thundering on the ground, and closes her eyes, unable to do anything to defend herself, and accepting her fate.

Suddenly, seemingly out of nowhere, a barrage of wind-bursts and spirit blasts slam into the great cat in mid-air, sending her landing on her back and stunning her for a moment.

A female voice speaks from close-by "Nekomata. Are you okay?"

Nyu opens her eyes and is shocked to see a Junmeri woman kneeling next to her. She helps Nyu sit up as she responds "Oh, umm. Yes. Thank you."

ETERNAL KNIGHTS OF EDEN II

Nyu spots a second Junmeri woman perched above them on a tree branch with an Elmeri sword in her hand. She looks down "Introductions later. Can you help us kill this abomination?"

Nyu pushes herself to her feet, grateful for the sudden appearance of the Junmeri huntresses. "Yeah. I'm good."

The first woman nods and stands up. Curiously, she does not appear to be carrying a weapon. She calls out "I'll keep her destabilized, and you two move in and finish her off. Her aura is fading. The Nekomata did a good job wearing her down. Let's help her finish it."

Nyu nods and readies her spear, somehow miraculously still in her hand. Her new partner in the tree tenses up to lunge forward.

As the Nekoshin shakes its head and climbs to its feet, the unarmed Junmeri stretches her arms out, and a glow envelops her arms and legs. Suddenly, she spins and twirls through the air as if dancing. As she does this, a barrage of fireballs streak out from her as she dances.

The Junmeri with the sword waits a split second, and dashes forward just as the fireballs hit the Nekoshin queen in the face and explode, knocking the great cat off its feet once again. She strikes the downed cat with a series of heavy sword strikes infused with ice magic, leaving multiple deep ragged gouge marks in the beast.

The cat manages to lash out with a giant paw, striking the Junmeri woman with enough force to send her airborne.

Nyu doesn't waste any time and hurls herself straight up into the tree. She leaps across the branches until she is right above the Nekoshin, and then grabs onto the branch. She spins herself around the branch several times before hurling herself even further into the air. At the apex of her jump, she gracefully backflips and aims herself straight down.

The Nekoshin looks up just in time to see Nyu drop down onto her from fifty feet in the air. The resulting impact drives Nyu's bladed spear through its neck and into the ground. Her aim was true, and she cleanly severed the beast's spine.

The great corrupted cat is so stubborn that, in spite of medical impossibility, it seems as if it may continue fighting for a moment. Nyu holds her weight on her spear, wondering for a moment just what it would take to kill this thing, but a second later, the great cat falls limp.

Nyu pulls her spear and runs over to the Junmeri who took the hit. When she reaches her, however, she finds her already climbing to her feet. She feels a great sense of relief as she asks, "Are you okay?"

The Junmeri nods "Yes, I am uninjured. Thank you."

The Junmeri mage reaches them about this same time "I am glad to see you both unharmed. Nekomata, what is your name?"

Nyu looks over and bows politely "I am Nyuralisiania, though most just call me Nyu. A pleasure to meet you."

The mage places and arm across her chest and bows in return. "Greetings, Nyuralisiania. I am Varofia, and my sword wielding companion is Hancer."

Nyu notes the non-Elmeri name of the second woman and asks, "Are you with the Ceraph Order, by any chance?"

Varofia shakes her head "No, we are simple huntresses from the nearby village of Children's Oasis. We were actually curious about the same, seeing as you do not appear to be native."

Nyu tilts her head, cat-like ear twitching indignantly "What do you mean, I do not appear to be native?"

Hancer actually answers her "You do not seem to hear the forest. You walk as if you are deaf to the world around you. It is a sign you have left the forests and joined the outside."

Nyu's ears flatten against her head sadly, and her tail lowers in shame "It is true. My mother fled from here when I was a small girl, and I am only now returning to my homeland."

Varofia nods, a suspicious or perhaps even disdainful look upon her face "So what brings you back here, after all this time? Outcasts do not typically return here once they had left."

Nyu continues to look ashamed "I never really knew my homeland. Nonetheless, when I heard of the complications with corrupted incursions being so much more frequent than normal, I could not contain my curiosity. I had to come home and find the truth for myself."

Hancer and Varofia exchange meaningful looks, before Varofia responds in a softer tone. "I see. It is not, after all, your fault that your mother took you away from here as a child. Perhaps you are not an outcast after all. Perhaps you are simply a lost kitten finding her way back home."

Nyu's ears perk up as she hears the change in Varofia's tone.

Varofia finishes "You felt the call of your homeland, and you answered it, returning to the place you lost. You may just be welcome here yet, child."

Nyu looks up, feeling slightly more cheerful now. "Thank you, Varofia."

Varofia nods and changes the subject "You are indeed correct about the corrupted incursions. We do not typically see corrupted up this far north, and certainly not in the numbers we have been seeing. This change, I fear, is a sign of some great evil that does not belong here. The forest speaks to us, and she tells us she is sick. But she does not know the source, and so we spend our time searching, hoping to uncover the source of the illness ailing our great mother."

Nyu raises her eyebrows slightly at the unusual way these Junmeri speak. She mumbles to herself "Man, these forest people are kind of weird."

Nyu jumps as Hancer replies to her muttered statement "We may be strange to you, but we revere the great forest and the spirit that watches over it. We have always known the forest, and she is like our own mother."

Nyu bows and apologizes profusely "I'm sorry, I did not mean to be rude."

Hancer waves her hand dismissively "Your ignorance gives me no offense. You speak your truth, after all. To you, who was raised around the people of Alastair, we must indeed be quite strange."

Nyu nods and coughs "Actually, there is another reason I came back here. Perhaps you may be able to help me?"

        A.S.GUINN

Varofia nods her head and replies "If we can assist in an honorable endeavor, then of course, stray one. What do you need?"

Nyu feels a sense of relief as she asks "I have heard of a temple that is sacred to my people that exists in this region. Dedicated to an ancient feline spirit that has been hailed as our guardian deity. My mother spoke of this temple quite often, and I wish to see it while I make my way to the village of my birth."

Varofia looks at Nyu with more curiosity now "Ahh, you seek the Temple of Tau?"

Nyu nods nervously and asks, "Would you be able to help me find it?"

Varofia shakes her head "Not now, stray one. We will return to our village tonight, where you are welcome to come as our guest. You are strong, to be sure, but I find it highly unlikely that you would survive for long in these forests alone. Come and share dinner with us and meet our village elder. She will teach you about our ways that you will need to make it in the forest, and if she deems you worthy? She may choose to reveal the temple of Tau to you."

Nyu flattens her ears nervously "And if she judges me unworthy?"

Varofia lowers her head "Then you will be escorted back to the Alastair border, where you would be unwise to return to our lands."

Nyu lowers her head and glares slightly at Varofia "Why couldn't I just take my chances if she dislikes me?"

Varofia shakes her head again "It is not a question of whether she likes you or not. This great forest is alive, my dear kitten. If you aren't worthy, and the forest does not accept your presence, then the very forest itself will seek to stop your progress. It is all but certain that you would be dead within two solar cycles. However, your progress thus far gives me hope that perhaps you could be accepted by our great mother."

Nyu narrows an eye, ears still flat against her head "I was nearly killed by a lone Nekonoshini. How is that a good sign?"

Hancer speaks up "A corrupted Nekonoshini. There is a great difference here. The corrupted beasts do not obey the will of the forest. Had a natural inhabitant of the forest bested you, our opinion would be different. There is no shame to losing to these unnatural demon-beasts."

Nyu relaxes her ears and nods, understanding their reaction to her somewhat now. "I see. That actually makes a lot of sense. Very well, I will join you for dinner. Teach me about my homeland that I have never known."

Varofia and Hancer exchange nods, and Varofia waves her along "I would be pleased to escort you to our village, stray one. Although an outsider like you may never fully embrace the forest as one who has always dwelled here, it is always a pleasure to teach those who are open minded to respect the forest."

Nyu nods silently as she follows the Junmeri huntresses through the forest towards their village. The two women fall silent as well, moving swiftly but silently through a path in the undergrowth. Nyu realizes just how noisily she moves and breathes when compared with the astoundingly silent movements of the two huntresses. As she hears her own footsteps, she feels a sense of amazement that she didn't find more trouble on her way here.

After two hours of travel through the undergrowth, they come up to a great wall of trees, packed so tightly together that they have begun to grow into each other. A large gap lies directly in their path, and the two huntresses lead Nyu towards it.

Varofia suddenly tilts her head back and makes an odd, loud chirping sound which echoes back from somewhere ahead.

As they reach the archway in the tree wall, Nyu observes multiple people in the trees above her, so well concealed that she would have never noticed them if she hadn't been looking for them.

Varofia walks through the archway and steps aside, waving her hand in a sweeping motion as if presenting something.

Nyu walks through the archway, and her jaw promptly drops in shock.

Children's Oasis is not the run down, quaint, primitive village she had been expecting. With the walls of a great circle of trees, the village was elaborate and beautiful. Literally hundreds of wooden huts lined the forest floor, ranging from small dwellings to shops and market stands. Above her, a spiderweb of catwalks link hundreds of tree-mounted shacks at various levels. And most astounding of all, hundreds of Nekomata and Junmeri populate the streets and catwalks around her. She looks around with her mouth open in shock and awe.

Hancer smiles at the young Nekomata's reaction "I'm going to guess, young one, that this was not what you were expecting?"

Nyu just shakes her head.

Varofia bows slightly and says "Nyuralisiania, welcome to Children's Oasis."

A moment later, a huge explosion occurs on the road behind where they came in. Varofia and Hancer ready their weapon, and Nyu spins around and groans "Oh, what now!?"

Someone outside the gate yells "BEHEMOTH!"

Hancer turns her head to Nyu "Could we trouble you for your assistance once more, young one?"

Nyu spins her spear around and nods "Bring it on, you big ugly bastard!" Lunging out of the archway.

*　　*　　*

[Half a continent away in Alastair]
Seventeen-year-old Reno Coltide sits in the troop barracks of the ARV *Stalwart Sentry*, looking at a hand of cards in front of him. To his right, Rayn Jarvis has his cards laying in front of him, looking bored, and to his left, Sergeant Garland looks at the young soldier, his face expressionless.

Reno lays out his cards nervously "Two pair."

Sergeant Garland nods, seemingly satisfied. "Not a bad hand, but..." he lays out his cards. "full house is better."

Reno groans as Garland take his money "I should have known better..."

Reno Coltide and his squad are currently onboard the Alastair warship *Stalwart Sentry* as part of a frigate wolfpack enroute to the city of Iron Veil. Similar to Broadspring, Iron Veil is a gateway city separating the civilized northern Alastair from the wilder southern reaches.

ETERNAL KNIGHTS OF EDEN II

Now third years in the Alastair Royal Military Academy, or ARMA, Reno and his class are being assigned to operate in Iron Veil for two months as part of an extended training mission. They will be operating alongside fellow Alastair military forces not as students, but as fellow soldiers.

Sergeant Garland shakes his head and grins "I think we're done, kid. I don't want to take ALL of your money, after all."

Reno grumbles unhappily, but he doesn't argue.

Rayn stands up and claps Reno on the back "Hey dude. Let's get some air."

Reno nods, gets to his feet, and follows Rayn out of the ship's barracks and into the hangar bay. When they arrive, Reno glances at the dropships and gunships lined up in the middle of the spacious compartment. He grins when he remembers Shaide's interest in any kind of ship. He almost doesn't notice two of their friends standing near the partially open hangar bay doors.

Celeste Wyatt leans against the pillar separating two of the drop doors, looking rather cool and disinterested. Her long white hair is pulled back in a ponytail, and her fair skin and ice blue eyes stand out against the industrial wall behind her. Wearing simple shorts and a tunic, in rather blatant disregard for uniform regulations. Reno's eyes are drawn to Celeste's rather ample bosom for a moment before he looks away.

Lania Howler sits cross legged on the floor of the hangar in a lightweight chain armor, her brown hair blowing gently around her face as her brown eyes survey the plains beneath them. The poor girl hasn't grown at all over the past two years, and as a result she still looks like she is fourteen. Nevertheless, she is a skilled support mage, and her proficiency with both support and healing magic has made her squad's life significantly easier.

The two girls look up as Rayn and Reno approach. Rayn for his part, is now a remarkably handsome young man, standing near six feet tall with a lean figure. He's a rapier specialist, so he has worked hard to maintain his agility, His wavy brown hair and green eyes are a source of distraction for the girls of the academy sometimes.

Reno stands in stark contrast to his squad. Shorter than Rayn, Reno has the build of a lumberjack. Heavily muscled and mildly overweight, he is a rather imposing sight to behold. Right now, he is wearing his casual uniform, but when he is in full plate armor, carrying a kite shield and a broadsword, his appearance can be rather frightening.

"Hey guys. Want to join us?" Lania indicates the deck beside her.

Reno shrugs and walks over to join her, sitting down on the deck and looking at the ARV *North Star* to the starboard side.

"What brings you guys to the hangar?" Celeste asks.

"Reno got tired of losing his money to sarge." Rayn replies with a smirk

Reno growls and mumbles "I could have won it all back…"

Lania, Rayn, and Celeste all break out laughing as Reno leans back on his palms with a reluctant grin.

Reno changes the subject "So, Celeste. How did your date go the other day?"

Celeste raises her eyebrows. "I blew him off." She replies indifferently.

"Seriously?" Reno asks, "That seems kind of…rude."

Celeste shrugs "Doesn't matter. I wasn't really interested anyway."

Lania grins "She likes someone else anyway."

"I don't like him, like him." Celeste rolls her eyes "I just recognize his reasonable attractiveness. That's all."

Reno's eyes dart between them, curiosity written all over his face.

Lania catches his expression and chuckles "Don't worry. It doesn't concern you."

He pouts but chooses not to argue.

Rayn leans against the pillar next to Celeste "Seeing that frigate brings back memories."

"Yeah, it does for me, too." Lania says with a nod "We went on our very first field exercise on that ship. A lot happened back then."

Reno gets lost in thought. *Yeah, I remember that ship. That was the last time Shaide and I were classmates. Now I barely see him anymore.*

Lania catches sight of Reno's face. "Is everything okay, Reno?"

Reno jumps when she addresses him. "Oh, yeah, I'm fine. Just lost in thought."

"I miss having him around too, Reno." Rayn says with a sigh "But he has his own path he has to follow. At least he makes sure to come see us sometimes, right?"

"Yeah, I guess that's true." Reno sighs "But I still miss having my best friend around sometimes."

After a brief silence, "What do you think we'll be doing when we get to Iron Veil?" Celeste wonders aloud.

Rayn contemplates her question for a moment. "I'm not really sure. This isn't a typical training mission. We're going there to operate as real soldiers."

"I hope we get assigned to something with a lot of fighting." Celeste says rather wistfully. "I've been getting kind of soft."

Lania raises an eyebrow and pokes Celeste in the belly. "You don't seem to be getting soft to me. You could probably grind meat on your abs."

Celeste lifts her tunic slightly and looks at her well-defined six pack. "You think so?"

Lania looks down and pokes herself in the gut "You're in better shape than me."

Reno rolls his eyes "You're in perfectly good shape, Lania. Don't get jealous just because she is a fitness nut."

"I'm not a fitness nut." Celeste says indignantly. "My halberd just requires a very high level of fitness to use effectively, so I have to stay in shape."

"You could have picked a less fancy weapon…" Reno mumbles

Rayn changes the subject "So Reno. How is your mom doing?"

Reno lets out a long sigh "She's still ill, last I heard. They're doing their best for her, but still."

ETERNAL KNIGHTS OF EDEN II

Lania puts a hand on his shoulder "It'll be okay. Your mom is getting some of the best medical care available. She'll be fine."

"Yeah. Thanks, Lania." Reno gets back to his feet. "I'm going to go be alone for a while. Excuse me." He walks off who knows where.

Lania watches him walk away with concern "Is he going to be okay?"

"He'll be okay." Says Rayn "He just need some time."

Reno walks down the hallway and comes to rest outside one of the gun batteries, where it is quiet. He pulls a letter out of his pocket from his father detailing his mother's slowly worsening condition. She had apparently been diagnosed with a rare malignant tumor that they were having difficulty treating. The prognosis isn't good.

Reno leans back and sighs. *Growing up sucks.* He thinks to himself. He takes a few minutes to compose himself and then he returns to the troop quarters.

*   *   *

The ARV *Stalwart Sentry* begins to slow as it and its four sister frigates approach the town of Iron Veil. There is already a heavy fleet presence in the area, as the military isn't taking any chances since the fall of Broadspring three years ago.

Commander Grail watches out the viewport with satisfaction as the allied fleet comes into view. In the airspace around the city, sixteen frigates, seven destroyers, three cruisers, and a single carrier are floating in the sky. Most imposing of all, however, is the presence of a single dreadnought, the ARV *Fire of Ifrit*; A massive warship over twelve hundred feet long, bristling with magicore cannons and even four railguns.

The military isn't taking any chances.

Down in the hanger bay, Lania, Rayn, and Celeste are all awaiting orders alongside a dozen of their classmates. Lania looks around nervously as Reno still hasn't returned from wherever he ran off to.

Captain Yuri Nikola, formerly Lieutenant, approaches the class with First Lieutenant Valerie Adeline. The fifteen military trainees all stand up straight when they see their instructors approaching.

"Sorry I'm late." Says an apologetic voice from behind Lania.

Lania turns her head to see Reno, fully armed and armored now, standing behind her. "Where were you?" she asks.

He shakes his head "I needed some time to myself. I'm okay now."

Lania sighs and reluctantly turns to face the front once more.

Capt. Nikola clears his throat "Jarvis. Is everyone accounted for?"

Rayn quickly counts heads and stands at attention. "Yes, Captain!"

Nikola nods approvingly "Very good. Class 3-B, today you begin your first official assignments. I'm not going to lie to you. All of your previous assignments had some degree of safety assurance to them. The days of holding your hands and walking you through your studies is over. You are soldiers now. While you have not yet graduated the academy, you will be expected to perform your duties to the best of your abilities and learn everything you can. There is no guarantee that all of you will make it back. In fact, out of every class of twenty, it is rare for more than half to survive to graduation."

The class shifts uncomfortably.

"That being said, this is one of the best classes I have ever seen. All of you are strong and intelligent. If anyone can break the odds, it will be you. Do your best and make me proud. Lieutenant? Please hand out the duty assignments."

"Yes sir." Lieutenant Adeline replies, and then she walks student to student, handing out letters detailing their individual orders.

When she finishes, Capt. Nikola salutes "Gather your gear if you haven't already done so and prepare to move out. Dismissed!"

The fifteen remaining members of platoon 3-B salute their instructor and fall out of formation.

Reno, Celeste, Rayn, and Lania all gather to compare orders. None of them are especially surprised to see that their orders are the same. Their orders are also rather alarming.

"We're assigned to a village security unit. That's unusual." Rayn frowns

Lania tilts her head in obvious confusion "Where is this town? Lone Ridge?"

Celeste speaks up unexpectedly "It's about a hundred miles south of here. It's a successful little village that was formed on top of a large ridge that has proven fairly easy to defend due to it only having one real ingress route. It's surrounded by sheer cliffs, so the defenses are all focused one direction."

"How did you know that off of the top of your head?" Reno asks, impressed.

Celeste looks at him with her usual disinterested expression. "Easy. I was born there."

Rayn looks back at his orders "It says we'll be flying there via dropship with gunship escort in about an hour, once everyone else is sorted out. Let's get our gear ready so we aren't late."

CHAPTER 2

WHITE CREEK

Shaide Darkmoon walks into a familiar looking chamber. He cannot say why it is familiar, only that he feels like he has seen it before. The chamber is vast, spanning a mile across, shaped like a perfect dome. The walls are not like that of an ordinary cave, however. A smooth, pearly black sheen of pure obsidian lines the chamber, along with many pillars of equal construction.

His eyes are drawn to intricate golden patterns on the obsidian pillar nearest to him. He runs his hand over them, and realizes the patterns are made of pure gold, laid into the black stone itself.

In the center of the chamber is an altar, different from that of the angels he has seen. This altar is made of pure obsidian, like the chamber around him, but it is also inlaid with green jade and blue sapphire trim and patterns. A stone table of the black stone sits at the base of a statue, and as he approaches, he sees the top of the table is made of pure blue sapphire.

He frowns. This chamber is incredibly intricate, easily costing millions of gold pieces to construct. Where did this place come from?

He suddenly sees movement out of the corner of his eye. He turns his head and sees a dark figure walk out from behind the statue, looking very similar to it in appearance.

Shaide takes a few steps back and observes as a strange woman walks into view. No, woman is the wrong word, but she is definitely female. She has deep purple skin, with black hair and red eyes. She has curved black horns wrapping around her head, and a black scaly tail projecting from the base of her spine. She is also wearing some kind of black scale armor that almost appears to be made of elegantly carved obsidian itself, made to look like dragon-scale.

Strangely, she seems slightly distorted, as if this wasn't entirely how she was meant to look. He notices strange black tattoo like markings on her exposed skin, and notices that it looks strangely out of place. Her sharp features seem slightly exaggerated as well.

Shaide is momentarily mesmerized. This creature is strange, but undeniably beautiful. He also senses a tremendous power radiating from her, its intensity magnitudes greater than anything he has ever sensed before. Yet, she doesn't seem hostile. She seems more curious than anything.

"What are you?" He asks her.

She smiles and stretches her arms up, and black feathered wings erupt from her back, stretching out to either side. She then simply shakes her head and extends a hand, beckoning him to come closer.

Shaide finds himself walking inexorably towards her. He reaches out…

*   *   *

"Shaide! Wake up!"

Shaide jerks awake as someone gently shakes him out of his slumber. He opens his eyes and looks up to see a pair of pink eyes looking into his own. He blinks a couple of times to focus, and then a familiar Elmeri face comes into focus.

"Hrm… Good morning, Amari…"

Amari sits back on her knees as Shaide sits up and looks around.

The two young Ceraphs spent the night in an abandoned shack out in the south-western plains of the nation of Alastair. They've been on a seek and destroy mission for a few days now, but they haven't been having much luck.

The shack is quite cozy. They aren't really sure who it belonged to, but they seem to have left long ago. Nevertheless, the shack was well built, and it provided adequate shelter against the elements. In spite of the rainy weather, the roof is not leaking.

Shaide gets up out of his sleeping bag and picks up his combat harness, pulling it on over his black leather armor. Once he finishes getting ready, he turns to Amari.

"Are you feeling okay?" She asks him, a look of concern on her face "You were mumbling some strange things in your sleep."

"Yeah, I'm fine." He says, eyebrows raised in surprise. "Just had a weird dream."

"The same one?" She asks.

Shaide hesitates for a moment, but then he nods his head.

Amari sighs audibly "I'm sure it's nothing. With everything we see, weird nightmares are kind of expected, I guess."

"I've been having this dream for years. I don't know where it's coming from. I can't imagine where I've seen that place before, or that creature."

Amari puts a hand on his shoulder and gently squeezes "I'm sure it will be okay. Come on. Let's eat breakfast and get to work."

"Hey, aren't I supposed to be the one watching over you, miss apprentice?"

Amari gives him an amused expression "I thought we promised to work together? I have to pull my own weight, don't I?"

Shaide rolls his eyes and grins in spite of himself. "Yeah yeah. I guess you have always been kind of take-charge."

Amari pulls some bread and some preserved meat out of her field bag and makes a couple of sandwiches. "It's not as good as home," she says, handing him a sandwich "but it will have to do."

Shaide takes a bite and nods approvingly. He's never been especially picky about his food, but Amari has been keeping him spoiled with her cooking. She apparently prepared and preserved the meat herself, and it has a pleasant flavor to it. He finds himself momentarily wondering why she goes so far out of her way to take care of him, but he chalks it up to him being her closest friend.

Once they finish eating, they pack up their camping gear and step outside of the shack, where they find the skies are still gray and overcast, but it isn't raining for the time being. They exchange glances and set off onto the plains.

Just over a week ago, they got a report that a pack of corrupted quillbulls had been harassing the southern village of White Creek, killing their livestock and even a few of their braver villagers. The two of them, along with Shaide's godfather and Aunt, Atondier and Lucy Norvus, departed to the village on the Ceraph frigate COV *Last Beacon*, and began the operation to exterminate the beasts.

Quillbulls are particularly nasty plains beasts on a good day. They are shaped like oversized bovines, but they are covered with spikey, scaly armor, with a line of spikes down their backs and a wreath of horns around their heads. In spite of their aggressive appearance, quillbulls are herbivores. Nasty tempers, but so long as you stay out of their way, they will leave you alone. Provoke them, however, and they will tear you to pieces without mercy.

These corrupted quillbulls are a different matter. According to villager accounts, they have mutated into larger, nastier, carnivorous beasts that will eat just about anything, and do not wait to be provoked to attack on sight.

The Ceraphs waited a few days in town for the quillbulls to return, but they never came back. As a result, they are now in their current situation. Aton and Lucy remained in White Creek to protect the village in case the quillbulls returned, while Shaide and Amari went onto the plains to begin seeking their quarry directly.

Over the past three days, they have been forced to fight a number of corrupted beasts, but there has been no sign of their targets. The village's relatively close proximity to the deadlands makes it an absolute wonder that they haven't had more problems, but they villagers are tough, and the small Ranger outpost is usually sufficient to keep most problems at bay.

Amari looks out over the plains "So, where do you think we should look today?"

Shaide assesses his surroundings as well and then consults their map. He once again notes the proximity of the deadlands but shakes the thought clear. They have a mission to accomplish, and he must put his discomfort aside to do so. Still, he doesn't like having Amari with him on such a dangerous mission.

"I would suggest we proceed further south." Amari says, "The villagers said they always saw them coming from the south, so maybe we just haven't gone far enough yet,"

Shaide reluctantly agrees with her. He readjusts his harness and starts walking "Alright, let's go then."

Amari enthusiastically jogs alongside him. The young Elmeri woman had only joined the Ceraph Order six months ago when she was tagging along with Shaide on a mission in Erita, and she accidentally activated an Angel's altar. After subsequently passing its test, she returned to the Citadel with Shaide to join the order and fight alongside her childhood friend.

　　　　　A.S.GUINN

She was very brave and headstrong. Danger did not usually concern her much unless she felt that she couldn't protect Shaide. Their mutual protective attitudes towards each other causes a few headaches, but ultimately, they work together extremely well, never allowing harm to befall the other.

Sometimes, however, her brave nature makes Shaide nervous. She is very strong, both with her spiritual powers and her martial prowess, but she tends to be overeager sometimes. He's worried she will get herself badly hurt someday. With this in mind he has resolved himself to look after her for as long as he can, and simply hope for the best.

The two of them walk south on the plains for quite some time, encountering nothing noteworthy. Eventually they reach a high ridged hilltop that overlooks the Fringe: The southernmost region of Alastair adjacent to the Deadlands.

Amari taps Shaide on the shoulder "Hey, is that what we're looking for?" She asks.   Shaide, however, isn't paying attention. He's looking at a black haze rising from the ground to the south.

The Temenos Deadlands.

Amari follows his gaze and looks out over the decaying lands within the haze. "I've never seen the deadlands in person before. It's kind of… dark and terrifying. You know? Shaide?" She pokes him again when he doesn't respond.

He jerks out of his focus "I'm sorry. Hey, let me see that map real quick."

Amari looks confused, but she hands the map to him.

He scans the map carefully and notices a major discrepancy.

"Hey, Amari? Look at this map, and then the plains. Tell me what you see."

Amari takes the map back and looks back and forth a few times before her eyes open wide.

"Do you see it?" Shaide asks her.

Amari nods vigorously "Yeah, I think so. The map shows the deadland haze quite a bit south of the river here, but it's well north of it…"

Shaide pats her on the head "Exactly. This map is probably twenty years old, but still. It looks like the haze is spreading. Slowly, but spreading nonetheless."

Amari takes a charcoal pencil and makes a mark on the map where the corruption appears to have spread. "There. I made a note so we could show it to the higher-ups when we get back."

Shaide nods approvingly, but he feels a creeping unease settling in.

"Well, anyways, mission first. Is that the pack we're looking for?" She repeats, pointing at a pack of creatures running north.

Shaide frowns. They came awfully far south. "We should try and follow them or lure them back to the village so Lucy and Aton can help us with them."

Amari has a rather mischievous look on her face. "Come on. Don't you think we can handle them?"

Shaide considers her. Truth is, she probably isn't wrong. They shouldn't be an exceptionally tough fight, but they did overwhelm the village's security detachment, so they aren't pushovers.

ETERNAL KNIGHTS OF EDEN II

"Umm, hey. Shaide?" Amari says with concern "They're starting to come this way."

Shaide looks up and sure enough, the pack of quillbulls is turning towards them. HE lets out an exasperated noise and says "You know? Somehow you seem to always get what you want."

"Not always…" she mutters cryptically.

The half dozen giant quillbulls charge directly towards them, and Shaide unsheathes his longsword. Amari takes a stance behind him as she glows with a blue aura.

"Steady…" Shaide says as they thunder along the ground. He repeats "Steady…"

They close to a hundred feet, and he yells "NOW!"

Amari swings her staff forward, and a large array of ice crystals erupts from the ground directly in the quillbulls' path. One of the quillbulls even gets speared from underneath, killing it instantly.

The remaining quillbulls are staggered by the eruptions, allowing Shaide to dive into their midst and attack. He attempts to stab the nearest beast with his sword, but his blade glances off of its hide.

"Oh crap." He mutters, jumping back as it whips around and attempts to spear him on its horns. He takes a couple of heavy wings, and his blade glances harmlessly off of its horns.

Suddenly he flies forward as he is unexpectedly kicked from behind. "DAMNIT!" He yells from the ground, a sharp jolt of pain crawling through his back. Normal quillbulls' hides aren't this tough. He was expecting them to be stronger, but this is nuts.

Amari sprints forward and casts three balls of light the curve around and slam into the side of the quillbuill that kicked Shaide. The three balls explode into starburst of ice that shatter almost immediately after forming, and the concussive force actually knocks it over.

She immediately casts another ice spell, and three arm-sized spikes of ice form and impale into the creature's belly, dropping their foes down to four.

Shaide feels something behind him and instinctively rolls over. He does so just in time, as a quillbuill rears back and rams its horned head into the ground where he was just a moment before. His hand finds his dropped sword, and he drives it through the beast's eyes before it can move.

"Hey, Shaide!" Amari yells at him "Let's try out that move you were talking about!"

Shaide immediately knows what she speaks of, and he jumps to his feet. This turns out to be a bad move, because his back was hurt by the kick, and he drops to a knee in shock.

"SHAIDE!" She yells, as a four-thousand-pound quillbull on the outer edge of the pack turns and runs towards him. Without thinking, she casts a thick bloom of ice between Shaide and the beast, causing it to slam headfirst into the ice rather than him. Unfortunately, the ice shatters, and Shaide is knocked forward several feet by the beast and the ice both slamming into him.

"DO IT NOW!" Shaide manages to yell after he slides to a stop.

Amari chants a short incantation of some kind, and an array of seven pristine ice crystals forms equidistantly around the three remaining quillbulls, and one taller one in the middle.

 A.S.GUINN

Shaide, flat on his back, channels a massive amount of spiritual power into his sword, and hurls it into the center ice pillar before falling flat on his back. On impact, the sword explodes with lightning energy, arcing between all seven surrounding ice pillars, causing the beasts to roar in pain.

Amari then casts a single supercharged fireball into the center pillar, and simultaneously dispels the ice pillars around it. When the fireball reaches the middle, a sudden explosion occurs as the dispelled ice explodes into a concussive blast of steam.

Amari runs over to Shaide, extremely worried about her friend. She slides to a stop along the ground next to him and shakes him gently. "Hey, Shaide? Are you okay?"

"Yeah, I'm fine." He groans "That damn kick hurt my back a little, but I think I'm okay."

Amari wipes a single tear from her eye. She lays the hand with her staff on his chest and channels a glowing green energy into him. As the steam behind her clears, the three beasts caught in the blast are lying on the ground. She ignores this and focuses her energy into him for a solid minute before relenting.

She removes her hand. "How are you feeling now" She asks, short of breath.

Shaide slowly sits up. His back is still a little sore, but he seems able to move without a problem now. "Much better, thank you."

Amari stands up and pulls him to his feet. He is unsteady for a moment and falls against her, his face uncomfortably close to hers. Their eyes lock awkwardly for a moment and they both feel their heartbeats speed up.

Shaide coughs and straightens up "Eh hem… Sorry about that. Now, where's my sword?"

Amari stands there in shock and confusion for a moment. *What was that? That had never happened before.*

Shaide limps into the midst of the fallen beasts and prods them with his foot. "Well, a thunder array and steam blast seem effective enough. These guys aren't getting back up." He kneels down and picks up his sword and looks back at Amari. "Hey, are you okay?"

Amari shakes her head and comes back to reality "Yeah, I'm fine. Sorry about that." She walks over and joins him. "So, what now?"

Shaide looks around and frowns. He makes his way back up to the ridge and looks south again, contemplating the strange anomaly. *Maybe the map is just inaccurate? The corruption can't be spreading on its own.*

"I vote we head back into town, personally. We're a day or two away."

Shaide turns around and rejoins her "Yeah, let's head on back."

Amari casts her staff away and walks alongside him, still confused about that strange feeling she had when they were face to face.

Shaide, meanwhile, looks wistfully at her hand that had been holding her staff.

She notices him looking and asks, "What's wrong?"

"Oh, it's nothing." Shaide says. "I just wish I knew how you could summon and dispel your own weapon like that. I don't know how to do it."

Amari smiles at the praise. She feels that strange flutter again. "I only learned how to do it recently. I can try and teach you later if you want. You certainly have enough spiritual energy to do it."

"I would really appreciate that." Shaide smiles.

The two of them walk until after nightfall when they finally reach the shack they had camped at the night before. It is only a few hours walk from the village, so it's as good a place as any to rest.

Shaide limps through the front door and groans.

"You're using the bed tonight. You're hurt."

Shaide shakes his head "I'm not letting you sleep on the floor."

Amari groans. Shaide's chivalry is usually something to be admired, but right now it's just ticking her off. "Fine, how about this. We both share the bed tonight. You're not sleeping on the floor either."

Shaide frowns, leaning against the doorframe. "Sleep in the same bed? Isn't that a bit… inappropriate?"

Amari suddenly realizes what she suggested and feels the heat rise in her face. Thankfully the cabin is dark, so Shaide can't see her face. "Just lie down, you stubborn idiot. We're on a mission. It's not like we're doing anything weird."

Shaide realizes she isn't going to budge any more than he is, so he limps over to the bed. She helps him take off his combat harness and ease back onto the fur-padded bed. It's rock hard compared to the beds in the city, but it beats sleeping on the floor.

Shaide seems to fall asleep before she even lays back on the bed herself. It's big enough for two people, and Amari is able to have her own space comfortably. She lies on her side and uses her field bag as a pillow. She stares at Shaide for a while as she gets lost in thought, thinking about all of the time they've spent together.

In truth, it has only been a few months since he came back into her life, and they had only spent a short time together before that, but there was an undeniable closeness or connection between them. They were natural best friends. Still, that feeling she had earlier. What was that?

*　*　*

Shaide wakes up the next morning still sore but feeling significantly better. He feels something warm and heavy lying against him, and he opens his eyes and looks down to find Amari lying back against him.

He smirks slightly, and gently rolls her over so he can get up. He swings his legs over the side of the bed and feels a slight twinge in his back, but he ignores it. He walks over to the front door to look outside, and discovers the sun is beginning to rise in the east.

"Hmm, Shaide? Where you goin?" asks a sleepy voice from behind him.

"Don't worry. I'm just looking outside."

She nods and slowly sits up "Okay, give me a minute. I'll get up."

Shaide frowns for a moment. She usually is up before him. It's not like her to be groggy like this. "Are you feeling okay?"

She nods slowly, taking a moment before speaking. "Yeah… I just had trouble sleeping." She gets up and checks her bag. "How is your back?"

Shaide stretches. "Much better, thank you." He decides not to mention the twinge.

Amari slings her bag over her back "Alright then. You want to eat first, or do you want to get moving?"

Shaide shrugs "Eat on the way?"

Amari yawns and pulls out a couple of pieces of fruit and tosses one to Shaide. "That works for me. *Yawn* I'm ready to get back."

She follows Shaide out the front door. They turn to the north and head towards where they know White Creek to be. It's actually not too difficult to find at the moment, because they can see their frigate in the sky even from several miles away.

The walk is quiet, and after about six hours, they reach the town. Several villagers greet them as they walk through the wooden outer wall into the town proper, and they make their way towards the inn for some proper food and rest.

"Hey Shaide! Amari!"

Shaide looks up to see his godfather Aton and his aunt Lucy approaching them from up the street. Shaide and Amari exchange tired grins before meeting their elders in the middle of the street.

Lucy predictably grabs Shaide and pulls him into a tight hug. "I missed you, kid. These villagers are fun, but it's just not the same."

Shaide shrugs her off and shakes Aton's hand "How are things here?"

"Quiet as the tomb. We took out a few stray beasts that wandered too close, but aside from that we haven't seen a thing."

Shaide smiles with satisfaction "You can probably thank us for that. Well, Amari mostly."

Aton looks at Amari "Did you find them?"

"Yeah, we found them alright." She says with a grin. "They were a bit of a hassle to take out, though."

Shaide chuckles "I think I only killed one of them. Amari literally blew up the last three with basically a steam bomb."

Aton surveys his young godson and Amari with pride. At one time, he was nervous about Shaide joining the military at all much less the Ceraph Order, but now it seems Shaide is where he belongs. Not only is he an exceptional Ceraph, even at his young age, but he brought another exceptional individual to their fold. He seems to be able to both fight and lead others to do the same. Shaide doesn't see it yet, but Aton is certain Shaide will become a leading Ceraph someday.

Lucy notices Shaide favoring his back. "Are you okay, Shaide?" She asks with concern.

Shaide nods "Yeah, just a bit sore. I got kicked pretty hard by one of the beasties."

"I thought you said you felt better…" Amari says with a frown.

Shaide rubs the back of his neck awkwardly "Well I DO feel a lot better. I'm just sore, Amari. I'll be fine, don't worry."

Amari gives him a slightly scolding look and doesn't respond.

Lucy chuckles "Careful Shaide. You don't want to go hiding things from your girly, you know. You'll regret it later when you get married."

Shaide ignores her entirely "So, dad. What's the plan now?"

Aton looks over his shoulder "Well, the innkeeper has offered to let us stay and even eat for free while we are here. Personally, I vote we stay the night here and head back in the morning."

"I'll have Yorlan send a report to Armstrong so we can get new orders." Says Lucy, referring to Shipmaster Yorlan Corolas. She looks slightly put out that Shaide and Amari both ignored her joke.

Aton nods. "Thanks Luce. I appreciate it."

Lucy waves and heads for the Ranger outpost where their dropship is parked.

Shaide rubs his back nonchalantly, but Amari notices. "Come on, Shaide. Let's get you to the inn so you can rest." She grabs him by the arm and steers him towards the inn, with Aton following close behind.

"By the way, Shaide. I thought you were fast. How did you get hurt, anyway?"

Shaide looks at his godfather and then lowers his eyes. "I underestimated them. Their hides were WAY tougher than I expected, and it threw me off."

Aton looks at Shaide's sword across his back with surprise on his face. "That sword wasn't able to hurt them?"

"Nope. Despite the Elmeri metal, their hides were just too strong. I was nearly useless out there this time." Shaide looks a bit disheartened as he says this.

"Don't worry about it, Shaide. You're usually the star of the show when we go hunting." Says Amari as they walk into the inn. "There was bound to be something you'd have trouble with, eventually. That's why I'm here with you."

"Thanks Amari." He replies as they walk into the inn.

"You know, she's right. You're usually the one with the highest damage output, for sure." Aton grabs them a table as he continues. "I wouldn't let one mishap get you down."

A barmaid walks over to them. "Ahh, the exalted heroes return. What can I get for you, on the house?"

Aton replies "Ale and the special."

"Tea, black, and the special as well." Says Shaide.

"Same."

The barmaid smiles and bows "Very well. I'll have it out as soon as I can."

As the barmaid walks away, Shaide lowers his voice. "There was also something else we needed to discuss."

Aton notices Shaide's serious tone shift and leans forward.

"The corruption from the deadlands doesn't match where the map says it is." Shaide pulls the map out of Amari's bag and lays it out, pointing at her mark. "The map says the corruption ends here, but we saw it around five miles north of there. Minor thing, I know, but it has me worried."

Aton silently considers the map for a moment, seemingly lost in thought.

"Hey, dad? You awake?"

Aton jerks out of his trance and looks back at Shaide. "We'll check it out ourselves before we head back. There is no record of the deadland corruption spreading as far as I know. It could just be a map error, but I want to be sure."

Amari looks at Shaide "A second look couldn't hurt. Eye in the sky and all that."

"Yeah, I think you're probably right. I don't want to start a fuss if we are mistaken. But Aton?" Shaide looks back at his godfather "Is it safe to fly that close to the deadlands? I thought magicore stopped working correctly over corrupted lands?"

Aton shakes his head "No, we won't fly over the lands. We'll just get a better look from above. We'll be fine."

"If you say so." Says Shaide.

The barmaid comes back with their drinks and stew. "Here we go boys, and lady of course. The house stew, an Ale, and two helpings of our famous tea."

Shaide take a sip, and his eyes open wide in surprise. "Wow this is really good. Where do you get the leaves for this?"

"We get them from Pandora. We trade a lot with the Junmeri village right on the border nearby. The tea leaves they grow are both nutritious and delicious, so we make sure to stock up on them regularly."

Amari nods her approval as well "I thought we Elmeri had good tea, but this is really good."

The barmaid bows. "I'm glad you like it. Is there anything else I can get for you?"

Aton shakes his head "No thank you, ma'am. I think this will be more than enough."

"Very well. Have a good evening. Let me know if you need anything else."

They eat in silence for a while. Shaide and Amari are both exhausted from their excursion. Amari used a lot more spiritual energy than normal, so she is feeling almost as much fatigue as Shaide with his injury. Nevertheless, all three of them are happy with how things have been going.

Around the time they finish eating, Lucy walks into the inn and joins them. She hollers across the inn "Hey, Maria! Let me have the special and an Ale!" And sits down with them.

"What's the word?" Aton asks her.

"Don't really know yet." Says Lucy. "We're a long way away from the Citadel. It will be a while before we get a response."

Aton shrugs and leans forward "Well, I DO have some news for you." Aton and Shaide proceed to explain the situation about the deadlands, and their desire to investigate further.

Lucy listens with rapt attention until they finish explaining, and by the time they are done, she is leaning back with her arms crossed, looking very serious now. "Is it going to be safe to take to frigate down there? You know the deadlands wrecks hell with magicore."

"I said the same thing." Says Shaide, raising his hand.

Amari frowns and looks between the other three before responding "I'm with Aton. I think it's worth checking out."

"We could take a dropship in. Fly close and get a better view. We wouldn't have to endanger the frigate that way." Suggests Aton.

Shaide shudders "I've already survived one crash in a hostile area. I'd rather not try my luck again."

"Well, do you have a better suggestion?" Aton asks with a frown.

Shaide thinks for a moment, and then shakes his head.

"We have to check it out one way or another." Says Aton. "It could just be a cartography error. It's so dangerous down here that I wouldn't be surprised if no one wanted to get close enough to make an accurate map. But I still want to see for myself."

Shaide gets to his feet and heads for the door.

"Where are you going?" Asks Amari, looking concerned again.

Shaide looks back over his shoulder and says, "I'm going for a look around town."

"Mind if I come with?" She asks.

Shaide shrugs and outstretches his hand, indicating she can join him.

"We'll see you two later." She says to Aton and Lucy before following Shaide out the door.

Lucy watches them go with amusement. "You know? I still can't tell if there's some chemistry there that they don't see, or if they are just really, REALLY good friends."

"Who knows." Says Aton with a shrug. "At their age, they probably wouldn't notice even if there WAS something there."

Lucy chuckles "They're basically attached at the hip though. They would make a cute couple, that's for sure."

Aton nods and turns his head "Hey, Maria? Can we get a couple more drinks when you get a chance?"

CHAPTER 3

NO REST FOR THE WICKED

Shaide awakens in the morning, slightly disoriented from a now familiar dream. It haunts him, because he feels like that place is extremely familiar, but he can't place why he knows it. He just feels like he's been there before, a long time ago…

He sits up and looks around. His godfather Aton, whom he is sharing the room with, is leaning against the window watching the rain outside. He clears his throat to get his attention.

"Oh, good morning, Shaide." Aton turns to look at him. "Sleep well?"

"I keep having this weird bogus nightmare." He swings his legs over the side of the bed and thinks for a moment. "Well, not really a nightmare, but just a really bothersome dream. I've been having it for years."

"Want to talk about it?" Aton asks with a frown.

"Well, there's this gigantic cavern, and an obsidian altar. And this woman." He considers his words and rephrases "Well, not really a WOMAN, per se, but a female figure. She kind of looks like a demon or succubus from those old stories. Violet skin, black armor, horns, dragon tail, the works."

"Does she torment you?" Aton asks curiously.

Shaide shakes his head vigorously "No, she just seems curious. Never says a word. Just watches me. Every time I try to approach her though, I wake up."

Aton walks over and claps him on the back "Well, it's just a dream, in the end. I wouldn't let it bother you too much."

Shaide just silently nods and begins putting his gear back on. He pulls on his black canvas pants and shirt, then straps his black leather armor over the top of it, finishing with his combat harness.

Aton looks at Shaide closely as he finishes getting ready. "Hey Shaide? Can I offer an opinion?"

Shaide looks up "Yeah, sure. What's up?"

"Well, have you considered wearing a little more armor that that? You're a sword fighter, and our kind typically wears a little more protection." He indicated his chainmail underneath his own leather armor. "Knife fighters can get away with the light armor because of speed, but you might consider a small upgrade."

Shaide looks down at his armor and thinks for a moment. It's true, he kind of does this out of habit from when he used daggers to fight, but he's more comfortable with the speed advantage like this.

"I appreciate the suggestion, Dad, but I like to stay fast and nimble. I'm worried that heavier armor will just slow me down."

"Your choice, in the end. Here take this." Aton throws Shaide a black hooded cloak.

Shaide catches it and pulls it on. "Thanks. Ready to wake the girls and go?"

"Yeah, Let's get moving."

The two of them exit their room and go to the room next door, but they find it open and empty. The girls must have already gotten up. They turn and walk down the hallway to the tavern section of the inn.

Amari and Lucy are indeed already having breakfast while enjoying a cheerful conversation of some sort. They are laughing and having a good time as the men approach.

"Hey boys. You're up early."

Aton raises an eyebrow. "You're up earlier than we are. Please tell me you're not drinking already."

"No, not today." Lucy pouts "The Elmeri princess here wouldn't let me."

Amari rolls her eyes "I figured someone needed to control her."

Shaide and Aton laugh as they sit down and order some bacon, biscuits, and gravy.

"What time are we going back to the ship?" Amari asks.

Aton takes a minute to swallow before answering "I figured as soon as we finish breakfast. We did what we came here for. No point in hanging around."

The door opens and the village elder walks in. Lucy looks up as he approached their table.

"So, I hear that you have taken care of our quillbull problem."

Aton jumps and turns around. "Yes sir. Our young friends here tracked them down south and took care of them."

The elder nods approvingly. "Well, I suppose this means you're going to be on your way soon?"

"Yes, I'm afraid so. We don't have the luxury of enjoying ourselves most of the time. Once we're done, it's generally right on to the next problem. We're actually planning to leave right after breakfast."

The elder bows "Well, we are sorry to see you go. You're welcome back any time."

"Thank you, sir. We'll keep that in mind." Aton responds with a smile.

The old man shuffles away without another word.

"Well, he's interesting." Says Shaide.

"These fringe villages are a different animal than the northern cities." Replies Lucy "The Ceraphs are like legends to these people. They spend every day isolated, working to survive on their own, and as such they have a different view of the world than we do."

Once they finish eating, they pick up their gear and head for the door.

A chorus of voices in the Inn call out to them.

"Good luck, Ceraphs!"

"Come back soon!"

"We'll miss you!"

The four of them turn around and wave to everyone as they walk outside, and the door shuts behind them.

"See what I mean?" Says Lucy with a grin.

"It's not just here." Says Amari. "Even in Erita the Ceraphs are like legends."

"Yeah, that's true." Says Shaide thoughtfully, "When I was there on the plague incident, I got virtually whatever I wanted, whenever I wanted it. It was kind of strange to me."

Aton nods and says "You have to remember. Even three thousand years later, the Ceraph Order is credited with saving the entire world. Even if you take that out of the equation, everyone sees the Ceraphs as these holy warriors who give their lives selflessly holding back the corruption. To the people who only see us once or twice in a lifetime, we are legends."

"I grew up around the Ceraphs, so I never really saw it that way." Says Shaide. "Even around three years after joining, I'm still surprised by how the world sees us."

Amari lays her head on his shoulder as they walk "Don't worry. You're still just Shaide to me."

"Wow, way to make me feel special." Says Shaide sarcastically

Amari makes a mock-offended look and says "Well, fine then. I won't try and make you feel special."

Shaide laughs as they reach the dropship pad.

"Miss Lucy!"

Lucy turns around and sees a bunch of kids running up the street to her.

"Miss Lucy! We don't want you to go!"

Lucy smiles and drops to a knee as she hugs the incoming kids "I'm sorry, little ones. We're needed elsewhere. I'll try and come back someday though."

"You promise?"

"Yes, I promise." She lets go of the kids "Now run along. We have to get going now."

"Bye miss Lucy!"

Lucy backs into the dropship with the other three as she waves at the kids. A moment later, the engines spin up, and the dropship rises into the air. When the kids are out of view, Lucy takes a seat.

"What?!" She says indignantly as she catches Shaide and Amari giving her a very amused look.

"We just…" Shaide looks at Amari. "We're kind of surprised to see that you're so good with kids. That's all."

Lucy looks almost hurt as she says, "Why would you say that?"

Aton coughs "You know, sis, you can't blame them. You DO act like a big kid yourself most of the time."

"Yeah, yeah. I know." Sighs Lucy "I'd like to have kids of my own, but I'm still young."

Amari looks at Shaide "Speaking of that. Shaide, how old WERE your parents? They'd have been a lot older than Aton and Lucy. Right?"

Shaide winces slightly, but he responds, "I think they were in their twenties when they had me, right?"

Amari looks extremely confused "But, aren't Mitera like the Elmeri? We can't have normally had children until we're nearly a hundred years old."

Aton looks away awkwardly "Well, Juvia WAS unusual. She shouldn't have been able to have a child at that age. Nonetheless, she was gone on a mission for over a year, working closely with Lodrick, and when she came back? She had a young baby in her arms."

"Lodrick?" She asks

"Shaide's father." Replies Lucy. "Lodrick Darkmoon. One of the toughest Exorcists the Alastair Military had ever turned out. Shaide's parents never officially got married, but she adopted his name and lived like they were."

Amari turns to Shaide "Yeah, I remember you mentioning something about that."

Shaide nods sadly "Yeah. They were good parents. I'm sad they're gone, but I'm proud of them."

Amari hugs him around the shoulder for a moment.

"Hey, Ceraphs! We're coming into the hanger bay!"

They feel a shift of inertia, and then a clang as the dropship lands on the deck.

"Come on. Let's get to the bridge." Aton says, leading them out onto the ship.

Shaide looks around at the familiar frigate. He spends about as much time on the COV *Last Beacon* as he does at home. Maybe even more. He feels as comfortable and at ease here as he does anywhere.

"Shaide, hey. Come on." Amari gently pulls him by the arm.

He shakes his head clear and looks up to see Aton and Lucy looking at him with concern. "Yeah, I'm okay. Sorry."

The four of them march out of the hanger bay and through the corridors until they reach the bridge. Here they find Shipmaster Yorlan Corolas waiting patiently while looking out across the plains.

"Greetings, Corolas."

Corolas, a middle aged Elmeri dressed in an unassuming white long coat, turns around and bows to them. "Atondier. Good to see you again. Lucy tells me your mission went well?"

"Of course, old friend. Our young companions here were the stars of the show as always." Replies Aton with a smile.

"Shaide, Amari. Very good to see you back safe and sound."

Shaide bows "Thank you, sir."

"Yes, thank you."

Corolas waves his hand dismissively "Oh come on, you two. How many times must I tell you that you don't need to be so formal?"

Shaide shrugs "Habit, Shipmaster. I was taught to respect my elders."

Corolas lets out a long sigh before replying "Your mother was always exceptionally polite as well. I guess I shouldn't be surprised. Miss Tamiel? Are you enjoying your work?"

"Always pulling Shaide's butt out of the fire?" Amari grins

"Of course, sir."

Corolas grins and nods approvingly "So, to business. I haven't heard back from the Citadel yet, so what are our plans?"

"Well, there is an anomaly to the south that we wish to investigate, but it could be hazardous to the safety of the ship. Can we see your charts of the local region?"

Corolas looks curious as he looks at a young human at a table "Navigator Switzer? Could you bring us the chart for this region please?"

The navigator riffles through his papers and pulls out a chart and brings it over to them.

"Thank you, son. Aton? What are we looking for?"

Aton closely examines the chart, and then pulls out the one he got from Amari. He sighs and turns to Corolas "That's exactly what I was afraid of. Even the military navigation charts show the same information."

"Is there something I am missing, Aton?" Asks Corolas.

Shaide, however, is the one to reply. "Amari and I witnessed with our own eyes that the corruption in the land is several miles north of what the maps indicate. It feels like it is spreading for some reason."

"That is concerning…" Replies the shipmaster, deep in thought. "I assume you want to move closer and get an aerial view?"

"Yeah, I think that would be a good idea. I know it's not safe for the frigate to get too close, but we could take a dropship in if we needed to."

Corolas shakes his head. "No, it won't be a problem. If we get some altitude, we should be able to get a good view from a safe distance without zeroing our magicores."

Aton nods "If you're certain. Thank you, shipmaster."

"This is a short flight. We should be there in only a couple of hours. No point in going full throttle. At this range."

"Thanks again, Corolas." Replies Shaide, feeling a bit relieved.

"You all get comfortable. I'll send for you when it is time."

The four Ceraphs bow and exit the bridge, heading down toward the Ceraph quarters.

"Hey, guys?" says Lucy "If I might ask, what exactly are you hoping to find down there, anyway?"

Aton stops walking and lowers his voice "I need to see if it is really spreading, and if it is an isolated incident occurrence."

Lucy nods "I see. So, you think something is happening?"

"There have been a lot of rumors flying around lately." Aton mutters, "A LOT of strange occurrences have been happening here in the southern regions, and even in neighboring Pandora, where we traditionally don't hear any news."

Lucy's eyes open wide. "Like the quillbull attacks. Even corrupted, they usually leave people alone."

Aton nods his head, resuming walking down the corridor. "Exactly. Something is brewing down here, and I want to gather as much information as possible."

"So that's why you came along, even though Amari and I could have handled this alone." He pauses, "Actually, we DID handle it alone."

Aton opens the door to their quarters "Correct. It gave me a ready excuse to come all the way down here, after all."

"I really hate it when you keep things from me, you know…" Shaide says with a scowl.

Aton shrugs apologetically "I didn't want to worry you over a suspicion. You had a mission to complete. I wanted you to focus on that."

"Fair enough, I suppose." Shaide pouts

Amari sits down in her bunk and pulls out a book, so Shaide sits down at the small communal table and tries to think about what they're dealing. "Trying" is the operable word, because Lucy chooses this time to torment him in her usual fashion.

"Your muscles are starting to get really big, Shaide." Lucy awkwardly caresses his arms as he tries to think. "You're really starting to look like a man now. You think Amari would let me borrow you for an evening?"

Shaide rolls his eyes and tries to ignore her. She does it because she knows it makes him uncomfortable, but even though he usually just ignores her, it's irritating him at the moment.

Lucy starts to pout when he doesn't react, and so she puts her head on his shoulder and whispers in his ear. "Come on, kid. You're not being any fun right now. You usually say SOMETHING back."

Shaide just growls at the invasion of personal space, but again chooses to ignore her.

"Hey, Shaide?" Amari calls out from out of sight "Do you need me to hit her with my staff? I'll do it, you know!"

Lucy leans back and looks over her shoulder, looking rather impressed "Girly? How do you always know?"

Amari calls back "Because I know you, Lucy!"

"Fair enough." Lucy laughs. She walks away and digs in the ration supplies and finds a can of salted nuts to snack on.

"Sis? As much as you eat when you're bored, I'm amazed that you're as fit as you are." Aton watches her in amusement.

Lucy just shrugs "What can I say? It's a gift,"

"Also? Please don't talk with food in your mouth. It's gross." Amari calls out.

Lucy just turns and sticks her tongue out at her.

After about an hour, Amari puts her book away and comes out into the communal area. "You know? I could really use a bath soon… I feel all icky from being outside for the last few days."

Lucy reasons "You probably have time. I'm sure you could even convince Shaide to scrub your-"

Someone knocks on the door.

"Come in!" Yells Aton.

A crewman comes in and stands at attention. "Sirs, Ma'ams. Shipmaster Corolas asked me to notify you that we are approaching the destination. He would like you to come to the bridge if you are able."

Aton nods "Thank you, crewman. We will be right there."

Lucy looks at Amari and fake-sighs "Well, there goes your chance. Sorry missy."

"I'm sure I'll have time for a shower later, you know." Replies Amari, missing Lucy's meaning.

"Not what I meant." Smirks Lucy.

The four of them follow the crewman as the warship decelerates to a stop. As they emerge onto the bridge, they see Shipmaster Corolas and several officers staring transfixed out of the main viewport.

"We're here, Corolas. What's up?"

Corolas turns his head and beckons them over. "Tell me what you see."

Shaide and Amari walk side-by-side up to the viewport, and they feel their jaws drop. In front of the warship, twelve-thousand feet below, they see a massive expanse of dead, barren land. Especially apparent from this high, a thick black haze hangs over the ground, stretching out as far as the eyes can see.

"It's pretty horrible, isn't it?" Aton says grimly. "You've never laid eyes on the deadlands before, have you?"

Shaide and Amari both shake their heads, too stunned to speak.

"This is the reason we fight. Three thousand years ago, when the Great War ended, Belial chose to sacrifice himself rather than be defeated, and went out in a massive, multi-thousand-mile blast of his corrupting miasma, poisoning the very land itself, rendering everything south of the terminal line completely uninhabitable and impassable."

The entire bridge is deathly silent as Aton continues.

"Millions of good men and women lost their lives on that very day, as they simply ceased to exist in the intense wave of corruption. The entire nation of our people, the proud Mitera, became an uninhabitable wasteland." Aton turns to face the two young Ceraphs. "We fight so that what happened that day will never happen again."

Shaide and Amari simply nod in understanding.

"By the way, Corolas?"

The shipmaster turns to face him "Yes, Aton?"

"Aren't we rather dangerously close to the deadlands?"

Corolas shakes his head "No, if we were to move any closer, we would be in danger, but I have the engines operating at 100% capacity to make up for any interference. By the way, Navigator Switzer. Please show them what we found."

The navigator from earlier carries over a local region map and shows them. "Sirs, you were correct. The corruption has indeed spread north by several miles, but only in this isolated area. Our instruments indicate that is has spread further north the closer it gets to Pandora, but it tapers back to the terminal line as you head east."

"Pandora?" Says Aton, thinking to himself. "That's strange."

"Shipmaster? We have an incoming message from the Citadel. Priority from Armstrong."

Corolas turns the communications officer "Play it, son."

"Shipmaster, Ceraphs? Good job in White Creek. I am pleased your mission was a complete success. Unfortunately, there is no time to rest. You are needed to relocate to Lone Ridge immediately. We have gotten some disturbing reports from our military contacts,

and I think they need your help. Meet with Sergeant Wyatt when you arrive. Armstrong out."

Aton lowers his head "No rest for the wicked, eh? Corolas. You heard him. Let's get to Lone Ridge ASAP."

Navigator Switzer consults the chart "We can be there within two hours at maximum output."

Corolas nods and barks orders "Turn to heading 040 and order the engine room to set engines to interception output. Warm up the magicore cannons and order the gunships to run their flight checks. We don't know what to expect when we arrive, so be ready for anything. Hop to it, men!"

*   *   *

In the early morning hours, Celeste Wyatt and Lania Howler are patrolling the outskirts of the town of Lone Ridge. Sitting up on a plateau, Lone Ridge is one of the few major settlements in the southern plains of Alastair.

With a sheer drop of over five hundred feet on three sides, and a narrow sloping incline on the fourth, Lone Ridge is ideally placed as a highly defensible location. Celeste has her halberd casually over one shoulder as she and Lania patrol the slope.

"Man, I am really bored." Lania complains.

"Yeah, me too." Celeste says with a sigh. "Nothing ever happens out here, just like when I was younger."

Lania reaches the drop off of the side of the incline and looks down. "You know? I never asked. How DID you get into the Academy, anyways?"

Celeste sits down next to her and explains "My older sister? The sergeant? She saw how proficient I was when I was younger and gave me a personal recommendation. Combined with my high test scores, getting in was really a cinch."

Lania nods "I see. I was born in the Capital, so they noticed my magic potential when I was younger. I didn't really want to join the military, but with my abilities, it seemed like a good road to follow. My parents pushed me pretty hard to do it."

Celeste nods "I get that, but still, if you didn't want to…" She trails off, looking to the south.

"What is it, Celeste?"

Celeste stares into the distance, and slowly stands up. She says in a low, flat voice. "Lania, we need to get back to the village. Now!"

Lania follows Celeste's gaze and her eyes open wide as dinner plates when she sees a literal cloud of something flying towards the town. "Yeah… I think you're right."

The two girls sprint uphill towards the village as they hear the warning bell ringing across the plateau.

*　　*　　*

Reno and Rayn sit on top of the watch tower playing cards and looking over the plains below. Reno's cuirass and helm are leaning against the wall with his broadsword and shield. Their duty today is one of the easiest, but also the most boring.

"Coltide, Jarvis. Status report."

Reno and Rayn jump to their feet as a white-haired woman reminiscent of Celeste walks into the tower. This woman is several years older than Celeste, and her hair is shorter and tied up in a bob on the back of her head, but she has the same white hair, ice blue eyes, and the same face.

"Sergeant. Skies are all clear, for the moment."

Sergeant Luna Wyatt nods approvingly. "Good men. Keep your eyes open. Carry on." She turns and walks back down the stairs to the town below.

"Man, I still cannot believe how much she looks like Celeste. I mean, I know they are sisters and all, but still." Says Reno in amusement.

Rayn deals out another hand of cards as they sit back down. "Yeah, I know what you mean. Gorgeous, but terrifying."

"I wonder if Lania has a hot older sister…" Reno wonders aloud.

Rayn laughs aloud "Don't let her hear you say that. She's self-conscious as is."

Reno chuckles back, looking at his cards.

"So how are you liking it working here in Lone Ridge?" Rayn asks.

Reno considers the question for a moment before replying. "It's not bad. A lot less interesting than I thought it would be, but I don't mind being safe either. Any day where I go home in one piece is a good day."

Rayn chuckles "Yeah, I can tell by your armor you like to be safe."

Reno scowls "Why do I feel like you are making fun of me?"

Rayn just shakes his head and changes the subject "Have you ever considered the Ceraph Order? Shaide is there, and he seems to have a good time."

"Shaide is nuts." Replies Reno. "He is my best friend and all, and I love the guy to death, but the psycho actually goes out LOOKING for trouble. I mean, come on. I love a good fight as much as the next guy, but I don't like to go LOOKING for trouble."

Rayn looks confused. "But you're training to be an exorcist. Our whole job is to look for trouble."

"Yeah, when we're older and more prepared. Shaide is our age, and he spends all day going to meet trouble head on. And the lucky bastard has that beautiful woman by his side every day."

"You mean Amari?" Rayn laughs "I can't argue with you there. That woman is gorgeous. I wonder if she and Shaide are a thing."

Reno considers this "I doubt it. Shaide is really, REALLY dense when it comes to girls. They're always all over him, but he never takes advantage of it."

"Maybe he's not dense." Rayn reasons, "Maybe he is just polite."

Reno shakes his head "No, trust me. He is dense. And he… What's that?"

"What's what?" Rayn asks, following Reno's gaze. A second later his jaw drops. "Ring the bell, Reno. NOW!"

Reno tears his eyes away from the incoming cloud of who knows what and grabs onto the chain attached to the massive bell in the tower, and he pulls it hard.

     A.S.GUINN

CLANG----------*CLANG*----------*CLANG*----------

A moment later, Sergeant Wyatt comes running up the stairs "What's going on!?"

Rayn points, and the sergeant's eyes widen. "Understood. Stay up here and keep ringing that bell!"

Rayn stares back into the sky as Reno keeps ringing the massive bell. He watches the cloud get closer and his heart fills with dread.

A massive swarm of hundreds of wyverns comes into view. Far too many for them to repel on their own. Rayn can only watch in horror as the civilians below retreat into their homes while the small company of soldiers guarding the town take to the streets.

"GET TO THE MAGICORE CANNON ON THE ROOF!" Reno yells over the sound of the bell.

Rayn shakes himself out of his daze and nods, jumping onto the ladder to the roof and taking his place at the large twin-barreled magicore flak gun on the rooftop. He rapidly spins the control wheels to turn the gun around the appropriate direction and takes aim with his hand on the firing crank.

When the wyvern close into range, Rayn takes a deep breath and starts turning the crank.

BOOOM--*BOOOM*--*BOOOM*--

All around him, the four other flak guns begin firing as well, and bursts of kinetic energy begin detonating in midair in the midst of the wyvern.

In response, the dragon-like beasts swoop down and begin assaulting the village, breaths of flame and lightning striking the town all around them. Rayn just grits his teeth amidst the sound of beasts screeching, people screaming, the bell clanging, and the sound of cannons firing all around town, and he continues operating his flak gun.

He watches a wyvern kamikaze-dive into one of the neighboring flak guns and smash the tower supporting it. He closes his eyes and blocks out the screams of his comrades as he continues firing.

Mages in the town below, both military and civilian, begin casting their magic into the sky as fast as they manage, and blast of fire, ice, lightning, and others he cannot identify being exploding in the sky amidst the flak cannons and the wyverns' breath attacks.

He spots Lania in the street below casting support spells to supplement the mages attacks, and those nearest to her cast more powerful spells.

A white blur sprints up the street, and he witnesses Celeste parkour run up the walls and launch herself from a rooftop, impaling a passing wyvern with her spear. As it goes down, she leaps to another nearby wyvern, repeating this pattern between rooftops and flying beast.

Reno stops pulling the bell, no longer necessary, and hears another, even more terrifying sound. He turns and looks down the slope and sees a large horde of land bound creatures climbing the slope towards town.

He grits his teeth and grabs his cuirass and helm, quickly putting them on and grabbing his weapons. He sprints down the stairs and out onto the street, yelling "LOOK TO THE SLOPES! INCOMING!"

Reno and a number of foot soldiers take off towards the south edge of town to meet the incoming enemy horde. Reno freezes for a moment as he spots a number of HUMAN looking monsters among the lobos and megantulas skittering up the slopes.

Sergeant Wyatt's voice roars over the noise "CHARGE! KEEP THEM AWAY FROM THE TOWN!"

Reno roars a battle cry and sprints forward into the incoming horde. He bull-tackles the nearest lobo with his shield and turns and immediately stabs a giant spider with his broadsword.

Something jumps onto him and knocks him to the ground, and without thinking he bashes it with his shield, and stabs it with his sword. His eyes open wide behind his helm as he sees a HUMAN face snarling and spitting at him, looking horribly distorted and almost half rotten. He roars and throws the creature off of him.

At some point, his helm is knocked off, but he continues fighting with everything he has.

CHAPTER 4

ANGEL OF DEATH

Atondier, Lucy, Shaide, and Amari all stare in shock out the viewport of the frigate as they see the scene unfolding in front of them. Swarms of flying beasts, buildings on fire, and explosions in the sky fill the sky in front of them.

"Aton. You know what we have to do." Says Corolas in the most serious tone.

"I do, Shipmaster. Good luck."

"You too, Ceraphs."

As the four of them turn tail and run for the Hangar, the ship-wide combat alert siren fills the air. Thy emerge into the hangar to find the gunships rocketing out of the hangar and the small contingent of ground troops loading onto the dropships.

 A.S.GUINN

Aton and Lucy run for the nearest dropship and turn around to find Shaide and Amari standing just outside of the troop bay.

"Come on. You two! What are you waiting for? Get in!"

Shaide shakes his head "I have my own way down. I'll see you there."

"Are you nuts?!" Yells Aton

Shaide looks at Amari and hollers "Get onboard! I'll see you down there!"

"No way, Shaide! I'm staying with you! Pilot! Get going!" Amari yells over him.

The pilot wave over his shoulder and rockets the dropship out of the hanger bay. Shaide and Amari slowly walk over to the edge of the hanger and watch as the vessel slows into an artillery support position just off of the edge of the town.

"Shaide? Are you sure about this?" She asks.

Shaide closes his eyes and nods. "Take my hand."

Amari takes his hand as the two of them walk backwards about twenty feet from the edge of the deck. Then, the two of them sprint forward, and Amari yells "Oh god I don't want to do this!" as they leap off of the edge of the ship.

*   *   *

Reno is covered in blood and sweat as he fights the beasts and formers in the middle of town, yelling with exhaustion after two hours of fighting as he struggles to keep moving, knowing that if he stops fighting, it's over. With a heavy grunt, he bashes a megantula in the face with his shield, and proceeds to stab it unnecessarily several times.

He moans and grunts as he has a momentary lull in the fighting. He looks around as he struggles to catch his breath, noting the terrible state the town is in. All around him, though, he can hear his comrades fighting. He takes several staggering deep breaths, and then runs up the street to find new foes.

He looks up and sees an extremely welcome sight. A frigate is in the air at the edge of town, and gunships and dropships are coming out of the ship! They have backup! He hears cheering in the streets around him as his allies are inspired by the sight of their new help, and feeling his second wind, Reno charges into the neighboring street to rejoin the fight.

*   *   *

Shaide stretches out the hand not holding Amari's, and she does the same. Glowing yellow and red glyphs respectively form around their outstretched arms as they plummet towards the town. The sound of two birds screeching fills the air, and just before they hit the ground, they are caught in the talons of their respective angels. Rho the Thunderbird, and Theta the Phoenix.

Shaide and Amari both use their momentum to springboard off of their angels and land softly on the ground. Shaide immediately assesses his surroundings and counts two dozen corrupted foes on this street, and three Alastair soldiers.

Cloak trailing behind him, Shaide leaps forward and hyper-aggressively dashes around the street at inhuman speed, not bothering to aim, and just dealing as much damage as he possibly can.

ETERNAL KNIGHTS OF EDEN II

Amari, likewise, aims her staff in the air and summons a storm of ice spikes which impale Shaide's wounded targets, pinning them to the ground.

Shaide spots a large corrupted drake at the end of the street fighting with a soldier in heavy plate mail and hurls himself towards them. Shaide slams into the corrupted drake's neck, and his momentum makes his sword tear a deep gash in its throat. It's not down yet, and it looks down at the heavily armored soldier with smoke coming from its mouth. Without thinking, Shaide runs and jump kicks the soldier in the breastplate, knocking him clear as the drake releases a massive breath of flame. Shaide ducks to try and cover himself from the blast, but a shield of ice forms in the air deflecting the fire around him.

Amari still has my back. He thinks to himself. *I've got this!*

Shaide swings his sword in mid-air, launching several arcs of lightning that slam into the drake, reeling it back and blasting scales off of its neck.

When did I learn how to do that? He wonders to himself.

Channeling his spiritual energy into his sword, he brings it around and swings it straight down, releasing a heavy blast of lighting that actually knocks the drake off of its front legs. Instinctively, Shaide slides forward and takes several heavy slashes at the beast's underbelly, before diving out the other side.

Right on cue, Rho swoops back down and fires a ball of super-compressed lightning from its mouth, hitting the drake and exploding, making it roar in pain.

A white-haired woman wielding a halberd sprints u the street towards him, and she screams "Ceraph! Together!"

The woman jumps off of the plate-mail soldier's shield and springboards to the Drake. Shaide simultaneously launches himself from the ground with a concussive blast from his feet, and the two reach the beast's neck at the same time. The woman takes a tremendously wide swing, and Shaide holds his sword out beside him, and the two slice clean through the beast's neck.

Shaide and the woman land on the ground as the beast falls.

The plate mail soldier gets back to his feet and yells "Holy hell, Ceraph! That was amazing!"

Shaide catches sight of the man's face and is stunned. "Reno!?"

Reno looks at his face and freezes "Shaide!?"

Celeste walks up behind him, covered in cuts and bruises, and a lot of blood that isn't her own, and claps him on the shoulder. "I can honestly say I have never been more happy to see you."

Shaide shakes his head "Come on! We aren't done yet! Catch up later!"

"Right!" Says Reno.

Shaide runs up the street and rejoins Amari, who promptly slaps him.

"OW! What the hell!?"

"Don't do anything that reckless again. Okay?!" She says. Firmly.

"No promises…" Shaide mutters.

She sighs explosively and turns around "Come on! We still have a town to save!"

With Reno and Celeste behind them, they work their way around town, assisting the local soldiers wherever they have a chance. The town is absolutely flooded with corrupted beasts and formers, and they seem to be fighting a losing battle. The town is in flames, buildings are collapsing, but everyone is still fighting.

Slowly but surely however, with the help of the Ceraph forces, the enemy's numbers dwindle.

Shaide snaps the neck of a former he had in a chokehold and tilts his head, listening. "Did you hear that?"

Amari finishes shish-kebabbing a pair of lobos and listens too.

The sound of a massive explosion fills the air, and Shaide feels the color drain from his face. "Oh god… No…"

* * *

Shipmaster Corolas begins to breathe easier as the number of wyverns in the air is whittled down by the cannons and gunships. It seems like they may be able to save the town after all.

"How is the situation on the ground?" Corolas asks his monitor.

"Sir, they seem to be slowly getting the corrupted under control. Shaide and Amari in particular seem to be especially effective."

Corolas nods, but before he can say anything more, he hears someone scream "BRACE FOR IMPACT!"

A split second later, a massive explosion fills his ears. The entire ship violently lurches to the side as the power flickers off. Corolas screams around the bridge as the vessel lists to port. "DAMAGE REPORT!"

"Sir! Power cores are offline, and the cannons have been disabled! We're running on one grav-core. We're dead in the air!"

"WHAT THE HELL HIT US!?" Corolas yells as the ship tilts slightly to the left.

"There! DRAGON!"

*   *   *

Shaide watches in horror as a dragon hits the COV *Last Beacon* with a massive blast of flame. Debris explodes from the ship as it lurches violently to one side, and all of its cannons cease firing at once. The dragon seems to be relatively small, maybe half the size of their airship, but it is a massive and dangerous foe, nonetheless. It appears to have disabled their frigate with a single hit.

Shaide grits his teeth and sprints up the street. "RHO!"

Amari screams Shaide's name as the thunderbird swoops down, and Shaide backflips, landing on its back.

"DAMNIT! THETA!" She screams, running up the street as her phoenix swoops down after her. She leaps onto its back and follows Shaide into the sky,

In the street behind them, Aton and Lucy come running out of an alley, accompanied by their own angels Zeta the Great Ape, and Io the Zephyr Steed respectively.

"SHAIDE! AMARI! GET BACK HERE YOU IDIOTS!" Aton screams.

          A.S.GUINN

Reno runs up to him and asks, "What the hell are they doing!"

"They're taking on that god damn dragon alone!" Yells Lucy, extremely distressed.

Celeste walks up calmly and mutters "Give 'em hell, Shaide."

One of their unnamed soldiers yells "We've got more company!"

In the air above, Shaide and Amari streak towards the one-hundred-and-fifty-foot dragon with a cold determination. Shaide spots Amari over his shoulder and groans, hoping that she had stayed on the ground. Nevertheless, she is here with him, so they may as well fight together.

"Amari! Speed and Strength!"

"Got it! And if we survive this, I am going to beat the crap out of you!"

"Fair enough! Let's make sure we survive first!"

"DEAL!"

Rho and Theta rocket towards the dragon and launch a salvo of thunder and flame attacks. The resulting impacts buffet the dragon around a little but don't seem to do any real harm to him. It gets his attention though, and that's what they really want. Keep its focus on them, and not the town or the crippled frigate.

Shaide lays low on Rho, and then leaps into the air as they pass. He strikes the massive beast hard with his sword, but he only manages to gouge the scales. Not penetrate them. "DAMN!"

Amari bombards it with a volley of heavy ice spikes, but they just shatter on impact. "DAMNIT IS RIGHT!"

The dragon turns its head and lets loose a massive ball of flame at her.

"AMARI!"

Instead of trying to avoid it, Theta suddenly turns up and opens its wings, putting itself between the dragon and Amari. The massive ball of flame seems to envelop Theta, and suddenly be absorbed by him. His eyes glow bright, and he returns the fireball at the dragon, twice as intense. The blast is so powerful, it rolls the dragon over in the sky and blasts a moderate patch of scales off of him.

Amari's eyes are wide with shock. "That's handy!"

Shaide breathes a sigh of relief as he sees Amari is okay. As the dragon rights itself, Shaide steers Rho towards the unprotected patch, and slams himself into it at high speed. He slashes deep and ferociously for a moment before falling, leaving deep bloody gouges behind as Rho circles back around and catches him.

The dragon roars in pain and turns its head to track him. It opens its mouth to let loose a ball of flame, when a barrage of ice spike bury themselves in its unscaled patch and explode, throwing off its aim and making the fireball soars past Shaide, singing his cloak and throwing ash in his face.

"Rho, this isn't going to work. We've got to think of something!"

Rho screeches in response and hurls several more thunder-balls at the dragon in rapid succession. The great beast roars in pain and tries to hit Amari with a fireball again, barely missing her due to

          A.S.GUINN

his attacks. Shaide notes the way it opens its mouth wide to attack and gets an idea.

Shaide closes his eyes, and feels a single tear roll down his cheek. "Are you with me buddy? To the end?"

Rho lets loose a sad, musical squawk, knowing what his partner has in mind.

"It's the only way, buddy."

Amari hurls another barrage of ice-spikes at the great dragon, making it absolutely furious as it turns its head to her.

As it opens its mouth, Shaide and Rho turn sharply towards its face from the front, and rocket across the sky.

Shaide turns his head to see Amari one last time, and she sees the sad smile on his face. For the briefest moment, all sound around her seems to shut off, and all she can see is his face. Everything seems to move in slow motion as her eyes open wide in horror, and Shaide and Rho fly into the fireball just as it forms…

Shaide and Rho fly down the dragon's throat at nearly supersonic speed and suck the fireball down in with them. Everyone watches in horror as a chain of explosions of fire and lightning erupt from the great beast's head, neck, and chest, spraying great fountains of blood into the air.

The dragon lets loose a pitiful, moaning last roar, and falls from the sky. Everyone's eyes are on the beast as it glides over the town and slams into the incline beyond. The ground itself shakes from the force of the impact as the dragon slides to a stop and moves no more.

Reno pulls his sword from the side of a large spider and lets his arm go slack. The last thing he saw was the blur of yellow streaking down its throat, and he knew instantly what happened.

He sees Aton and Lucy, and even Celeste sprinting up the street towards the incline, and he sees their mouths moving, but strangely, he cannot hear a sound. Everything seems to have gone mute as the shock sets in.

Up above, a phoenix dive and slams into the ground, and Amari rolls to her feet alongside Aton as they sprint to the dragon's remains. They come to a stop next to the great beast and just stare in shock, looking for any sign of life but knowing there was no one who could have survived that.

As Reno shuffles his way out of the town and onto the incline, Amari falls to her knees, too deep in shock to even cry. She just stares at the remains of the beast he had sacrificed himself to defeat.

Aton tries to compose himself as Reno walks up behind him. "I can't believe it. The crazy son of a bitch… I don't…"

Lucy puts a hand on her brother's shoulder, tears running down her own face. "He just saved all of our lives. That thing would have killed us all. He's a hero, Aton… The biggest I've ever known."

Aton closes his eyes "I would rather have him here than him be a hero…"

"I know…" Says Lucy. "Come on. Let's not make it in vain. We still have to finish cleaning up the town."

Behind them however, dozens of citizens and their fellow soldiers are filing out of the town to look at the great fallen dragon that nearly killed them all. The remaining corrupted beasts seem to be fleeing and ignoring them entirely. It seems that seeing the great corrupted dragon fall was enough to scare even them.

Aton reaches down and gently pulls Amari to her feet. "Come on kid… We have to go…"

"Shaide…" She says.

They turn away towards the town and slowly make their way towards the townspeople. Lania and Rayn are among them, just observing the Ceraphs and friends returning. Lania and Rayn's eyes open wide in shock when they realize what happened.

They get no more than twenty feet from the beast when they suddenly hear movement behind them. Aton freezes, but Amari turns around, staff in hand, anger and rage boiling in her face.

What happens next is beyond what anyone could have ever anticipated.

A black clad figure roars with exertion and forces its way out of one of the ruptures in the dragon's chest. A black, blood-soaked cloak and a hooded face of pure white stumbles out, looking the very image of the grim reaper from old storybooks.

It flicks its sword, throwing offal from it, and looks up at the gathered crowd with a stunned look on its face.

At this point Amari realizes this is no specter. Its Shaide. He's alive!

"What the hell-" Says Aton, staring at him in shock.

Amari lets out a howl and sprints at him, tackling him to the ground with her arms around his neck, crying in earnest.

Reno just starts clapping his hands, and Celeste quickly follows. Before long the entire crowd is clapping along with them, and the sound of a few people cheering fills the air as well. Their town may be severely damaged, but that can be repaired.

Sergeant Wyatt walks out of the village with her squad's survivors in tow. She walks up to Shaide and stands over him as he gives in to Amari and allows her to cry over him.

"Come on, sweetheart. Let him breathe." Lucy pulls Amari off of Shaide as Sergeant Wyatt pulls him to his feet.

"You, Ceraph. What is your name?"

Shaide wipes his face revealing that the white coloration was just ash. "My name? I-uhh. I'm Shaide. Shaide Darkmoon."

Sergeant Wyatt turns to face the crowd and hollers "Everyone! Listen up! LISTEN!"

The gathered crowd falls silent as she continues "Let's hear it for Shaide Darkmoon, the Ceraph Order's Angel of Death!"

The crowd cheers once again as they chant his name.

Aton smiles "Angel of Death, huh? Nice nickname. Whoa Shaide!"

Shaide suddenly sways and falls over. Amari quickly catches him and holds him up. "Shaide! Are you okay?!"

Shaide nods slowly "I'm fine… I'm just exhausted, sore, and I think a little burned…"

Amari pulls him a bit closer and mumbles "Come on, you crazy lunatic. I'll take care of you."

Sergeant Wyatt call out to her troops "Come on, boys. We can't let the Ceraphs do all of the work! Let's make sure the town is

     A.S.GUINN

clear and begin damage control. We can rebuild, but let's make sure the monsters are all gone first!"

Reno and Celeste look at Shaide with concern for a moment.

"Go on, you two. I've got him. I promise." Amari still has tears running down her face.

The dropship Aton and Lucy rode in on circles over to them and lands nearby. The remaining aircraft otherwise pursue the retreating handful of wyverns as they flee west.

Aton hesitates as he looks at Shaide, and he runs in to talk to the pilot. "Pilot! What's the status of the *Last Beacon*?"

"Crippled, sir, but she can remain in the air. It will be some time before she can move again."

"Can we use the medical facility?"

"Afraid not, sir. The ship is still unstable. The gravity field is fluctuating, so we can't safely land in the hanger yet."

Aton balls his hands into fists "Understood. Take us into town to the clinic, if it is still standing."

The pilot salutes, and Aton waves Amari and Lucy on board. They half carry Shaide into the back, and the dropship takes off into the burning and wrecked town.

*   *   *

Several hours later, Celeste finishes her patrol of the town and returns to the Alastair military garrison. There she finds her older sister resting off duty at her desk.

"Hey Sarge. How are you feeling?"

Luna looks up "Exhausted, Wyatt, but I'm okay. Report?"

Celeste stands at attention "Patrol is completed, ma'am. Mages have the fires under control, and the town appears to be clear of any further corrupted threat."

"Very good. You may relax. Have a seat, Celeste."

She complies and sits across from her sister.

"So, kid. How are you doing, yourself? It seems like you know those Ceraphs."

Celeste nods. "Yeah, Shaide: the one who took out the dragon. He used to be a student at ARMA, and we're pretty good friends."

"I see. You seemed a bit more concerned for him than just a friend, though." Luna nods "If I am making an observation."

Celeste shakes her head "No, no. Just friends. Actually, I think he may have something going on with that Elmeri girl, Amari. I've met her once before, and they seem very close."

Luna nods sadly "Well, that's probably for the best. A Ceraph would make a poor husband. They don't have the longest life expectancy, and that one seems especially brave."

Celeste chuckles "The Angel of Death. I like the nickname you gave him."

"Well, it fits. He dropped out of the sky and nearly single handedly stopped the corrupted invasion."

Celeste raises her eyebrows "That might be a BIT of an exaggeration."

"Not really. He dropped into town, took out several dozen corrupted in the span of a few minutes, including an especially nasty drake, and THEN took to the sky and killed a dragon that managed to disable a warship. His kill count may be even higher than yours."

Celeste grins "Now, I doubt that,"

"He killed an eight-hundred-thousand-pound dragon. I think that beats ANYONE's kill count." Luna reasons with amusement.

"Still only one kill…" Celeste mumbles grumpily.

"Well, anyways. You should go to the clinic to visit your friend. I think Coltide should be heading there soon as well. Speaking of…" Luna looks off in thought for a moment. "Coltide is a hell of a soldier too. He led the initial counterattack against the ground invasion, and he kept fighting until it was over. You have a good bunch of classmates, Celeste."

"Yeah, I really do." She replies with pride, getting to her feet. "Thanks, sis. I'll go check on him now."

Celeste turns and walks out the door onto the street. The frigate managed to limp to the town and is hovering just off of the plateau on the incline as the make repairs. She can see part of it at the end of the street. She shakes her head and turns towards the town's clinic and walks through the front door.

The clinic is packed with injured civilians, but miraculously, most of the injuries weren't serious. The town is well used to this kind of thing, and although this was many times more severe than any attack in living memory, they knew what to do.

She walks up to the desk. "Excuse me, I'm looking for Shaide Darkmoon?"

"The Ceraph?" Replies the nurse. "Yes, he's down in 113."

"Thank you, ma'am." Celeste bows and walks down the hallway until she finds room 113. It was actually easy to find, because two order foot soldiers are standing guard on either side of the door.

"May I enter?" She asks politely. The two soldiers bow and step aside, allowing her to enter the room. When she goes inside, she finds Shaide is unconscious, his black cloak and armor beside the bed. Not too surprisingly, Amari is laying across him, fast asleep. Celeste walks up and gently touches Amari's back, and she jerks awake.

"Celeste? Oh, hey. What's up?" Amari asks sleepily.

"How is he doing?"

Amari looks at Shaide for a moment with a gentle smile. "He's okay. Somehow, he is virtually uninjured. Some superficial burns and bruises, but nothing serious."

"What's wrong with him, then?" Celeste asks, confused.

"He nearly achieved what they called spiritual zero." Amari says with a sigh. "He nearly drained his energy to the point of death. It's normally impossible, but he tends to go into a kind of overdrive state in combat. He can push himself beyond what most can manage."

Celest pulls up a chair and sits down. "That's good. After I saw him fly down that thing's throat, I was sure it was over."

Amari tears up a bit "I was sure it was too…" She sniffles as she tries to hold back from crying again.

Celeste starts to see why Shaide and Amari are so close. They are both immensely loyal people. They care deeply about their friends. Celeste never understood his attachment to Amari before, but she can see it now. She pulls her into a gentle hug. "Hey, he's okay. Everything's okay."

Amari get a hold of herself, and Celeste lets go. "Thank you…" Amari says. "It's just kind of hard. Shaide is always doing these reckless things, and it always seems to work out, but I'm just worried that one day, his luck will run out and that will be the end of it."

Celeste looks at Amari with pity and understanding. The poor girl doesn't even understand her own feelings for him, but Celeste can see it. "Well, as long as you are there to protect him, he will be fine. Right?"

Amari shakes her head "I can't protect him from everything."

Celeste stands up and kneels in front of Amari, looking her square in the eyes "As long as you are there for him, he will always pull through. So just make sure you always do one thing."

"One thing?" Amari asks.

"Always stay by his side."

Amari blinks a couple of times, then she smiles. "I will. Thank you, Celeste."

Celeste sits back down "He's a good guy, Amari. Never have I seen anyone willing to do the things he's done for people. Keep him close."

"Hey, let me in, assholes! That's my friend in there!"

Amari turns around and walks to the door "Hey is everything… Oh, hi Reno!"

"Do you know him ma'am?"

Amari nods "Yeah let him in."

The two guards release Reno "Apologies, sir."

Reno glares at the two of them before walking into Shaide's room. He looks at Amari and asks, "How is he?"

"He's fine. He overexerted himself, so he's out cold for a while." Amari says, resuming her place at his bedside. "Give him a day or two, and he'll be fine."

Reno leans back against the wall. "That's good. He literally flew down a dragon's throat and blew it up.

Celeste frowns "You know? That's kind of bothering me, now that I think of it. How DID he survive that? That shouldn't have been physically possible."

The three of them sit in silence for a moment.

"I'm not going to complain." Says Amari. "I'm just glad he's okay."

"Yeah I'm not complaining either, but still- "

Reno puts a hand on Celeste's shoulder "Let it go, Celeste. With the Ceraphs, there's honestly not much that surprises me anymore."

Shaide twitches suddenly, and his eyes open.

"Shaide!" Amari exclaims "You're awake!"

He slowly sits up and looks around, confused and disoriented.

"Whoa, bro. Take it easy." Says Reno. "You're in the hospital."

"I'm in the hospital? What happened?" Shaide looks around at Amari.

"You drained your spirit almost to zero against the dragon." She says, tears welling up again. "I don't know how you managed, but you killed it."

"Dragon?" Shaide says slowly. Suddenly his eyes open wide "Wait, that really happened?!"

Reno reaches over and squeezes his shoulder. "Yeah, dude. You literally flew down the thing's throat."

Shaide's eyes move between his three friends, stunned. "How… How am I alive right now?"

"I don't know." Says Amari "But you are, and I am so glad you're okay."

Shaide is frowning, however. "I don't get it. I shouldn't have survived that."

The grin falls from Reno's face as he says "What do you mean? Were you intending to die there?"

"Well, not intending to die, exactly…" Shaide speaks slowly and deliberately "But I knew when I made my decision that it was a one-way trip."

"You were just going to leave me here?" says Amari, anger starting to form on her face. "Even after the promise we made?"

Shaide lowers his eyes "It was the only way, Amari. You know that. The *Last Beacon* was crippled, two of the four flak cannons were destroyed. That thing was going to kill us all. I just figured…" He shakes his head and looks back into her eyes. "If I was going to die either way, I chose to save everyone doing so."

Amari looks like she wants to hit him for a moment, and Reno and Celeste watch them with their breaths held.

"Idiot…"

Shaide chuckles "Hey, it all worked out, didn't it?"

"Yeah, this time." Amari replies, her face completely serious. "But this luck of yours won't last forever. If you keep behaving recklessly like this, some day it really will be the end of you."

"I'm prepare for that." Says Shaide. "When I chose this life, I knew it was going to end badly one way or another."

"And what about me?" Says Amari, looking hurt. "Would you really just leave me behind here?"

Shaide looks ashamed as his eyes fall to his chest.

Reno looks out the window "Hey, guys. The fleet is arriving."

Outside the window, to the north, over a dozen warships approach the town. Several frigates and destroyers, a cruiser, and even…

"Whoa! They brought the *Fire of Ifrit*!" Reno exclaims "Why are they bringing a Dreadnought?"

"Well, a dreadnought is the best weapon against a dragon." Reasons Celeste "Maybe they figured with one already here, they shouldn't take chances?"

A knock on the door, and Aton walks in. "Hey how is Shaide… You're awake?!"

"Hey dad…" mutters Shaide.

Aton doesn't look happy, however. He looks at his godson in utter shock, as if he can't believe his eyes.

"What's wrong?"

Aton shakes his head and a smile breaks across his face. "I can't believe you're awake. The docs said you'd be out for a couple of days, at best."

 A.S.GUINN

Shaide shrugs "I feel fine, honestly. I'm not sure what the big deal is."

Aton seems to accept this at face value now that the shock has passed. "Well, I have some news, since you're awake."

Amari turns to face him, and Shaide sits up straighter.

"We did some tracking, and we found where the corrupted beasts came from."

"The deadlands?" Asks Shaide.

Aton shakes his head and leans against the door. "No, surprisingly. They came from the west. Pandora."

Shaide and Amari exchange glances.

"Yep. Exactly what I thought when I found out." Says Aton. "Those were jungle lobos, marsh drakes, and the dragon was originally an Emerald Dragon."

Shaide frowns "I see. All Pandora beasts."

"Exactly." Aton nods "We took a dropship to scout the area and found something else interesting."

Four sets of eyes are locked onto him now.

"The corruption from the deadlands has extended into Pandora as well. Pretty far, by the looks of it."

Shaide swings his legs out of bed and moves to get up. Amari, however, grabs him by the shoulders and tries to force him down. "Shaide, no. You're not ready to move yet."

Shaide takes her hand and gently removes it from his shoulder. "I'm okay, Amari. Trust me." He gets out of bed and walks to the bedside table to pick up his gear.

"Are you sure you're okay?" Asks Reno, looking doubtful.

"At least let the doctor take a look at you first..." Says Amari, looking very concerned.

Shaide lets out a long sigh and sits back down. "Alright. Fine. But I'm ready to move."

"I'll get the doctor." Says Celeste. She grabs Reno by the arm and drags him outside with her.

"What?! Hey!"

The door shuts behind them. Aton sighs and sits down next to the bed. "The townspeople have a new nickname for you, you know?"

Shaide looks over at him, intrigued.

"They call you, Eden's Angel of Death. The Grim Reaper of Lone Ridge."

Shaide can't help but grin. "Angel of Death, huh? I kind of like it."

Amari sighs in exasperation "Don't give him ideas, Aton... It's hard enough to keep him alive as it is."

"Hey, I'm just the messenger." Says Aton, looking amused. "They're the ones who gave him the nickname."

Amari just sighs and crosses her arms.

A moment later, the doctor enters the room with Celeste and Reno.

"I must say, I thought they were playing a bad joke when they said you were awake, but it seems they were telling the truth. Our Angel of Death seems to live up to his reputation." He walks over to Shaide "So, how are you feeling, son?"

"I'm okay." Says Shaide "Honestly, I feel pretty good. Maybe a little tired and sore, but I feel fine."

The doctor's aura spikes for a second, and his eyes glow green as he analyzes Shaide with a perception spell. A moment later, his eyes revert to normal, and he looks extremely impressed.

"Well?" Shaide asks "How am I?"

"I wouldn't believe it if it was anyone else, but it seems your spiritual core has nearly recharged already. Your injuries are healing at a massively accelerated rate as well, so it seems to me as if you are good to go."

Aton looks stunned even further. "You're saying he's back to normal? After all of that? It hasn't even been a full day!"

"Well, his physical injuries were relatively minor." Explains the doctor. "I heard about him flying down the dragon's throat. Perhaps that angel of his protected him?"

"He has a point." Says Amari. "Theta absorbed a massive attack from it, and even sent it back twice as hard. Maybe Rho did something similar."

"I suppose that makes sense." Aton relents "It's just that… Shaide? Do you have any idea the significance of what you did?"

Shaide tilts his head to the side "I saved the town?"

Aton shakes his head "No. Not that. Shaide, no one has ever killed a dragon like that. I mean, sure we've taken them out with capital ships or large-scale Special Forces assaults, but no one has ever gone two-on-one and killed one before."

"It wasn't even me." Mutters Amari. "It was all Shaide."

"That's not true." Says Shaide "You were the one who hurt it. You did more damage to it than I could manage. And without you, I'd have never gotten a clean shot at its face. I couldn't have done it without you."

Amari blushes at the unexpected praise.

"Well, anyways…" interrupts the doctor. "I would prefer you to rest here another night, but you are free to leave, if you wish."

"Thanks, doc. Really." Says Shaide.

The doctor goes to leave but pauses at the door. "By the way. The blacksmith, Gorba, wants to see you before you leave. He says he has a gift for you." The doctor walks out the door.

"Gorba?" Asks Shaide

"He's a Termer blacksmith who moved here about forty years ago." Explains Celeste. "He's the one who helped design our flak guns and some of the buildings."

Aton looks impressed "A Termer wants to give you a gift? That's pretty high praise."

"What do you mean?" Asks Shaide.

Aton just shakes his head. "You'll have to find out for yourself."

Shaide shrugs and gets out of bed, pulling on his tattered outfit and armor.

"Hey, Shaide." Says Celeste "Make sure you wear the cloak."

"Why?"

She smiles "It's what the town knows you for now. Just do it."

Shaide pulls the cloak over his head and stands there, fully equipped again. "Well?"

"Definitely scary looking." Says Amari. "I'm glad I know you."

"You look awesome, bro." Remarks Reno.

The five of them make their way down the hall of the clinic, as nurses and civilians bow to them respectfully.

They make their way through the town streets, and Celeste leads them to a shop that somehow survived the attack. "Gorba is in here." She says.

The other four hang back, so Shaide shrugs and walks into the store.

"Well, I'll be. You're already awake!"

Shaide looks at the low counter and sees a stocky a stocky man of around five foot or slightly shorter. He smiles and walks over. "Gorba, I presume? I was told you wanted to see me?"

"Yes." He says. "I have a gift for you. Just finished, in fact." He walks to the back of his store and as Shaide waits patiently. A moment later, he returns to the front of the store with a long fancy looking box.

"This was a personal project I made recently, as kind of the crown jewel of my work, but I decided you had more than earned it. I spent all of last night making some modifications to better suit you." He pushes the box across the counter. "Take it. I hope you like it."

Shaide opens the box and slowly picks up a beautiful black broadsword.

"The hilt is made of Ebony Steel, and the blade is made of a secret tungsten alloy infused with obsidian and a special channeling variety of magicore."

Shaide removes the sword from its scabbard and examines it more closely. A medallion in the shape of the Ceraph Order sigil: a winged sword, has been inlaid into the hilt on each side, and the elegant blade looks as smooth and sharp as a razor.

"The blade will never dull, never rust, and will cut through just about anything."

Shaide hefts the sword. It is remarkably light.

"This is my gift to you, Shaide Darkmoon. A sword befitting Eden's Angel of Death. Use it well and continue to do what you do best."

*   *   *

In the skies around Lone Ridge, Alastair, the nation's Royal Military Fleet sits in defensive positions. Seven frigates, three destroyers, a heavy cruiser, and a rare dreadnought form an impenetrable wall around the city. On the plateau below, the Ceraph Order's COV *Last Beacon* undergoes rapid repairs to its hull and power systems.

When the Alastair 3rd Naval Fleet at Iron Veil received word of the assault on Lone Ridge, they deployed a battle group immediately. However, by the time they had arrived, the battle was already over, and now they are reinforcing the town's defenses while they help rebuild.

There is another vessel in the sky, however. One that does not belong to the Ceraph Order or the Alastair Navy.

The heavy destroyer *Spear of Zion* hovers in the skies to the south of the city, cloaked in a powerful optical camouflage that conceals it from the nearby Alastair fleet. Manned by three hundred true Formers, rather than the mindless thralls Alastair is used to dealing with, the stealth destroyer is prepared for virtually any battle situation.

On the bridge of this vessel stands a single Fallen, in addition to the Former crew.

"Excuse me, Lucien?" Asks the first officer.

The black haired, black clad Fallen turns to face him. "Yes, what is it?"

"Forgive me for speaking out of place, but are you certain allowing the village to survive was the right move?"

Lucien releases a low cackle before explaining "Oh, my dear Former friend. You do not understand the purpose of this mission, do you?"

"Sir?"

"Could we have taken the town? Of course, we could have, but we learned something quite interesting." He cackles loudly, sounding quite demented. "They have an especially capable young Ceraph in their midst. The very same one whom I witnessed in the mountains above that blight of a town, Broadspring, and I suspect the very same one who defeated our agent, Justice."

"I don't understand, sir. Then why let them live?"

"Simple, my narrow-minded friend. We have gleaned valuable information, and we cannot risk revealing ourselves to the Ceraphs just yet. Let them live for now. They will all fall before the might of Belial soon enough."

"Yes sir, I understand."

"No, no you don't." Sighs Lucien "But it makes no difference. Take us to the rendezvous. I do not wish to be late reporting to my father."

*   *   *

Shaide walks out of the store with his new sword to meet his eagerly awaiting friends. He catches movement out of the corner of his eye and looks to the sky south of town. He swears he sees a ripple in the clouds for a moment, but then it passes.

"Hey, Shaide? You okay?"

Shaide shakes his head "Yeah, I'm fine."

Reno looks eager and says, "Well then, show it to us!"

Shaide smiles and removes the sword from the box. Amari. Aton, Celeste, and Reno all look at the sheathed sword in awe. Shaide grins and slowly pulls the sword from its scabbard, carefully holding it out for them to see.

"I can honestly say that is one of the most beautiful swords I have ever seen." Says Celeste, her eyes twinkling at the shiny black blade.

"A true Termer sword." Says Aton "Having this is really something to be proud of."

"Can I hold it?" Asks Reno, enthralled by the beautiful sword.

"Be careful." Says Shaide as he gently hands it over, "This is the sharpest blade I have ever seen. Don't hurt yourself."

Reno hefts it a couple of times "This is light. REALLY light for its size."

"Yeah, he said it was made of a special alloy." Says Shaide. "Never dulls, never rusts, cuts through nearly anything. I guess a blade doesn't need to be heavy when it is so sharp."

Reno hands it back to him "No kidding."

Shaide looks at Aton "Where is Lucy? And Lania and Rayn, for that matter?"

"Lucy is aboard the *Last Beacon,* helping to oversee the repairs." He replies, "As for your other friends, I cannot say."

Reno coughs "They are likely still on guard duty."

"I see." Says Shaide. "Can we return to the ship for now? I can't believe I'm saying this, but I want to see Lucy."

Aton raises his eyebrows, looking amused "As much as she gives you a hard time, we all know you love your aunt, Shaide. "

"What's with this, Shaide?" Amari asks "Is everything okay? You're acting a little odd."

Shaide mutters to her "I think I'm just a little shaken up. That's all."

Amari hugs his arm and smiles "I understand. I'm still going to beat you up later, though." She finishes seriously.

"Yeah, yeah…" sighs Shaide. "I know. I deserve it."

"Aww, you two are so cute…" jeers Reno.

Shaide and Amari exchange nods, and then simultaneously turn and punch Reno in the face.

"OW! WHAT THE HELL!?" He yells, rocking back and grabbing his nose.

"You know you deserved that…" Celeste chuckles.

Reno pinches the bridge of his nose and pouts.

When they walk out of the busted village gates, they find Lania and Rayn standing guard outside of the still-under-repair *Last Beacon*.

Lania sees Shaide first and calls out "Shaide! You're okay!"

Shaide smiles and jogs over to meet his friends.

"Shaide! I can't believe you're on your feet after that!" says a stunned Rayn, extending his hand. "How are you feeling?"

"I'm good, Rayn." Says Shaide, shaking his hand "I didn't see you in the battle. Where were you?"

"Operating one of the flak guns. Someone had to, and I was closest."

Shaide nods and turns to Lania, who promptly gives him a tight hug.

"Whoa, Lania!" Says Shaide, slightly alarmed "Where did this come from?!"

"You idiot." She says, releasing him. "I seriously thought we were going to lose another friend. I'm glad you're okay."

Shaide nods "I'm glad you two are fine also. What are you doing out here?"

"Sergeant Wyatt instructed us to guard the *Last Beacon* while it undergoes repairs." Rayn explains "She said after everything you Ceraphs did to help us, it was the least we could do."

"What's going on out here? What's with the gaggle? We have work to do, people, and- Oh! Shaide!"

Shaide looks behind his friends and sees Lucy coming over to greet him. She walks up and pulls him down into a hug, smashing his face into her chest. "I'm surprised you're up already! I thought for sure you'd be down for a few days!"

Shaide rolls his eyes and says in a muffled voice "Auntie, I can't breathe…"

She releases him and looks at Aton "No time for a happy reunion I'm afraid. There's been a new development."

All eyes turn to her.

"Pandora is asking for help."

CHAPTER 5

REUNION

Onboard of the bridge of the COV *Last Beacon*, the four Ceraphs gather around the communication console with Shipmaster Corolas, listening to a rather frantic transmission from a village in Pandora.

"Ceraph Order, my name is Nanilina, acting chieftain of the village of Children's Oasis. We need assistance as soon as possible. Our village has endured daily attacks by mutated beasts that are not normal to this region. We don't know how much longer we can hold out. We have already lost sixty percent of our defense force, and each raid brings more civilian casualties. It pains us to request outside assistance, but we have no choice. As servants of Eden, and enemies of the corruption, please send help as soon as you possibly can manage.

     A.S.GUINN

We must find the source of this new corruption, and snuff it out, or else there may soon be o Children's Oasis left to defend."

Aton looks at Corolas "How soon can we be underway?"

Corolas sighs "All four gravity cores are now back online, but our electrical system is still significantly damaged. We can move, but not very fast. Weapons are still offline too, so we cannot fight either. That dragon's attack was more than just fire. It overloaded our systems as well.

Aton frowns, considering their options.

"Children's oasis isn't THAT far. We should be able to manage in a dropship, shouldn't we?" asks Shaide.

Corolas shakes his head "No, even if you could keep the engines from overheating, you'd be defenseless. You likely wouldn't make it in one piece."

"Couldn't we ask the Alastair military for help?" suggests Amari. "If it's an emergency, is there any reason they wouldn't help us?"

Aton and Corolas exchange impressed looks. Aton turns to Amari "They would not normally dare to cross international lines, but if a Ceraph squad has an emergency…"

"It's worth a try." Says Shaide.

*   *   *

"You want me to take the four of you across Pandora's national border to investigate a corrupted incursion in sovereign Pandora territory?" Asks an amused Captain Winslow of the ARV *North Star*. Coincidentally, the same frigate that took Shaide to Broadspring just before he became a Ceraph.

A.S.GUINN

"Yes, sir." Replies Shaide "I know it is a great deal to ask, as it is technically illegal, but as we believe this incident is related to the attack here, we cannot ignore it."

Winslow turns to face away from them "Son, I remember when you were on this ship, oh, three years ago. I remember searching for you when your dropship was downed by a wyvern." He turns back to face him again. "And now you are Eden's legendary Angel of Death. Son, if there is anything that I can do to help you, you bet your ass I will do it. Give me an hour to get permission from Admiral Arale, and we will depart."

"Thank you, sir." Says Shaide. "It will be an honor to serve on your vessel again."

"Don't thank me, son." Says Winslow "It is my honor to host a prestigious squad of Ceraphs such as yourselves." Captain Winslow boards his dropship, and it lifts off towards the ARV *Fire of Ifrit*.

"I suppose letting you talk to him was a good Idea after all." Remarks Aton "He seems particularly fond of you. I remember talking to him back when your dropship crashed in Broadspring. He was very helpful that ay as well."

"Good man." Says Shaide.

Amari looks uncomfortable. "I feel so out of place."

Lucy squeezes her shoulder "Don't, girly. We're ALL going to feel out of place soon. Even I have only been to Pandora twice, I think. And both times it was REALLY awkward."

Aton seems like he can barely contain himself.

"What's so funny?" Shaide asks curiously.

"I really shouldn't tell you…"

"Aton…" Lucy warns him.

"But last time we were there, Lucy got a little drunk and got rather…friendly…with one of the local Nekomata girls." Aton's face is brick red from restraining his laughter. "Oh god, it was hilarious when she kept saying 'hey kitty kitty' and petting her…"

"I will kill you, Aton…" Lucy growls.

Shaide and Amari exchange rather alarmed looks. "Oh god, and I live with her." Says Amari.

Lucy waves her hands frantically "Oh god, no. I don't go for girls! Relax! I was just really, REALLY drunk, and she was so soft and… I'm going to shut up now."

Shaide and Amari bust out laughing so hard they double over.

"Anyways," Aton changes the subject "Shaide. Are you sure you're up for this?"

Shaide stretches a little and nods "Yeah, I feel like I'm back to a hundred percent."

"If you say so…" Says Aton.

*　　*　　*

One hour later, they are waiting on the dropship from the ARV *North Star* to come down and pick them up. They are rather surprised, however, when five familiar faces come to greet them at the incline.

"Shaide! Amari!" Reno calls out.

"What on earth…" Shaide says. He sees them carrying all of their gear.

Sergeant Wyatt salutes reflexively when she approaches. "Angel of Death, it is good to see you on your feet again. I was sure you'd be down for a while."

"Yeah, everyone keeps saying that." Says Shaide.

"My Exorcist squad has new orders. They have been instructed to join you aboard the ARV *North Star* and assist you in whatever way you deem necessary."

Aton frowns "That's really not necessary, sergeant."

Wyatt shakes her head. "I'm afraid it is, sir. The order came from Admiral Arale. He recognizes the importance of your mission and wants to assist however he can."

"I understand." Says Aton "Happy to have you all join us."

"The pleasure is ours, sir." Says Rayn "Working alongside you again will be valuable experience for our training."

"Agreed." Says Celeste

"Looking forward to it!" Says Lania with enthusiasm.

"Meh…"

Shaide looks at Reno, who just grins.

"Men. Your attention for a moment."

Reno, Rayn, Lania, and Celeste all face Sergeant Wyatt at attention.

"Follow the Ceraph's orders no matter what. They know what they are doing, and I am sure they will get you back in one piece." She says "Do your best to support them, and come back even better than you were when you left. Understood?"

"Yes ma'am!"

"Dismissed, squad. Good luck."

A lone dropship descends on their position and settles onto the ground. The rear hatch opens, and the pilot calls out "Come on, Ceraphs! Captain Winslow wants to depart immediately!"

"Understood!" calls out Aton. The eight of them board the dropship and sit down.

"Good luck! Take care of yourself, sis!" Sergeant Wyatt calls out.

The dropship's engines scream as the pilots takes them back into the air. They hang on tight as the dropship spirals upward until it reaches the hanger bay of the awaiting Alastair frigate. They ease into the open bay doors and settle down onto the deck.

They find Captain Winslow waiting for the in the hanger bay. "Good afternoon, Ceraphs and Exorcists."

"Request permission to board, Captain?" Says Aton.

"Granted. It is good to see you again. We will be getting underway in just a moment, but I wanted to greet you in person."

The eight of them disembark from the troop bay and line out in front of Captain Winslow. Celeste, Lania, Rayn, and Reno all salute the Captain.

"At Ease, you four."

They relax.

"Sir, where would you like us to stay during the voyage?" Asks Aton.

"Use the unused crew barracks aft of the hangar." The captain replies. "The ARMA crew already knows where it is."

"We do, sir." Replies Rayn

Aton nods "You six, go on down there and wait for us." He says. "Lucy and I need to speak alone."

Shaide and the others bow and walk away back to the aft exit of the hanger. The captain likewise bows and says "I will leave you to it, Ceraphs. I will be on the bridge if you need me. We need to get underway."

"Of course, captain. Thank you."

Captain Winslow departs the fore of the hanger, and Aton turns to Lucy. "We need to talk."

"I think I know." Says Lucy. "It's about Shaide, isn't it?"

Aton nods "Yes. Something about Shaide isn't right. Not only did he survive against impossible odds, but he recovered impossibly fast as well."

Lucy shifts uncomfortably "I noticed. The shape he was in, it should have been three days at best before he regained consciousness, but he woke up after a simple night's sleep."

"I think we're seeing the anomaly Armstrong warned us about." Says Aton. "Shaide is dangerously well-attuned to spiritual energy. It flows through his body inhumanly efficiently."

"Is that really a bad thing?" Says Lucy "It means he is strong."

Aton shakes his head. "No, Lucy, that is exactly the problem. The way his body is channeling spiritual power is increasing too fast. Armstrong seems to fear that it may exceed his ability to control it. If that happens before he has the means to control his power…"

"He could become a walking time bomb." Lucy says, understanding now what her brother is saying. "But I don't get it, why is he such a special case?"

"I don't know…" Says Aton. "I feel like Orville knows more than he is telling he. He has taken an unusual interest in Shaide."

"Did you notice the side effect of his growing power?" Lucy asks.

Aton tilts his head inquisitively.

"Amari's power is growing unusually fast as well." Says Amari "Her spiritual signature greatly resembles his own, when you scan her."

"I hadn't noticed." Says Aton. "She's been strong since I met her years ago."

Lucy frowns "Is it possible that her own energy is feeding his growth?"

"I don't know." Says Aton. "But if we ever make it back to the Citadel, I'm going to have a long talk with Armstrong, and find out what he knows."

*   *   *

"So, come on, you two." Lania pokes at Shaide and Amari. "Are you really going to sit there and tell us there is nothing romantic going on between you? Nothing at all?"

The six teenagers are milling around the empty troop barracks on board the *North Star*, having a rather intense discussion about the two resident Ceraphs.

Amari and Shaide exchange glances, and she says "No, really. We're just really good friends. That's all."

"Huh." Says Lania, looking surprised "I was sure that there was something going on, but I guess I was wrong."

"Yeah, to be honest, I was kinda wondering about that myself." Interjects Reno.

"So, Amari." Says Lania, a mischievous look on her face. "Are you honestly telling me that if Celeste here; Gorgeous, busty eighteen-year-old Celeste, was to grab Shaide by the face and stick her tongue down his throat, right here in front of you, that it wouldn't bother you?"

Celeste and Reno look at Amari with intense curiosity all over their faces. Shaide and Rayn on the other hand seem rather disinterested.

"Well, I don't see why it would." Amari replies. "Aside from it being rather inappropriate, anyways."

Lania and Celeste exchange looks, and without hesitation, Celeste leans forward and grabs Shaide by the neck and plants her lips on his. Shaide's eyes open wide in shock as she legitimately kisses him wholeheartedly.

As Amari watches this, she feels a strange twinge of pain in her chest, and an inexplicable feeling of anger. *Am I jealous?* She finds herself thinking.

On the outside, however, she shows no reaction whatsoever, and when Celeste pulls away, leaving Shaide stunned and dazed, Lania frowns. "Huh. I guess there really IS nothing going on between you."

"What the hell was that!?" Exclaims Reno, looking almost as stunned as Shaide.

Celeste looks at him "What? I wanted to see if she would react."

"That looked pretty enthusiastic to me." Rayn mutters, laughing quietly to himself.

"Shut it." Celeste shoots back at him.

Shaide finally finds his words again "I, uhh… What the hell, Celeste? Did you have to use tongue if you were just going to test us?"

Again, Amari feels that twinge of jealousy. *What is this?*

"Well, I figured if I was going to do it, I might as well enjoy myself." Celeste replies. "Why? Are you complaining?"

"Celeste, leave the poor guy alone." Rayn interjects "If you're going to get friendly with Shaide, do it somewhere more private."

Although externally calm, Amari is feeling a sense of panic inside. Her heart is racing, she feels a tightness in her chest, and she is having trouble thinking straight with the image of Celeste kissing him in her mind. *What the hell is wrong with me? He's my best friend! Why is this upsetting me?!*

"Hey Amari? Are you feeling okay?" Shaide asks, looking concerned.

Amari jumps and nods "Yeah, I'm fine. I think something was wrong with the sausage at breakfast. My stomach is a little queasy." This is an outright lie, of course.

"If you say so." Says Shaide. "Need to lie down?"

Amari shakes her head, hair flopping in her face. "No, I'll be alright."

Shaide gives her a look, not quite sure if he believes her or not, but he decides not to push the issue. "So, yeah. Anyways…"

Amari sits back quietly and tries to calm herself over what just happened. She had never felt that before. Not even when that Drameri girl…

"Hey Shaide?" Celeste looks at him curiously "Was that not the first time you ever kissed a girl?"

Reno answers for him "Oh hell no. First girl he kissed was back in our first year. That Nekomata girl?"

"Oh yeah! Nyu!" Shaide exclaims "I never did find out what happened to her."

Lania claps her hands together "I remember her! The one I saw you with the weekend before we went to Broadspring!"

Shaide rubs his neck awkwardly "Yeah, THAT was a thing. I wonder what ever happened to her. I never saw her again."

"Hey bro?" Reno turns to face him "Anyone else other than that?"

Shaide sighs in exasperation "Yeah, a couple. Girls tend to be REALLY grateful when you save their town from monsters, you know."

Amari forces herself to join the conversation to avoid seeming out of place "Oh yeah, like that Drameri girl, Kara, who tried to get you to go home with her a month after I joined!"

"Right, yeah. Her." Shaide looks slightly embarrassed for some reason. "She was REALLY pushy. I think she wanted to take me home for good. You had to pretend to be my girlfriend to chase her off for me!"

"Yeah. She was really quick to believe it too." Amari lets out a hollow laugh "That was an interesting week all around."

Reno looks confused "Why wouldn't you go home with her? Was she ugly or something?"

Shaide shifts uncomfortably "Well, actually she was pretty cute, and really sweet. I just wasn't interested."

"Are you telling me that you STILL have trouble around attractive women?" Rayn says, looking intensely amused. "You're brave enough to fly down a dragon's throat, but you're still scared of women?"

Shaide shrugs awkwardly.

"He doesn't seem uncomfortable around us or Amari." Lania mumbles "Are we ugly or something?"

Celeste and Amari both look at Shaide pointedly as if expecting him to say something.

Shaide, on the other hand, looks extremely alarmed and uncomfortable. "Oh god, no. I don't think ANY of you are ugly at all. Well, except Reno." He cracks a grin. "I just have known you all along time, so I got over it a long time ago."

"Well, you DID seem uncomfortable when you first saw me after I got these." She bounces her chest slightly "So I guess that makes sense."

"Lucy still makes you uncomfortable though." Says Amari suspiciously. "Even though you're around her all the time."

"She keeps shoving my face in her chest!" Shaide retorts "OF course she makes me uncomfortable!"

Amari chuckles, but she has a rather downcast look on her face. Shaide notices, but he can't imagine what is bothering her.

"So Shaide. Tell us." Celeste inquires forcefully "How DID you survive going down that dragon's throat? Did you use some kind of special technique? What did you do?"

Shaide looks around and finds all five sets of eyes on him now. He rubs his neck uncomfortably and hesitates to answer. *The truth is, even I don't know how I survived that.*

"Yeah Shaide, tell us." Reno says eagerly "It's not classified, is it?"

Shaide sighs in defeat "The truth is, I don't really know how I survived. When I flew down its throat, the slipstream pulled the fire blast in with me. I never felt like anything really touched me. Maybe Rho was reinforcing my aura, or maybe I was just impossibly fortunate."

"Shaide," Rayn leans forward "Come on, man. You have to give us more than that."

Shaide looks at Amari uncomfortably, but she just looks away from him. "The truth is, I was fully expecting to die. I went down to sacrifice myself and take it with me. I did not plan to be here now."

An awkward silence fills the room. Reno and Celeste were already aware of this, but they remain silent. Several sets of eyes move to Amari as she refuses to look at Shaide, evidently still upset with him.

The door clicks open "Well, this is certainly an unpleasant atmosphere. What the hell happened?"

All eyes look up and see Aton and Lucy entering the room. Shaide takes advantage of this to ask "Hey, dad? How WOULD someone survive a kamikaze attack down a dragon's throat?"

All eyes lock onto Shaide's Godfather. He considers the question carefully. "Best guess is that it had something to do with

Rho. Angels are very special existences, being sentient lifeforms of pure spiritual energy. It is possible, even likely, that Rho simply shielded Shaide inside of the dragon, exploding its energy and diverting all harm from Shaide, destroying the beast in the process."

Everyone in the room, aside from Shaide, nods in understanding, seemingly satisfied by this explanation. Shaide, however, looks at his godfather suspiciously for a moment, not quite believing this explanation himself. His expression is not lost on Amari, who looks at him curiously.

*   *   *

Several hours pass aboard the *North Star* as they travel to Pandora. All four Ceraphs are standing on the bridge as they fly over the jungle, watching three approaching warships of an unusual design.

Captain Winslow watches the incoming ships nervously, unsure of their intentions.

"Relax, Captain." Says Aton "When they contact us, we'll explain the situation. They'll understand. Even in Pandora, Ceraphs are held in high regard."

Captain Winslow stares out the front viewport. "As I understand it, they do not worship Eden in Pandora. Am I wrong?"

Aton shakes his head "Not completely, Captain. The Nekomata worship Diosia, the living planet. The Junmeri, however, still practice the worship of Eden, and even the Nekomata recognize Eden's importance. They just believe the planet is more important."

Captain Winslow nods reassured "We have few dealings with Pandora. Even in the military, it is almost mythological in nature."

"Captain. Short-band transmission coming in."

"Put it through." The Captain replies.

A female voice comes over the short-band communication's equipment. *"Unidentified Alastair warship, this is the PDF* Forest Guardian. *You are trespassing on the sovereign nation of Pandora. State your business immediately or you will be treated as hostile."*

Captain Winslow walks over to the console and hits the transmit key. "Ma'am, this is Captain Winslow of the ARV *North Star.* Due to a damaged airship, I am transporting four Ceraphs in response to a distress call from the village of Children's Oasis. Please acknowledge."

A good minute passes by as the three odd looking frigates form a phalanx around the *North Star.* Even the Ceraphs are a bit nervous by the delay in response.

"ARV North Star, *the Ceraphs' business is confirmed as legitimate. I must inquire, is Alastair offering additional support as your warship is present?"*

Captain Winslow keys up and replies "Yes ma'am. I am providing four exorcist-class warriors and support craft if needed."

The uncomfortable delay fills the air again as the Pandora Defense Forces seem to be discussing something.

"ARV North Star, *your assistance is unexpected but appreciated. Turn heading 330 and proceed to Children's Oasis. We will escort you until you arrive. Acknowledge?"*

Captain Winslow lets out the breath he was unconsciously holding. "Acknowledged PDF *Forest Guardian.* Turning heading 330 with escort. Thank you."

The ARV *North Star* adjusts to the appropriate heading and moves to the north-northwest. Captain Winslow turns and addresses the Ceraphs. "I was concerned that they may not be so willing to let us proceed, but I see what you mean about Ceraphs."

"Yes, Captain." Aton nods in response "If they were desperate enough to ask for our help, they will not dare get in our way. They are a very insular people. If they reach out, it's a big deal."

"That's what worries me." Mutters Lucy.

Shaide walks up to the domed viewport at the front of the bridge and looks down. The density of the forests here is quite amazing. On one of the navigation panels he can see they are over three thousand feet in the air, but the treetops seem so close beneath him.

After a moment, Amari's curiosity overwhelms her irritation with Shaide, and she joins him in looking out over Pandora. This was, after all, her first time in this nation.

"Beautiful, isn't it?" Shaide asks her.

She just nods, mesmerized by the sheer density of green.

"The most beautiful things are usually the most dangerous, though." He says thoughtfully.

"Captain. Docking spire in sight ahead." Says the navigator.

"*ARV* North Star, *dock with the illuminated docking pier and stand by in your hanger until security forces greet you.*"

The communications officer responds "Acknowledged, ma'am."

The docking spire ahead isn't especially large. It's designed to accommodate merchant and supply ships. Not full fleets of warships like the air docks in Alastair and Erita. Nevertheless, it is more than sufficient to accommodate their frigate.

Aton walks up and puts a hand each on Shaide and Amari's shoulders and says "Come on. Let's go down to the hanger and wait for our greeting party."

The four of them make their way through the corridors of the ship and back down into the hanger bay. As Shaide, Amari, and Lucy wait near the bay doors, Aton runs off to retrieve Reno, Rayn, Celeste, and Lania.

"So Shaide, I've been meaning to ask." Lucy grins mischievously "How did it feel to be inside your first woman?"

Shaide and Amari both look at Lucy in complete alarm and shock.

"The dragon was a female!" Lucy laughs "So, technically you were-"

"LUCY SHUT IT!" Amari yells at her.

Lucy and Shaide both look at Amari in shock now. Everyone nearby in the hanger bay gives them uncomfortable looks.

"Jeez, I'm sorry." Says Lucy "I didn't realize it was a sore subject."

Amari looks surprised at her own outburst, and quickly looks ashamed "No, I'm sorry. It's just… I'm still shaken up about the incident in Lone Ridge."

"I understand…" Says Lucy. "Sometimes I forget how young you two are. This was your first fight like this, with such high stakes. I hadn't considered the possible trauma."

Shaide sighs in relief. He was worried that might escalate. Amari has definitely been acting strangely. She'd been moody and short tempered ever since he woke up, sometimes just staring blankly into space.

"Good lord, what happened in here?" Celeste's voice says behind Shaide, making him jump.

"Oh, don't mind us." Shaide says dismissively "Lucy is just making some bad jokes, and it's getting on people's nerves. That's all."

Lucy sticks her tongue out playfully.

"Can I not leave you alone for even five minutes?" Aton says to his sister.

Lucy just winks at him with her tongue out before turning back to face the open sky.

"So, Ceraphs. Friends." Rayn corrects himself "What do we need to know?"

"We'll be docking at Children's Oasis shortly." Lucy explains. "We'll stay here until we're cleared to enter the village. The Pandorans aren't especially happy to have the Alastair military here, but they're being polite and accepting the additional help, so BEHAVE YOURSELVES."

"They're not the ones I'm worried about, Lucy..." Aton mumbles.

"HEY! I was DRUNK, okay!?" Lucy says indignantly "Let it go, please!"

Aton grins and chuckles "Not as much fun when it's you, is it?"

Shaide chuckles under his breath, and even Amari cracks a smile in spite of herself.

"So, we've been kind of kept in the dark here." Says Celeste "What exactly are we doing here?"

"You know as much as we do, Celeste." Shaide replies "They sent a distress call requesting Ceraph help, but we don't really know what to expect."

"Going in blind and playing it by ear?" She says "Simple. I like it."

"Sometimes I think you two get along way too well." Rayn laughs

Again, Amari feels that strange tightness in her chest. She does her best to ignore it, though. She can't get distracted right now.

"You okay, Amari?" Shaide asks, looking concerned. He noticed her expression.

"Yeah, I'm fine." Amari lies, forcing a convincing smile on her face. "Just lost in thought. That's all."

"If you say so." Shaide says suspiciously.

At this point, the spire from Children's Oasis comes into view, extremely close. The deck officer takes control of the ship from a console near the hanger doors. The ship eases slowly against the docking pier until they hear a soft *thunk*, and the ship makes contact with the gantry.

Waiting on the pier is a contingent of six individuals. Three of them are obviously Drameri, although these are Drameri who left their home of Erita to live in Pandora, so technically they are called

ETERNAL KNIGHTS OF EDEN II

Junmeri. The other three individuals are drastically different in appearance.

Humanoid in shape, though slightly smaller in stature, these three have a distinctly animal-like appearance. They have pointed ears atop their heads, long tails coming from the base of their spines, and their eyes are colorful with slits for pupils. In addition to this. They each have a thin layer of fur on their bodies with distinct stripes or spots, depending on the individual. These are the Nekomata of Pandora.

The Nekomata in the lead is dressed in a fancy fur outfit complete with a fur cloak and a circlet embedded with gemstones. Shaide is having difficulty guessing, but she would appear to be in her thirties or forties. The two Nekomata females accompanying her are obviously bodyguards, dressed in more practical furs and carrying partisans: polearms with a bladed spear on the end.

The Junmeri, on the other hand, seem to be huntresses of some kind. Shaide finds it odd that no male Junmeri are present.

"Greetings, Ceraphs and Alastair forces. I am Nanilina, the acting chieftainess of Children's Oasis. While we usually do not welcome outsiders, the current crisis has me very happy to see you."

Aton bows politely, and the others all follow suit. Captain Winslow approaches from the front of the hanger bay with two officers.

"Ma'am, it is my pleasure to return to Children's Oasis, though it has been some time since I was here." Aton greets her, then he looks up suspiciously "May I ask, what happened to Chieftainess Analisia?"

Nanilina lowers her head, and her ears flatten sadly against her skull. "That, Ceraph, is why I am acting chieftainess now. My sister Analisia was killed in the current crisis, and I was forced to take her place."

"I am sorry to hear that." Says Aton.

Captain Winslow approaches "Chieftainess Nanilina, I presume?"

"I am she."

Captain Winslow bows "I am Captain William Winslow, commanding officer of the ARV *North Star*, and I am here at your service."

"A pleasure, Captain. Please, come with me and we can enter the village proper, and I can explain the situation and why I called you here. Come." She turns and walks back towards the spire itself.

The Ceraphs, the Exorcist candidates, and the Captain and his accompanying officers all follow Nanilina onto the pier, while the Junmeri huntresses escort them. Shaide looks over the edge and notices the village below appears to have significant damage. He frowns, getting an ominous feeling about their mission.

As they walk down the spiral staircase inside the spire, which they now see was once a titanic tree, Nanilina explains some about the village.

"Children's Oasis was once a prospering Pandoran village. We maintained necessary trade with Alastair and Dorim, we defended ourselves from the dangers of the forests with little difficulty, and everyone worked together, living happy and healthy together here." She is being unusually open for a Nekomata. "Recently, however, everything changed. We've been suffering increasing attacks from corrupted beasts that are far stronger than anything we have dealt with before. As you can see from the damage…"

They walk out of the tree into the village proper, and they can see that indeed, the village is in sorry shape. What was once clearly a beautiful, extravagant village is now half in shambles, burned or crushed by who knows what.

"We are no longer able to keep them out when they attack. The worst by far was the behemoth attack. We lost many warriors and civilians to that monster, and it is still an absolute miracle that we were able to stop it at all.

Before she can continue any further, someone interrupts. "Shaide? SHAIDE!"

Shaide is flattened to the ground as someone tackles him with an unexpected hug.

CHAPTER 6

PANDORA

Shaide lies on the ground in shock for a moment as something warm and soft pins him to the ground. He feels like this unexpected person is choking him to death. She finally lets go of him and pushes her upper half off of him, awkwardly straddling the lower half.

Shaide is still slightly dazed as he looks up into the face of a very happy looking Nekomata woman about his own age. "I'm sorry, do I know you?"

She frowns unpleasantly "Do I really look that different? I recognize you, you know. You smell the same."

Shaide's eyes open wide "NYU!?"

Amari's eyes open in shock at the fact that Shaide knows this girl. She tries to think and place where she's heard this name before.

ETERNAL KNIGHTS OF EDEN II

A smile breaks across Nyuralisiania's face once again as he recognizes her. She looks significantly different from the last time he saw her around three years ago. She's grown up. A lot.

Reno exclaims excitedly "Nyu?! Is that really you?"

Nyu looks up at Reno curiously, and then brighten up again "Hey! Reno! You're here too?"

Shaide coughs "Umm, Nyu? Can you get off of me, please? This is REALLY awkward."

Nyu looks down for a moment, confused, then it clicks. "Oh right. Sorry!"

Shaide allows her to help him to his feet before dusting himself off. He looks around at everyone for a moment and then freezes when he sees the slew of amused expressions. "Oh, umm, everyone? This is Nyuralisiania, also known as Nyu. She is an old friend from before I joined the Ceraph Order."

Nanilina clears her throat, and then Aton says, "I'm sorry to interrupt the reunion, but we are here on urgent business, after all."

"Right…" says Shaide, looking ashamed "Sorry, Aton."

Nanilina looks at Nyu "Actually young lady, you may wish to join us for this too. After all, you have been a significant help in protecting the village."

Nyu's ears perk up "Thank you, chieftainess."

"Well, then, shall we continue?"

The party resumes walking, heading for a large longhouse-style building at the end of the main pathway. Nyu falls in line rather enthusiastically beside Shaide, leaving Amari scowling on his other side.

As they walk through the village, Shaide makes a few observations. One of which is that there are indeed a significant number of male Junmeri in the village, and they are all occupied with rebuilding. The second observation is that every Nekomata he sees is female. He had always heard that males were very rare, and even heard rumors that there were no males at all, and that they bore children by reproducing with males of other species.

"Hey Nyu?" Shaide whispers "Why are there no male Nekomata in the village?"

Nyu answers quietly "There are three here in the village, but I'm not sure where they are. Only one in fifty Nekomata are male, so you don't see them often."

They reach the longhouse and proceed inside where they find a comfortable, welcoming atmosphere. Nanilina and her escorts take a seat at the table, and she indicates they should do the same. When Shaide sits down, Nyu and Amari take their places on either side of him. Reno notices and looks at him with an amused grin.

"Ceraphs," Nanilina begins "In the last month, forty-one villagers and warriors have lost their lives, including our previous chieftainess. We always suffered some degree of attacks in the past, but they never accomplished anything. Now. However, we are facing a near daily siege by corrupted monsters of varieties we have never seen before, in numbers we have never seen before, with a ferocity and coordination we have never seen before. Varofia?"

One of the Junmeri huntresses (presumably Varofia) sits up straighter "The attacks all seem to be originating from the south. We have not been able to find the source, but as dangerous as it is here, it

     A.S.GUINN

gets even more so as you head that direction. Nekoshin, drakes, basilisk, lobos, decantula, nightstalker, you name it. We've been searching for anything that could be the cause, but so far we have found nothing."

Nanilina nods and inquires curiously "So, master Ceraphs. What do you make of this information so far?"

"Well, Chieftainess, this would not appear to be an isolated incident." Replies Aton "To the east, in Alastair, we recently faced a similar problem. The village of Lone Ridge suffered a horrific assault by unnaturally coordinated corrupted forces. Every regional beast you can imagine, along with a small army of formers assaulted the village, culminating in a very unpleasant visit from a small corrupted dragon."

The chieftainess, her bodyguards, and the three Junmeri huntresses all look extremely shocked. You don't very often hear of anyone surviving dragon attacks when they occur.

Nanilina clears her throat "If I may ask, Ceraph. How did you fend off the beast and survive? When dragons are involved, destruction is normally absolute."

Aton extends a hand and indicates Shaide "This is Shaide Darkmoon. He took on the dragon himself and earned the nickname Angel of Death during the battle of Lone Ridge. You can piece together what happened, I am sure."

All Nekomata and Junmeri eyes turn to Shaide, including an extremely wide-eyed and impressed Nyu.

"Mr. Darkmoon, does this man speak the truth?" Nanilina asks, astonishment filling her face. "Did you face down a true corrupted dragon and defeat it?"

Shaide nods rather shyly, uncomfortable with the amount of attention he is receiving, especially from so many women.

"How did you do it?" Nyu whispers audibly.

Lucy speaks up proudly "He flew his angel down its throat, literally, and killed it from the inside. He came out with barely a scratch."

All eyes are on him again, and he coughs uncomfortably "I really don't like all of this attention. Can we please return to the matter at hand?"

"Yes, of course, master Ceraph." Nanilina says respectfully "I could not help myself. Aton, is it? Please continue."

Aton's grin fades as he continues his explanation. "We discovered that the corruption in the land seems to be spreading north in certain regions. While we have been unable to verify due to the density of foliage, we believe that the corruption has spread into Pandora, and could very well be impacting local wildlife."

"It is as I feared…" Says Nanilina "Allow me to finish my explanation of our problem now."

"Of course, chieftainess." Says Aton.

Throughout all of this, Reno, Rayn, Lania, and Celeste, as well at Captain Winslow and his attendants, remain silent, listening intently as all of this is a little beyond their understanding.

"Four days ago, we lost contact with a sister village to the south." Nanilina explains "We sent our scouts to investigate and made an alarming discovery."

Varofia picks up "The entire village had been completely leveled. Nothing left standing. When we followed the trail of what did it, we were shocked at what we found."

A second Junmeri continues "The great elder wyrm, guardian of the forests for centuries, was terribly corrupted. It never bothered the village before, and in fact seemed to protect it at times. Now, however, it was something horrible, and it killed everyone."

"Varofia and Hancer speak the truth." Nanilina says grimly "The great elder wyrm was once a symbol for our people. An agent of Diosia sent to protect those who worship the living planet. But now it seeks only to destroy."

"I am a good fighter," Says Nyu "But I do not have even close to what it will take to kill the beast."

"That is why we called you, Ceraphs." Nanilina stands up and bows, almost pleading "We need you to do what you exist to do. Take out this elder wyrm before it claims even more lives and find the source of the corruption that threatens our village. Please, Ceraphs. I beg this of you!"

"Relax, Nanilina." Aton says in a calming voice "There is no need to fear. We came here to help you. That is what we do. We will seek out this corruption and purge it like we always do."

"Chieftainess Nanilina. May I make an offer myself?"

Nanilina turns to Captain Winslow "Yes Captain, you may."

"I will send my exorcists with the Ceraphs to aid in the hunt, but I would also like to offer you the services of my ship and crew to aid in defending you and your village. I have a modest company of soldiers aboard my vessel, and they could aid in defending your village while the Ceraphs are away."

Nanilina seems to contemplate this heavily for nearly a full minute. She finally closes her eyes and drops her head, and replies "It pains me to allow outside soldiers to defend our village, but the well-being of my people must come before my pride." She raises her head "Captain Winslow, I graciously accept your offer of assistance. Thank you."

Captain Winslow bows "I know of a time in history when Pandora rose to aid Alastair in its greatest time of need. I feel it is only proper to honor that friendship now and offer you the same that you gave us so long ago."

"Very wise, Captain." Nanilina replies "Perhaps there is honor among outsiders after all. Thank you. Nyuralisiania!" She turns to Nyu suddenly.

"Y-Yes ma'am?"

"I would like you to accompany the Ceraphs on their mission. There appears to be a great trust between you, and your…abilities…could prove useful to them."

"Yes ma'am! I would be honored!"

Varofia turns to Nyu "Kitten. Do you remember where we last saw the great elder wyrm?"

"Yes, ma'am." Nyu replies "I can show them the way."

"Very good." Varofia smiles "Do Pandora proud, former stray. Do us proud."

Nyu turns to the Ceraphs "When do we leave?"

Aton and Lucy exchange glances before he says "We can leave immediately, if everyone is up to it. Everyone is fully geared, so we can leave any time."

"I'm ready." Shaide says immediately.

"As am I." says Amari, glancing uncomfortably at Nyu.

Rayn looks at his classmates "I believe we are ready to go as well."

"Chieftainess Nanilina?" Aton says "Leave the wyrm and the corruption to us. You just focus on defending your village."

"Thank you, Master Ceraph." Nanilina bows again and begins walking to the door "This means a great deal to us. Allow me to escort you to the village gates. A proper send off for the brave warriors."

"It would be my honor, Chieftainess." Aton bows in return.

Captain Winslow stands "I will return to the *North Star* and prepare the troops to defend the village alongside the Nekomata and Junmeri. I wish you luck, Ceraphs and soldiers. Make us proud."

Everyone stands and makes their way to the door. As they emerge into the village, citizens on all sides stop what they are doing to observe the procession going by. As they pass the spire, Captain Winslow breaks off and proceeds up to his ship as the Ceraphs and Exorcists follow Nanilina and her bodyguards to the village gate.

As they walk through the village again, Shaide gets a better look at the surrounding scenery. The village itself is built around the trees. Few structures are not attached to the trees in some form or another. All of the buildings on ground level are constructed of wooden logs, though some have stone incorporated in their design as well. Above him, he sees many buildings further up the trees, connected by catwalks, and some smaller building are even suspended in mid-air.

A second inspection, however, reveals the extent of damage the village has suffered. Many buildings are severely damaged or even destroyed, and many of the catwalks have been damaged and are hanging freely

Shaide and Amari both simply shake their heads as they observe the damage.

"Here is where I leave you, brave heroes." Nanilina stops and turns to them. "I look forward to your return. If you succeed, we will have to throw a grand party in your honor. Should any of you fall, know that you will always be remembered as heroes to my people. Before you leave, may I please hear all of your names, so we may honor you?"

Aton nods "Atondier Norvus."

"Lucy Norvus."

"Shaide Darkmoon."

"Amari Tamiel."

"Rayn Jarvis."

"Celeste Wyatt."

"Lania Howler."

"Reno Coltide."

"Brave Ceraphs and Exorcists. And dear Nyuralisiania." Nanilina bows deeply, and her bodyguards, and then the gate guards all follow suit. "May Diosia be with you."

*   *   *

"So, Nyu?" Shaide asks quietly "How did you end up back here in Pandora? I was under the impression that they don't usually welcome back those who leave.'

The party of nine is walking slowly along the forest floor. Typically, Pandorans will move through the treetops at a rapid pace due to their skill with stealth in the forests, but the Ceraphs and military party don't have such skill, so they are forced to move more slowly on the ground to avoid attracting attention.

The party is also watching the reunion with interest. In spite of the mixed feelings she has been dealing with, Amari is intrigued by the presence of Shaide's old friend as well.

"They usually don't," Nyu explains "but after explaining that my mother left with me as a child and that it wasn't my choice to leave, they decided to give me a chance. Especially as the village was in dire need of assistance, and I helped defend them."

"But why did you come back?" Shaide asks curiously "I was under the impression you were happy in Corallina."

"I was." She said "But after I heard the Ceraph Order had taken you in, I decided to go on a bit of an adventure myself. I began working as essentially a bounty hunter, slowly working my way west and helping villages deal with their problems on my way. When I neared the border of Pandora a couple of months ago, I began hearing rumors of trouble in my homeland among other things, so I decided to come back and see what I could find."

"Hey, Nyurali…Nyuralish…" Aton struggles to pronounce her name.

A.S.GUINN   133

"Just call me Nyu."

"Yes, of course, Nyu." Aton shakes his head clear. "How far are we from the location of the village that was destroyed?"

Nyu tilts her head, thinking. "Moving at our pace, it should take us around three days to get there."

"Can't we pick up the pace a little?" Lucy asks, frustrated.

"Not if we want to avoid trouble." Nyu shakes her head "You bigger lot with your heavier armor and gear make a lot of noise if you move fast. If we make too much noise, we'll attract all kinds of trouble."

"I understand." Says Shaide "The creatures of the forest are well evolved to live here. They know how to stay quiet and hidden. We'll stick out ad attract anything hungry."

"Exactly." Nyu nods approvingly. "We should probably talk as little as possible, too. We can catch up more later."

Shaide nods and stops talking.

For the next several hours, the party moves along the forest floor. Nyu keeps flinching every time someone's chainmail rustles, or every time Reno's plate mail clanks, but they move along, nonetheless. They encounter a few predators, but it seems their numbers are discouraging any attacks. Finally, as night falls, they come to a small pond in the middle of the forest where they decide to set up camp.

Nyu and Celeste work on catching fish from the pond as Lania sets up a campfire. Meanwhile, Shaide and Reno, along with Rayn and Aton split off into pairs to scout the area around them while Amari and Lucy hang back to guard the camp.

As the scouts head into the forest, Amari sits down alongside Lucy.

"What's bothering you, girly?" Lucy asks, noticing Amari's unhappy expression. "Would you rather have gone along with Shaide?"

"No, that's no… Well yes, but that's not what's on my mind." She says. "Can we talk?"

Lucy raises her eyebrows and nods.

"Well, lately I've been feeling…strange." Amari explains. "I keep getting a strange feeling in my chest sometimes when I'm around Shaide. A tightness, like I can't breathe. And when I see him around other girls, it almost hurts."

Lucy closes her eyes and smiles. She saw this coming the moment she first met Amari. "You've never had a crush on a boy before, have you?"

"A crush?" Amari's eyes widen "You mean like attracted to someone?"

"Yeah, that's what I mean." Lucy opens her eyes and says with a smile.

Amari doesn't look amused. In fact, she looks borderline horrified.

This isn't lost on Lucy "It's a normal thing, Amari. The two of you are so close, and the two of you spend so much time together, it was inevitable that some kind of feelings would develop."

"But, Shaide is my best friend!" She says, voice quivering with borderline panic. "I don't want to think of him that way! I want things to stay the way they are!"

"Relax and take a breath." Lucy puts a hand on her shoulder "You're seventeen years old, Amari. Now, I don't know much about Elmeri, but as your body and mind develops, these things will happen. I'm actually surprised you haven't crushed on someone before now, but still. It's a normal thing, and you can't always control it."

"Sometimes it really hurts though…"

"I know it does, Amari." Lucy leans back and looks at the canopy of trees above her. "For a Mitera, I'm little more than a child myself. Aton seems to forget how young we really are in the scheme of things and takes life too seriously. I know the feelings you're dealing with all too well, though."

Amari looks up at her in surprise. "You do?"

Lucy nods, her eyes closed as she remembers. "I once had a major crush on a young Mitera named Lodrick. Our families were close, and we spent a lot of time together when we were younger."

"Lodrick?" Amari frowns "That name sounds familiar."

Lucy chuckles "Lodrick Darkmoon. Shaide's father."

Amari's eyes open wide, and she is stunned into silence.

"Yes, Aton and I were very good friends with Lodrick and Juvia from the time we were small." Lucy smiles sadly "I could never bring myself to tell him though, and before I knew it, he had fallen in love with Juvia Edenkin."

"I'm sorry, Lucy." Amari says sympathetically "I had no idea."

"Something was special about those two. That is certain." Lucy nods. "We were stunned when they came back after a long joint mission seventeen years ago with that baby in hand. It shouldn't have been possible at their age. After all, we Mitera are much like you Elmeri. But destiny had something different in mind."

Amari listens, her eyes wide as she in stunned by Lucy's story.

"When the two of them died seven years ago, I had long made peace with my feelings." Lucy smiles sadly "But I will never forget the feeling when I heard Lodrick had died. It felt like my heart had been ripped out and torn to pieces before my eyes."

The two of them sit in silence for a moment as Lucy relives all manner of old memories, happy and sad. A single tear runs down her cheek.

"How did you do it?" Amari asks, "How did you manage knowing how you felt about him?"

"I made a decision." Lucy explains, coming out of her reverie "If he ever showed that he reciprocated my feelings, I would have jumped on him in a heartbeat, but I resolved to do something simple."

"That is?" Amari asks, leaning forward expectantly.

"I resolved to support him and protect him as best I could." Lucy explains. "Regardless of my feelings for him, the fact that we were friends would never change. I wasn't prepared to act on my feelings, so I chose to channel them into being his friend. And when he chose to be with Juvia, it hurt, but I accepted and celebrated his decision, because I truly cared about them both, and I really just wanted them to be happy."

Amari looks at Lucy like she had never seen her before. She had always seen Lucy as a fun-loving troublemaker. She had never considered that there was so much more to the woman. She finds she has a great deal more respect for her now.

"That's…very honorable Lucy." Amari says in awe. "What should I do, then?"

"That is your decision." Says Lucy. "You can act on your feelings. Even if Shaide doesn't realize it, and face it, he DOESN'T realize it. The boy is as dense as that sword when it comes to women. Even if he doesn't realize it, I would bet my very life that he has similar feelings somewhere inside. If you act on your feelings, I am certain that you would get what your heart desires."

"And if I'm not ready for things to change?"

"You can try and control your feelings." Lucy says simply. "You can set them aside and continue being his friend until you are ready. But you must be prepared to see him with other women, and if you choose not to act, you must be prepared to lose him to someone else, doomed to forever remain his friend."

"That's not very comforting…" Says Amari, a pit forming in her stomach "What should I do, then?"

"That is your decision to make." Lucy says. "I cannot make it for you. Only you can decide what is best. You shouldn't force it if you are not prepared. Just be aware of the consequences of either choice."

"Hey Lucy?"

"Hmm?"

"Thanks." Amari says gratefully

"Anytime, girly." Lucy smiles. "I'll be here if you need anything. Remember that."

Amari turns and looks out into the forest, feeling a little better. She still feels that sense of panic from her unexpected feelings, but she feels like she will be okay now.

*   *   *

"You know, bro?" Reno says to Shaide as they walk through the forest around the camp. "We haven't hung out just the two of us in a very long time."

"I know." Says Shaide. "The others are always with us."

Reno stops and leans against a tree "So tell me bro, really. Is there honestly nothing going on between you and Amari?"

Shaide shakes his head "There is really nothing between us, dude. We're really good friends, but that's it."

"Are you honestly saying the thought has never crossed your mind?" Reno inquires "I mean, she is very strong but very sweet. At least to you. She is absolutely gorgeous, with that silky pink hair, that smooth face, and that phenomenal body. If I had even an inkling of a chance, I would be all over that if I were you."

Shaide just shrugs "She is beautiful. And amazing. That's true. But she's my friend, Reno. We've been together virtually constantly since we were reunited. I can't imagine anything more than that."

"If you say so." Reno says doubtfully "But, can you honestly tell me there are no feelings there? I find that hard to believe."

"Well, maybe…" Shaide says uncertainly "There have been times, when we were very close, that I've had weird impulses, but nothing ever comes of it. I don't know, Reno. We're just always so focused on the corruption, and on our missions, we've never really had time to think about it."

"Well, I know one girl who has a thing for you." Reno says with an odd mix of jealousy and humor.

Shaide raises an eyebrow.

"Celeste." Says Reno, grinning. "That polearm-wielding fiend is obsessed with you. I don't know if she has feelings for you, but she is definitely attracted to you."

Shaide chuckles, remembering her kissing him to make Amari jealous.

"I bet if you asked her," Reno says mischievously "She'd probably be willing to get down and dirty with you."

Shaide rolls his eyes "I would like to see a world in which that could even possibly end well."

Reno shrugs "If you say so. What about Nyu?"

"I hadn't really thought about it." Shaide says "We just reunited a few hours ago."

Reno grins "There's another one that I think would jump you if she got the chance. She was so upset when she found out the Ceraphs had taken you, I was kind of worried about her."

"Well, she did seem to really like me."

"Dude, she was LITERALLY all over you!" Reno exclaims "If you hadn't gone to the Citadel, she'd probably be having your babies by now!"

Shaide rolls his eyes "You seem so obsessed with my love life, but what about you? You have a girl somewhere you're interested in?"

 A.S.GUINN

"Maybe." Reno mutters quietly.

Shaide leans forward and gets in his face "You've been harassing me about the girls enough. Now it's your turn. Spill it."

"Well…" Reno says rather bashfully "What do you think about Lania, really?"

Shaide is taken aback for a moment. "Lania? Well, she's kind of underdeveloped, but she is really kind and sweet. She's good at support magic both because she is very intelligent and because she cares deeply for her friends and allies. Also, I GUESS she's kind of cute, although she still looks like a kid to me."

"I'm not concerned with how she looks." Reno says, looking embarrassed. "I agree with you, though. She's really smart and sweet. Even though she tends to be quiet, she's pleasant to be around."

"So, you've got a thing for Lania, then?" Shaide says, looking amused. "With how much you stare at the big-chested ladies all the time, I would have never guessed you'd have a thing for washboard."

"She's not a total washboard…" Says Reno, looking slightly disgruntled "They're there. They're just small."

Shaide chuckles and doesn't respond.

"Bro, it has been WAY too long since we got to just hang out like this." Reno sighs "I missed being able to just shoot the crap with you like this."

Shaide puts a hand on Reno's shoulder and squeezes "I know, man. It's been way too long."

The two of them resume their patrol through the trees. Strangely, this part of the forest is very quiet. It seems Nyu knew what she was doing when she chose to camp here.

"How does it feel to be out on actual missions now?" Shaide inquires

"Honestly? I wasn't expecting to be out on our own like this. Especially as Academy students."

Shaide nods "Yeah, I get that. I'm surprised myself that they sent you along on such a dangerous mission. Have you even learned the exorcism arts yet?"

Reno shakes his head "No, I'm afraid not. We've started learning anti-corruption magic and techniques, but we are far from done. We are supposed to buckle down and focus on that once our training deployment is complete."

"Still, dude." Shaide says skeptically "I'm surprised they sent you out here without supervision."

"We are supposed to be functioning as soldiers while on this deployment." Reno explains "We do whatever our orders are regardless of whether they make sense or not. Besides. I know I wasn't going to turn down an opportunity to work alongside my buddy again."

"Good point." Says Shaide.

"That whole move against the dragon though." Reno looks at him seriously "Were you really trying to kill yourself?"

"Oh god, no." Shaide shakes his head frantically "I didn't WANT to die. I just didn't see any other way to kill that thing and save all of you. The frigate was crippled, the gunships don't have nearly enough firepower, and Amari and I may have been able to hurt it, but we certainly weren't going to kill it the way we were fighting."

Reno puts a hand to his chest and sighs in relief "Good. I was worried you may be suicidal for a while. That who maneuver was insane, bro."

"I know it was." Shaide mumbles. "I'm glad it worked out too."

"Just make me a promise, bro."

"Yo?"

"NEVER do something that crazy again."

"I can't promise that." Shaide chuckles "But I promise never to do it again unless there is no other choice."

Reno sighs in exasperation "I guess that's as good as we're gonna get."

Shaide just sticks out his tongue.

*   *   *

Nyu thrusts out her partisan and impales a large fish on the end. She pulls it back and looks at it with satisfaction. "Another good catch."

"So, Nyu? Can I ask you a question?"

Nyu looks up at Celeste as she puts the fish in the bucket. "Yeah, sure."

"Did you and Shaide ever… You know…"

Nyu's eyes open wide "You mean mate? No, of course not. We were too young, and the Ceraphs got to him just a few days after we met."

Celeste goes into thought for a moment. "So, if he hasn't been with Amari, or you, and judging from his stories..." Her eyes open wide "I don't think Shaide has EVER been with a girl."

"Wait. Shaide and Amari aren't together?"

Celeste shakes her head.

"Huh." Nyu says thoughtfully "I could have sworn I smelled a bonded scent."

"Bonded scent?" Celeste asks, confused.

Nyu nods "Yeah. Humans and Elmeri can't smell it, but we can. When someone is attracted to a specific mate, their scent changes to indicate they aren't receptive to advances by the opposite gender."

"Are you sure that's not just a Nekomata thing?" Celeste laughs

"Of course I am." Nyu says indignantly "The married couples I met in Corallina all had the same scent, and so do the Junmeri in the village who have found partners."

Celeste looks amused and impressed "I never knew that before. Huh."

"Have you ever been with a man?"

Celeste shakes her head "I'm afraid not. I've been too focused on my studies and my martial arts. Never had time. I figure I've got my whole life ahead of me. I can put of that stuff for a while."

Celeste thrusts a wooden spear she made from the wood grass on the shore and impales two fish in one thrust. Her halberd is ill-suited to fishing.

"Nice catch!" Nyu says, impressed.

"Thanks." Says Celeste

                    A.S.GUINN

"So, what's your story?" Nyu asks.

"Me? Really?"

Nyu nods.

"Well, I was born in the town of Lone Ridge. My father is in the military, and my mother was a nurse at the village clinic. I spent my childhood watching the village fend off attack after attack, and watched my older sister go off to join the military herself. When I was old enough, I applied with ARMA, got accepted, and you know the rest. Why?" She asks curiously.

Nyu shrugs "I don't know. You just seem a little different than your military buddies. You remind me more of Shaide, actually."

"What do you mean?"

"Well," Nyu replies "You have more of a sense of purpose than the others. More of a relaxed, 'ready for whatever comes' type of feel to you. You just seem more like the Ceraphs than a soldier."

Celeste looks up in thought "I've entertained the thought of joining the Ceraphs from time to time. It seems like I would get more bang for my buck. It's not a light decision though."

"I get that." Says Nyu, spearing another fish. "I'm going to try and go back to the Citadel once all of this is resolved myself."

"To be with Shaide?" Celeste ribs her.

"No, no." Nyu shakes her head "I wouldn't mind that, but I truly want to make a difference, and I can't do that just hunting on my own."

"I can respect that." Celeste nabs another fish.

"What about you, white one?" Nyu asks "Are you planning on going back to the Citadel when this is over?"

Celeste runs her hands through her white hair and shakes her head. "No. I wouldn't mind the Ceraphs, but my team needs me. I cannot leave them behind."

"I understand." Says Nyu, leaning on her partisan for a moment. "You seem to be the strongest of the four of you. At least overall. You're worried they would have trouble without you?"

Celeste nods.

"Take care of those you care about. That's not a bad philosophy." Says Nyu.

"Still, though." Celeste reasons "If the offer was made, it would be difficult to turn down."

"Yeah, I can understand that too."

*   *   *

Rayn and Aton are scouting the outside of the camp opposite of Shaide and Reno. Aton's eyes are carefully, thoughtfully scanning the trees as they slowly explore the perimeter. Rayn has a certain degree of respect for the way Aton is able to focus so carefully on their surroundings. The level of experience this man has is immediately apparent to anyone who sees him work.

"Hey, Mr. Norvus?" Rayn says in a low voice. "May I ask you a question?"

"Please, just call me Aton."

"Yes sir, Aton. May I ask you a question?"

Aton sighs "Not what I- Never mind. Yes, of course."

"How did you become a Ceraph?" Rayn asks him curiously.

"Well, it's a bit of a long story." Aton says, leaning back against a tree. "Lucy and I both grew up in the capital. Our friend,

Juvia, was from a long family line of Ceraphs, an it seemed inevitable that she would end up one as well. To our surprise, when that day came, Order Master Armstrong made us the same offer as Juvia."

"We entered the Order as support staff, essentially, following along on airship missions as we learned alongside live operatives. When each of our days came, we each acquired our angels and joined their ranks as true Ceraphs."

"What happened to Juvia?" Rayn asks "Is she still a Ceraph?"

"I am afraid she passed away." Aton says sadly. "Juvia Edenkin, also known as Juvia Darkmoon, died with her lover seven years ago, saving the village of new watch from corrupted attack."

Rayn's eyes open wide "Juvia was Shaide's mother?!"

"Of course." Aton nods, still smiling sadly "His father was a childhood friend of ours as well, but while we went the Ceraphs, he chose to stay at ARMA."

"I thought that name was familiar." Rayn mumbles.

"What about you, Mr. Jarvis?" Aton asks curiously. "You seem like a smart young man. How did you end up in ARMA?"

"Military family." Rayn smirks "My father is Colonel Lim Jarvis of the Alastair Army, and my Grandfather is Lieutenant-General Roy Jarvis. It was pretty much decided from birth that I would be attending ARMA."

"I had no idea." Aton replies, impressed.

"It's not a big deal." Rayn scowls slightly. "Neither of them was happy when I chose to join the Exorcist corps. They wanted me to do something safer, and more in line with command advancement, but I wanted to do something I found meaningful so, here I am."

Aton nods his approval "Parents are important, but you should choose your own life. It's better that you choose something that makes you happy rather than what makes them happy. You're the one that lives with the consequences."

*　　*　　*

"Hey guys, dinner is just about ready!" Lania calls out as Shaide, Reno, Aton, and Rayn return to camp from their patrols. Lania has a couple dozen fish up on spits cooking over a reasonably large fire.

"How did you manage that?" Shaide asks curiously "We didn't even smell the food or the fire until we were right here!"

"That was my doing also." Lania says proudly. "I laid a sensory suppression field over the fire so that the smell wouldn't filter through the trees and attract the wildlife."

"Very smart." Aton says approvingly.

Celeste and Nyu are visiting by the fire, and Shaide notices Amari sitting with Lucy. He walks over and sits down next to her. "Hey, you. You seem like you're feeling a bit better."

"A little." Amari replies. She does indeed look less stressed and anxious.

"What was bothering you?"

Amari just shakes her head "Girl problems. I talked it out with Lucy. She's really a good person, you know?"

Shaide nods, smiling "Lucy is an obnoxious, perverted, total pain in the ass-"

"I'm right here…" Lucy grumbles

"-but she is also one of the most caring, loyal allies you could hope for. If you can get past the constant drinking and flirting." Shaide pokes fun at her with the last bit.

Lucy opens her mouth to argue, but then she just shrugs, conceding the point.

"Point is, you can trust her if you ever need anything."

"I see that." Says Amari with a smile.

Everyone sits around the fire for a while, eating fish and otherwise relaxing. Once they finally finish eating, and they move to visiting and getting to know their new allies, Amari turns to Shaide.

"Hey, can I use your shoulder for a bit?" She asks quietly

Shaide nods, and she leans over and lays her head on his shoulder. Across the campfire, Nyu sees this and smirks, giving Shaide an unreadable look of some kind. They sit like this for some time.

Finally, Aton stands up and says "We've got a long journey ahead of us tomorrow. Everyone should get to sleep. Lucy? Do you mind taking first watch?"

Everyone shuffles around as guard duty is assigned to various individuals. Shaide lays back against a large tree to sleep and closes his eyes. He hears movement and opens them again, noting Amari leaned against the tree near him on one side, and Nyu leaning against him on the other. Amari fell asleep almost instantly, but he notes Nyu looking at him before she winks and closes her eyes.

Shaide shrugs and closes his own eyes, drifting off to sleep, happy to be surrounded by so many friends once again.

CHAPTER 7

TRAGEDY AT TORCHLIGHT

The next two days of their journey is largely devoid of any unexpected complications. They deal with several attacks by local wildlife including lobos, nekoshin, and a memorable carnivorous plant. This is an absolutely expected occurrence.

What was strange about these attacks was the proof things weren't normal here. Every one of the creatures that attacked them was corrupted, and far more vicious than the usual beasts found out here. However, this was completely expected as they were seeking the cause of the corruption, and it does little to hinder their journey. Now they are on a well-worn path that leads to the village of Torchlight.

"The way I understand it," Nyu explains quietly "Torchlight wasn't an especially large village, but it was still home to a few dozen

Nekomata. There were no Junmeri here, though no one would tell me why."

"Anything in particular we should expect?" Aton asks.

Nyu's face falls "It's... horrible."

Nyu has been mildly flirty with Shaide over the past two days, walking close to him and picking on him quite a bit, but now she is behaving with absolute seriousness. She leads the Ceraph and Exorcist contingent up the path as they approach the village.

"Prepare yourselves." She says sadly, her ears flattened against her skull. "It's just up ahead. It's not pretty."

Shaide walks out of the trees into the large clearing and feels his stomach drop. Several dozen huts once stood in this clearing, but now they are nothing but smoldering piles of wreckage. Shaide looks around in shock as he realizes that not a single building remains standing. His eyes don't immediately register the worst part of the scene.

"Shaide..." Amari crouches next to something, looking up at him with tears in her eyes.

He walks next to her, and inhales sharply as he sees what she is looking at. The remains of a young Nekomata girl, probably no older that ten to twelve is lying on the ground, being sheltered by the remains of who is presumably her mother.

"Oh my Eden..." Shaide breathes. He looks around the clearing and realizes that a number of remains are scattered throughout the ruins of the village.

Amari stands up and turns around, wrapping her arms around Shaide and crying silently onto his chest. All he can do is just pat her head softly as she deals with what she has seen.

"This is horrible." Aton says, the first of them to be able to speak. His eyes are wide with shock.

Nyu asks him quietly, a sad expression on her own face "I would have thought that the Ceraphs would be used to this kind of thing."

Lucy kneels next to the same girl as Amari and shakes her head. "No, not this. We've seen destroyed villages before, but never a village of women and children. Not this."

Rayn and Reno both hang back, neither of them with any clue as to what to do. Lania bravely walks through the rubble nearby, tears running down her face as she searches for she knows not what.

Celeste, however, is kneeling next to a Nekomata huntress, looking like she is intrigued by something. After a moment, she calls out "Hey, Shaide! Come here and look at this."

Amari lets go and takes a step back. "I'm okay. Go see what she needs."

Shaide nods and approaches Celeste "What is it? I've seen enough of this."

"Trust me." She says grimly. "Look at this wound and tell me what you see."

Shaide kneels and closely examines a fur-armored Nekomata. He looks closely at her torso wounds and notices something strange. He runs his hand across a strangely straight and clean slash.

"There's no tearing…" He mumbles. He looks at a smaller wound directly over her heart. "Hey, Celeste? I'm guessing you noticed too."

"Yeah," She scowls at him "These aren't cause by any creature I've seen."

Shaide grimaces "You might want to look away for this." Shaide pushes two fingers into the chest wound and finds no bottom. He rolls the body over and sees an exit wound the same size as the entry wound.

"That's…disturbing." Celeste frowns, ignoring his probe of the body and observing the exit wound. "She wasn't killed by a monster."

Shaide shakes his head. He then calls out "Aton! Come here!"

Aton slowly walks over to him and kneels down. "What is it?"

"This wound. Look at it."

Aton examines the wound for only a few seconds before standing up, looking alarmed. "This girl wasn't killed by that wyrm. This is a weapon wound."

Shaide and Celeste both stand up too, looking around nervously.

The rest of the party comes over to join them, all looking curious about their findings.

"What did you find?" Nyu asks

"Someone killed these villagers." Shaide says "Someone, not something. At least some of them, anyway."

"I know it's not pleasant, but fan out and check the bodies." Aton says grimly "Look for wounds that look like they were caused by weapons instead of teeth or claws."

All nine of them reluctantly undertake the task of examining the bodies in the village. Their findings only serve to further raise suspicion.

As they all gather together again, they reveal that the majority of the villagers were killed by weapons rather than creatures. A tense silence fills the air as everyone contemplates their findings.

"So, the majority of these villagers were murdered." Aton concludes "Although a few fell to some kind of creature, this was no accident. Someone attacked them."

"Why would someone do that!?" Nyu bursts out angrily

Amari and Lania both hang back from the conversation, still nauseous from their unpleasant investigation.

"When you're dealing with the corruption," Lucy mutters "sense and reason go out the window."

Shaide looks at the upset expressions on Amari and Lania's faces, the angry look on Nyu's face, and the disturbed expressions on Lucy and Celeste's, ad he decides to make a suggestion.

"We should bury the villagers." He "We shouldn't leave them like this."

Reno looks around "That's a lot of graves…"

"Yes, thank you, Reno." Shaide interrupts him. "It's not right to leave them like this. They deserve a proper burial."

Amari, Lania, Nyu, and even Celeste all look at Shaide with grateful expressions, as if they were thinking the same thing. Lucy and Rayn even give him a respectful nod.

"Good idea." Says Aton. "I know I wouldn't want to be just left here like this."

"Let us handle the graves." Lania says, looking at Amari "We mages can knock that out without a problem."

Amari nods "Yeah, we can handle that."

"Then we'll handle the rest." Says Aton. "Men, help me gather the remains so we can bury them properly."

It takes them almost two hours, but they eventually have all one-hundred and three victims resting peacefully in their graves. They have nothing to mark them with, but they are happy to have done what they could.

"Villagers of Torchlight," Nyu says to the graves "Although I never knew any of you, we were all from Pandora. We were all Nekomata. The forest is our home. It is where we are born, and it is where many of us will die. It saddens me to see that so many of you fell before your time, but it brings us comfort to know that you have rejoined mother Diosia and become a part of the forest once again. For we are never truly gone, but we simply return to mother's loving embrace. Farewell."

"That was beautiful." Rayn says respectfully.

"So, what do we do now?" Celeste asks, looking seriously at Aton.

"We hunt down the cause of this." Aton replies. "Most of these villagers were murdered not by creatures, but by someone. I find it difficult to believe that this was some bandit raid. Right in the middle of a corrupted hotspot, I am certain that we are dealing with a band of Formers."

"Formers?" Reno asks, confused "Those mindless zombie-like people we fought in Lone Ridge?"

Shaide looks uncomfortable as he says, "The aren't always like that."

"Like the one in Mt. Kasai?" Amari asks

"Sometimes they can be remarkably intelligent." Aton explains grimly "The bulk of them are mindless zombies, to be sure. We still aren't certain where exactly they come from. But it's not unheard of to encounter more intelligent corrupted people capable of more strategic attacks."

Reno looks a little sick as he hears this.

"So, where do we go next?" Rayn asks.

Aton contemplates him for a moment before responding "We should set up camp for the night. It's going to be getting dark soon, and in spite of what happened, this is a well sheltered place to camp."

Lania and Reno both look around uncomfortably. Reno says "Are we sure we want to camp here? This is…well…"

"Well, it's either in here where we are somewhat protected," Lucy reasons "Or out there where we are in the open."

Shaide looks around. The outer walls of the village are still somewhat intact, so they ARE more protected here. It still feels creepy though, even to him.

"I don't want to stay here." Says Amari, tugging on Shaide's armor. She is a very brave woman. It's kind of alarming to Shaide to see her scared like this.

"Aton," Shaide braces himself, and he firmly states "I don't think we should stay here in the village. Whether it's safe or not isn't the problem. No one is going to be comfortable enough to rest. We should move on and stay somewhere nearby."

"If you feel that strongly about it, Shaide, I guess I won't argue." Aton sighs "Come on. We need to find a new campsite soon."

"Thank you, Shaide." Amari whispers.

"Not much scares you." Shaide whispers back "I'll trust your instincts."

A short time later they find a suitable campsite about a hundred yards from the village. Celeste and Nyu hunt and kill a venite (A deer-like creature that roams the forest) and bring it back for dinner while Lania and Shaide help cook it.

While they're eating, Amari comes over and sits next to Shaide like usual. She seems to have something on her mind this time, however. "Hey, Shaide? Can we talk?"

Shaide looks at her in surprise and nods. She's usually very casual with him.

"I feel like we're getting close to something."

Shaide tilts his head "What do you mean?"

"Well, it feels a lot like when we went after that Fallen in Erita." She explains. "IT just feels like there's more going on here than we are seeing."

"I get what you mean." He replies. "This whole mission is beginning to look a lot more complicated than we initially thought."

"When is it ever that simple?" Lucy says, making him jump. She sits down on his other side. "Whenever us Ceraphs get involved, you can just about guarantee it's not as simple as it first looks."

Amari nods "That's what I mean. I feel like there's something we should be seeing, but we're overlooking for some reason."

"Well, we'll worry about it tomorrow." Lucy says, "You two get some sleep. Rayn and I will take first watch."

Shaide leans back against a nearby tree to get some rest. He isn't relaxed enough to lay down. After he closes his eyes, he feels something shuffling, and finds Amari scooting up to lay against him presumably for comfort after the unpleasant evening. He puts a hand on her head, not noticing her smile as they drift off to sleep.

*   *   *

A loud howling sound fills the air, making Shaide jerk awake. Amari is fast asleep with her head on his lap and doesn't seem to notice. He looks around, heart pounding. Now that he's awake, he feels like something is watching him. Like something is coming. He can FEEL spiritual energy of some kind moving towards them.

"Amari. AMARI. Wake up!" He whispers urgently.

She jerks awake and he puts his hand over her mouth. "Shh… Something's wrong. Stay quiet."

She rubs her eyes and nods, looking around in alarm.

Shaide climbs to his feet and walks over to where Celeste is perched on a tree branch, staring into the darkness.

"Something is out there." She whispers.

Shaide draws his sword and stares into the darkness as well. Amari behind him summons her staff into her hand. Out of the corner of his eye, Shaide sees Aton in a bush looking the same direction.

A shuffling sound comes through the trees. Shaide narrows his eyes and sees movement. Something is slowly walking towards them, standing upright.

Nyu stirs and sits up, her ears perked up in alarm. She sniffs the air for some reason as well, as if she can smell something strange.

Amari illuminates her staff, and the whole area lights up. They are all shocked to see a Nekomata woman stumbling towards them. She looks exhausted and injured.

Shaide steps forward and whispers "Hey, ma'am? Are you okay?"

She doesn't respond, and she just keeps shuffling towards him. She closes to ten feet and he begins to repeat "Ma'am. Are you-"

Without warning she lets out a bloodcurdling scream and leaps at him, knocking him to the ground.

"WHAT THE HELL!?" Shaide yells, trying to throw her off of him.

"Get off of him, you crazy bitch!" Amari yells, hitting her with her staff like a hammer, knocking her off of him.

Shaide scrambles to his feet "Thanks, Amari."

A sleepy voice yells from the camp "What's happening?!"

The woman flails back to her feet, and Shaide grabs her by the throat, pinning her against a tree. "CALM DOWN, LADY!?"

"Shaide!" Amari screams, shining her light on the woman "LOOK!"

Shaide looks and realizes the woman looks like a corpse. Her skin is mottled and necrotic, and she is covered in weapon marks.

"WHAT THE HELL!?" He yells again. Without thinking, he throws her to the ground by the throat and rams his sword through her chest. To his alarm, this has no effect.

A chorus of bloodcurdling, inhuman screams fills the forest, and they are suddenly surrounded by movement.

"EVERYONE UP NOW!" Aton roars "WE'RE UNDER ATTACK!"

Everyone asleep in the camp scrambles to their feet and grab their weapons as more Nekomata charge into their midst and attack them.

"WHAT IS HAPPENING!?" Reno screams, swinging his greatsword around in a panic.

Shaide rams his sword through the downed woman several more times, alarmed at the lack of impact. Amari steps in and hits her with an intense flame attack, and she seems to disintegrate.

"USE FIRE!" She yells. "Shaide, stay next to me!" She summons a wreath of flames around them, encasing them in a protective fire shield. Another of the psychotic attackers tries to leap through the shield at them, disintegrating in mid-air.

Shaide looks at his sword for a moment, and concentrates. His blade lights up with electrical energy, glowing from the spiritual energy flowing through it.

"Shaide?"

"Amari, let me out of the shield!" He yells.

With a reluctant look on her face, she drops a section of the shield, and Shaide leaps out into the fray.

In the few seconds they were in the shield, they find themselves surrounded by dozens of insane attackers. They seem to be trying to bite, claw, or otherwise just tear them apart in any way they can.

Shaide roars and slashes violently with his lightning-imbued blade. The sword he received from the Termer blacksmith is indeed a wonderful conduit of spiritual energy. With little effort, he cuts through every attacker he can see. The violent lightning energy that assaults his targets from the blade has a similar effect to the fire, as everything he hits burns up and disintegrates.

"CRAP! HELP!"

Shaide sees a pile of the attackers and realizes Rayn is buried beneath them. Shaide sprints over and jump kicks the pile, knocking them off of his friend. He backwards rolls to his feet and delivers a great upward slash, releasing an arc of lightning energy that fries the three who were on Rayn.

"Are you okay?" Shaide asks, pulling him to his feet,

Rayn cradles his left arm with a deep bite wound, and his leg seems to be injured. He shakes his head and says "Enemies first. Me later."

Shaide nods and spins around, instinctively slashing one of the things leaping through the air at him.

Lania has managed to climb a tree at this point and is raining fire and lightning spells down on the assaulting force as they wind through the trees. Shaide realizes in alarm that they are getting separated as the things stream in around them. Shaide spins around and sees another one in his face-

thkt!

A halberd pins it to a tree just before it hits him, and he turns to see Celeste holding it in place, halberd through its neck.

"Shaide look!" She yells at him "I think this was one of the villagers! The villagers became freaking zombies!"

Celeste channels a vicious wind attack through the blade, ripping the zombie apart from the inside, making it disintegrate like the rest.

He sees bright flashing a hundred feet away, and he rushes through to trees to find Amari flipping and twirling, wielding a rope of flame emanating from her staff like a whip, striking any undead villager within reach.

In spite of their valiant counterattack, the undead just seem to keep coming. Aton is alternating fireball and sword attacks in the distance to keep them at bay, and Lucy is presumably somewhere nearby with her daggers.

Shaide looks around in mild panic as he sees the undead charging him from all sides, and he roars with fury. He feels a great well of spiritual power rise up inside him, lighting up his blade like a beacon. He stabs the sword into the ground, and a large wave of lightning explodes outward, frying a dozen undead in a single shot.

He stands there for a moment, breathing heavily as he gains some respite, before he runs alongside Amari. "Are you okay?"

"Yeah, I'm doing FINE!" She yells the last word as she brings the whip of flame down on a stray undead, leaving their area clear. They can hear their comrades fighting around them in the forest.

"Good to hear." Shaide leans back against her for a moment "Rayn was injured but he was okay. Celeste is fine. I don't know about anyone else."

Amari turns to face him with a nauseous look on her face. "Are those what I think they were?"

Shaide puts a hand on her shoulder and shakes his head "Don't think about it right now. Let's just make sure everyone is okay."

She nods, still looking slightly sick.

The two of them work their way through the trees, where first they find Reno sitting against a tree, greatsword in one hand, shield in the other, trying to catch his breath. He jumps as they approach.

"Easy, Reno!" Says Shaide. "It's just us!"

"Oh, thank god…" says Reno, relieved. He holds out a hand and Shaide pulls him to his feet. "Where are the others?"

"Still looking for them."

The three of them make their way back to the camp where they find Lucy binding up Rayn's injured arm and leg. Lania is sitting with her knees against her chest, rocking back and forth as Celeste rubs her back to calm her down.

"Oh, thank Eden, you're okay!" Nyu suddenly appears out of nowhere and hugs Shaide around the neck.

"We're fine too…" Reno grumbles.

Nyu lets go of him and puts a hand each on Amari and Reno's shoulders.

Aton walks back into the camp across from Shaide. He looks intensely relieved to see his godson and friends in one piece.

"Dad!"

Aton nods "Good. Everyone made it back okay."

Lania looks up, eyes wide and tears running down her face. She looks like she is in borderline shock. "Wh-what in the hell were those things?!"

Aton sits down next to the fire "It's bad. REALLY bad."

Lucy looks equally as grim as her brother as she explains "This hasn't been seen in our lifetime. Actually, not for hundreds of years, if not thousands."

Shaide frowns "I feel like I'm missing something. This has been seen before?"

"Yes, I'm afraid so." Says Aton, getting back to his feet and pacing. "Reanimated corpses supposedly gave the allies a mass of trouble back during the war. Somehow, corrupted forces were able to reanimate fallen enemies and friends alike and use them as invincible suicide troops."

"They haven't been seen in so long." Lucy says, a sick look on her face. "We're not even taught about them anymore. The only reason we even know about them ourselves is that we stumbled across some notes about them in the library."

Shaide's eyes widen as he remembers "Yeah, I thought that was just a myth!"

　　　　

Aton shakes his head "No, apparently it really happened. No one ever found out HOW they were doing it. They didn't know if it was the corruption itself or if it was some kind of magic, but part of the reason their numbers were so high was their ability to reanimate bodies."

Now it is Shaide's turn to feel nauseous "That's sick. It's bad enough to try and take over and corrupt everything in your path, but they also desecrated those who gave their lives? That's just…"

"Sick." Says Amari, matching his feelings.

"Rayn. How is your wound?" Aton asks

Rayn shakes his head "Thanks to Lucy it's clean and bandaged. I'll live. But I can't move my arm right now."

Aton paces around, thinking.

"We're in a bit of a pickle." Lucy says.

Aton nods "Yeah, we are. We can't take Rayn with us. His injury makes it too dangerous for him to continue the mission."

Rayn starts to stand up "No. I can continue the mission. I-"

Lucy puts a hand on his shoulder and sits him back down. "No, you can't. You can't even move that arm." She sighs and looks him in the eyes "Sometimes part of being a soldier is realizing your limits and that you would only hurt the mission. You can't fight, Rayn. You would put us all at risk."

Rayn opens his mouth to argue, but then he relaxes. Defeated.

"The problem is, we're three days from town as well." Says Aton "So we can't take you back either."

"We could split up." Shaide suggests. All eyes turn to him.

"What do you mean, split up?" Reno asks incredulously.

"A small group escorts Rayn back to the village." Shaide explains. "The rest of us continue the mission. We could probably move faster in a smaller group anyway."

Aton scowls heavily. "I don't like it, but I think you're right."

"I'll go with Shaide and Amari onward to the objective." Says Lucy. "Nyu should come with us too."

"I'll take the Exorcists back with me." Aton responds. "With Rayn injured, I could use the extra help."

Reno looks at Shaide with a pained look on his face, but Shaide just lowers his gaze and shakes his head.

"Good luck, you guys." Says Celeste "Make sure you make it back to the village in one piece."

Reno steps forward and holds out his hand "Yeah. We haven't gotten to hang out nearly enough yet."

"We'll do our best." Shaide replies, shaking Reno's hand.

Reno pulls him into a brotherly hug "Be careful. This forest is giving me the creeps. Don't get killed out there."

"Alright, alright…" Shaide laughs, breaking away from his friend. "We'll be fine. We do stuff like this all of the time."

"Take care!" Lania waves.

"Lucy. Take good care of them." Aton says seriously "I don't like this place, and I'd rather not split up if we can help it. Be careful."

Lucy smiles and shakes her head "Relax, bro. We'll be fine. You look after the injured one."

"I'm sorry to be such a burden." Rayn says rather miserably.

Lania shakes her head "Nonsense. I'm surprised ANY of us got away uninjured. I was sure we were going to bit it back there."

"We'll meet you back at Children's Oasis when we're done." Lucy says. "Deal?"

Aton nods. "Let's go, guys. We need to get back."

Aton watches Lucy, Shaide, Amari, and Nyu walk away before he turns back towards Torchlight. Because they were awakened early, the forest is still dark, so they set off back towards the ruins at a careful pace.

They weren't far from the village, but it takes them a few minutes as Aton is supporting Rayn. In the short walk to the ruins, Rayn starts to groan in pain. The bites from the undead were very deep, and every movement strained them.

"Hey, set him down against something." Says Lania. "I'll see if I can't treat that wound some and ease the pain."

Aton nods and lowers Rayn against a tree on the edge of the village.

Celeste and Reno look at Rayn with concern. It's only been a short time since he was injured, and he already looks mildly feverish.

"Try to relax, Rayn." Lania says soothingly. "Healing works better if your spiritual power can flow more freely." She holds out her hands, and a green glow comes from her palms and engulfs his injured arm and leg.

Aton, meanwhile, proceeds further into the ruins with Celeste and Reno to take a look around. The empty ruins of the village are even creepier this time around after what happened. He feels like very footstep is amplified, and an undead could be hiding in any shadow.

They come around a corner and see what Aton feared. The ground where all of the villagers had been buried was disturbed, and it appears that every one of the villagers had risen from their graves.

"That is just screwed up." Celeste says with a sickened look.

Aton kicks the overturned dirt absentmindedly "There isn't much that surprises or bothers me anymore, but yeah. This is wrong."

"Haven't they been through enough?" Reno says "They were already murdered. Did they have to disturb their final rest too?"

"They weren't dug up." He states, examining the ground closely. "They came from underground. And this earth…"

"What are you thinking?" Celeste asks curiously

Aton closely examines a clump of dirt from which the undead had risen, his eyes glowing green with sensory magic. "This ground is saturated with corruption, and that wasn't here before."

"That sounds bad…" Reno mutters.

Aton pulls his sword back out and looks around. "Keep your eyes open, you two. Someone did this on purpose, and not too long ago. They may still be here."

Celeste looks over her shoulder "We should get back to Lania and Rayn."

"Good idea." Says Aton.

Celeste, Reno, and Aton walk back through the village to where Lania is attempting to heal Rayn's wounds. The two younger Exorcist students nervously watch their surroundings as they approach, while Aton focuses ahead and observes his dark surroundings with his ears rather than his eyes. By learning the sounds normal to the forest as they travelled, he can ow easily pick out the sounds that shouldn't be there.

Lania is still focusing on Rayn's leg, trying to get him at least more mobile. Aton can because the glow around his leg is more intense than the glow on his arm. As he watches them, something catches his eye. Is something moving behind them? He can't tell.

Meanwhile, Rayn leans back and tries to relax while Lania channels her spirit energy into him. The feeling of being healed isn't unpleasant, but it does feel strange. All of a sudden, his sixth sense starts to tingle. He feels like he is being watched.

Without any warning, a black cloaked figure seems to materialize directly behind Lania. Aton can be heard yelling "LOOK OUT!"

Without hesitation, Rayn leaps to his feet and grabs Lania, throwing her out of the way. A long, shiny dagger misses her be less than an inch, and Rayn feels a heavy impact on his chest. He and the assailant stand there for a moment as a splitting pain courses through his chest, and then it fades.

The assailant steps back, holding a blood-stained dagger while at the same time, Rayn feels something warm and wet running down his chest and back. He suddenly feels weak and drops to a knee, putting a hand to his chest. As he takes his hand away, even in the dim light he can see the red covering his hand. HE feels himself fall face first to the ground.

He sees Aton run in front of him with his blade drawn, and the cloaked figure disappears into the trees. Reno grabs him and rolls him onto his back as Lania desperately tries to heal him. Curiously, he cannot hear them, and the pain he was expecting never came. He sees their mouths moving, but no sound comes out.

He feels an overwhelming sense of exhaustion. The need to rest. The need to sleep. Rayn closes his eyes for the last time and falls still.

*   *   *

"RAYN! RAYN NO!" Reno screams, shaking his friend with tears in his eyes.

Lania focuses desperately on her healing magic, determined to close the wound and save her classmate and friend. His eyes close, and she makes a strained sound as she channels everything she has into the wound, but the energy won't go into him anymore. She feels her energy give out and she stops, sobbing uncontrollably as she lays her head on his chest.

Celeste just drops to her knees and stares, her eyes blank with shock.

Aton comes running back and skids to a stop next to them. "The bastard got away! How is…he…" Aton's face falls when he sees their faces.

"He's…gone…" Lania sobs.

"I'm so sorry…" Aton says quietly…

CHAPTER 8

KNIFE IN THE SHADOW

Shaide, Amari, Nyu, and Lucy all move through the forest at a faster pace than before. With only four of them, and none of them in heavy gear, they are able to move much more quietly.

"Hey, Nyu?" Shaide asks "Where are we going exactly?"

Nyu's ears are turned back to him while her head stays on a swivel. "There's a village further ahead. The inhabitants here are much in tune with the forest than back at Children's Oasis. If there is something wrong here, they will know about it."

"So, we'll find out what they know about the Wyrm?" Lucy asks.

Nyu just nods.

Shaide looks at Amari beside him with some concern. He lowers his voice and says "Hey, are you okay? That was a pretty nasty situation back there."

Amari closes her eyes for a moment and shudders. "I'll be fine. Just promise me that you and I will never end up like those poor people."

Shaide puts a hand on her head and reassures her "It won't. We have to die before that can happen, and I don't plan on either of us dying anytime soon."

"That's reassuring." She smiles.

Nyu makes an amused expression. Although there is nothing going on romantically between Shaide and Amari, their behavior is a bit perplexing. Nyu is considering trying to get close to Shaide again, but she can't get a read on the dynamic between the two Ceraphs, and it's throwing her off.

They're powerwalking through the forest for a few hours until it is roughly noon, and Lucy finally speaks up. "We should stop here and take a break."

"Yeah, we're making good time." Says Nyu. "We can afford a break."

The four of them find a small clearing and settle down. Lucy and Shaide are both carrying preserved rations, and they pass out a small meal to Amari and Nyu. They eat in silence, even now still a little unnerved by the events of the morning.

"Hey, Shaide?" Amari quietly gets his attention.

"Hmm?"

"Do you want me to start teaching you to summon and dispel your sword?"

Shaide looks up at her and chuckles "I had actually forgotten about that."

"Come on." She stands up and holds out her hand. "I'll get you started."

Shaide shrugs and lets her pull him to his feet. They walk a short distance away and find some room.

Amari stands behind him and explains "I've come to realize you store a weapon in much the same way the angels are bonded with us. It only works with a weapon or object capable of channeling spiritual energy, like your sword, my staff, or even certain armors, but with compatible objects, you can break them down into spiritual energy and basically store them within yourself, and then summon them back into their original state."

Shaide blinks in confusion several times.

She sighs "Okay. Stand behind me and put your hands on mine. I want you to feel the spiritual energy when I summon and dispel my staff."

Shaide raises his eyebrows as they turn around and he stands behind her. She reaches out her right hand, and Shaide puts his hand on the back of hers. She blushes and feels her heart speed up, but she remains focused.

"Okay, now feel the flow of energy as I summon my staff."

She channels her power slowly so that he can perceive it, and her staff materializes in her hand from a stream of spiritual power.

"And now as I dispel it away."

The staff likewise seems to turn into pure energy and disappear into her hand.

"See what I mean?" She looks up over her shoulder at him. "You'll be able to do the same with your sword. Now let me stand behind you, and I will guide your energy as you try."

They turn around again, and Amari stands behind him. She realizes how tall he is when she can just barely see over his shoulder.

Shaide draws his sword from the scabbard in his back and holds it out. "Okay, now what do I do?"

Amari controls the shy embarrassment she feels at being so close like this and she reaches out, putting her hand on his. "Okay, let me guide you, and try to learn the feeling of the energy as I help you dispel and summon."

Shaide nods and begins channeling his energy into his blade. He feels the energy flow being manipulated, and he allows her to guide the energy as she sees fit. It's a very personal feeling, letting her actually guide and control his energy like this. It's a strangely pleasant feeling, though, as well.

She changes the energy flow from going directly to the blade, and instead makes the energy cycle through it and back into Shaide. She then constricts the energy flow, pulling it back into him.

His eyes open wide with shock when the black broadsword seems to break down and disappear into his hand. "Whoa. That's cool!"

She nods. "Okay, now visualize your sword, and try to do the reverse of what you just did."

Shaide nods and, with her hand on his to guide him, he focuses on his sword and tries to direct his energy back into his hand. A swirling ball of energy forms in his palm, but it doesn't take form. Shaide tries hard to focus, but he isn't quite sure what he is going for.

Amari sighs and manipulates the energy, correcting the flow that was only slightly off, making the sword materialize in his hand.

"Oh, I see!" He says excitedly.

"We can practice again later." She says with a smile, her face slightly flushed. "It's easier to learn when you have someone guiding you. Less guesswork."

Shaide turns around and hugs her unexpectedly. "Thank you, Amari. I really appreciate the help."

She hugs him back, a little flustered. She hugs him all the time, sure, but it's very rare that he hugs her first. She closes her eyes and enjoys it for a moment before they break away and return to Lucy and Nyu.

"Did you two have fun?" Lucy grins "Is it my turn to take Shaide somewhere private for a few minutes?"

Shaide gives her an *Are you serious* look, but otherwise refuses to even acknowledge that she said anything. Amari just rolls her eyes and looks the other way.

"We can take turns with him?" Nyu says jokingly "When do I get my turn?"

Shaide looks at Nyu with borderline alarm. "That is not a very funny joke."

"Who said I was kidding?" She smiles and sticks her tongue out at him. "Seriously, we need to talk once we're done with this whole mess."

Amari feels a sense of rising panic in her chest. She doesn't REALLY want to change the way things are between her and Shaide, but the thought of another girl getting close to him still makes her jealous. She now knows Lucy is just screwing with him for kicks, but she's not even remotely convinced that Nyu is kidding at all.

Although she manages to hide her panic from her face, Lucy still gives her a meaningful look as if she understands what she's thinking, and she just shakes her head.

Nyu gets back to her feet and stretches. "Come on. We should get moving."

"Agreed." Says Lucy.

The party sets aside their jokes and resumes their journey.

*   *   *

Aton, Celeste, Reno, and Lania all stand in silence as they observe the body of their fallen comrade. Aton determined that the assassin had stabbed Rayn directly in the heart, and that there was nothing they could have done to save him.

Reno trembles with anger and grief as he tries to come to terms with what happened. Celeste still has that look of wide-eyed shock, while Lania just stares at the body looking lost.

"Mr. Aton?" Reno says, his voice trembling "What are we going to do about the bastard that killed him?"

Aton shakes his head "I lost him in the woods. I don't think we can find him unless he wants to be found."

"Aton?" A timid voice says.

He looks and finds Lania looking at him. "What is it?" He asks softly.

"What will we do with him?" She asks with tears in her eyes. "We can't just leave him here. He needs to go home, to his family."

Aton frowns. They are days from the nearest settlement with transport. They have no real way to get Rayn's body back to Alastair. In addition, they are in an extremely dangerous forest region, and that assailant is still out there. If Aton's fears are correct, that assailant is likely moving on to deal with Lucy and Shaide's party, but he cannot possibly catch up in time to warn them. He finds himself in a serious pickle.

"Could you fly him on your angel?" Reno suggests

"No, I'm afraid not." Aton says sadly "Mine does not fly, after all."

"What about Shaide? And Amari?" Celeste asks with concern "That assassin is still out there, and if he's not coming back for us, then he'll be going after them."

Aton looks at her for a moment. *This girl is sharp. She'd make a good Ceraph.* "I'm worried about that as well. I know you don't want to leave the body here, but if we're going to help our friends, we can't take him with us."

"The reason we were headed back in the first place is kind of moot now…" Celeste says in a flat, emotionless tone.

"What is wrong with you?!" Reno says angrily. "Rayn is our friend! We can't just LEAVE him here like this!"

Celeste looks at Reno slowly with pity, and she responds in that same flat tone. "I don't want to leave him here either, Reno. But I also think he'd rather us worry about the friends we can still help. He was a leader." Celeste's flat tone breaks, quivering with her masked grief. "There's nothing else we can do for him now, anyways."

"God damnit this sucks!" Lania cries "I don't want to leave him here, but I know you're right. Why does it have to be this way, though!?"

"Because this is the terrible reality of war." Aton replies grimly. "They never tell you this part when they recruit you. You never find out the realities of war and loss until it is too late, and you are already in the middle of it."

Reno has his hands balled into fists as he shakes with anger, but he doesn't say anything. The truth is, they are well acquainted with losing friends. They lost two of their friends their first year in the academy. It's not any easier, though.

Aton walks away to a half-collapsed hut and looks around. He comes back a few minutes later with a decorative Nekomata-made blanket, and he gently wraps Rayn's body in it. When Reno realizes what he is doing, he helps him finish.

When he is done, Aton carries Rayn to a large tree in the middle of the square where they stand and places him underneath.

"We'll come back for him when we're done." Aton says firmly "For now, we have to try and help the friends we can still help. Any objections?"

 A.S.GUINN

Reno and Lania look reluctant, but they nod in agreement. Celeste stoically stands up straight, choking back her own tears as she too nods in agreement.

"Okay then. We have to move. It's already going to be a total pain to track them down."

"I can follow them." Says Lania. "I know tracking magic."

Aton nods his approval. "Good. We're already a ways behind them, so we have to catch up."

*   *   *

After moving swiftly through the forest for most of the day, Shaide's party comes to a stop near a lake in the forest. They are growing tired, as traversing the forest is much more difficult than travelling the plains of Alastair.

"Amari, can you get a campfire going for us?" Lucy asks, "It's getting a bit chilly."

Amari nods and begins gathering wood and leaves to start a fire.

"I'll scout the perimeter." Shaide says "Don't want anything sneaking up on us."

Nyu runs up beside him "I'll come with you."

Amari looks at Shaide with a pained look on her face for a moment, but she decides not to cause a fuss.

Lucy nods "I'll see if I can't get some fish from the lake. Don't be gone too long."

Shaide waves and walks into the trees with Nyu.

The forest here is a bit denser than it is up around Children's Oasis. The trees seem older, like this part of the forest hasn't seen much activity. Some of the trees are several feet thick, and they have obviously been here for hundreds of years.

"Hey, Shaide?"

"Hmm?" He looks at Nyu

"I'm glad we finally get some time alone." She says, "I'm really glad to see you again, but I haven't had a chance to talk to you."

Shaide gives her an amused look "I'm honestly surprised you even cared after this long. We literally only knew each other for a couple of days."

"What can I say?" Nyu shrugs "When we get attached to someone, it sticks."

Shaide stops walking and looks at her "Why would you be attached to me?"

"You saved me from the bullies, you basically save the world for a living, and you're really enjoyable to be around." She smiles "Why WOULDN'T I be attached to you?"

Shaide looks up for a moment, thinking about her words. She raises a good point.

"The only thing that kind of bothers me is Amari." She says, he ears lowering against her skull.

Shaide looks at her, confused "I don't understand."

"You really haven't changed much…" She smiles sadly "I know you said there's nothing going on between you two, but I don't think she really feels that way."

Shaide raises an eyebrow.

"How do I explain…" She sighs explosively. "When she's around you, I can smell that she is attracted to you."

Shaide shakes his head violently "Say WHAT?! You can *smell* it?"

Nyu leans back against a tree and crosses her arms, rolling her eyes. "Listen. It's not as strong with humans and Elmeri, but when a person is attracted to someone, their pheromones change. I doubt Amari is attracted to me or the Mitera woman, Lucy, so the only explanation is that she likes you."

Shaide just stares at Nyu in disbelief.

"Well, tell me honestly. What DO you think of her?" Nyu asks

Shaide shrugs "Well, she is very smart, almost terrifyingly so. She's very hard working, very brave. I've never met anyone as loyal as she is. She's very strong, I think she could even keep up with me in a duel."

"Do you think she is attractive?" Nyu asks. She isn't defensive. Her ears are perked up like she is just extremely curious.

"Well…" Shaide considers the question "She IS very beautiful. I won't deny that. Objectively speaking, she has a beautiful figure. I had never really thought about it before."

"Yeah, you have." Nyu grins, her tail flicking playfully. "You cannot tell me you've never thought about it. I've caught you looking at me, and even I'll admit the girl has a better body than me. No way you haven't noticed her."

Shaide just shrugs "She and I are old friends. Her father entrusted me to look after her. I've just never thought of her that way."

"You are really no fun." Nyu sighs "I was sure there was some unspoken love between you, but you're not reacting like I'd hoped at all."

"I'm sorry." Shaide shrugs "I guess I've just been too focused on being a Ceraph."

Nyu walks over to him and stands face to face with him. Shaide stands his ground, looking her straight in the eyes. She very seriously considers just doing what she wants to do here and now.

"You have grown up." She whispers, "You used to get nervous."

Shaide just stares back, heart beating faster, waiting to see what she's going to do.

rustle

Nyu's ears perk up and she turns her head "What was that?"

Shaide shakes his head clear and follows her gaze.

"I swear I just saw something over there."

Shaide puts a hand over his shoulder and onto the handle of his sword and slowly walks over to where she was looking. When he gets there, though, he finds no sign of any activity.

"Anything?" She calls out.

"No." He replies, "Must have been the dark playing tricks on you." He walks back over to her where they both stand rather awkwardly now.

Nyu pouts a little, her ears flattened in disappointment. She had been hoping to push herself on him and get closer to him since he doesn't seem interested in Amari, but the mood has been completely ruined, and now she is just paranoid that they aren't alone.

Shaide notices her disappointment and smiles slightly to himself. The amusement quickly passes as once again the feeling of being watched settles in.

"We should head back to camp."

She nods without a word.

When they arrive back at the campsite, Amari and Lucy are already cooking dinner. Lucy seems to have caught quite a few fish, and Nyu's eyes open wide as her mouth drops open.

"Help yourself, you two." Lucy smiles "You must be hungry after, well, you know."

Shaide rolls his eyes "Lucy, could we not?"

Lucy catches the tone. "What is it? What's wrong?"

"There might be something out there." Shaide says in a low voice.

Nyu nods "Yeah, I swear I heard and maybe even saw someone."

Lucy lets out a long sigh before responding "Alright, then we'll take watch in shifts. We don't want anything sneaking up on us."

"I'll take first watch." Says Shaide, helping himself to fish.

All the while, Amari is being oddly quiet and distant. It hasn't gone unnoticed by Shaide that she has been acting strangely this entire trip, but he doesn't have any clue what's wrong, nor does he have any idea how to ask her about it.

"Come on, girls. Let's get some rest." Lucy says once they finish eating. "Shaide? Don't get any ideas about doing anything to them while we're asleep. Do it to me instead." She winks.

Shaide lets out a long, exasperated sigh and climbs into a tree without a word.

Lucy smiles and lies back. Many things change as her nephew gets older, but he's still fun to pick on.

Inwardly, Shaide thinks, *scary part is, even though she's kidding, I don't think she'd complain. She scares me sometimes.*

Nyu winks at him too as he settles down in the tree, but he doesn't notice. His attention is on Amari, who seems to be developing an increasingly bad mood. She's always been so happy. Her behavior is unsettling.

Before long, the girls seem to be asleep, and Shaide sits lonely in the tree, looking through the forest. He channels some spiritual energy into his eyes, improving his night vision slightly. This technique requires a lot of focus, so it's impractical in combat, but it's very useful when on watch.

The forest is remarkably quiet tonight. He was expecting all kinds of insect noises and trees rustling, but everything is quiet. He finds it rather unnerving. In addition to the silence, he also feels as if he is being watched, just like earlier. He even feels a somewhat familiar presence, though he can't place it.

After around an hour, he observes a nekoshin come uncomfortably close. It sees him in the tree and seems to consider him for a few minutes, but this nekoshin is of the natural variety rather than corrupted, and eventually decides to move on.

Two hours into his watch, he hears rustling, and he looks down to find Amari looking up at him. He quickly leaps down from the tree and notices her exhausted look.

                    A.S.GUINN

"You ready to switch?" She says.

Shaide looks at her with great concern "Did you even get any sleep?"

She just shakes her head.

"What's bothering you?" He asks her gently, leaning close and looking her in the eyes. "You haven't been acting like you this whole trip?"

"What do you mean?" She asks

Shaide puts a hand on her shoulder "You're usually glued right to my side. You're cheerful and friendly. Energetic. But since even before Children's Oasis, you've been acting strange. Distant. It's not like you."

His concern for her lifts her spirits slightly. In fact, she had been beginning to feel as if he was drifting away from her, but she realizes she may just be being paranoid. After all, he has reunited with several people he doesn't see very often. Still, she liked it better when it was just the two of them most of the time.

Shaide looks expectant, and Amari decides to answer him with bold honesty. "I'm just used to it being just you and me, you know? Just the two of us against the world. Sure, Aton and Lucy are sometimes there, or other Ceraphs, but it's still you and me. This trip has been weird. I don't know, I guess I'm so used to it being just us, I feel a bit neglected..." She looks down, face burning with embarrassment.

Shaide's response is entirely unexpected. He wraps her in a tight hug and pats her head. She closes her eyes, puts her arms around his back, and enjoys his warmth.

"I guess in all of the commotion of the emergency mission, and the unexpected reunions, I have been kind of neglecting you." He sighs "You're not going to lose me, though, you know? We made a promise that we would do all of this together, and I intend to keep it. Cheer up, okay?"

Although this isn't her only concern, she does feel herself cheering up significantly.

"Come on. I'll be right here while you're on watch." He sits down and leans back against the tree, and she sits down beside him, feeling quite a bit better for now.

Nyu watches them with one eye and frowns. *Getting him from her is going to be a lot harder than I thought,* before falling back asleep.

*   *   *

The cloaked man watches the party carefully through the trees. The Elmeri girl whose face he will never forget is guarding them while they sleep. He considers the possibility of attacking them now, in their sleep, but four Ceraphs would be far too dangerous for him to take alone, even if they are asleep. He also notices the man beside her. He was certain this man was dead, but here he is.

No, he will follow them until he has an opportunity to take them out. His mission may require him to eliminate any witnesses to what he is doing, but this is also personal.

He pulls out a dagger, stained with blood. He had been aiming to take out the support specialist, but that damned young man got in his way. Nevertheless, it was extremely satisfying to kill him.

He almost wants to wait for this bunch to find out about it before he kills them, because their anguish would be far too satisfying.

No, no. He must be patient. They appear to be heading in a fortuitous direction. They'll be coming across the perfect location to spring a trap before long. He should probably get ready.

He chews his lip, fighting off the urge to attack them now, and dashes off through the trees.

*   *   *

Aton pulls his sword out of the side of a corrupted nekoshin. "God DAMNIT! We'll never catch up with them if we keep fighting these things all night!"

Celeste stabs a second nekoshin with her halberd as Reno brings his sword down on its neck with perhaps a bit more force than was necessary.

"You don't think he's already gotten to them, do you?" Lania asks, full of concern.

"No, not likely." Atone shakes his head and scans their surroundings. "I can't speak for the Nekomata, but I don't think anyone could take Shaide, Lucy, AND Amari simultaneously."

Reno growls as he stabs his fallen target again in anger. "I just want to catch up to that prick and run my sword through his heart."

"I'll take that action." Says Celeste, back in her cold emotionless mode again. "He was my friend too. Save some for me."

Aton looks at Lania, who just shakes her head "As long as the others are okay. I just don't want to lose anyone else."

Aton quickly sets off into the forest again, leading the pack as they follow Lania's tracking magic. They're determined to catch up to their friends before the assassin has a chance to hurt them, but Aton can hear the heavy breathing of his young companions and realizes that they are getting tired. Adrenaline can only fuel you for so long.

He slows to a stop and looks around.

"What's wrong?" Celeste asks.

"We'll camp here for the night." He says, "No point in continuing on if you are all exhausted."

"I can keep going!" Reno exclaims. In spite of his bravado, though, Aton can tell that he is growing tired.

Aton shakes his head "No. We stop for the night. We won't do them any good if we're half dead when we find them."

Lania puts a hand on Reno's plated shoulder "Listen to him, Reno, please. We don't need to lose anyone else. Keep your strength up."

Reno looks down at her in frustration, but he feels the fight drain out of him when he sees the tears in her eyes. Although she is technically a soldier, Lania isn't as hardened as the rest of them. Her personality is well suited for her role as a support mage. She is trying to maintain a brave face, but she is taking Rayn's death harder because she cares deeply for her friends, possibly more so than him or Celeste.

"Celeste? You're being quiet." Aton remarks

She just shakes her head. "I want to put my halberd through him and make sure Shaide and the others are okay too, but I'll trust your judgement, *master Ceraph*." She emphasizes the last two words, subtly expressing her displeasure eve if she is following his lead.

          A.S.GUINN

"I'll take first watch." Aton says, "You three get some rest while you can."

Celeste sits down against a tree with her halberd in her lap.

As Reno does the same, Lania sits next to him and says meekly "Can I use you?"

Reno looks at her in mild surprise, but he nods. She leans back against him and seems to relax a little, taking some comfort in him.

Aton looks at them and smirks. They remind him a lot of his own friends when he was their age in a way. They are strong, determined, and brave, but at the end of the day they are still kids.

"I would give anything to find those archangels and put an end to this corrupted madness…" He mutters to himself, referring to the prophecy of Bahamut.

He looks back at his charges and is amused to find them all already asleep. They're tough indeed, but they were more tired than they would admit. He smiles and keeps a close eye on his surroundings.

*   *   *

A few hours into the night, Reno wakes up to relieve Lania from her watch. When he walks up to her, he sees that she is practicing an unusual technique by sharpening her daggers with spiritual energy.

"How're you doing that?" He whispers.

She looks up at him and shows him as she continues the process. "I channel my energy into the blade, using the pressure to subtly reform the blade and make it sharper without wearing it out."

He looks at it, impressed, as she shuts it down and dispels her blade, making it vanish into nothingness. She looks up at him "What's up?"

"It's time to change shifts, if you're ready." He whispers. "Are you doing okay?"

She shakes her head "No, not really. I said before I never really wanted to be a soldier. It was more like it was expected. Losing Bryon and Joslin was one thing. That was a freak crash. Losing Rayn, right in front of me like that, though…" Her eyes water up again.

Reno finds himself instinctively pulling her into a hug against his armor. In spite of the cold metal, she seems to accept the hug and let her tears flow.

"I feel almost like it's my fault." She whispers "He was going for me, not Rayn. He was stabbed trying to protect me."

"It's not your fault, Lania." Reno says, trying to suppress his own anger remembering what happened. "Any one of us would do the same to protect each other. We're a team. A family. I know Rayn would never blame you for what happened. You shouldn't either."

"I know," She whispers, "but it doesn't make it any easier. He's always been with us. Our leader, holding us together. What will we do now without him?"

Reno sets a heavy gloved hand on her head as he hugs her with the other. "We'll go on and do our jobs." He says, "We'll do it for him, so that his sacrifice wasn't in vain."

She nods and steps back, her brown eyes looking up into his green. The two of them just stand there for a moment, looking into each other's eyes.

Reno feels his heart rate increase. He's never had a girl look at him this way before. Before he knows what's happening, Lania reaches up and puts her hand on the back of his neck and pulls his face down, kissing him.

Reno feels his mind go blank as he enjoys his first kiss ever. His hands just kind of hang there as he doesn't really know what to do.

After a moment she breaks away, her face bright red. "I, uhh… I'm sorry. I'm going to go to bed now. Have fun on watch." She walks away and lays down facing away from him. Her eyes remain wide open for a while as she feels a mixture of sadness and confusion. She didn't really MEAN to do that, but it didn't exactly feel wrong.

Reno, meanwhile, leans against the tree, looking at her back with great confusion of his own. Was that what was supposed to happen? She gives him his first kiss and then she just walks away awkwardly and goes to sleep?

He looks out into the trees and contemplates. Lania is very sweet, and smart, and in spite of her undeveloped appearance she is cute in her own way. Would it really be so bad to have a relationship with a squad mate? Technically the academy prohibits it, but they won't be there forever.

Reno shakes his head and tries to clear it. He needs to focus on his duties right now. He has to watch the forest and make sure that nothing sneaks up on them. In spite of the events of the past twenty-four hours, however, he cannot help but smile slightly at what just happened.

Celeste looks at him with one eye open and a smile on her face. She had been predicting for a while that Reno and Lania MIGHT end up dating. It looks like she would have won her bet with Rayn, if only he were still here.

Celeste drifts back to sleep, getting some more shuteye before her watch, while Lania lies awake for quite some time, contemplating what she just did.

CHAPTER 9

FATED VILLAGE

Early the next day, Shaide's party rapidly approaches the village of Wyrmwood, where Nyu hopes to gather some information on the location of the rogue Elder Wyrm which they believe is at least partially responsible for the decimation of Torchlight.

"What should we expect when we get to the village?" Lucy inquires.

Nyu stops walking and turns around to face Lucy, Shaide, and Amari. "I really don't know. I'm sorry."

Lucy makes an unpleasant face "Well, that's lovely. We're in hostile territory and we don't even know what we're walking into."

"Isn't that how it always is with us?" Shaide remarks

Lucy shrugs in response and says, "Good point."

"Anyways, I've never actually been there before." Nyu says indignantly, ears flat against her head "I know that they worship the great Elder Wyrm, and for reasons that no one is quite certain of, the Elder Wyrm does not harm them.

Lucy, Shaide, and Amari all exchange glances without a word. After a moment of awkward silence, Shaide extends a hand and says "Well, shall we continue?"

Nyu nods and turns around, resuming leading them down the path. Shaide and Amari exchange amused glances before continuing behind her.

The sound of thunder echoes above the treetops, and rain starts to drip through the canopy overhead. Nyu looks up and groans, flattening her ears against her head again in displeasure.

The three Ceraphs, on the other hand, continue walking as if the rain made no difference to them. They are well accustomed to working in less than ideal weather conditions, so the rain dripping on them is little more than a mild annoyance.

"Ugh, all this rain screws with my sense of smell." Nyu complains "All I can smell is my own wet fur."

Shaide and Amari look at each other and grin, trying not to laugh.

Lucy leans over and mutters jokingly "Hey Shaide? Haven't you always wanted to play with a wet-"

"Shut it, Lucy!"

Lucy grins and looks straight ahead again. She squints her eyes and says "Oh, hey! Isn't that the village just up there?"

Nyu squints and looks too. "Yeah, that would be it. Do yourselves a favor and put your weapons away. Hancer warned me that these Nekomata and Junmeri aren't the friendliest in the world, and visitors should be very cautious.

The three of them nod. Amari dispels her staff and Shaide sheathes his sword across his back; he hasn't gotten the hang of weapon summoning yet. Lucy's sword and dagger are already sheathed.

As they approach the edge of the village, they notice a couple of very unfriendly looking guards at the perimeter. They are both carrying polearms and watch the approaching party warily. They do not move or otherwise react to their presence, and simply watch them as they pass.

As they enter the village, Shaide looks over his shoulder at the guards still staring at them. He's getting a very bad feeling, but he can't quite place why.

"Where is everyone?" Lucy asks quietly.

The village is more primitive looking that Children's Oasis. Wyrmwood is the Pandora equivalent of a rural town, it's construction and culture very different from the larger hub village. The huts here are more subdued and simpler, and there is no complicated network of elevated catwalks and shacks. Everything is on ground level, and the size of the village is significantly smaller.

What's strange is the near absence of villagers out and about. There are a few armed and armored guards out, but they are just standing at their posts. There are no civilians out as far as they can tell at all. It could just be because of the rain, but Shaide somehow doubts that explanation.

"Something's not right here." Says Lucy, giving voice to Shaide's uneasiness.

Amari looks around uncomfortably as they walk further into the village. "Where is everyone? Shouldn't there be someone outside?"

Nyu grumbles "I wouldn't want to be out in the rain either."

Shaide sees eyes looking at them through windows as they pass. There are a lot of eyes just staring at them. It's making him very uncomfortable.

"We're going to that temple." Nyu points at the end of the path where a larger wooden hut stands, built much more neatly than the rest, with twin statues of some kind of great lizard on either side of the door. "The priest there should be able to help us."

"I wouldn't count on it." Shaide mutters "These people don't seem especially happy to see us."

Shaide looks at the twin statues as they pass, and he notices that rather than a lizard or drake, the statues are scale models of a large quadrupedal dragon with large flightless wings tucked against its sides. As they pass, Shaide's eyes are drawn to a large crowd of Nekomata and Junmeri coming out into the open behind them, watching them with unhappy looks on their faces.

A moment later they pass through the double doors of the temple, and the gathering villagers drop out of view.

The inside of the temple is very different than they had expected. The walls are lined with elegantly carved decorative wood with scriptures in some unknown language covering their surface. Pillars made of a smooth, golden wood bracket the great hall, and in the center of the great room, an enormous statue of the Elder Wyrm is carved from an unknown translucent and phosphorescent green stone bathes the entire hall in a mild green glow.

Shaide finds himself transfixed by the great statue, and beside him, Amari cannot take her eyes from it as well. The statue is carved with such fine detail, the wyrm almost appears to be alive.

Footsteps echo across the hall, and the four of them look around to see a hooded figure in green robes and a brown hooded cloak approaching them with two young female Nekomata in similar robes on either side. They quietly approach before the hooded figure pulls back his hood, revealing what is unmistakably a Nekomata male, wearing a subdued but elegant circlet with green stones similar to the statue. Shaide notices that the male's face is more animalistic than the female Nekomata. While the females look more or less human in the face, other than the fur and the eyes, the male's face looks slightly more beastlike, with an ever so slightly elongated snout and mouth giving him a more catlike appearance.

"What brings you outsiders to our temple?" He asks simply, no emotion in his voice or on his face.

Nyu explains carefully "The village of Torchlight was attacked recently. In fact, the entire population of the village was killed. The evidence suggests that the village was attacked by a great wyrm, along with some inexplicable wounds that appear to have been inflicted by weapons rather than beast."

"Ahh yes, Torchlight. The heretic village. I know of what you speak."

Nyu and the three Ceraph's exchange alarmed glances.

"We attempted to spread the good word of our savior to the people of Torchlight, but they refused to heed our words. They refused to submit to our master. As a result, our master instructed us to eliminate them. So, we did."

Lucy and Shaide both look at each other, extremely alarmed. If this priest speaks the truth, then these people slaughtered the villagers.

Amari speaks up, her voice quivering slightly. "Who is your new master? What is his word? We are new to this area and have not had a chance to learn of this yet. Please, tell us."

Shaide glances at her, impressed. She is playing along to stall for time and learn as much as possible. Lucy seems to catch on as well, adopting a faux-curious expression as if she wishes to learn as well.

Nyu looks back at them as if she can't believe they aren't taking action, but she seems to realize after a moment that they are up to something, so she remains quiet.

"Ahh yes, it pleases me to see you are open minded." The priest bows slightly. "We were spreading the word of our master, Borealis. His acolytes have brought us his word, and so we work to spread it."

"Master Borealis?" Amari inquires.

ETERNAL KNIGHTS OF EDEN II

"An emissary from the south." The priest explains "He offers us salvation and a world free of war, once all who oppose him no longer do so."

Lucy looks very uncomfortable now. "I believe we have heard all that we need to." She says. "We simply needed to know what had transpired in the village. Now that we know, we should be getting back."

"ARE YOUN INSANE?!" Nyu loses her temper and screams "THESE BASTARDS MURDERED AN ENITRE VILLAGE AND YOU WANT TO JUST LEAVE?!"

The two on either side of the priest summon partisans into their hands and take a battle stance.

"Damnit Nyu…" Shaide mutters

"I'm afraid I cannot allow you to leave this village without Borealis's blessing." The priest says firmly. "If you do not receive his blessing, then you are heretics and you must be destroyed."

The two temple guards lunge forward with their weapons, aiming for Amari. As a look of shock crosses Lucy, Amari, and Nyu's faces, Shaide reacts instinctively. Fast as lightning, he pulls his blade from his back and slashes downward, cutting the partisans in half. In a continuous fluid motion, he delivers a second swipe, fatally cutting down the two guards.

The priest quickly backpedals, powerful magical auras forming around each hand "I see you are no weaklings. Nevertheless, I still cannot allow you to leave."

Amari summons her staff and quickly assaults the priest with a barrage of fireballs, but he seems to absorb them with his own magic. Lucy dashes forward and attempts to run him through with her own sword but is repelled and knocked down by an unknown force. She shakes her head clear and climbs back to her feet as she watches the aura intensify around him.

"I am sorry, my new friends. But Borealis's word is law. Goodbye."

"LIKE HELL IT IS!" Nyu screams. Glowing purple glyphs engulf her arm, and a glyph appears in midair just inside the front door of the temple. Without warning, a great black blur appears from the portal and dashes across the temple. It grabs a hold of the priest and slams him to the ground with a loud snap.

Shaide is so shocked by the sudden appearance that it takes him a moment to notice he is looking at a giant black cat, the size of a sleipnir, with great big fangs and a glowing purple aura.

"Nyu, is that what I think it is?" Lucy asks in a flat tone.

The glowing purple-black cat slowly walks over to them. The arch of its back is over seven feet high, and its head is enormous. Nevertheless, it walks over to Nyu and stands beside her patiently, dwarfing her in size. Behind him, the priest lies on the ground in a pool of his own blood, four fang holes torn into his neck.

"Yes, the is Tau." She says proudly. "He was one of the reasons I came to Pandora in the first place, but then I heard about the attacks, and I ended up staying to help my people."

"Tau?" Shaide asks, nonplussed.

"Tau the Shadow Cat." Lucy explains "He hasn't had a master in a while due simply to the near impossible to reach location of his altar."

A.S.GUINN

Shaide nods "Oh. I see." He suddenly shakes his head violently and looks at Nyu "What are you doing with an angel?!"

Nyu looks down, embarrassed for the first time he can remember "I wanted to join the Ceraphs, and I thought if I got my own angel like you, I would be able to join."

Amari interrupts "Hey, I know this is amazing and all, but we should probably get moving."

"Right." Says Lucy. "We'll discuss this more later. We should go. Damn Formers…"

"Well now. Isn't this an amazing surprise?"

Five sets of eyes look up into the rafters. A man wearing a tattered black hooded cloak was sitting unnoticed above them. The voice sounds strangely familiar to Shaide.

"Once again I find you meddling Ceraphs in the middle of my business." The man looks down on them from up high and continues "Not only do I get to see you two LOVELY Ceraphs again, but you've brought two friends this time as well!"

Shaide realizes with a start he is addressing him. "What do you mean? Have we met somewhere before?"

The man pulls his hood back, revealing a badly scarred face that looks like he had been severely burned. Even through the scarring, Shaide feels like he is familiar.

"Of course we have met before!" The man yells angrily "I drove a sword through your chest, and your little girly there knocked me stupid and gave me a lava bath at Mt. Kasai! I am amazed that you survived that wound."

"Oh god, Justice." Shaide mutters.

Amari yells up at him "I can't believe you survived that! But we beat you before. We'll beat you again!"

"I wouldn't be so sure of that!" He yells. He casts a fan of flames, igniting the walls of the temple. He then leaps through the window at the top of the second floor as the flames rapidly engulf the temple.

"Come on! Let's move!" Lucy yells, leading them out the door. Amari, Shaide, Nyu, and her Angel Tau sprint out the front door, but are quickly brought up short.

In front of them, what seems like every single villager and guard is facing them, armed and angry. Behind them all stands a truly gargantuan wyrm, its scales resembling moss, its great leathery wings tattered and torn, rendered flightless. Even on all fours, the great wyrm is twenty feet high.

On its head stands Justice, smiling down at them with a victorious face. "You see? I brought friends too. And mine are much stronger than yours!" He raises his arm, and a summoning circle appears on the ground. Moments later, a fifteen-foot-high minotaur wreathed in a red aura and carrying twin battleaxes appears on the ground in the circle.

"Well, hell..." Lucy breathes. She looks over her shoulder. "Shaide? Amari? Nyu? I have instructions for you."

The three of them look at her, confused.

"Take Rho and Theta and flee this place." Lucy says "I will buy you some time. The Citadel MUST learn of what happened here."

Shaide shakes his head "I can't leave you here, Lucy."

Lucy shakes her own head in return. "Shaide. You MUST. Are you willing to stay here and send Amari to certain death because of me?"

Shaide looks at Amari, and she looks Lucy in the eyes "We're not leaving."

"I'm afraid I cannot let you live after what you have seen here!" Justice calls out. "You have seen the army we are building, and I cannot allow you to tell anyone what you have seen! Goodbye, Ceraphs!" He looks down at his corrupted army "KILL THEM!"

The horde of former villagers charges at them en masse. There are probably close to six hundred of them.

Shaide charges forward, sword in hand "RHO!"

A golden glyph forms, and a golden thunderbird streaks through the treetops, spitting out a huge ball of lightning into the oncoming horde.

Amari, right by Shaide's side, summons Theta, and the great phoenix divebombs through the canopy and releases a great wave of flames.

"GOD DAMNIT YOU FOOLS!" Lucy yells "IO! I NEED YOU!"

A cyan glyph appears behind Lucy, and a four-legged equine with a golden horn on its head materializes through the glyph. With a loud whinny, a massive shockwave of wind erupts from him, fanning Theta's flames and knocking the former villagers to the ground.

"Tau!" Nyu yells "Do your thing!"

The great Shadow Cat dashes forward and stops just short of the line of formers and lets out an earsplitting lion's roar. When it does, everything seems to go black for a second as a devastating shockwave rips through the air, distorting reality and pulverizing slews of their enemy.

In spite of the tremendous opening assault, their enemies still number in the hundreds, and they still have an angry Daemon, a Fallen, and worst of all an enormous wyrm to deal with.

As the surviving formers get to their feet, the three Ceraphs and Nyu charge into their midst and tear them apart with everything they have.

Justice, meanwhile, sits stop the clearly corrupted Elder Wyrm, watching the battle below with interest. Even Taurus seems to be hanging back, waiting for the command to attack.

Shaide leaps and twists through the horde of formers, slashing and cutting them down without hesitation or mercy. None of these formers are a match for his own skill, and they fall around him in droves.

Amari uses her staff like a war-hammer, while simultaneously casting barrages of ice and fire magic at her opponents, keeping them at bay and thinning their numbers quickly. She brings her staff around and freezes. A young Nekomata girl stands in front of her, and Amari's eyes open in horror.

As she hesitates at the sight of the child, her aura falters, and the young former stabs her in the leg with a long dagger.

Amari screams in pain and drops to a knee. She closes her eyes as the girl moves to finish her off.

"NOOO!" Shaide roars in anger. Amari doesn't see what transpires, but a loud thud occurs directly in front of her, and when she opens her eyes, Shaide is standing in front of her as a shield.

Amari looks down at her leg, bleeding profusely.

"Amari! Are you okay?" He yells over his shoulder, fending off aggressive formers that try to rush them.

"Yeah, I don't know! My leg is hurt!" She cries, still shaken from the child.

Shaide channels his aura into his blade and stabs it into the ground, sending a great shockwave out fifty feet and knocking down every former in that range. "Heal yourself! Quick!" He yells, energizing his blade with lightning.

Amari nods, shaken, and begins channeling a healing aura into her leg wound. When she does, she notices something strange. Shaide's own aura is unusually strong, and he seems to be getting stronger. While her own aura is depleting from use, Shaide's aura is INCREASING beyond normal human levels. She shakes her head and focuses on at least stopping the bleeding.

Nearby, Lucy and Nyu are fighting back-to-back, repelling their attackers with brutal efficiency.

Justice raises a fist into the air, and the attacking formers back away from the Ceraphs. Amari is still healing her leg, though the bleeding seems to have stopped at least. Nyu and Lucy are breathing heavily, worn out from fighting full force non-stop. Shaide stands stoically, carefully watching his surroundings in case of a sneak attack, guarding Amari with his life.

"Bravo, Ceraphs. Bravo." Justice claps "I didn't honestly expect these villagers to be able to defeat you alone, but I must say I am impressed, nonetheless. Four hundred villagers down in only minutes, and you have only suffered a single wound? That IS impressive. I see now how you defeated me before I was what I am now."

"You really like talking, don't you?" Shaide grumbles. "Amari, how's your leg?"

"Still working on it." She says, tears of frustration running down her face "I'm sorry Shaide, I saw the little girl and I froze and-"

Shaide reaches behind him and puts a hand on her head "It's okay. Don't apologize. Former or not, it was a child. I can't blame you."

She nods and focuses on healing her wound.

"-will return. Now, though, I am afraid it is over. You are worn and tired, and you cannot stand against my Daemon." Justice grins "Taurus! Finish them!"

The red minotaur bull-roars and charges forward through the formers, and Shaide raises his sword, braced. Rho, circling ahead, divebombs down, but movement catches Shaide's eyes...

A great ape bounds from seemingly out of nowhere and tackles Taurus from behind. Taurus skids along the ground and rolls to his feet, spinning around to face the great ape.

Shaide recognizes the ape. Zeta Wu Kong.

"WHAT THE HELL?!" Justice and the great wyrm look behind them.

Aton, Reno, Lania, and Celeste coming running from behind the Elder Wyrm. Lania hammers the wyrm with non-elemental magic blasts, while Celeste and Reno bury their blades deep in the wyrm's side. Aton sprints forward to join Shaide and Lucy as Zeta and Taurus launch at each other with great ferocity.

"WHERE DID YOU COME FROM!?" Justice screams at them.

"Shaide! Lucy!" Aton yells, running to join them.

Lucy calls back "The entire village is corrupted! Stay on your guard!"

Aton turns and looks at the former villagers now walking forward angrily to resume their attack. "I see that! Amari! Are you okay?"

"Leg wound! I'll be fine!" She calls back.

"Shaide! You look after her until she can fight! I've got this!" Aton leaps forward and joins Zeta in fighting Taurus as Shaide raises his sword to defend Amari from the incoming horde.

Justice seems to have other ideas. The great wyrm raises its head and seems to draw in a great breath.

"TAKE COVER!" Lucy screams

The Elder Wyrm lowers its head and releases a gigantic wave of black corrosive flames. Zeta dives and covers Aton from the wave, while Theta and Rho dive and shield Amari and Shaide with their wings. Tau and Io shield their partners from the wave as well. The black flames consume the villagers, the village itself, and everything else in their path.

Shaide kneels and shields Amari with his own body as the rushing sound and the heat engulf them, fanning around them thanks to their angels shielding them. He cannot hear anything except for the great rushing sound, until the flames finally subside...

Shaide opens his eyes and looks around. Rho and Theta and glowing and fading, the sheer power of that attack forcing them to dispel for now. As he looks around, he is stunned by what he sees.

The entire village has been razed to the ground. Literally everything in a great fan behind him has been burned from existence, a great black charred swath of destruction. In front of him, Io, Tau, Zeta, and even Taurus are all glowing and fading as they could not withstand the attack of the Elder Wyrm.

Shaide looks around and sees that, thankfully, Aton, Lucy, Nyu, Reno, Celeste, and Lania are all unharmed. He realizes a split second later that Rayn is not among them.

"Rayn! Are you okay!" No response "RAYN!"

Aton looks back at Shaide with pained eyes, and Shaide looks back at him, not understanding what he is trying to say.

"Oh! Are they missing one of your friends?!" Justice yells with glee "He must be the one I killed! I was aiming for the girl, but he was just as satisfying!"

Aton closes his eyes and looks down.

Shaide feels a boiling rage and a simultaneous sense of shock wash over him. This freak, whom they failed to kill last time, killed Rayn? That can't be right...

"I ran my dagger right through your friend's heart!" Justice taunts him "I killed him like a lobo, and I did it just because I wanted to! My elder friend here is going to do the same to all of you!"

Shaide slowly turns to face justice and the wyrm, rage boiling inside of him, shutting everything else out except the Fallen murderer standing atop the great Elder Wyrm.

Lania stares at Shaide with shock as Reno clenches his sword tightly in anger. "Hey, uhh, something is wrong with Shaide." Lania says, looking at him with her aura vision.

"He's pissed…" Says Celeste quietly. "We all are."

Reno adjusts his grip on sword and shield, grinding his teeth as he stares at Justice.

"No." Says Lania. "Something is wrong with his aura. It's pulling spiritual energy from everything around him. His own aura is stronger than the angels' auras were."

"It's okay. You'll all be joining him soon." Justice exclaims with glee

The great wyrm draws another great breath, pulling in both air and energy from the environment.

In spite of her injury, Amari scrambles to her knees and channels every bit of energy she has. She yells at Shaide "GET DOWN!" as he stretches out his arms to shield her.

Aton, Lucy, and Nyu all sprint out of the cone of attack just as the great Elder Wyrm releases the earth-scorching flames across the battlefield.

The great wave of flames engulfs everything in front of it once again, consuming the corrupted villagers who survived the previous attack. Aton, Lucy, and Nyu just barely clear the blast zone, their clothes and fur still getting singed from the heat.

Shaide and Amari take the absolute brunt of the attack, dead center, and all six of their companions watch in horror as the air burns with corrupted flames where their friends once stood.

This attack, more powerful than the last, consumes everything in its path. Trees and brush, stray fauna, even stone is burned and melted to nothing in the wake of the attack.

A moment that feels like an eternity passes, and the Elder Wyrm lets up its attack. Flames, smoke, and ash fill the air as the beast observes the results of its carnage.

In the midst of the desolation, however, a subtle glow can be seen. A moment later, the dust begins to clear, and something leaps from the ashes as a magical barrier falls.

"WHAT!?" Justice yells, pulling his sword just in time as none other than Shaide himself lands on the wyrm's head and launches a vicious assault on him. The sound of metal on metal rings through the air as Shaide and Justice cross swords. As the two of them lock blades and roar face to face, Shaide takes a quick step back and kicks Justice in the chest, giving him some space.

Shaide yells over his shoulder at Reno "DON'T JUST STAND THERE! GET HER OUT OF THERE!"

Reno realizes with a start what Shaide is talking about, and he runs across the burned ashes and skids to a stop next to Amari. "Can you walk?" He asks.

She shakes her head, so he picks her up with a grunt and takes off running back to where his friends are.

Shaide's attacks are inhumanly ferocious as Justice's expression quickly turns from amused glee to frustrated anger.

"You were NOT this strong when we fought last time!"

Shaide delivers a series of heavy blows, Justice struggling to just barely deflect them. "YOU MURDERED MY FRIEND!" Shaide roars, losing all sense of reason as he tears into Justice with nothing but murder in his own heart.

Aton looks at the wyrm and realizes that the beast is not attacking while Justice is distracted. He taps Nyu on the shoulder and jerks his head, and the two of them sprint towards the enormous beast. He delivers a series of non-elemental blasts to get the beast's attention and then leaps through the air, driving his blade into the side of its face.

Nyu takes a running leap at the trees near it and manages to parkour-jump into the air and drive her partisan into its head. The beast is so massive, however, that the spear cannot penetrate deep enough to do any real damage.

Lania and Amari take shelter behind a tree as Lania resumes Amari's healing on her leg. "How did you two survive that?"

"I threw up a barrier with everything I had." Amari says, still sounding out of breath.

"Just how powerful are you?" Lania remarks with amusement.

On top of the great beast's head, Shaide and Justice are still crossing blades. Shaide has him on the ropes, but he can't seem to land a hit. Justice, likewise, is trying to counterattack, but Shaide's own speed is making it difficult to find an opening.

Shaide staggers as the great wyrm swings its head back and forth, trying to fend off the attacks coming from the Exorcists and Ceraphs beneath him. He falls to his knees trying to maintain his balance, and Justice takes his opening. As Shaide's arms open wide, Justice manages to deliver a deep cut to his left arm, making him roar in anger.

Shaide immediately counters with an arc of energy from a downward swing, hitting Justice and knocking him backwards.

Amari observes that the lightning arcing across its back seems to aggravate the seemingly invincible Elder Wyrm, and she has an idea. "Lania, can you do ice magic?"

"I can," she replies, "but I'm not especially proficient at it."

"Damn…" Amari grumbles. She pushes herself to her feet. "I'll do it myself then."

"Amari, don't!" Lania exclaims "Your energy is almost out!"

Amari gives her a determined smile as she says, "I have enough for this." She channels her dwindling spiritual power into a rapidly growing single ice spike of super-condensed ice power, making it spin faster and faster until she launches it into the wyrm.

The ice spike finds its mark and manages to penetrate deep into the scales in its neck. A split second later it explodes and blossoms with additional ice blooms, blowing scales off of the great beast's neck.

Aton realizes what she is doing and bounds off of a tree, driving his sword into its neck and making a large bloom of ice explode on the opposite side.   He yells "CELESTE! RENO! DO THE SAME UNDERNEATH!"

            A.S.GUINN

Reno and Celeste get the message and sprint underneath the great wyrm's head as it rears back in pain. Shaide grabs onto a horn to maintain his position as Justice struggles to maintain his own on the thrashing beast.

The two Exorcists candidates drive their sword and halberd into opposite sides of the underside of its jaw and channel their own power into exploding ice blooms. They don't understand why as they aren't doing an especially high amount of damage, but they follow the Ceraph's advice.

Amari slumps against the tree and manages to yell "SHAIDE! FRY IT!" before collapsing to the ground.

"Amari!" Lania squeaks, resuming her healing immediately to try and restore her lost energy and injured leg.

Shaide draws on his drained angel and channels a massive amount of lightning energy into his sword and drives he obsidian-steel blade deep into the dragon's neck. He roars and discharges every bit of the energy he had been channeling through his sword, making a violent cross-arc of lighting bounce through the beast off of the multiple ice blooms buried in its neck.

The beast thrashes hard and launches Justice off of its back and out in front of it. As the Elder Wyrm falls on its belly, wounded, Shaide tracks the Fallen warrior as he hits the ground. With a great running leap, Shaide throws himself into the air.

Justice can do nothing but watch as Shaide comes down on top of him and sinks his sword hilt-deep into his chest.

The two lock eyes for a moment as Justice struggles to breath. Shaide's teeth are bared as he twists the sword in his prey's chest, and Justice squirms with pain as he struggles to breathe. A moment later, the Fallen agent ceases to move, his eyes locked on the tree canopy above him.

Satisfied, Shaide plants his foot on Justice's chest and wrenches his sword out. He turns to face the great Elder Wyrm, but without Justice controlling it, it seems to have no interest in them anymore. It struggles to its feet and turns to depart through the trees, leaving the Ceraphs and Exorcists to watch it simply walk away.

The battle is over.

The other seven slowly make their way over to Shaide, with Lania supporting Amari as she limps over. Reno, Celeste, and Lania look down at the man who murdered their friend with a mixture of satisfaction and resentment.

Nyu, meanwhile, turns around and looks at the Elder Wyrm as it shuffles away. "Are we really just going to let it go?" She asks, watching it leave.

"Yes, we are." Aton replies, also watching the great beast lumber away. "That Elder Wyrm is probably tens of thousands if not hundreds of thousands of years old. The fact that it is walking away when it could kill all eight of us is proof enough that it isn't completely corrupted."

All eight sets of eyes return to their enemy's corpse as they try to wind down from the fight.

"How did he die?" Shaide asks suddenly.

Reno and Celeste look at him uncomfortably. Lania is the one who answers "He came out of nowhere. I never even saw him. I was healing Rayn's bite wounds when he suddenly jumped up and threw me out of the way. I hit the ground and I looked up…" She chokes, unable to continue.

Reno pulls her into a hug and finishes for her in a flat, emotionless tone as he tries to suppress his own feelings of grief that he hadn't had a chance to process yet. "That dagger there, on his back. He drove it through Rayn's chest, right through the heart. It was over so fast."

Shaide nods and claps Reno on the shoulder. He has a fleeting suspicion about him and Lania, but he chooses to leave it for another time.

"I really wish you hadn't killed him, Shaide." Aton carefully weighs his words. "We could have really used any intel he could have given us."

Shaide just shrugs "I don't think we'd have been able to bring him alive. He can control a dragon, for Eden's sake. He was too dangerous to leave alive."

Aton sees a coldness in Shaide's eyes that he's never seen before. Angel of Death indeed. Aton can almost feel the cold aura of hate coming from him. Shaide is getting to be a little terrifying sometimes, even to a hardened veteran like himself. He pities anyone who takes his godson's friends from him.

Shaide's expression softens when he finally notices Amari though. He takes a couple of quick steps and relieves Lania of her. "Are you okay? How's your leg?"

Aton is a little disarmed by the sudden change in Shaide's personality. Keeping the two of them together was definitely not a mistake. She has a calming influence on his hotheaded nature.

"I'm fine." She says with a weak smile. "It's sore, but Lania did a good job on it."

Shaide turns to thank Lania, but she is still holding onto Reno, so he decides to thank her later. He asks Amari "You had to have drained your energy badly after all of that. Are you sure you're going to be okay?"

She silently nods and rests her head on his shoulder.

Nyu's mouth twitches unpleasantly. Her face is half annoyed and half amused. *It is going to be REALLY hard to get him from her.*

Lucy stands next to her brother and whispers "You know? Give those two five more years, and they may become the strongest Ceraphs we've ever seen. Their spirit and strength are way beyond their age."

Aton mutters back "Did you notice what Shaide did though? It's the second time I've seen that."

"You mean where he seemed to absorb a portion of the energy around him and use it for himself?"

Aton is careful to keep his voice low "Yeah. I'm pretty sure he did the same thing with that dragon in Lone Ridge. Obviously, Amari put up a barrier to block that attack, but no lone barrier could block an attack of that magnitude. Especially not a corrupted attack. No, I think he somehow absorbed some of it."

Celeste claps Shaide on the shoulder and says "That was impressive, Ceraph. Fighting that guy on the back of a great wyrm. That was a hell of a fight."

"So, I'm 'Ceraph' now?"

Celeste sticks her tongue out at him.

"Something bothers me." Says a troubled-looking Amari "These villagers that were corrupted. They were still people, weren't they? Corrupted or not, we just killed an entire village of people."

"It's not that simple, Amari." Lucy replies gently. The others start listening too. "When the corruption takes hold to this degree, any trace of their former selves is gone. These weren't as bad as thralls, but they were completely under Justice's control. They couldn't even really be considered Nekomata or Junmeri anymore."

"The priest spoke to us." Shaide points out. "He had some sense of awareness."

Lucy nods sadly "Yes, that is true, but even his guards did not any longer. They knew what they were supposed to do, at the cost of everything else."

Amari nods and doesn't ask any further questions, but Shaide can tell that she is still troubled. He doesn't really know what to say right now, though, so he tries to ignore it. She is right. These formers didn't seem normal.

"You say you met this guy before?" Reno asks Shaide curiously, finally letting go of a red-faced Lania.

"Yeah. Amari and I fought him in Mt. Kasai a few months ago." Shaide replies "I was sure he was dead, but apparently not."

Amari looks a little nauseous as she asks, "Is there any way to be SURE he doesn't come back?"

Lucy holds out a palm and strikes the body with a bright blue fireball. The bod bursts into flames as they stand and allow the body to burn to ash.

After a few minutes, Shaide asks Lania "Can you do me a favor and help Amari finish with her leg?"

"Yeah, of course!" Lania says. As Shaide eases Amari to the ground, Lania crouches next to her and focuses her healing magic again.

Shaide motions to Aton and Lucy that they should follow him, and they walk a short way away so they can talk in private.

"Things are getting worse." Shaide says bluntly.

Aton and Lucy exchange glance before Aton replies "You've noticed too, huh?"

"Yeah, how could I not?" Shaide replies. "Village attacks are growing more frequent, and more severe. And the Fallen have returned. Justice can't be the only one. He's strong, but he can't be pulling the strings."

Lucy leans in and lowers her voice "I'm with you, Shaide. Corrupted attacks are quickly growing to numbers similar to just after the war. Something is brewing, and we need to find out what before it is too late."

"You know…" Aton says "No one really knows what lies south of the deadlands border. I've wondered for years if everyone really died when Belial kamikazed at the end of the war."

Shaide looks at him, slightly bewildered "How could anything survive in that hellish wasteland of corruption?"

"We can't survive down there." Aton points out. "But who is to say that there is any reason they couldn't if they are corrupted?"

Shaide nods, admitting Aton has a point.

"Come on." Lucy says "We'll worry the others if we stay over here by ourselves. We can talk about this when we get back."

"We needed to scout the corruption, but considering everything we've been through…" Aton looks at the wounded Amari, the exhausted Exorcists, and his currently unstable godson. "We should get Rayn's body back to the military and rest up to plan our next move."

The three of them walk back to join their companions before returning to Children's Oasis.

CHAPTER 10

A HERO'S FAREWELL

Captain Winslow stands aboard the bridge of the ARV *North Star* surveying the village beneath him. The Nekomata and Junmeri had been very hospitable in spite of their dislike of outsiders, but he still didn't want to intrude, so he spent most of his time aboard his frigate.

Nearly two weeks had passed since the Ceraphs and Exorcists had departed to seek the source of the attack and put a stop to it. The village of Children's Oasis endured multiple attacks by corrupted monsters, and even a handful of Formers, but with the help of the *North Star's* troops, the village was able to end off the attacks with minimal casualties. In the past forty-eight hours, there had been no attacks at all.

"Sir? The scouts report that the Ceraph party is approaching. They'll be at the gates in a few minutes." A messenger reports.

Winslow straightens up. "I suppose I should go down and greet them. Lieutenant? You have the bridge."

"Yes sir."

Captain Winslow proceeds out of the bridge and down to the hanger bay where he disembarks the *North Star* onto the village airship spire. A few short minutes later he is approaching the gate, where he finds the village chieftainess, Nanilina, waiting as well.

"Chieftainess." He greets her with a bow.

"Ahh, Captain." She bows in return. "Your men should be arriving shortly."

They wait for only a few minutes before the party comes into view. The captain smiles for only the briefest moment, but it falters. There are only eight of them.

As they get closer, the crowd at the gate draws a collective breath. Shaide and Reno are carrying something wrapped in blankets and enchanted with ice magic between them. Captain Winslow does a quick headcount and realizes he one missing was Rayn.

He quickly approaches them and receives a prompt salute from Celeste and Lania, while Reno looks around awkwardly.

"What happened?" He asks them.

Shaide and Reno ease Rayn's body to the ground. Reno salutes "Sir, Rayn Jarvis fell in the line of duty to a corrupted Fallen, trying to save the life of one of our squad mates. His sacrifice was brave, sir."

Captain Winslow adopts a grim expression as Nanilina puts a hand to her heart.

"The Fallen responsible for the corruption has been terminated, and the Elder Wyrm, while still alive, is not likely to be a threat any longer." Reno finishes.

"At ease, Coltide. You've been through enough." Captain Winslow says.

Nanilina steps forward "What of the Elder Wyrm, Nyuralisiania? What happened out there?"

Nyu steps forward and speaks face-to-face with the chieftainess. "A corrupted agent was orchestrating the whole thing. It appears that the Elder Wyrm was not responsible for the attack on Torchlight. Rather, it is likely that the villagers of Wyrmwood had fallen under the corruption and killed them. We were forced to exterminate Wyrmwood when we faced the corrupted asshole and his enthralled Elder Wyrm. Actually, he killed most of them himself, and wiped out the village with them."

Nanilina shakes her head in disbelief. "He took all of those people under his control and just sacrificed them?"

Nyu nods sadly "It seems he knew Shaide and Amari, and he had a personal grudge against them. Something about them leaving him to die in a pit of lava last time they met."

"Good goddess…" Nanilina breathes.

Meanwhile, Captain Winslow signals over two troops "Men, take Jarvis's remains to the medical bay. We have to get him home to his family."

"Sir!" The two soldiers gently pick up Rayn's body and start carrying it to the airship spire and the *North Star*.

"All of you." Captain Winslow indicates the gathered heroes "You should return to the ship as well. You have been through quite an ordeal. You've more than earned the rest."

"Thank you, Captain." Reno says, unusually take-charge. The younger majority of the group proceeds to return to the airship behind the soldiers carrying Rayn, but Aton and Lucy remain behind to speak with the Captain and Chieftainess.

"Umm, Captain?" Nyu asks timidly "May I board the ship to stay with my friends?"

Aton answers before the captain "That depends. Since you have that Angel, are you coming back to the citadel with us? Or will you remain here in Pandora?"

"Is that an option?!" She says rather excitedly. She looks at Nanilina for guidance.

"Dear kitten, this path is laid out for you." The chieftainess says gently. "Should you choose to leave Pandora this time, we will all know it is for a greater cause. It is one thing to leave the forest for selfish reasons, but it is another to leave out of selflessness. Should you leave this time, you will be welcome here."

Nyu nods gratefully. "Then I would like to come to the citadel."

Aton looks at Captain Winslow and asks "Well, sir? Since she is with us, may she board?"

The captain sighs and closes his eyes "You Ceraphs really do play fast and loose with the rules sometimes. But yes, I know better than to interfere with your business."

"Thank you, sir!" Nyu hugs the Chieftainess goodbye and runs to join her friends.

The four of them, meanwhile, slowly walk back towards the longhouse.

"So, what really happened out there?" Nanilina asks seriously.

Aton weighs his words carefully. "We don't yet know how he managed it, and we will have to return later to investigate further, but he was somehow rapidly corrupting the local population of people and fauna and directing them to attack and spread the corruption to anything nearby. He even managed to take temporary control over the Elder Wyrm itself."

"Now that he is dead, what will happen?"

"It seems that they were being directly influenced." Aton replies. "The reason for the attacks was that he was somehow directing them to do so. Am I correct in assuming the attacks have nearly stopped?"

"Yes." Says the captain. "We haven't seen a corrupted beast in over two days."

"I thought so." Says Aton. "Without him directing them, they are little more than feral corrupted animals now. They should be more than manageable."

Nanilina sighs with relief "That is good to hear. We must get in touch with the capital and let the council know what has transpired.

We are most grateful for your help. All of you." She hesitates for a moment, then finishes "I am sorry it cost the life of one of your own. Will his friends be okay?"

"They're a tight group." Lucy says. "It will take some time for them to get over it, but they will, and they will be stronger for it.

*   *   *

"Hey guys, wait up!" Nyu says, running to catch up with her new friends.

Shaide looks at her in surprise "I'm sorry, Nyu. We're going back up to our ship. I don't think the military wants a civilian, especially a foreigner, on board its warships."

Reno nods his ascent.

"It's okay. I'm coming back to the Citadel." She smiles. "Mr. Aton wants me to consider joining the Ceraphs, so the Captain said I could come aboard with you!"

Shaide looks at Amari, who gives him a pained look, but she nods.

"If you say so." Shaide says warily "Welcome aboard."

"Jeez. Don't look so disappointed." Nyu pouts "I thought we were really good friends!"

"I'm pretty sure she wants more than just his friendship." Celeste whispers quietly. Reno and Lania can't help but grin.

"No, no. It's fine, Nyu." Shaide says with some exasperation. "It's just been a stressful couple of weeks. Please, PLEASE promise me you'll behave yourself and keep your antics to a minimum."

Nyu raises a hand "I solemnly promise to TRY to behave myself most of the time."

Shaide lowers his heads and sighs "That's as good as it's going to get, isn't it?"

"Pretty much!" Nyu says playfully.

As they climb the spire and subsequently board the *North Star,* Reno turns to Lania "Hey, can I talk to you in private?" He asks.

Lania looks a little surprised, but she nods and follows him across the hangar as their friends head for their quarters.

Reno and Lania stand next to each other at the edge of the hangar bay looking away from the spire for a while. However, he is having trouble finding the words he wants to say to her.

For her part, Lania is waiting patiently. She knows what this is likely about, but they haven't had a chance to discuss it in light of recent events.

"So, listen. About that night…"

Lania shakes her head "No, no. I'm sorry. I really shouldn't have done that."

Reno looks at her, confusion etched into his face. "Don't apologize. That makes ME feel bad. What I mean to say is, was that out of grief? Or did you mean it?"

Lania's face is growing red with embarrassment. "I, well…I, um…"

Reno sighs and turns to look back out into the sky, hiding his face from her. In spite of the dangers they've faced, THIS is what is scaring him. He weighs his words carefully. "I liked it, and I feel like we've gotten close working together. If you wanted to…"

Lania's face is bright red, and it seems like she wants to speak, but is unable to. Reno turns around to face her when she doesn't respond and is surprised to see a face that looks as nervous and scared as he feels.

"Well, I…" Lania manages to stutter.

"Oh, screw it." Reno says. He goes for broke and kisses her, putting his hand on her face. Her eyes widen in shock for brief moment, and then the she closes them, reciprocating the kiss from the guy she has silently crushed on.

Someone whistles in the hanger, but they ignore it. After a moment they break apart, and Lania says quietly "Wow. I guess that just happened."

Reno smiles gently "I thought it was easier to ask what you wanted that way."

Lania admits to herself he has a point. Still, she's concerned about one thing. "If we're going to do this, let's keep it out of the Academy. Okay? I don't want any trouble."

"Of course." Reno agrees with her. "Military regulations on fraternization and all that. I get it."

She smiles awkwardly at him "We should probably join the others before we get into trouble. We have witnesses."

*   *   *

Shaide, Celeste, Nyu, and Amari all walk into the makeshift Ceraph quarters and grab seats around the compartment. They have it all to themselves, so they have a bit of room to spread out.

Celeste strips off her chain armor and leathers, basically down to her underwear, and lounges in one of the beds. "God, I could really use a bath SOO bad right now. It's kind of muggy in here."

Shaide rolls his eyes. For the second time recently, he's trapped alone with a group of women. On the mission he distracted himself with said mission, but here in the dorms, he feels a little out of place.

Amari rolls her eyes and sits a little closer to Shaide. "Hey, Celeste? I know it's muggy in here, but do you mind keeping your clothes on? There IS a boy present, you know."

Celeste turns her head to Amari from the bunk and sticks her tongue out and says playfully "What's wrong, Elmeri? Afraid your boyfriend will like what he sees?"

"HE'S NOT MY BOYFRIEND!" She yells defensively. Shaide leans his head back and rolls his eyes. This isn't a rare discussion.

Nyu raises her hand "Hey, if she can strip down, can I strip my furs also?"

Shaide looks at her curiously. "Do you even wear underwear under your furs?"

"Not on top, no."

Shaide's eyebrows rise as high as they can go.

"NO! Everyone please keep your clothes on!" Amari cries rather desperately.

"But it's so hot in here!" Celeste mock-whines.

"Hey, Amari?" Nyu says playfully. "If you're worried your boyfriend will get jealous, you COULD strip down too."

"FOR THE LAST TIME, HE'S…," She sighs, fanning herself "It IS kinda hot in here."

"Take it off! Take it off!" Celeste chants.

     A.S.GUINN

"I have a better idea." Amari says. She summons her staff out of mid-air and casts some kind of magic. The cabin becomes quite windy for a moment as the temperature drops from ninety degrees to almost sixty before the breeze dies down.

Celeste shivers and pulls her armor and clothes back on. "Jeez, Amari. You're really no fun. Although, I never knew you could use magic as an air cooler."

"How do you think we keep our homes cool?" Amari says "It's a frost magicore with and electric blower. Magic can do the same thing."

Celeste looks impressed "I never knew that. Still, you ruined our fun."

Shaide makes a joke "I was kinda wondering who was going to get naked first. OW!"

Amari slaps him in the chest.

"Hey guys, sorry we... Wow. It's kinda chilly in here." Reno pauses as he and Lania walk in.

"We were taking bets on whether you two were doing it or not." Celeste says. "Looks like I lost. That wasn't nearly long enough."

"Kiss my ass, snow woman." Reo retorts.

Celeste makes a mock-offended face "Oh wow. Scathing."

Lania takes a seat next to Nyu, while Reno sits by Shaide's unoccupied side. "So, what did we miss?"

Celeste pouts "Well, we WERE trying to strip for Shaide, but Amari ruined our fun."

"Sad thing is she's not exaggerating by much." Amari says resentfully.

Reno looks around in surprise "Wow. What did I miss?"

"The usual." Celeste replies simply.

Lania rolls her eyes "So… trying to make Shaide uncomfortable. Got it."

Celeste sits up "Hey, Lania. Maybe YOU should strip for him. Maybe he likes petites."

"Why the obsession with stripping?!" Amari says in frustration.

To her credit, Lania completely ignores Celeste. "Hey Shaide? I have a question."

"As long as it's not about stripping, go ahead."

Reno chuckles as Lania continues "When we were fighting the wyrm and that Fallen guy, your aura did something really weird. It was like you were drawing spiritual energy from the environment, and even more surprising, directly from the wyrm. How did you do that?"

Five sets of eyes turn and lock onto Shaide. He tilts his head in earnest confusion "What do you mean? I didn't do anything."

Four sets of eyes swing back to Lania.

"I was watching everyone's auras, in case anyone over exerted. It's normal for an aura to resonate with the environment, but your aura was most definitely drawing massive amounts of spiritual energy from the environment and using it, rather than using your own reserves. Honestly, your aura more closely resembled your angels' auras rather than a Mitera or a human."

Shaide slowly shakes his head, utterly nonplussed. "I have no idea what you're talking about. If I was doing something weird, I wasn't doing it on purpose."

"Damn…" Lania sighs "That would be a hell of a technique if it could be learned."

"I'm sorry, really." Shaide says apologetically.

The six of them spend the next hour visiting and decompressing after their especially taxing mission. Their unusual behavior is just a coping mechanism to help the young and inexperienced warriors readjust to a more peaceful life after rough missions, and although they seem to be giving each other a hard time, they are all really friends. Even in spite of the tension between Nyu, Celeste, and Amari as they compete for Shaide's attention. The three girls are friends as well.

After a while, Aton and Lucy join them in the cabin. Aton asks everyone "How are all of you doing, considering what has happened?"

Reno looks around at his fellow warriors and nods "I think we're okay, sir, umm… Aton. We're sad about losing Rayn, sure. Devastated, honestly. But we knew what we were getting into when we chose this life."

"Very good." Aton nods with satisfaction. "Well, I have some good news for everyone. We just got a message from the *Last Beacon*, and she is airworthy again. Her repairs aren't complete, but she can make the journey back to the Citadel."

"So, does that mean we'll be saying goodbye?" Shaide says, looking at his friend Reno sadly.

"No, not yet." Says Aton. "I wish to attend the services for Rayn as well, so we will be returning to Alastair with the *North Star*. That bring me to my second bit of news."

"There's more?"

Aton nods. "Queen Nasha has been told of your heroics in defense of her people. The arrangements will be made at a later date, but she wishes to bestow upon you all the greatest honor they will grant to outsiders. It has not been awarded in over fifteen hundred years, in fact. An award ceremony will be arranged for you all in the future."

The six younger occupants of the room exchange shocked glances. They had never expected to be recognized by the queen of this nation.

*   *   *

A few short days later, the ARV *North Star* and the COV *Last Beacon* are parked on one of the spires to the Alastair Royal Military headquarters in Corallina.

In the base below, a significant number of personnel were gathered in the Alastair National Memorial Cemetery, attending the service of Rayn Jarvis, who is being granted posthumous honors for his sacrifice.

Standing at the head of the casket are Colonel Lim Jarvis, and Lieutenant General Roy Jarvis; Rayn's father and grandfather respectively. His mother also stands beside her husband, along with his younger brother.

ETERNAL KNIGHTS OF EDEN II

Queen Nasha of Pandora and her guards have managed to attend the event, as well as Chieftainess Nanilina of Children's Oasis. Rayn was receiving a grand send off.

Reno, Lania, and Celeste were all present in their dress blue uniforms, along with all members of their class not currently on other assignments. Captain Nikola and Lieutenant Adeline even managed to attend.

Also at the front of the crowd, Shaide, Amari, Aton, and Lucy are all wearing their nicest black outfits to honor the occasion, and much to everyone's surprise, Orville Armstrong of the Ceraph Order also is in attendance.

"Every soldier enters the service knowing that every day could be his last." Captain Nikola delivers the eulogy "They do so hoping that their risk and sacrifice can provide the people of Alastair with a better future. Few have embodied the meaning of being a soldier as well as Rayn Jarvis."

"Rayn was a hard-working student, and a natural leader. He never complained about what he was asked to do, and always tried his hardest to keep his comrades together. Even in his final moments, he gave his life to save that of a fellow soldier."

Tears run down Lania's face as Nikola says these words, feeling guilt for the death of her friend.

"Rayn made the greatest sacrifice not for Alastair, but for Eden as a whole. In defense of our neighboring ally, he was selflessly serving the needs of the world itself above his own. Never in my years in the service have I ever been as proud of a comrade as I am today.

Rayn Jarvis, The Alastair Royal Military has lost one of its finest. Goodbye, friend."

Captain Nikola steps down, and High-General Alexander Edenkin steps forward to the podium. "Rayn Jarvis exemplified the very qualities that define a soldier of Alastair. He was brave, honorable, and most importantly, selfless. In light of his service, I grant him the posthumous rank of Captain, and bestow upon him the Alastair Medal of Valor." He turns and hands a small box to Rayn's mother and father as they exchange salutes.

Queen Nasha takes the podium and looks around at all of the human and Mitera faces. She smiles gently and speaks "I never met Captain Rayn Jarvis, but I know of what he has done for my people. His sacrifice gave way to the safety and salvation of a great many of my people. Never have we known an outsider to do something so selfless for us. In light of the unparalleled honor and integrity of this man, I, Queen Nasha of the sovereign nation of Pandora, grant him the Crest of Pandora. An honor never before given to an outsider."

Queen Nasha walks over and places a Medallion bearing the Pandora royal crest on his casket and bows deeply with her hand across her heart. Her guards at the podium mimic her salute, and then she turns and takes her place by the other officials.

The honor guard marches in from either side of the casket to stand facing it

"Honor guard. Salute!"

The six members of the honor guard draw silver ceremonial sabers and point them up at an angle, forming a kind of archway as the

　　　　　　　A.S.GUINN

casket begins lowering to the ground. The band present begins playing a traditional funeral song.

Tears run down the faces of Rayn's mother and brother, along with Shaide, Reno, Amari, Celeste, and Lania, among several others. The cemetery is silent aside from the sound of the band.

Moments later, the casket is settled at the bottom, and the band brings their song to an end.

Silence fills the air until General Edenkin calls out "Alastair personnel! Dismissed!"

As the bulk of those present filter slowly out of the cemetery, Shaide, Amari, Celeste, Reno, and Lania all approach the grave as Rayn's parents and grandfather approach as well.

"Mrs. Jarvis… I am so sorry…" Lania says timidly.

Mrs. Jarvis just shakes her head "No, dear. Don't be. He would have never been able to live with himself if he hadn't saved you. This was the way things had to be, and I know it. It's just…"

Colonel Lim Jarvis, his father, says in a flat voice "No parent should ever have to bury their own child."

Lieutenant General Roy Jarvis turns to Shaide and bows unexpectedly. "Ceraph, I would like to offer you my thanks."

"Your… Thanks, sir?" Shaide asks in confusion.

"Yes. For being my grandson's friend, and for avenging his death by killing the one responsible." He says "Rayn would be proud knowing that his death helped bring peace to those people. I do not think he would have any regrets."

"Thank…Thank you, sir." Shaide says awkwardly.

Queen Nasha walks over with Aton and Lucy. "Jarvis family. Allow me to offer my personal condolences once again. I know it brings little comfort, but your son will always be remembered as a hero to my people."

"Thank you, your majesty." Lt General Jarvis says.

"Ceraphs and Exorcists? I would like to speak with you later, before I depart to return to my nation."

"Of-of course, your highness." Shaide stutters nervously.

She shakes her head "You are the heroes of my people now. You of all people need not express such formality. Especially you, Grim Reaper of the Ceraphs."

Shaide raises his eyebrows.

"Of course, ma'am." Reno interjects "But it is the way we were taught. Please accept our respect and courtesy."

"Of course, young Exorcist." She bows. "Master Norvus, Mistress Norvus."

Aton and Lucy watch the queen walk away. Aton then turns and bows to Rayn's family "We will let you be alone for now. Come on, everyone."

After a quick final offering of condolences from everyone present, the group marches out of the cemetery and towards the gate leading to town.

"The academy is giving us a few days off to grieve." Says Reno. "They did the same when we lost Bryon and Joslin."

Celeste nods "It's not unusual for a class to lose a few students before graduation, but this has definitely been a first."

Reno looks wistfully at his side "I still can't believe he's gone. He's always been by our side, since our first day with the academy. He was a little bit of a tight wad, but he always looked out for us and kept our spirits up. Kept us in line, but he kept us alive."

"Now he's gone." Lania says gloomily.

Shaide puts a hand on Reno's shoulder "He was a good guy. Right through the end. Would any of the rest of us have had the balls to sacrifice ourselves like that?"

Amari gives him an amused look "Didn't you fly down a dragon's throat?"

The group manages a weak series of laughs.

"I only knew him a short time, but I was very impressed with him." Aton says, "I was considering trying to recruit him into the Ceraphs, in fact."

"Indeed." Lucy nods. "He was brave, smart, and strong. He was not tied down to Alastair. He was more than happy to protect anyone who needed it."

The mood in the crowd is still fairly somber. Aton looks around as they head off the base and into town. "Why don't we grab lunch. We're not far from that diner Shaide likes."

"I could go for lunch." A familiar voice says unexpectedly. Nyu runs up to meet them. She's not wearing her usual furs, but is instead wearing a sort of leather dress outfit similar to that of the other Nekomata at the funeral.

"Where were you?" Shaide says, sounding mildly displeased.

"I was at the ceremony, but they made me stay with the Pandora personnel." She says, "I'm not military, and I'm technically not with the Ceraphs yet either."

Aton nods "That's right, Armstrong hasn't been able to meet with you yet."

"Speaking of which," Shaide inquires suspiciously "How DID you end up with Tau, anyway? That's a little strange."

"Well, it's a long story." She replies "I actually went into Pandora looking for him, and ended up helping defend the village of Children's Oasis after Hancer and Varofia saved me from an ambush by some nekoshin. They helped me find the altar in exchange for helping them defend the village."

Shaide's suspicion deepens. "How did you BEAT the thing?"

"He's not a thing." She says indignantly "He's the Shadow Cat, and he is my friend. Anyways, I summoned him, and had to use every bit of agility I possessed to dodge him. He was relentless, and his sonic attacks were particularly nasty. I felt like my bones would shatter. I never technically BEAT him, exactly. After dodging his attacks long enough, and even managing to land a few blows myself, his aggression suddenly faded. He bowed to me and, well, kind of went inside me."

Aton nods approvingly "That sounds about right for Tau. He has always favored particularly agile partners. It's no secret that most of his partners have been Nekomata."

They turn down the street and proceed to the café that Shaide favors. Their sharp-dressed appearance immediately draws a number of looks from the other guests.

"Oh Shaide! I haven't seen you in a while!" The waitress, Ashlie exclaims. She looks around at the others "It's good to see all of you again. I feel like someone is missing though…"

Reno nods and looks down "Yeah, actually… Rayn passed away. We just came from his funeral."

"Oh…" Ashlie says, her face falling. "I'm really sorry to hear that. I liked him."

The party moves over to a larger unoccupied table to sit down. After taking their order, Ashlie retreats to the kitchen.

"She's really nice." Nyu remarks. "Hey Shaide? Did you and her ever,,,?"

Shaide shakes his head.

"Oh, I see." Nyu smirks for some reason.

A young man walks over to the table "Excuse me, did she say your name was Shaide?"

Shaide look at him in surprise. The kid is probably around fourteen or so. "Umm, Yeah, I'm Shaide. Why?"

The kid looks excited for some reason "Are you Shaide Darkmoon? The Grim Reaper of the Ceraph Order?"

Shaide's eyebrows rise into his short hair as he looks around the table at everyone else's amused expressions.

"Shaide, it looks like you're becoming famous for your stunt in Lone Ridge." Aton says with a slight grin.

"It IS you!" The kid says excitedly "Can I get you to sign this for me?"

Shaide looks down at the paper the kid is holding. It's a newspaper article about the averted disaster in Lone Ridge.

"Umm, yeah. Sure, kid." Shaide signs the news article for him.

"Thank you, sir! Keep protecting us!" The kid runs away excitedly to show his family.

Amari smiles at Shaide "You're becoming a bit of a hero, Mr. Reaper."

"You know there is no way in hell I could have done it without your help…" Shaide mutters embarrassedly.

Amari shakes her head "Maybe, but you can keep the fame. I'm fine without it."

"Shaide, don't cast off the importance of what you did." Aton says rather sternly "Being a hero is a great service in itself. The people need hope, and having a figure to look up to gives them that hope they need to keep going."

Ashlie returns with their drinks "By the way. I told my dad about what happened. He said your meals are on him today. A thanks for the sacrifices you make, and an offering of condolence for your loss."

Lucy nods gracefully "Thank you, miss Ashlie."

Reno raises his drink in the air "To Rayn. A great friend, a fantastic leader, and a true hero. Rayn, although you are gone, your spirit will remain with those of us who remain. Your sacrifice will forever inspire us to follow your example and help anyone in need. Your sacrifice reminds us that no act of heroism is too small, and that we should all be willing to do whatever it takes to save those we care about. To Rayn!"

"To Rayn!" Everyone else raises their glasses and clinks them together. Even the tables around them, while unaware of what transpired, recognized the significance of the toast, and raised their glasses as well.

Everyone drinks deeply for a minute in honor of their fallen friend. A hero's goodbye. Shaide sets his glass down and looks at Reno, and they exchange meaningful glances. They too will do whatever it takes to serve and protect the people of Eden.

"Goodbye, Rayn."

CHAPTER 11

ACT TWO

In the extreme southern reaches of Alastair, just inside of the Deadlands, a young woman lies unconscious in a lone cave, under a lone plateau. She doesn't seem to be injured in any way, but she lies motionless.

"Awaken."

The young woman's eyes open, and she stares at the ceiling overhead for a few moments. She sits up and looks around, getting a bearing on where she is. The woman is very fair. She has pale skin, blonde hair, blue eyes, and has a well-developed frame. She doesn't appear to be older than her early twenties.

She looks around the cavern in curiosity. She notices where the cavern once appeared to be sealed, but some kind of seismic activity has broken the seal on the entrance. Overhead, cracks in the thick roof of the cavern reveal traces of sunlight filtering in.

　　　　A.S.GUINN

She turns around and looks behind her and sees an altar of some kind. Curious. It has a very ornate statue standing over it.

"Bring the child of Eden here..." a voice whispers to her. She nods and climbs to her feet. She is completely naked, but she has no memory of who she is or why she is here. As such, she feels no need for modesty.

She walks out of the cavern and into the sunlight.

Strange. The sun is oddly diluted, as if a thick haze hangs in the air. All around her, a black haze slowly rises from the ground in places. It doesn't seem to be harming her, however. She turns north and begins walking. She doesn't know exactly why she is going this way, but she has a feeling that something is this way.

She walks for hours upon hours. Day turns to night, and night again turns to day, and she just continues walking. She sees numerous animals along her way, but they give her a wide berth for some reason.

For three days and nights she continues walking without rest, food, or water. Exhaustion sets in, yet she feels compelled to continue walking. She doesn't even notice when she departs the haze of the corruption into more fertile land.

On the third day, an outpost comes into view. An extremely heavily defended military post on the southern edge of the habitable lands of Alastair.

She looks up at the heavily fortified base, with multiple heavy capital ships parked above it, and continues walking towards it.

A soldier in a watchtower sees her and calls an alert, and soon five squads of special forces Exorcists spill out of the base and surround the woman. The men and women of Hell's Doorstep look in confusion at the woman as she just stands there, naked and dazed.

"Excuse me! Why are you here? This is a restricted area!"

The young woman focuses on the man in charge who addresses her, and she simply says "I need… the child of Eden…" she immediately passes out and collapses.

"What in the hell?" The commander says, utterly confused "Get her inside the base, and contact Iron Veil!"

Another of his troops stands over her as one of the women covers her naked body with a tarp she was carrying. "Who is this girl? What is she doing here?"

As several troops pick her up and begin carrying her inside, the rest of them stand around, looking completely lost and confused.

*   *   *

Shaide, Amari, Nyu, Celeste, Reno, and Lania are all gathered at the usual restaurant in Corallina, for today is a special day. Ashlie and her father reserved the whole place for them today in honor of their favorite customer.

"Happy birthday, Shaide!" Everyone says, raising their glasses to clink together. Shaide turns eighteen today, and as such is legally a full adult in the eyes of Alastair.

Reno hands Shaide a decent sized box. "Here, this is from Lania and me. We had it made specially for you."

Shaide opens the box and finds a jet-black buckler. Elongated and narrow, it looks like a skinny pointed shield. He straps it on his arm and finds it is surprisingly light. The material looks very familiar.

     A.S.GUINN

"We had the smith in Lone Ridge make it for you." Lania says "He even gave us a discount when we said it was for you. They remember the Reaper of Lone Ridge very well."

"Thank you, guys!" Shaide says, looking admiringly at the buckler. Of course it looks familiar. It is made from the same material as his sword.

Celeste holds out a box as well "This is from me. I had it made at the smith up the street."

Shaide opens the box and finds a balaclava style mask in it, with holes for the eyes. The image of a spectral face is embroidered into the front, making it look like a ghost or skull.

"I thought it was fitting for the 'Grim Reaper of the Ceraphs'" She says with a smile.

"Thank you, Celeste!" He says.

Amari summons a heavy box from seemingly nowhere. "Here. My dad had this made for you at my request." She says, red in the face.

Shaide opens the heavy box and finds a beautiful black magicore-forged steel scale-mail cuirass in the box. The overlapping scales provide superior protection while maintaining light weight and easy flexibility. Underneath it is a fitted black-leather vest to go over it.

"Oh my god, Amari…" He says, picking it up and examining it with reverence. "This is absolutely amazing! This is royal-forged armor…"

Amari nods, glowing at the fact that he likes it so much "My father was able to convince the empress to allow her personal smith to forge this for you. It is basically the best lightweight armor the Elmeri make. Only the Termer could do better."

Shaide looks it over with great admiration. He cannot believe she did this for him, or that her father would do this for him. He was under the impression that General Tamiel was still pissed at him for running off with his daughter. Apparently not.

Shaide picks up a not from inside the box,

Shaide,

I had this made for you at the request of Amari. The man I have trusted with the life of my youngest daughter needs the best protection I can provide. After all, you cannot protect her if you cannot protect yourself, and I would hate for someone else to kill you before I get the chance myself.

Take care of yourself, Shaide. Although I disagree with the life you and Amari have chosen, it is your lives to live. I have heard of the heroics you two have committed together, and I cannot deny that, in spite of my misgivings, this may be what Amari was born for.

If anything happens to her, you had better hope that you die trying to protect her, otherwise no one in the Ceraph Order will be able to protect you from my wrath. This being said, I love you both. Take care of each other and continue doing what you do best.

Maj. Gen. Koraru Tamiel

Shaide rubs his neck awkwardly. Apparently Koraru is still a little angry. He smiles to himself in spite of this though. The man

A.S.GUINN

treats him as his own son much of the time, and Shaide is still happy to hear from him.

"I see my dad still hasn't changed." Amari says, reading the letter over his shoulder.

Shaide sets it down and sighs "Well, I DID take you out of Erita without talking to him first. I wouldn't expect him to forgive that just yet."

Amari smiles at him "He's not as mad as he pretends to be. He just has to keep up appearances."

"I wonder if your dad would start a war with the Ceraphs if you died." Celeste wonders aloud.

"Let's not find out." Shaide mutters. He takes the cuirass out of the box and carefully puts it on. As expected, the material is remarkably light. Even the spaulders (a lightweight shoulder covering similar to pauldrons) are very light and flexible. He pulls the top on over the armor, and looks down.

"Looks good." Reno says with a smile.

"I've been trying to get you to wear SOME kind of armor forever." Amari says with a sigh. "Maybe you'll actually wear it?"

"Absolutely. It's surprisingly light." He jumps up and down a couple times. "A little working out to get used to the weight, and it should be just fine!"

Amari can't help but smile. He really likes her gift.

In the box is a matching set of greaves that scales the hips and outside edge of the legs without sacrificing mobility. He puts everything back in the box. "I'll figure out how to dispel and summon it later."

"Oh hey! Mind if we join you?" A familiar voice reaches his ears. He cautiously turns to look at the street, and Amari mimics his apprehensive look.

"Oh, hey Amber. Vargas. What brings you here?" Shaide says.

The redheaded Drameri and the Elmeri outcast walk in to join them.

Vargas holds out a hand, shaking Shaide and Amari's in turn. "We heard you were having your eighteenth birthday celebration, and we thought we would come see you since we have some free time."

"Of course!" Amber nods "I could never pass up the chance to come and celebrate with my favorite Miteran Ceraph! We don't get to spend NEARLY enough time together, after all. And here I was hoping to get to spend a LOT of time with you after the mission in Erita, but no, you had to go running around all over the world while I'm stuck at the lab with Vargas and Ronoa, missing my hot little Miteran-"

"AMBER!" Vargas barks "You're doing it again!"

"Oh, sorry." Amber coughs. "Anyway, Eighteen, huh? A grown man now. Has miss Amari made a man out of you yet?"

"AMBER! I SAID SHUT IT!"

Amber grins and shuts up. The Exorcists in the group look extremely amused at the interactions between these newcomers and Shaide. He and Amari exchange amused glances. It's nice to see that some things never change, even if they are a bit annoying.

"Anyways, we at the research department got together a little gift for you." Vargas says with a smile. "Here. Take it."

Shaide takes a small box and opens it to find a small pocket watch.

"It's a magicore powered global watch" Amber says proudly "It automatically adjusts the time based on the position of the sun, so you are always in the right time zone. Also, if you channel a trace amount of power into it, it will light up like a lantern, giving it an extra use in dark places."

"Wow. Thank you!" Shaide says.

Amber leans in close to his ear "I can give you another present in private if you want, now that you're grown."

"AMBER!" Shaide yells.

She backs away and winks, sticking her tongue out at him.

"Did she say what I think she said?" Amari whispers to him.

Shaide nods, trying not to laugh.

"Lecherous old broad…" Amari mutters, smiling in spite of herself.

"Hey, I'm not that old, you know." Amber says. "I'm still a young woman by Drameri standards."

Vargas sighs "I know, and you definitely act like it…"

"I'm not even old enough to have kids yet!" She pouts "Why shouldn't I have fun?"

Vargas looks extremely exasperated "I'm not even going to dignify that with a response…"

"Okay, okay. I'll behave now…" she says, still pouting.

Shaide mumbles only loud enough for Amari to hear "I'll believe it when I see it."

Amari snickers slightly.

Shaide leans back with a smile. It's times like these that make all of their fighting worth it, when they can just sit together with their friends and enjoy themselves.

"Where are Aton and Lucy?" Vargas asks curiously.

Shaide's face falls slightly "They're away on a mission. They were supposed to be back already, but you know how often that actually happens."

"Indeed. I'm sorry to hear it."

Amari looks at Shaide with great affection. She feels like she is getting a handle on her emotions, but she cannot deny that part of her still wants to be more than friends. She's accepted that this is unlikely to happen, and it might even be a bad thing, but she still finds herself longing for it sometimes.

She shakes her head and looks away. Everyone seems to be happy right now, and even she has to admit she is feeling pretty good right now.

*   *   *

"I'll see you all later!" Amber says to Shaide, Amari, and Nyu as they climb out of a helicar at the Citadel. "Shaide? I'll catch you later to give you my…personal…present." She says with a wink.

Vargas rolls his eyes "Amber? If you're going to jump the young man, just do it and get it over with, will you? Good lord, woman."

Amber puts a thoughtful hand to her chin. "Hmm. Maybe I should!"

Amari turns to her and growls "Amber? I know you're our friend, but will you shut the hell up for once?"

"Ooh! I'm getting to Amari now, am I?" She winks "Are you that afraid that I'm going to steal your-"

Shaide, Amari, and Vargas all simultaneously yell "AMBER! SHUT IT!"

Amber just chuckles "Okay, okay. I'll see you guys later, I'm sure."

Vargas puts his face in his hand and says "That woman is going to be the death of me. Happy birthday Shaide! See you all later."

Vargas and Amber set off in the opposite direction as Shaide. Amari, and Nyu set off towards the residential district of the Citadel. They had a fun day hanging out with all of their friends, but it had been a long day.

"What's the story with that Amber chick?" Nyu asks "Her scent is all KINDS of excited and…well… yeah, around Shaide. Who is she?"

Shaide rolls his eyes "She's a Drameri biologist who works for the Ceraph Order as a researcher and science expert. She is ridiculously intelligent, surprisingly strong, a lot older than she looks, and is a total and absolute pervert."

Nyu nods "Yeah, I kinda got that part. It seems like you guys know her pretty well."

"She was the lead biologist on the team that came to Erita last year when I joined the Ceraphs." Amari explains "Like Shaide said, she is incredibly smart, but she seems to have the libido of a rabbit. She could hardly stop hitting on Shaide while she was around him. She was studying how to combat that strange illness that was claiming

Elmeri lives. We worked with her for well over a month, so yeah, we got to know her pretty well."

Nyu looks extremely amused. "When your aunt Lucy acts like that, I can tell she is mostly kidding, though if given the actual opportunity… Well, anyway. That Amber, however, she literally smells like a lobo in heat."

Shaide bursts out laughing at Nyu's candidness. That was what he liked about her. She straight up spoke her mind regardless of what it was.

"Well, anyways. I'm going to head home for now." She yawns and stretches "I could use a nap after today."

"Later Nyu." Shaide says.

"See you."

Nyu waves at them and walks away to her dorm. In the past few weeks since they returned from Pandora, Nyu had been granted entry into the Ceraph order. Shaide was under the impression she was his age, but it turns out she was a little older. The petite nature of the Nekomata just made her seem younger. She had participated in a couple of minor missions with the two of them since their return, and it turns out that the three of them make a pretty good team.

"You know? I can never quite read her, but she IS a really nice girl." Amari says thoughtfully.

Shaide nods in response as he says, "She's different, that's for sure."

"She's all over an awful lot, though." Amari says, a hint of jealousy in her voice. "Is there anything low-key going on between you two?"

   A.S.GUINN

Shaide shakes his head "No. We were kind of dating for a few days back when I was in the academy, but there's nothing right now."

"Right now…" She says, trailing off.

Shaide notices her face and smiles gently. "Hey, why you come in and hang out, just you and me? We haven't gotten to spend much one-on-one time together lately, have we?"

Amari seems to perk up a bit "Are you sure?"

Shaide opens the door to his and Aton's house "Yeah, of course. Come on in."

Amari and Shaide enter his house, and she sits on the couch as Shaide gets them both a glass of water.

She looks around the living room. She hasn't been in here in a while. It had been non-stop missions and activity for quite a while, and their personal lives kind of fell by the wayside. She sees there are a number of photographs in here, and while a couple of them are of Shaide's other friends, most of the photographs are of him and her together. She sees an old photograph of them when they were ten, and she can't help but smile that he had kept that photo for the past eight years.

Shaide walks back in and hands her a cold glass of water. "Man alive, after all of the missions we've been running, I'm surprised how tired a simple party made me."

Amari looks at the small stack of boxes Shaide had carried all the way from Corallina. "Well, you DID have a bunch of stuff to carry."

Shaide nods and sits down next to her "Yeah, I suppose so."

Amari yawns widely. She's pretty tired too, now that he mentions it. "Hey Shaide? Can I borrow you for a bit?"

"Hmm?" He says

She scoots over next to him and lays back against his chest and closes her eyes, and falls asleep almost instantly.

Shaide smiles to himself. He puts an arm around her shoulder and lays his head against hers and falls asleep himself.

*   *   *

Several hours have passed since the mysterious young woman appeared at Hell's Doorstep Alastair military outpost. While the soldiers try and figure out what to do with her, she lies unconscious in the infirmary with a fever.

"Strange." Says Dr. Vorzech, looking at the woman's appearance "She's definitely human. She only shows trace symptoms of miasma exposure; no more than any of our soldiers, at least, so she can't have been out of the Deadlands."

Brig. Gen. Warsaw frowns as the doctor looks her over. "You're saying she's not corrupted, then. Am I correct?"

"No more than our own people down here." Vorzech replies. "Aside from that, she is remarkably healthy, albeit dehydrated. I couldn't tell you where the hell she came from though."

Gen. Warsaw scratches his chin thoughtfully. "There are no settlements for miles, and she came from the south. Who the hell is this woman?"

Her eyes suddenly open, and she looks around in confusion.

"Take it easy. You're safe now." Vorzech says gently "You're in a military hospital. Can you tell me your name?"

The woman sits up slowly and shakes her head.

"Can you tell me where you are from?"

The woman looks as if she is thinking, and with a pained look on her face, she says "I don't know."

General Warsaw and Dr. Vorzech exchange glances, and the doctor continues "What can you remember? Take it easy, there is no rush. Just tell me."

The woman seems lost in thought. It is a good minute before she finally speaks "I remember a cave… and I remember walking for days and nights. No rest. And I remember seeing some people, and a camp or base…"

Vorzech looks at Warsaw "Days of walking with no rest? No wonder she collapsed."

Warsaw nods his head at the woman, indicating Vorzech should continue.

"What else do you remember. Anything at all, no matter how small." Vorzech asks gently.

The young woman looks like she is struggling to think. Her eyes widen in some kind of realization. "The… child of Eden. I need the child of Eden."

Warsaw waves the doctor over and they speak in private. "Doctor, she came from the south, and she said she was walking for days, and now she says she needs a child of Eden? I believe she might have come from near the deadlands after all."

"Her words would definitely seem to indicate this." Vorzech says thoughtfully "Perhaps she was with a party of Ceraphs and something happened? She mentioned a cave, and she has some mild exposure to the miasma. Might I suggest we contact the Citadel?"

"I think I will consider this." Warsaw nods "I will wait to hear back from Lieutenant General Jarvis first, and see what Iron Veil wants to do."

The doctor salutes "Understood sir. I will continue trying to speak to our patient."

Warsaw returns the salute. "I leave her in your hands for now."

As the General leaves, Doctor Vorzech summons a glass of cold water and takes it to the patient. "Now, drink this, and take it easy. Let it come to you. I need to know what happened so I can help you."

The woman takes the glass and takes a slow sip.

"Were you here with the Ceraphs?" Vorzech asks gently "Why do you need a Ceraph?"

The woman stares off into space. "Ceraphs? I don't remember why I was there. When I woke up in the cave, I was alone. I only remember that I need the child of Eden. I need to take him there." She strains, struggling to remember.

Vorzech sits back and frowns. This woman turns up at their base, naked and alone, and the only thing she can remember is that she needs this child of Eden. She cannot remember her own name, or where she's from. She only remembers a cave, and what sounds like the Ceraphs. A strange case if she has ever seen one.

"So, you need the Ceraphs?" Vorzech asks again, trying to get any detail she can.

To her surprise, the woman shakes her head "No, I need the child of Eden."

"Who do you need? Do you know their name?" Vorzech asks curiously. If she can get a name, they may have a clue who this mysterious woman is.

The woman seems to be struggling. "I- I don't remember. I just need to take him there."

"Where do you need to take him?" Vorzech asks, her curiosity piqued to the max.

"There." She says simply, struggling to remember.

The doctor isn't able to get any more information from her for now.

*　　*　　*

Shaide wakes up a few hours later on the couch to find Amari is still asleep against him. He finds himself grinning involuntarily. *She's so cute when she's asleep.* He thinks to himself. They had been back together for over a year now. They are just friends, but Shaide finds himself thinking that he can't imagine his life without her now.

He doesn't want to disturb her, so he leans back and relaxes, letting her sleep. Everyone else makes their jokes about them being together, but as he realizes just how content he is, being alone with her, as relaxed as he can be, he wonders. *Would I really be such a bad thing if we were more than friends?* After all, their lives essentially revolve around each other. They go on every single mission together whether it is needed or not. Sure, Amari is the one who decides to come along every time, but truthfully, he has never considered leaving without her since she joined him.

He feels a great sense of apprehension though as this thought passes through his mind. *What if things didn't work out?* He frets. *What if we don't work out, and we end up unable to even be around each other anymore?* Shaide isn't certain he could handle losing her entirely. He finds himself starting to panic as these thoughts run through his head, but then Amari shift and snuggles closer to him with a yawn, and he finds his stress melt away. *Maybe I shouldn't worry about it right now.*

*knock*knock*

Amari jerks awake "Hmm? What time is it?" She sits up and looks around sleepily.

Shaide gets up and walks to the door "Who is it?"

"It's Nyu."

Amari blinks at him sleepily.

He opens the door "Yo. What's up?"

"Hey Shaide. Sorry to bother you." She peeks inside "Oh! Amari, you're here too?"

Amari nods sleepily "Hey, Nyu."

"Well, anyways. I was bored and I wanted someone to hang out with." She says, "I went to Amari's, but obviously she wasn't home."

Shaide suspects she is lying. Nyu likes to try and get him alone when she can, and while it doesn't bother him, he also doesn't quite feel like he used to about it.

"You guys want to go and get some food?"

Shaide looks over his shoulder at Amari, and she stands up and says "Yeah, sure. I'm kind of hungry."

Shaide shrugs "Sure, I'm game."

The three of them head out of the house and head to the edge of the residential district of the Citadel. Shaide looks around now that they are wound down and relaxed. He hasn't really appreciated the Citadel in a while. The residential district is comprised of a large number of modest wooden houses and apartment buildings or dorms, but it is a nice and peaceful place. The support personnel live in the Citadel as well as the Ceraphs, and altogether including families, there are over a thousand people residing in the citadel itself.

The docking spire looms overhead, casting a long shadow in the dusk light, and Shaide's eyes find the COV *Last Beacon* parked overhead as it continues repairs and retrofits from the dragon. He heard that Armstrong ordered the *Last Beacon* to be fitted with a prototype railgun similar to the heavy-destroyers and dreadnaughts, only smaller in scale. A metallic projectile the size of a human head made with a magicore center is accelerated along a magnetic rail powered by the ships electric magicore circuits and fired at over twenty-five thousand feet per second. The cannon would be capable of taking on heavier tonnage warships and, more importantly, it would be capable of knocking a dragon out of the sky with pinpoint accuracy. As it stands, a frigate does not have enough firepower to take a dragon.

"Hey, Shaide." Amari waves her hand in front of his face. "We're here. Wake up, silly."

Shaide shakes his head and realizes he had been staring at the ships overhead and nearly walked right past the pub.

"You haven't stared at the ships like that in a while." She giggles. "What's up?"

"Just thinking about the new gun they're putting on the *Last Beacon.*" Shaide replies. "That's all."

Nyu rolls her eyes "Alright, gear brain. Let's eat."

The three of them proceed into the pub and are greeted by several people they are familiar with. They take a seat near the back as the middle-aged Termer waitress walks over to greet them. "Hey kids. What'll you have tonight?"

They place their orders, and she winks "I'll have Barch get it started for you. Make yourselves at home."

As she walks away, Nyu stretches and yawns "You know what? The Ceraph Order may be a demanding life, but I cannot say it's bad."

Shaide nods in agreement "I've been here for over three years now. I can't really imagine doing anything else."

Amari claps her hands together "Hey! We should go to the lake tomorrow. Go swimming and relax, maybe cook some fish by the campfire."

Nyu's ears perk up "Well, I'm not really much for swimming, but I hear fish. Count me in."

Amari and Shaide exchange glances and start laughing.

"I wonder if we could get Reno, Lania, and Celeste to come along?" Amari thinks aloud.

"Maybe. It's worth a shot."

* * *

ETERNAL KNIGHTS OF EDEN II

The patient is resting, so Doctor Vorzech returns to her office. This young woman just keeps going on about this child of Eden, though to her it sounds like she is looking for the Ceraphs. It seems important, whatever it is. For her entire memory to be blanked out, yet be able to remember this one critical detail, it MUST be important.

She sighs and unstoppers a bottle of scotch on her desk and pours herself a couple of fingers and takes a drink. The burn is pleasant, and it helps her relax after dealing with something stressful.

She starts reading a history text about the great war, wondering if the child of Eden is an old term for the Ceraphs or not.

As she reads, she stumbles across a statement from none other than the first Edenkin. It reads:

"Eden said that she had a sacred place near the border of Temenos, but it was lost when Belial decided he was a sore loser. This place supposedly housed something of great importance, but she warned that we were to never approach it. The contamination of the Deadlands was a death sentence for anyone who strayed into it, and the power of what was contained there was far worse than the contamination. It was something no mortal could hope to best. I don't know, but I will follow Eden's will, and we will declare this place off limits. It would be nice if we knew WHERE this off-limits location was though."

Doctor Vorzech smiles in amusement. That Edenkin refers to Eden as she is comical to her. Everyone knows Eden is male. She starts reading again but feels a tremor in the ground. She sets down the book and looks around curiously.

She jumps as the raid sirens start whining up all around the camp, signaling an attack. She hears yelling outside, and returns to the patient room.

The young woman looks around, scared. Doctor Vorzech walks over to her and tries to calm her down. "Shh, shh. It's okay, this happens down here from time to time. The soldiers outside will protect us. Just stay calm and keep your head down."

The young woman nods and tries to remain calm. The sounds outside of men running around, the sirens blaring, and the occasional sound of some kind of beast roaring make it difficult, however.

The sound of warship cannons firing fills the air, and Dr. Vorzech starts to feel some concern herself. If the warships are providing artillery support, then what the hell is attacking them? They haven't seen a behemoth or dragon for months.

The ground trembles as airborne artillery pounds the area around Hell's Doorstep trying to take out whatever it is attacking them. Hell's Doorstep has its name for a reason, after all.

*   *   *

The next morning, Shaide, Amari, and Nyu are waiting outside the gates of ARMA for their friends to come meet them. They're planning to try and go to the lake outside of the city and relax for the day to decompress from their busy schedules.

Shaide looks up at Corallina's military spire like usual, and notes the unusual number of ships at dock.

"Hey, guys!" a familiar voice calls out. Shade, Amari and Nyu all look down to see Reno, Lania, and Celeste coming to greet them. They are in full field gear, which is highly unusual for a weekend.

"Hey Reno, buddy!" Shaide says casually, shaking hands and giving him a brotherly half-hug. Everyone exchanges a series of hugs and handshakes in greeting.

Celeste looks at them in surprise "It's good to see you guys, but what are you doing here?"

Nyu sticks her tongue out and says "Well, we WERE going to invite you guys to the lake with us, but if you don't want to see us…"

Reno shakes his head "It's not that. We've got new orders."

The mood tenses up really fast.

"I was afraid of that." Shaide says "You'd never be all geared up if something wasn't up. So, what's wrong?"

"Alastair High-Com is deploying a large battlegroup to deal with some situation all of the way south." Lania explains, looking nervous. "The border fortresses are all reporting an unprecedented surge in activity, and they need additional manpower to defend the fortresses"

Celeste leans back against the outer wall of the academy compound "Apparently Hell's Doorstep is taking an especially hard beating. They're losing men fast because they don't have the numbers to stem the tide."

"Do we have that many corrupted crossing into Alastair now?" Amari asks with some alarm.

Reno shakes his head "No, this is apparently different. The corrupted almost seem to be focusing their attacks on the fortresses themselves."

The three Ceraphs exchange glances.

"That sounds like they're being coordinated." Shaide says with concern. "Is there a Fallen leading them?"

Reno and Celeste shrug. "We only know the basic situation and our orders. We won't know more until we get down there."

Shaide feels an odd sense of foreboding, like something terrible has been set into motion. He looks at his friends and wonders if he is ever going to see them again.

"We always knew this was going to happen someday." Reno says, looking at Shaide with sad eyes. "You're a Ceraph, and we're Alastair military. We lead two different lives. But you know? I really hoped we'd have more time before we separated like this."

Celeste nods and hugs the three of them "This isn't a short deployment either. From what it sounds like, it's going to be a warzone down there."

Lania mimics Celeste and says, "They're sending the entire Exorcist class down there to finish our training alongside the active duty Exorcists, so there IS a silver lining, I guess."

Celeste looks at her pocket watch "Hey, Reno?"

"Yeah, I know. We're out of time." He says. He pulls Shaide into a tight hug and slapping him on the back as he says "You take care of yourself, bro. It's getting nasty out there, and it's only getting worse."

     A.S.GUINN

Shaide slaps him on the back in return "You take care of yourself too, Reno. If everything you said is right, then you're heading right to the frying pan."

The three of them start to head back into the academy. As they cross back through the gates, they all say "Goodbye, you guys!"

Shaide, Amari, and Nyu all wave back, and say halfheartedly "Goodbye!"

*   *   *

Several short hours later, Shaide, Amari, and Nyu are all lounging at the giant lake outside of Corallina, relaxing and trying to enjoy their day. Enjoy being the operable word here, as their concern for their friends is great.

The region around Corallina is peaceful as usual. The grand lake is sparkling blue in the sun, and the water is so clear you can see all of the way to the bottom, even in the deeper water. The water is full of fish.

Nearby, a patrol of Alastair soldiers passes by, the men eyeballing Nyu and Amari, who are both rather scantily dressed to enjoy the water. Amari has on a swimsuit consisting of a fairly tight pair of shorts made of some kind of elastic spun fabric, along with a cotton top padded around the breast to avoid showing through when wet. Nyu on the other hand is outright wearing a bikini style outfit made of hide that leaves very little to the imagination, but this is due more to her people's lack of modesty rather than any desire to show off.

Nyu sees the soldiers looking, and she rolls onto her stomach to pose seductively in response. One of the soldiers walks face-first into a tree while staring at her, and she giggles before rolling back over to look at Shaide and Amari.

Shaide is wearing a pair of heavy black canvas shorts, and no shirt. His slender muscular physique is quickly growing to that of a man rather than a boy, and he is catching a few glances from neighboring women himself.

"I wonder…" Amari thinks out loud "Do you think they'll be okay?"

Shaide lays flat and stares straight up into the sky. "I don't know, Amari. I hope so. Reno is strong, and Celeste is terrifying, and even Lania knows how to take care of herself. I'm still worried though."

"Me too." Amari nods.

"I find something about that a little strange." Nyu pipes up.

Shaide and Amari both roll over to look at her.

"Well, they're dealing with a corrupted invasion, right?" Nyu reasons "So why aren't the Ceraphs down there helping them?"

"There probably are Ceraphs down there." Shaide replies "Just because WE haven't been sent doesn't mean they aren't there. They have to keep enough of us up here to respond in case of emergency."

Amari leans back and closes her eyes "I think there's a Ceraph cruiser, the COV *Enlightenment* that is almost permanently stationed down south." She rolls to look at Shaide "Didn't you tell me that?"

Shaide nods, impressed that she remembered. "Yeah, the *Enlightenment* and the frigate *Twist of Fate* usually stay down there together. There are eight Ceraphs between the two ships."

Amari nods and her eyes pass over the city to the west. She notices a lot of movement in the sky. "Hey, I think the military is departing."

Shaide and Nyu follow Amari's gaze, and indeed two Alastair cruisers, two destroyers, four frigates, and a carrier are slowly accelerating south in formation. Shaide would be more impressed with the small flotilla if his friends weren't on board.

They watch the ships flying away for a few minutes. The sheer size of them keeps them visible in the sky for many miles, and their eyes stay glued as their friends fly off to danger without them.

Once the ships drift out of sight, all three of them let out a semi-depressed trio of sighs and lay back. Amari closes her eyes and enjoys the late afternoon sun, her pink hair laid across the towel beneath he, the sun shining off of her surprisingly pale skin.

Shaide finds himself looking at her, his thoughts drifting. He had never really considered it before, but she really is quite beautiful. He had noticed, sure, but he had never really THOUGHT about it.

He shakes his head. *No. She is my best friend. I can't let myself think about that,* He turns and looks up at the blue sky overhead, the occasional cloud drifting across his view.

Amari, unaware he was watching her, turns to look at him. She has begun getting a handle on her unrequited feelings for him, but she still finds herself pining or longing for him sometimes. Nevertheless, she made the decision to remain friends, fearing that telling him how she feels might cause a rift between them when she finds out that he did not return her feelings. She is unaware that he too is developing feelings for her.

"Hey, Shaide?" Amari says suddenly, sitting up. "Let's go for a swim."

Shaide opens his eyes and snaps out of his thoughts "Hmm? Yeah, sure. Why not."

"Come on!" She says. She pulls him up by the hand and walks him to the water.

Nyu sits up and pouts "Hey! What about me!?"

"You can come too, if you want."

Nyu deliberates heavily for a moment, but she makes up her mind and chases them into the water.

Amari and Shaide walk out into the deeper water and find the temperature to be surprisingly pleasant. They swim around for a while, and splash each other, dunk each other under water, and play all kinds of games, relaxing and enjoying themselves for once while they drive everything else from their minds.

Amari finally smiles, really smiles, for the first time in quite some time. Their constant missions, stress, the loss of Rayn, and just the knowledge of how quickly things are falling apart has kept her in a distracted or even sad mood, her feelings for Shaide only aggravating the problem. But now, relaxing, having fun, and just playing with Shaide like they haven't done since she first came back, she finds herself feeling happy finally.

Shaide, for his part, notices her earnest smile, and feels his own spirits rise greatly. He had not seen her smile like that in a long time, and it had been concerning him. As she dunks him under water with a martial art move, and he retaliates by grabbing her from underwater and flipping her upside down, he finds her laughter and smile as she resurfaces to be an elating sight.

Nyu joins them after a few minutes of getting used to the water. She considers trying to make a move on Shaide; playing around in the water is a good time to do so, but when she sees how the two smile when playing around, she realizes that she may be fighting a lost battle. She wants Shaide for herself, sure, but seeing the two of them together, relaxed and happy, she wonders if it would really be a good thing to take him for herself.

The three of them play around and enjoy themselves until dusk, when they finally climb out of the water and walk back to their towels to lay down and dry off. In spite of the knowledge of their friends' departures, all three of them feel a great sense of happiness and contentment. Days like this were so rare for them, Shaide knew to enjoy it while it lasts.

After drying off, the sun setting on the horizon, all three of them whistle sharply, and their sleipnir, Shaide's own midnight-black Twilight come to their masters. Shaide pats his mare, now fully grown, and strokes her shiny black coat. The three of them load up their belongings on the saddle pouches and set off for the Citadel.

*　　　*　　　*

"Sir, we've just gotten word, the battlegroup from Corallina should be on its way right about now with our additional personnel." A young lieutenant addresses Brigadier General Warsaw.

Brig. Gen. Warsaw nods approvingly "Very good, lieutenant. Thank you."

Hell's Doorstep, the widespread nickname for the south-central fortress responsible for coordinating all counter-corrupted operations at the border of the Deadlands, had been enduring frequent attacks by corrupted forces for days. If communications are accurate, the other fortresses along the border are taking a hit too. Gen. Warsaw cannot help but feel as if the young woman they found has something to do with it. Nothing concrete, but the attacks started around the time she turned up.

Warsaw heads outside and looks up at the sky. Their support fleet remains uncompromised, and for certain they would have fallen by now if they did not have their air support, but the sheer numbers of their attackers have been overwhelming the airborne artillery defenses, and they are still being forced to engage the wild beasts and the hordes of zombie-thrall-like formers on the ground as they get through the artillery defenses. They are losing men, and they can't hold out forever. The attacks are getting worse.

As Warsaw contemplates this, the warships overhead open fire again, and looking out over the ramparts of the outer wall of the fortress, Warsaw can see another massive horde coming in.

"Son, let me borrow those for a moment."

"SIR!"

Warsaw borrows a monocular from a wall-top sentry and looks out across the warzone. Hundreds of disfigured lobos, nekoshin, terraswine (oversized hog-like beasts with hides like rock and razor-sharp tusks), and even a decent sized behemoth, along with a couple of hundred of zombie-like formers bare down on the fortress as the navy enacts its response.

Artillery batteries open fire overhead, magicore cannons firing their explosive payloads into the swarm below. The gunships fly through in wolfpack groups, raining automatic fire on the ground beneath them. On the walls of the fortress, magicore artillery guns are manned and ready to attack anything that gets too close. As fire fills the air, and the mindless corrupted beasts push on, the General's eyes are on the behemoth. Nothing seems to be taking it down.

The heavy-cruiser turns into position, and the prototype railgun rotates on its gimbal, acquiring its target. Lightning arcs along the firing channel, and with a bright flash of light and a hypersonic crack that is deafening even from the fortress below, the behemoth explodes in a shower of meat and gore.

The general looks up and nods. Yep, they would not survive without the naval support.

He watches as his wall cannons open fire on the horde, and after several minutes, the battle seems to be won. Ground troops move out to clean up the stragglers, and the general decides to pay a visit to someone.

He enters the infirmary and finds Dr. Vorzech treating some of the injured soldiers along with several of her assisting staff. She sees the general and jumps to salute.

"At ease, Vorzech." Warsaw returns the salute. "How is our resident amnesiac doing? Any changes?"

Vorzech shakes her head "I'm afraid not, sir. She doesn't seem to remember anything. It may be a side effect of the contamination. Her exposure to the corruption was mild enough that her body is fighting off the pathogen, but it could still explain her memory loss, if not for the other discoveries."

"Other discoveries?" Warsaw says, intrigued.

Vorzech hands off the bandages to one of her staff to finish, and she leads Gen. Warsaw into her office, where she pulls some notes out of her desk. "Her body is extremely unusual. Her spiritual energy is unnaturally high, and I'm talking ridiculously inhumanly high. Higher than should be physically possible with a human or even a Mitera body. And then there is her eating and sleeping habits."

The general's interest is growing, but so is his confusion. "Eating and sleeping habits?"

"Yes, sir. She barely eats or sleeps at all." Vorzech explains "She eats on a little, maybe once a day, and she only sleeps at most a couple of hours a night. She just sits there, staring out the window, muttering about the 'child of Eden', whoever that is."

Warsaw contemplates what he has heard so far. "That is strange, but not unheard of. She is fairly small, and she isn't very active. That alone isn't exactly alarm worthy."

"That's not all, sir." Dr. Vorzech continues "Her body is completely flawless. I don't mean this in an aesthetic way, or in any metaphorical way, I mean literally. She is perfectly symmetrical, her skin is completely unblemished, her teeth are straight and white, her eyes are devoid of any bloodshot, her finger and toenails are identical mirrors of each side, and then there's her internal workings. Flawless digestion, perfect heart rate, perfect blood pressure, only a slight fever

     A.S.GUINN

from the contamination. She's more like a carefully handcrafted doll than a person, sir. It's bizarre."

Warsaw narrows his eyes, unsure how to feel about this.

Dr. Vorzech finishes "It's like she was handcrafted or something. I can't explain it, but this woman is not like any human or Mitera I've ever seen."

Warsaw peeks out the window and sees the young woman in a hospital gown, staring out the window at the courtyard of the fortress. "Keep a very close eye on her. High-Com doesn't want them involved, but I am going to contact the Ceraphs. Maybe they can make sense of this."

"High-Com doesn't want the Ceraphs' help?" Vorzech asks, confused.

"Something strange is happening, all over." Warsaw keeps his voice low "High-Com is becoming distrusting of the Ceraphs for some reason, and they're keeping them out of the loop more and more. I don't like it."

Out in the patient area, the young woman stares out the window, and a flash of yellow crosses her eyes…

CHAPTER 12

SEEDS OF DISCONTENT

Shaide is in a familiar dark cavern with elegant decorations. The cavern isn't someplace he has ever seen in his life, but rather a place he has dreamed about for a few years now. The domed canopy overhead, and the pillars laced with gold, and the obsidian altar are all quite familiar to him by now.

Shaide walks into the spacious area and looks around. Something IS different this time. The place feels more lucid. Vivid. He can feel the black stone beneath his feet, and when he looks closely, he sees that it is not a natural occurrence. The stone appears to be some kind of tile made from polished volcanic rock. The walls are lined with veins of a dimly phosphorescent material that gives the cave an odd eerie feel.

ETERNAL KNIGHTS OF EDEN II

He shakes his head and proceeds deeper into the cavern, his feet taking him to the altar of their own accord. The ceiling overhead is different now as well, and it has odd glowing glyphs and patterns made of the same phosphorescent material, giving the cavern its dim light.

Shaide knows what this place is. He has seen its kind before. It is the sanctum of an Angel, but the almost demonic statue behind the altar is not one of any angel he has ever heard of, though he admits he does not know of them all.

As he approaches the altar, a glowing purple glyph-circle, more intricate than any he has seen before, forms on the altar and the ceiling above it. Shaide stands back patiently, knowing this is a dream and it cannot hurt him. Moments later, a familiar feminine figure appears in front of him.

The unknown angel, with her purple skin, her horned head, her scaled armor, and her black feathered wings appears before him. This is unusual as well, for she is usually sitting on the altar waiting for him.

Then she speaks.

"It is time. Come to me, child. You are mine, and it is time for you to return here, though you do not remember being here. Follow my messenger, and she will bring you to me. Then we shall be together once more."

Shaide, utterly and completely confused, tilts his head, unable to respond.

"You will know where to go. Now come back to me, child of Eden."

*   *   *

Shaide wakes up wide-eyed, his heart beating rapidly. The dream was so real, and so vivid. Nothing like the dreams he had had about that place before. He sits up and looks around his room. It's very lonely with Aton gone. He sighs and lies back, staring at the ceiling.

*knock*knock*

Shaide sighs and sits up, swinging his legs out of bed and heading for the front door. As an afterthought he grabs a shirt on his way so he doesn't answer the door in nothing but his shorts.

"I swear, Nyu, if this is another one of your-" He opens the door "Oh! Sorry, I thought you were someone else. What do you need, Sam?"

One of Armstrong's assistants was waiting at the front door. "Mr. Darkmoon? Master Armstrong wishes to speak with you as soon as possible. It's urgent. He says to come prepared to deploy."

Shaide frowns. What could have happened since last night?

"I'll be getting miss Tamiel and miss, umm, Nyu, and they will be joining you."

Shaide shakes his head "No need, Sam. I'll get them."

"As you wish, Mr. Darkmoon."

As he turns away, Shaide calls out "Hey, Sam. What's this about, do you know?"

Sam shakes his head "There's something going on to the far south. That's all I know. Sorry."

"Don't worry about it. Tell Armstrong we'll be there shortly."

Sam bows and walks away.

          A.S.GUINN

Shaide frowns and closes the door. THAT'S unusual. They don't usually come get him first thing in the morning unless it's really important. He pulls on his black canvas and leather field outfit, and puts his new armor on over the top. The scale mail and tunic are a perfect fit, and he privately thanks Amari for the gift. He straps the bracer to his left forearm and sheathes his sword across his back. He can dispel and summon his sword now, as well as his bracer, but he still likes to keep the scabbard handy. He's even working on dispelling and summoning his armor, but he hasn't mastered that yet.

He picks up his field duffel and heads out the front door with a sigh. It's only perhaps seven in the morning, and even in the middle of summer, the air is cool in the citadel streets. Amari's house isn't far, so he walks over and knocks on the door.

When the door opens, much to Shaide's surprise, Nyu answers sleepily.

"Hmm? Hey, Shaidy. Why're you up so early?"

Shaide looks around in confusion. It's the right house. "Nyu? What are you doing at Amari's?"

"Hmm? Oh, Amari said she didn't want to be in the house alone, so I crashed here to keep her company."

Shaide raises his eyebrows. Makes sense. "I see. Well, I hate to disturb you both this early, but Armstrong said he needs to see us as soon as possible. It seems urgent. He said to come ready to move out."

Nyu yawns, and her ears flatten against her head in displeasure and mumbles "You know, I really hoped that when I see you first thing in the morning, we'd be in the same bed…"

"Hmm?" Shaide didn't quite catch what she said.

She shakes her head violently "Nothing, never mind. I'll get Amari."

A short time later, Amari and Nyu sleepily join him on the street. Shaide notices that Amari has a new outfit. She's wearing an odd hybrid outfit that is half mage, half warrior in appearance. Covering her breast and upper chest is a form fitted lightweight plate mail cuirass, and she is wearing a flexible scale mail skirt, with armor plated shin boots and vambraces over the forearms. Underneath all of this is a fitted chainmail underlayer covering her legs and midriff to maintain maximum flexibility. This is all finished by a dark violet cloak.

"Where did the new armor come from?" Shaide asks with interest.

Amari looks herself over "Oh, daddy had it made for me when he commissioned yours. You know he wouldn't allow me to go without the best protection too."

"Isn't it heavy?" Shaide asks curiously, wondering about her martial abilities.

Amari just shakes her head in response "No, it's infused with a special magicore based alloy that makes it barely heavier than my old outfit."

Shaide raises his eyebrows, impressed.

"Do you like my new outfit?" Nyu says, spinning around.

Now that Shaide looks, Nyu has ditched her usual fur outfits for new leather armor. Heavy brown and black leather covers her entire body, providing her with reasonable protection against glancing blows.

　　　　A.S.GUINN

"I figured it was time for me to get something a little more in line with what everyone else around here wears." She says, "With all of the dangerous stuff we do, I wanted some protection."

Personally, I'm just impressed that you're finally fully clothed. Shaide thinks to himself with a chuckle.

Shaide spots the newly retrofitted *Last Beacon* docked with the spire overhead as they walk out onto the Citadel grounds and turn towards the temple, where the Order Master's office and quarters are located. Only a handful of Citadel citizens are up at this time of morning, and they find their walk to be fairly quiet.

As they enter the temple, they all three take a quick bow and praise Eden, before proceeding to the adjacent building addition and climbing to Armstrong's office.

Shaide knocks on the heavy wooden door and receives a "Come in.", before the three proceed inside.

Shaide notices several things almost instantly. First, there are four white-armored Corallina temple-guards standing along the back wall. Second, an unknown young woman is present, sitting next to Armstrong. Third, Armstrong is looking much more anxious than normal.

Shaide observes the woman and frowns. She has pure white hair that, unlike Celeste, seems to have a subtle glowing quality to it. Her eyes are a bright silver, almost white, and her skin is pale and flawless beneath her white priestess robes.

Armstrong waves them in. "Shaide, Amari, Nyuralisiania. Allow me to introduce you to the Grand Priestess of the Temple of Eden. She goes only by the name-"

"That is unnecessary, Orville. It is okay." She says gently.

Shaide, Amari, and Nyu all three exchange very alarmed looks. The Grand Priestess? Here? She almost never leaves the Great Temple in Corallina.

"Please, have a seat."

The three Ceraphs awkwardly take their seats across from Armstrong, next to the Grand Priestess.

"Would you like to tell them yourself, Excellency, or should I?" Armstrong asks her respectfully.

She bows her head, indicating he should speak.

"Shaide. Amari. Nyuralisiania." Armstrong addresses them seriously. "What I am about to tell you is of the utmost level of classified. We are not even supposed to be aware of this due to some…mistrust recently with the Alastair military. Just over a week ago, a strange young woman stumbled out of the deadlands and onto the doorstep of the Hell's Doorstep fortress. She had no memory, her body was oddly resistant to the corruption, and she was completely naked when she found them."

"Her appearance and biology defy normal human or Mitera norms. They described her as a hand-crafted doll, the very image of artistic perfection, and doesn't even seem to need to eat or sleep nearly as much as a normal person. Strangest and most suspicious of all, her appearance was immediately followed by an unceasing wave of corrupted assaults on all fortresses ever since, and Hell's Doorstep in particular has been taking an extra hard beating."

The three Ceraphs wait patiently for Armstrong to continue, but he remains silent.

Shaide finally asks "Sir, I understand this is extremely unusual, but I fail to see why you called us here, or why this is a Ceraph concern if Alastair is handling it."

Armstrong bows his head "At first glance, this would seem to be a military concern, but there is a single detail which our Grand Priestess and I both find very distressing."

The Grand Priestess speaks, her voice gentle and soothing. "The young woman keeps saying she needs the child of Eden, that she must speak with the child of Eden, and take him somewhere." She shakes her head slowly and deliberately, a certain elegance to her motions "Eden has no living children that we would know of. That this woman speaks of this is highly alarming, and it must be looked into. I asked Armstrong for the three best Ceraphs he has available, and he has called you here to me."

Shaide sits forward, fully alert and asks "Grand Priestess. What do you ask of me?"

Amari and Nyu exchange glances but say nothing.

"Child, I need you to go to Hell's Doorstep and speak with this woman. Do whatever it takes to convince her to take you to wherever she needs to take this child of Eden. See what is so important that it is the only thing she can remember."

Armstrong nods "Yes, it is imperative that we find out what is so important to this strange woman. We suspect that by child of Eden, she may simply be referring to the Ceraphs, but we aren't sure. Either way, we need to find out who she is."

Shaide looks at Amari and Nyu. "What do you two think?"

Without hesitation, Amari says "Shaide, I don't really understand what is happening, but you know that wherever you go, I will follow you."

Shaide shrugs and looks to his other side. "Nyu?"

Nyu looks a little more nervous "I don't like the idea of going so close to the deadlands, but I feel it would be hypocritical of me to refuse to help now, after the sacrifices you made for my people. I'll go."

"Very good." Armstrong says approvingly. "The *Last Beacon* is preparing for departure. Shaide? I am giving you command of this mission. Even should you encounter any other Ceraph personnel, you are in charge. Understood?"

"Yes sir." Shaide says "Will we have any backup on this mission?"

Armstrong consults a notebook tracking all of the Ceraphs and their current missions. "I will contact several Ceraphs in the local area in case you need assistance, but you should assume you will be on your own."

Shaide nods "Yes sir."

"Let me stress one thing to you." Armstrong leans forward, emphasizing his seriousness "The Grand Priestess here believes that this woman, and whatever she wants, is extremely important. It is absolutely imperative that, whatever she wants, or whatever she needs, you must ensure you do whatever it takes to find out who she is and where she came from. Even if you must travel into the deadlands themselves to find out. Understood?"

　　　　A.S.GUINN

Shaide, Amari, and Nyu all exchange alarmed looks, but they each nod their agreement to each other.

"Yes sir." Shaide says confidently. "Whatever it takes."

"On your way, Ceraphs. Good luck."

As the three Ceraphs exit the office, the Grand Priestess looks at her bodyguards and says simply. "Leave us. I must speak to Orville in private."

The four temple guards bow and exit the room behind the Ceraphs and stand guard outside. Armstrong waits until the sound of footsteps dies away before addressing the priestess.

"Eden, are you certain we shouldn't tell them the truth? You know as well as I do who makes their home down there. This cannot be a coincidence."

The Grand Priestess, revealed as Eden herself, shakes her head and smiles sadly "There are secrets we must keep even from our most trusted friends, my dear Telos. Still, that young man, Shaide. He is interesting."

Armstrong, aka Telos, nods. "He is one of the strongest Ceraphs I have ever seen, and his companion Amari is no pushover either. Their powers seem to be at a superhuman level, and at their age…"

Eden shakes her head slowly "No, Telos. That is not what I speak of. His power is great, this is truth. His nickname as the Grim Reaper of the Ceraphs; our very own Angel of Death, is well earned. But no, I refer to his magnetism."

"Eden?"

She smiles widely at Armstrong "People are naturally attracted to him. Drawn to him. I do not speak romantically if course, but more generally. People naturally trust and follow him. Even when they know what he is doing is dangerous and suicidal, they will follow him."

"This is true." Armstrong says thoughtfully. "I have never met a soul who did not like him. His friends have followed him into the jaws of death more than once."

Eden nods and looks out the window "I wonder, Telos. I wonder if Shaide is the one who may very well be able to save us all from the darkness that is coming."

*   *   *

"I've never seen the Grand Priestess before." Says Amari "What is she?"

Shaide tries to remember what he had been told. "The Grand Priestess is a Miteran woman who is over three-thousand years old. She was appointed to her post by Eden at the formation of the Ceraph Order. It is said that Eden has gifted her with youth, and so even at her age, she looks no older than us."

"She feels older, though." Nyu says "You can feel from her demeanor. From the deliberate nature of every movement, that she has far more experience than anyone I have ever met."

"Yeah, I noticed that." Shaide says, looking up thoughtfully as they haul their equipment into the spire and up the lift. "I can't help but feel, though, that she is strangely familiar. Like I've met her before, a long time ago."

Amari giggles slightly for some reason.

          A.S.GUINN

"What is it?" Shaide asks indignantly "What's so funny?"

"I don't know." Says Amari. "It's just funny for some reason,"

Shaide shakes his head.

"I don't really see the big deal." Nyu says "In Pandora we recognize how important Eden was in saving the world from the corruption, to be sure, but we never really worshipped him as a god. Just a savior and protector."

Shaide and Amari turn to look at Nyu in amusement. Shaide asks her "Who do your people worship, then? I know it has something to do with the forest, but they don't like to talk about it."

Nyu's ears flatten defensively. "Well, I really don't…"

"Oh, come on, you can't do that." Amari says "You can't bring it up and drop it like that. That's just rude."

Nyu sighs and looks down as they exit the lift "Well, you see, my people believe the planet itself is our goddess. Not in a figurative sense, mind you, but they believe the planet is literally a living thing, and the source of all of our spiritual energy. We believe that are a product of the planet, and we owe everything to it."

Before they can say anything else, Shipmaster Corolas greets them at the hanger. "Shaide, Amari. It is good to see you again. You as well miss Nyu."

Shaide shakes his hand and smiles "You can't get rid of us, Yorlan, can you?"

"Shipmaster, it is good to work with you again." Amari smiles

Nyu just stands there awkwardly, not as familiar with the man as they are.

"Come on aboard, Ceraphs. We're waiting for you." He says, turning to lead the aboard "So, we are literally travelling to Hell's Doorstep, is that right?"

"Unfortunately, yes." Shaide says warily "We are travelling right to the edge of the Deadlands. There is an asset of extremely high value we must meet with, and find out exactly what we are dealing with."

Corolas raises his hands "No need to worry, Shaide. Armstrong already told me this mission is a directive from the Grand Priestess herself. I will not question a mission such as this. Tell me what you need, and it will be done."

Shaide shakes his hand earnestly "Thank you, Yorlan. I'd be lying if I said this mission didn't make me nervous. Knowing you have my back makes me feel a little better."

"Shaide, Amari? When have I ever failed to have your back before?"

Amari smiles as she says "Never, Shipmaster. You've always been there for us."

They stop off at the Ceraph quarters to drop off their gear, then proceed with Corolas to the bridge of the frigate.

"This sweetheart has more punch than she did before." Corolas says proudly as a few of his bridge crew wave in greeting to the Ceraphs. "Our engines have been upgraded in power, and we have a new railgun. Not as powerful as the ones on the cruisers and dreadnoughts, mind you, but she should be able to go toe to toe with a dragon now, unlike our last encounter."

Shaide looks around the bridge in interest. It certainly looks like the warship got some special treatment. "How long before we reach Hell's Doorstep?"

"Well, assuming we can fly straight through without interruption," Corolas consults the chart "We won't be arriving until well after nightfall. We're flying all the way to the south border, after all."

"Without interruption?" Shaide repeats curiously.

"Indeed." Says Corolas "There has been some tension with the Alastair military recently, though we aren't certain why. We may get held up at Iron Veil."

Shaide sighs "This is not the time for the higher ups to be fighting. What's the problem?"

Corolas shrugs and looks out the forward viewport. "The young Queen seems to think the Ceraph Order should report to Alastair, since we are based within the borders. She and the higher ups in the capital seem displeased that we have been giving so much aid to foreign nations. They feel we should focus our efforts here."

Shaide sighs. Ever since the King and Queen died of illness a few years ago, their daughter, the new queen, has been causing all kinds of trouble. She is almost never seen in public, and it is rumored that she will not speak to Eden or the Grand Priestess. He didn't know the full extent of the trouble, though.

"Are we ready to get underway?" Corolas asks Shaide.

He snaps out of his reverie and nods "Yes, let's get going."

The turbines of the frigate roar to life as the vessel sets off to the south. Shaide watches out the front viewport for a moment before he feels someone tug on his arm. He looks over and sees Amari jerk her head towards the door, and he gets the hint.

"Shipmaster? We'll be down in our quarters if you need us."

Corolas bows slightly "As you wish."

Shaide, Amari, and Nyu all three exit the bridge and head down to their quarters in silence. Once inside, Amari sighs loudly "I hadn't realized things were getting as bad as they are."

Shaide opens the bunkroom at the end and moves his bag inside. "Yeah, I'd been hearing rumors that Queen Ilium was at odds with the Ceraph Order, but I'd never seen any sign of it myself until now."

"I thought King and Queen Ilium got along well with the Ceraphs?" Nyu says in confusion.

"No, her parents got along well with the order." Shaide shakes his head "But for some reason, ever since the King and Queen died of an infectious illness a year ago, their daughter feels differently."

"I see." Says Nyu, looking troubled "I had no idea."

Amari dispels most of her armor, leaving her shorts and a plain top. "Well, I see no reason to fret about the politics. We have a job to do, right Shaide? Leave all that crap to the politicians and such."

Shaide smiles. "Yeah, I guess you're right. I'm just worried our job will become more difficult in the future."

     A.S.GUINN

Amari sits in the couch in the lounge area and lays back with a book and starts reading, while Nyu heads straight for the pantry to grab a snack.

Shaide finds himself watching Amari again. He feels a bit troubled by his feelings. He had always felt a kind of brotherly protectiveness towards her, but he finds his feelings changing. *When did she become so beautiful? And smart? And...mature?* He'd been attracted to girls before. He's even fairly fond of Celeste, and Nyu. This is a different feeling though.

He turns his gaze to Nyu, and finds his heart doesn't race the same way. He finds her attractive, sure. Very attractive, in fact. He likes her very much as a friend, and really enjoys her company, but when he tries to picture more than that, he just doesn't see it.

He turns his gaze back to Amari, and finds those thoughts come forward on their own, without his provocation. Would he even be able to live without her now? She's become such a central part of his life that no matter what future he tries to picture, she is always right there in the middle of it. When did this happen?

"Shaide? You okay?" Nyu asks suddenly.

Shaide jumps and shakes his head. "Hmm?"

She laughs "You were kind of spacing out there, and you looked a little distressed."

Amari turns to look at him as well.

"No, no. I'm fine." Shaide says evasively "Just thinking about what we're dealing with." This isn't entirely a lie.

"Oh, okay. If you say so." Nyu says, and she returns to snacking on some preserved meat.

Amari locks gazes with Shaide, and she gives him a fond smile. Shaide feels his heart flutter when she does, and he manages to return the smile before she resumes her reading. Unaware that Amari wrestles with the same feelings as he does, he retreats into his bunk and tries to distract himself.

*   *   *

A few short hours later, Shaide feels the ship decelerating. It hasn't been nearly long enough for them to be arriving at Hell's Doorstep yet, so why are they slowing down?

Nyu looks around curiously as well, and Amari sticks her head out of her bunk "Hey, why are we slowing down? Are we there already?"

Shaide peeks looks out the small porthole and notices they are in a mountainous area. "Let's go to the bridge and see what's going on."

The three Ceraphs depart their room into a long corridor leading up to the bridge. As they emerge onto the bridge, they hear shipmaster Corolas arguing with someone on the communications terminal.

"-with the Ceraph Order. This is the COV *Last Beacon*. I demand to be allowed passage immediately. The Citadel will not be pleased to hear the Alastair military is holding us up without due cause."

"I'm sorry, sir, but orders are orders. We have been ordered that absolutely no vessels are to be allowed to cross into South Alastair without express permission of Admiral Harris. Please, dock with the spire and await further instructions."

A.S.GUINN

A very irritated Corolas notices the Ceraphs on his bridge and waves them over "Maybe you can talk some sense into them, Mr. Darkmoon. They are refusing to allow us to pass Iron Veil."

Shaide leans his head back and closes his eyes. So, the tension between the Ceraphs and Alastair wasn't exaggerated. He sighs explosively and walks over to the console, gathering his wits.

"This is operative Shaide Darkmoon of the Ceraph Order. We are on a mission given to us by the grand priestess of the Temple of Eden. By what authority are you interfering in our operations, in direct violation of the Pact of Aderfia?"

There is a significant pause on the other end of the channel before a nervous voice finally responds *"Sir, I am sorry, but my orders from Admiral Harris are that no ships nor personnel be allowed to pass through Iron Veil, even the Ceraph Order. Please sir, he has instructed that you dock with the spire until he authorizes you to proceed."*

Shaide roars in frustration before responding "Very well, Alastair vessel. We will comply with your order after contacting the Citadel. Rest assured there will be consequences for interfering with a Ceraph Order operation."

Another long silence *"Understood, sir. Control out."*

Amari walks up and whispers "Was that entirely necessary?"

Shaide grinds his teeth in frustration and doesn't answer her. "Corolas? Contact the Citadel and let them know what happened, and then take us to the spire. We will go down to the hanger and sort this out."

Corolas looks slightly nervous at Shaide's attitude. "Yes sir. I'll take care of it."

Shaide jerks his head to the door, and Amari and Nyu follow him out as he heads back to the hanger.

"So, what is that all about?" Nyu asks.

"Well, you heard." Shaide says, his voice full of irritation "The Alastair military isn't wanting to let us pass. I intend to get to the bottom of this."

They emerge into the hanger and proceed near the edge in full combat attire. Shaide even pulls on his skull-embroidered facemask and summons his sword across his back for maximum effect.

Amari notices that Shaide is fidgety, and starts to feel concerned herself. "Shaide? Is this really that big of a deal? You seem upset."

Shaide growls "Of course I'm upset. The crown of Alastair is supposed to serve Eden, the being I've worshipped my whole life. Now suddenly they are defying the temple's orders and stopping us from doing our job? Yeah, I'm a little upset."

Amari recoils slightly, taken aback by his tone. She knows this tone well, and it is extremely threatening. He's ready for a fight.

Shaide finds himself still seething in anger. He has never been the most pious of Eden's followers. Although he fully believes in and worships their guardian deity, he has never been the kind to go to the temple every morning or anything like that. However, he has been given a mission under the direct orders of the grand priestess, presumably at the request of Eden himself, and now the very nation that owes its existence to Eden is interfering? He is indeed upset.

As the *Last Beacon* moves in to dock with the spire, Shaide sees an arrogant looking army colonel alongside two very uncomfortable looking junior officers. As the frigate eases to a halt, the colonel begins to approach.

Shaide feels an instant dislike of this colonel for some reason and reacts impulsively. "STOP!"

The colonel freezes, looking stunned, one foot hovering over the threshold of the frigate's hanger deck.

Shaide, still seething, barks out "This is a sovereign Ceraph Order naval vessel, and you do not have permission to board! Now tell me immediately why we are being held up!"

The colonel grinds his teeth in irritation as he eyes Shaide and his companions. "I was not aware that the legendary Grim Reaper was aboard this vessel."

"Save the flattery and answer my question."

The colonel bows his head and replies, his voice dripping with arrogance "Admiral Harris has ordered that no additional Ceraph personnel be allowed to cross into southern Alastair, and that we are to detain all vessels here at Iron Veil until we receive orders to the contrary."

Shaide's fists tighten, a gesture that doesn't go unnoticed by the colonel's escorts. "And on whose authority does the Admiral order this? May I remind you that under the Pact of Aderfia, interfering in a Ceraph Order operation is a capital offense, punishable by death?"

The colonel looks at him with amusement "As I understand it, these orders came from young Queen Ilium herself. As you know, disobeying a direct order from the queen is also punishable by death."

Shaide steps forward and gets in the colonel's face just on the edge of the hanger. The colonel stands his ground as his escorts take a step back and put their hands on their weapons.

"Ceraphs do not belong to Alastair, or Erita, or Dorim, or Pandora. We are sovereign, and not subject to the rules of the crown, as laid out in the Pact of Aderfia."

The colonel narrows his eyes "And after the recent suspicious deaths of her parents, the former king and queen of Alastair, she believes that it is time for this to change. She believes that you are an outdated order, no longer needed with the might of the Alastair military protecting the land. She seems to feel, as many of us do, that if the Ceraphs are going to reside in this land, then they should be a part of Alastair."

Amari and Nyu's eyes widen in alarm as Shaide's sheathed sword sparks a little with lightning.

"But alas, how I feel is a moot point." The colonel sighs. "The Admiral is the only person who can clear you to proceed, so in the meantime you will have to wait. You are welcome to proceed down into town if you wish, but you may not proceed south into the plains."

The colonel turns and walks away without another word.

Shaide stares at his retreating back as Amari walks up and puts a hand on his shoulder, speaking to him gently "Come on, calm down. It's going to be okay. We're on a mission for Eden, so they can't detain us forever."

Nyu peeks out over the edge of the deck and looks at the town below "Well, I vote we take a look at this town while we wait. I've never been here before!"

Shaide grumbles "I'd really rather stay close to the ship in case we get cleared to leave."

Nyu grabs his other arm "Oh, come on! I'm sure we've got at least a little bit of time before we go!"

Shaide looks at Amari for support, but she says "I don't know. Might not be a bad idea to take a look around."

Shaide relents "Okay, fine. We'll go speak with Corolas and let him know the situation, and then we'll go down to the village.

*   *   *

Reno takes a wide, powerful swing with his sword at a charging corrupted blacktusk boar, cutting a deep slash down the side of the thousand-pound pig. With an aggressive spin, he finishes driving his sword into its side, bringing it to the ground. Once it stops moving, he pulls his sword out and lifts the visor on his helm, wiping the sweat from his brow.

Nearby, Celeste takes a running jump and vaults off of a charging Temenos Lobo, driving her halberd deep into the underbelly of a low-flying wyvern. A flash of light blue, and a blossom of ice explodes from the wyvern's underbelly, and it spins in the air, coming to a crashing halt on its back. Celeste yanks her halberd from it and hits a passing lobo with a pair of wide and powerful swings, crippling the lobo with the bladed edge of her polearm.

Lania for her part is performing emergency medical treatment on injured soldiers who have been dragged to cover, focusing her spiritual energy while a pair of elite soldiers protect her from stragglers who slip through the lines.

"WE COULD REALLY USE A CERAPH RIGHT ABOUT NOW!" Reno roars, taking three wild and vicious swings at a charging lobo. His whole body aches from the time he has spent on the battlefield today while fighting nearly constantly. He feels like he is going to give out at any time, but he keeps pushing himself knowing he and his friends will die if he does not continue fighting.

Celeste spears a charging Agrigato (A type of giant dessert wildcat related to the nekoshin) through the chest as its momentum seals its fate. It nearly tears her weapon from her hands as it flips over. "NO KIDDING! I'M HAVING FUN, BUT I'M EXHAUSTED!"

A few hundred soldiers are on the ground around the Hell's Doorstep military outpost, as thousands of corrupted beasts and former people charge the compound. The navy overhead is overtaxed trying to keep the monsters at bay as this most recent attack is the most aggressive yet. Word of their guest has spread through the ranks by now, and many soldiers are starting to think she is connected to these attacks. The unrest among the ranks grows by the hour.

Reno takes a knee, breathing heavily, and looks around the plains now littered with thousands of corpses, both friendly and corrupted. The one good thing to be said for the corrupted is that their bodies do not remain long, and even those brought down in the current battle are beginning to disintegrate.

He raises his head in time to see a charging lobo, and with no time to react, turtles behind his shield as the massive reptilian wolf slams headfirst into it. Reno feels the shock and throws his sword aside, grabbing his shield with both hands and bashing the creature repeatedly in the head with it, many more times than is likely necessary. As he looks around once more, the battle seems to be tapering off rapidly. The warships overhead still their guns as the soldiers further out stop the last of the creatures trying to get to the fortress.

Reno flops flat on his back, breathing heavily from exhaustion. His heavy plate armor makes fighting even more of an exertion for him than his friends, but it serves him well, and although he has taken several hits, he has suffered no injury behind his heavy steel.

He hears crunching footsteps and opens his eyes. He sees Celeste holding her hand out. "Come on, Reno. Let's get back to the fortress wall. It looks like this one is about over."

Reno closes his eyes and takes her hand, letting her pull him to his feet with a grunt. He walks over and picks up his discarded sword and re-sheathes it, before following Celeste back to the wall where Lania is treating the injured.

"Reno! You're okay!" Lania says, looking pleased to see him. "Is everything alright?"

Reno nods, breathing heavily.

"Just exhausted." Celeste answers for him. "They were not kidding when they said this place was in deep."

Lania hands Reno a canteen of fresh water, and he downs it like a man dying of thirst. Celeste drinks her own canteen slowly, watching Reno's adam's apple bob up and down like a yoyo with amusement.

"Ahhhhhh." Reno sighs "That hits the spot. Thanks, Lania."

"Not a problem." She smiles "I can't have you dying on me, can I?"

Celeste rolls her eyes and looks across the battlefield, where many of the other soldiers are making their way back to the wall, mopping up a few stray beasts along the way. "You know, I'm fine too, by the way."

Lania takes Reno's helm off and examines his head "You're burning up, Reno. Are you sure you're okay?"

Reno nods, fanning himself. The plains down this far south are very warm with little to no shade across the wide-open stretches of grass and dirt. Reno's plate armor is extremely hot and uncomfortable, but it beats the alternative.

Lania frowns "Let me try something. It won't last forever, but it should help a little, at least."

She puts her hands on his armor, and an icy blue glow emanates from her hands, enveloping the armor. Almost instantly, Reno feels the armor cool significantly, becoming almost borderline chilled.

He closes his eyes and smiles, feeling instant relief as the chilled armor siphons off his excess body heat and cools him.

"Feel better?" She asks

He nods with a broad smile, his eyes closed.

"Good." She says, "It won't last forever, but it'll keep you cool for now."

Celeste pokes the cooled armor with a raised eyebrow "How did you do that? I know how to enchant my halberd with ice magic, but I didn't know you could do armor that way."

"It's actually very similar," Lania replies proudly "But not very many people are brave enough to do it. If you over-enchant the armor, you can end up killing the person. Too much ice or fire enchantment and you freeze or cook yourself."

Celeste raises both eyebrows "Good point. I'd probably freeze myself to death. I can't throttle my magic very well."

Lania reaches out and channels a small amount of ice magic into Celeste's chain armor.

Celeste closes her eyes and grins "Oh the cold metal feels wonderful on my skin…"

Lania raises her eyebrows "Are you not wearing underwear again?!"

"Of course I am." Celeste chuckles "But I ditched my bodysuit because of the heat, so the metal is right on my skin."

"Weirdo."

As several additional soldiers reach them, Lania hands starts handing out rations to everyone. "Come on, boys and girls, eat up. The day is still young and there may be plenty of fighting left to go around."

A series of groans and moans come from the gathered men and women. Reno scarfs down a pair of pork sandwiches like a starving man and downs another canteen of water. Lania and Celeste observe this with amusement and manage a couple of weak laughs. In spite of all of the fighting, he is still acting like himself, and that alone helps raise their spirits.

"Why aren't the Ceraphs here?" Reno asks no one in particular. "I'm pretty sure that this is exactly their kind of thing."

A nearby sergeant responds unexpectedly "There's some unrest higher up. The Ceraphs and the crown aren't getting along right now."

Reno sits up, and everyone's eyes turn to the sergeant. "What happened?"

"I don't know." The sergeant replies "But it doesn't bode well for us. Corrupted activity is surging like I've never heard of before. This is a piss poor time for them to be having a quarrel."

The soldiers around the camp groan, everyone thinking the same thing. If they don't get some major help soon, they may not be around much longer.

"Come on, Shaide…" Reno mutters "Where are you when I need you?"

CHAPTER 13

KNOCKING ON HELL'S DOOR

Shaide, Amari, and Nyu are all three strolling through the main portion of the village after speaking with Shipmaster Corolas about their interaction with the Alastair Colonel. Corolas understood the situation and gave Shaide a mobile signal receiver that, while not capable of vocal communication, could alert them to a signal received from the frigate if they receive clearance to leave.

Iron Veil is surprisingly different from Broadspring. While the latter was nestled in the mountains, built inside of a broad valley surrounded by fresh mountain springs where it gets its name, Iron Veil is a large fortress town built on a plateau-like area protruding out into the plains. Sloped roads lead to the south, southeast, and southwest gates of the village from the plains below, and to the north, a massive iron gate seals the eastern mountain pass from the town.

Iron Veil seems to be larger than Broadspring as well, both in size and population. Ever since the disaster at Broadspring, the military ramped up its presence significantly at this town to prevent a repeat incident.

Broadspring still remains overrun by the corrupted beasts and formers, and for reasons unknown to the rank and file, the military has yet to mount a full-scale attack to reclaim it and rebuild. Instead, they continue to man their temporary base at the north end of the pass, which after four years is beginning to look more and more permanent.

Nyu happily licks her ice cream while Amari nibbles on a sweet pastry they picked up at a shop back up the street. Shaide chose not to get anything, still feeling a sense of anxiety and anger at the disruption of their mission.

While Nyu obliviously enjoys her cold dairy treat, Amari notices Shaide's unrest. She leans close to him and whispers "What is it? What's wrong?"

Nyu perks up and looks at him, her sensitive hearing picking up the whisper.

Shaide hesitates and points to the large pond they saw from the docks overhead. Amari looks for a moment and nods, following him. A short time later they come out of the buildings and into the large park surrounding the pond.

Shaide hesitates for a moment before speaking "Last night, I had that weird dream again, but it was different this time."

"Different?" Amari asks, sounding confused.

"Dream?" Nyu asks, looking even more confused. He had never spoken to her about the dream.

Shaide nods, thinking back "You know about the cave that haunts my dreams a lot of nights, and that strange demon, but this one was different. More vivid. The first time this ever happens, we get sent on a mission by the Temple of Eden only a couple of hours later? I find it hard to believe that it is a coincidence."

Amari frowns "How do you figure that? It's just a dream."

Shaide shakes his head "I'm honestly not sure that it is. I've never seen the place before in my life, but from the very first time I remember having the dream, that place and that…demon, seemed familiar."

Amari looks slightly troubled. She never likes it when he talks about the dream. It gives her the shivers to hear about it. She doesn't understand why, but she feels like something is WRONG with the place in his dream.

Nyu tilts her head in polite interest, absentmindedly licking her ice cream.

"Do you honestly feel like this woman is connected somehow?" Amari says skeptically "Shaide? Are you feeling okay? You've been under a lot of stress lately. Maybe it's getting to you."

"I'm not crazy!" Shaide says firmly "Those dreams I've been having mean something. The same dreams of the same place for over four years. It can't be a coincidence that it changes the morning we meet Eden's Grand Priestess."

Amari and Nyu both look at Shaide uneasily, taken aback by his tone.

"I'm sorry…" Shaide softens his tone a bit "Please, Amari. Trust me. I don't know if this mission is connected to my dreams, but

I want to find out. Even if they aren't, the Grand Priestess seems to believe this is important. So please, just trust me."

Amari looks Shaide in the eyes for what seems like quite some time. She feels that old sense of great affection rise up, and senses something more behind his own gaze. She thinks back on their time together, and he hasn't steered her wrong yet.

"Amari?"

"Okay. I trust you." Amari says, smiling gently "I think this is all very strange. Every bit of this. But I trust you."

Shaide feels a great sense of relief in his chest. He had felt some odd tension between him and Amari for some time, and he was growing concerned. That she would still trust him over something so crazy eases his mind significantly. He doesn't even realize they are still looking in each other's eyes.

"Oh, just kiss already." Nyu says, licking her ice cream.

Shaide and Amari both jump and look away, both feeling a sense of embarrassment.

"So, someone want to fill me in on this dream?" Nyu asks, her ears aimed forward in curiosity.

Shaide rubs his neck "It's…a long story. I've been having dreams about some strange fancy cave for years, but nothing ever came of it. It's been driving me nuts."

Nyu licks her ice cream and shrugs "Ahh, I see. Well, my people believe that repeat dreams can actually be lost memories, like there was something or someone you once knew, but you forget about them in your conscious mind, so your subconscious mind brings it up in your sleep." She looks down at her now empty ice cream, and her ears droop in disappointment. "Maybe you've been there before, and you just can't remember?"

Shaide and Amari exchange surprised glances.

"I HAVE always felt like that place was strangely familiar." Shaide says.

Nyu shrugs and crunches down the crispy cake cup her ice cream had been served in "Merbey ert merns sermtherng." She swallows and coughs "*ahem* Sorry… Maybe it means something."

Amari looks at Nyu uneasily. She doesn't like entertaining the idea of these dreams; it makes her very uneasy. But Shaide and even Nyu seem to think it's important, and who is she to say they're wrong?

"Well anyways… Hey Shaide!" Nyu says abruptly "Doesn't this pond remind you of the little lake up by the Academy?"

Shaide looks across this water. The tree-rich park around the large pond does indeed remind him of the recreational spring lake in Corallina's upper tiers. He feels a slight smile when he thinks back to those days, before everything was so complicated.

"Ahh, to think…" Nyu says rather sadly "If you hadn't been dragged off by the Ceraph Order, I was going to make you my boyfriend back then."

Amari jerks out of her contemplation "Say what, now?"

Shaide looks away awkwardly as Nyu says "Yeah, not gonna lie. I really had a thing for him after he saved me from those bullies. I hogged him all to myself that weekend, and I was planning to make him mine when he came back, but he never did. We had a LOT of fun at the lake…"

Amari feels that burning sense of jealousy rise up in her chest again. She tries her hardest to remain polite as she says carefully "Fun? What kind of fun?"

Shaide looks at Amari and feels a sense of alarm. The usually sweet and innocent girl has the tiniest shadow of a dangerous look on her face. Shaide only sees it because he knows her so well, but her nostrils are flaring like she is angry, in spite of her politely curious face.

"Oh, nothing like you're thinking, I promise." Nyu says, smiling with her tongue out. "No, we just hung out a lot, and I kept ramming my tongue down his throat."

Amari's mouth and eyes twitch slightly, and to Shaide it looks like she might be slightly broken. Why does she look angry all of a sudden?

Nyu's nose twitches, and she actually smells Amari's anger. In spite of this, she continues to antagonize her, a mischievous look on her face as she says "Don't worry, Amari. I never touched his naughty bits. Those are still yours if you want them."

Amari's face twitches for a moment, Shaide legitimately worried. After a moment, however, Amari simply closes her eyes and says "Nyu... I really hate you sometimes..."

Nyu just sticks out her tongue and winks at Shaide. "You two really need to just do it already. I could cut the tension between you with my partisan."

Shaide coughs so hard he chokes for a minute, and Amari stares at Nyu with wide eyes. After a moment, the three of them begin laughing, the tension disappearing from the air all at once.

          A.S.GUINN

Nyu sits down against a tree "I feel like relaxing here for a bit. Want to join me?"

Shaide and Amari exchange glances and shrug. They both sit down by the tree, a little more distance between them than normal due to Nyu's teasing. For her part, Nyu grins at the result. Everyone but the two of them can see the tension between them, and she just wonders how long it will take for them to see it themselves.

* * *

The mysterious young woman is standing by the window in the infirmary. Dr. Vorzech is certain that she is getting fidgety, being trapped in the hospital wing for so long, but she seems unusually agitated. Vorzech has observed the young lady is normally very calm and composed, but it seems like something is bothering her now. She still won't say much besides needing to see the child of Eden. Vorzech suspects the woman may just be suffering from severe emotional trauma.

General Warsaw walks in the office "Vorzech."

"Sir!" She says, jumping to her feet and saluting. "What can I do for you?"

Warsaw looks out the office window into the infirmary. The base hospital is nearly at capacity due to the recent attacks, and General Warsaw is growing concerned about their chances to survive. Even with the Exorcist reinforcements, their numbers are steadily dropping. Meanwhile, high command doesn't seem to be taking their situation seriously.

"Vorzech, how is our guest doing?" He asks quietly.

She looks out the window at the lady "She seems very agitated right now. I'm not sure why. She still doesn't say much."

The young woman places a hand against the window, and she seems to be shaking. Dr. Vorzech and the General exchange glances, and slowly walk out into the infirmary.

"Dr. Vorzech, we need-"

Vorzech raises a hand and indicates she should wait, and they walk over to the young woman.

"Young lady, what is bothering you? Why do you seem so afraid?"

She slowly turns and looks at the two of them, and a look of sheer terror is on her face. She simply says "He is coming…"

The ground seems to shake slightly in a slowly growing crescendo. The General asks her urgently "Who? Who is coming?"

She doesn't answer, the sheer look of terror on her face telling him everything he needs to know.

A siren begins to wail on the base, and all of the sirens soon follow.

The General frowns. This isn't a standard raid signal. This is…

*   *   *

Reno, Celeste, and Lania are sitting back resting after yet another enemy raid. This last attack seemed unusually small. All of the raids so far had been steadily growing in size, but this last one was almost refreshing. It has Reno feeling uneasy.

Lania leans against Reno's broad back, taking some comfort in resting with her boyfriend. Military protocol is very clear about romantic fraternization while on duty, but right now, after all of the hell of the past couple days, she is saying to hell with protocol.

"You two are really cute together." Celeste grins "The big chunky tank and the cute little washboard. It seems to fit."

Lania pouts again "Washboard? Really? I'll remember that when you get hurt."

Reno rolls his eyes "Don't mind her. It doesn't make much difference to me."

"I still see you looking at the bigger chested girls…"

Reno coughs awkwardly, but Lania doesn't really look upset. They always play around like this.

Celeste leans her head back and stares at the reddening sky. "I don't know how these guys down here do it. These constant raids are wearing me out fast, and I don't know if I'm going to be able to hold up under all of this."

Reno nods lazily, his eyes closed as he tries to micro-nap. "I know what you mean. I've never had to work half this hard in my life. I hope my body can hold out."

"It's testing the limits of my spirit too." Says Lania. "I hope I can keep treating the wounded without killing myself."

A ripple rolls across a nearby puddle. Reno looks at it in curiosity.

Ripple. Ripple. Ripple. Ripple.

He feels the ground begin to tremble slightly beneath him, and he looks around in curiosity. The other soldiers in nearby camps are looking around as well. The rumbling slowly but steadily intensifies, and Reno slowly gets to his feet.

In the distance far to the south, a large dark mass seems to be coming their way, but something is different about this one. The warships overhead are turning their guns on the distant mass, but they are holding fire for some reason.

Celeste and Lania are on their feet now, as is everyone they can see.

Suddenly the sirens start blaring, but this isn't the usual raid siren. This siren is a tone he has only ever heard in the academy. It's…

"It's an army! All units form up!" The sergeant yells. "COME ON! GET MOVING!"

Reno looks around in confusion as soldiers haphazardly begin getting into formation, lining up into columns of companies. "EXORCISTS! GET ALONGSIDE COMPANY BRAVO!"

Reno and Celeste look at Lania and the pained look on her face.

"GET MOVING!"

Reno jumps and puts a hand on her head for a moment before running alongside one of the companies.

"What's happening?"

"An invading army?"

"What are we doing?"

Voices of confusion ripple through the ranks of the neighboring company of soldiers. Behind them, hundreds of soldiers are streaming out of the base behind them, forming into additional battle companies.

Reno feels an extreme sense of unease. They've never treated any of the previous attacks like this. They just charged out and defended the base. This time, they're organizing like the armies of their textbooks. What's happening?

The approaching mass becomes more visible, and Reno squints. It looks like it's in some kind of formation. They're not charging en masse like they normally do.

Reno looks around and sees that in no time at all, an entire battalion has lined up outside the base behind them.

"ALL UNITS! HOLD FAST!"

Overhead, as the approaching force gets within range, the fleet overhead opens fire. Every frigate, destroyer, and cruiser opens up with a small salvo of artillery fire directed at the unknown force. Balls of fire streak through the air at tremendous speed as the earth-shaking booms of cannon fire, and they watch the resulting impacts on the incoming army.

Flares of fire from the impacts stretch across the plains in front of them as they watch with anticipation. The Alastair army cheers with elation as they watch their artillery support rain fire on whomever approaches.

The cheers quickly subside however, as the flames clear, and they see some kind of semi-transparent barrier that is flaring. Something blocked the incoming fire.

Overhead, the fleet opens fire in earnest, firing multiple salvos of artillery rounds at the incoming forces. Dozens if not hundreds of rounds of high-explosive magicore shells rain down on the enemy, bombarding the barrier with a barrage that nothing could live through. They maintain fire for a full sixty seconds, before ceasing their barrage.

Flames roar across the plains in the distance, and the Alastair forces watch in anticipation for the artillery barrage to decimate their enemy. The flames seem to rage for what seems like eternity before subsiding.

The incoming mass, which can now be seen as an army of unknown origin, is completely unharmed, some kind of barrier preventing the artillery from reaching them.

"ALL UNITS! PREPARE TO MARCH! WHOEVER THESE GUYS ARE, WE CANNOT LET THEM REACH THE BASE! FORWARD MARCH!"

The Alastair forces nervously begin their march forward, hearing the war cry of the approaching forces. Their leaders see that their men are nervous and unprepared. They begin calling out motivational chants to fire the men up.

"MEN! WE DO NOT KNOW WHOM WE FACE, BUT IT DOES NOT MATTER. THIS IS OUR BASE, AND THIS IS OUR LAND. WE WILL NOT GIVE GROUND TO THIS TRASH, AND WE WILL NOT SURRENDER. FOR THREE THOUSAND YEARS, THE ALASTAIR MILITARY HAS HELD BACK THE TIDE OF THE DEALANDS, AND THAT WILL NOT STOP TODAY! WE WILL DEFEAT THIS ENEMY, AND WE WILL PROTECT OUR NATION! FOR EDEN!"

The army chants back "FOR EDEN!"

"FOR EDEN!" The commander repeats.

Several hundred voices chant in unison "FOR EDEN!"

"FOR! EDEN!"

The army chants back one last time "FOR EDEN!"

"ALL UNITS! HALT! ARCHERS AND LONG-RANGE MAGES, FRONT AND CENTER!"

Several dozen archers and mages rush forward to the front of the line as the enemy forces close within range.

"PULL AND CHARGE! HOLD!"

Archers draw their arrows and infuse them with energy. The mages spin up various spells in front of them, holding them back for the command.

"FIRE!"

A volley of arrows, fireballs, ice spikes, lightning balls, and various forms of offensive magic rip through the air. The approaching army hunkers down behind shields and blocks much of the incoming volley. To their surprise, a massive volley of arrows and magic comes back at them.

"INCOMING!"

Those with shields raise them to block the incoming fire, but many of the archers and mages are caught by surprise and unable to defend themselves. Reno watches in horror, anger building in his chest as many of his comrades fall to the incoming volley.

"ALL UNIT! CHARGE!"

Inspired by the rage of watching their comrades fall, Reno and all of his fellow soldiers sprint forward past their mages and archers, roaring a battle cry. The incoming army, dressed in black and gold, does the same.

Reno pulls down his visor and raises his shield and sword, and the two armies close on each other rapidly. As soon as it begins, the forward lines smash into each other. Dozens of men again on either side fall as the first wave collides.

Shields clang. Weapons pierce flesh and break bone and armor. Reno roars as he cuts everything not wearing the blue and silver of Alastair. He slashes, stabs, and bashes everything in sight as he is surrounded on all sides.

The adrenaline kicks in full force, and the fear of death pushes him to fight harder. As he knocks an unknown soldier to the ground, its helmet comes off, and he sees a human face looking back at him, black veins lining his face. Reno hesitates for a moment. This isn't like the corrupted he is used to. This guy still looks…human.

He shakes his head and drives his sword into the man's chest, and spins around, bashing another newcomer with his shield before deftly decapitating him cleanly.

Nearby, Celeste is performing her acrobatic fighting routine, keeping her enemies out of range with her halberd. Not concerned with individual targets, she stabs, sweeps, and slashes anyone within range with her polearm, aiming for quantity over precision.

This battle is like nothing they have experienced thus far, however. Their enemy is intelligent and creative, far different from the usual corrupted forces they have been fighting. Certain individuals like Reno and Celeste and doing well, but the Alastair forces are being overwhelmed by the enemy's ferocity.

The sound of turbine engines roars in the distance, and Reno watches for a moment as a few dozen dropships come out of the navy overhead, but Reno's attention is quickly returned to the battlefield as he continues fighting for his life.

A.S.GUINN

Behind the Alastair army, the dropships from the navy overhead deploys over a hundred additional men onto the battlefield to reinforce the soldiers of Hell's Doorstep. The name has never been more fitting than it is today.

*   *   *

"Shaide Darkmoon?"

Shaide turns around from the table where he is eating dinner to find a young soldier his own age nervously greeting him. "Yes?"

"Admiral Harris wishes to speak to you at the spire. He says it is extremely urgent. Will you come with me please?"

Shaide, Amari, and Nyu all exchange glances. "That's pretty rich of the Admiral to request us after causing so much trouble, but yes, we'll come." He throws some money down on the table.

The four of them look walk down the street at a rapid pace towards the military section of Iron Veil, laid out in a wide arc around the three south gates constructed of nearly solid iron, which where the town gets its name. On their walk, Shaide once again admires the robust architecture of the town, much like Broadspring once was. The houses and shops are all constructed of heavy, sturdy wood and strong stone, some of them even having iron pillars reinforcing them. The streets are arranged in a grid-like pattern, giving the forces of the town easy access to any place there may be trouble.

The military gatemen give them no trouble as they approach, apparently being away that the Admiral is expecting them. As they approach the spire, they see a heavily decorated Navy Admiral standing there waiting for them, escorted by four assistants and the army colonel they met previously. Shaide notices that fully armed

A.S.GUINN   315

soldiers are moving in very large numbers, all of them heading for the vessels docked overhead. Shaide is getting a bad feeling about this.

"Admiral, Sir! The Ceraphs whom you requested."

"At ease son. Ceraphs? It pains me to speak to you so briefly, but we are short on time. I am Admiral Harris, the commanding officer of Iron Veil Forward Defense Base."

Shaide looks at the Admiral's outstretched hand for a moment, and then chooses not to shake it. An expression of his displeasure. "Admiral, I am Shaide Darkmoon of the Ceraph Order. I am here on an operation ordered by the Temple of Eden in Corallina directly. I am not in the mood for polite formalities at the moment, so just tell me what you want."

Amari and Nyu look at Shaide in shock with the level of disrespect he is showing this seasoned Admiral. The colonel looks daggers at Shaide. "Look here now, *Ceraph.* This is Admiral Ja-"

"SILENCE Colonel!" The Admiral barks. "These Ceraphs have every right to be upset with us. Do not make things worse by running your mouth!"

"But Admiral! The disrespect-"

"I SAID AT EASE!" The Admiral yells loudly, every nearby soldier cowering in fear. The colonel looks miffed, but holds his tongue. "Ceraphs, I am sorry about the detainment. It has been ordered by the crown, and I cannot disobey an order from the Queen, regardless of my feelings on the matter. That is a moot point, however. We need your help."

　　　　　　　A.S.GUINN

ETERNAL KNIGHTS OF EDEN II

Shaide narrows his eyes, breathing heavily and clearly angry. To his credit, he maintains his composure this time as he responds. "What do you need, Admiral?"

The Admiral, while stern in the face, looks grateful that Shaide calmed down. "Hell's Doorstep has come under attack by an unknown enemy army. I hear that your mission is to that base anyways, so I would like to request your assistance in repelling the enemy and retaking the base. If you will do this, I will give you free reign down here, and the crown can deal with it."

Shaide's anger disappears all at once. "An…Army? Isn't Hell's Doorstep coming under constant attack anyway?"

"No, this is different." The Admiral shakes his head. "A literal army has descended on Hell's Doorstep. We have no clue where they are from, but they seem to be corrupted in nature. They are bearing black and gold uniforms we have never seen before."

Amari puts a hand on his shoulder and whispers "Shaide…"

"I know." He mumbles back. "Our objective is in that base. We don't have a choice but to help them."

She nods, while Nyu just looks around nervously.

"Okay, Admiral. We will help you." Shaide says "After we save that base, we are going to have a serious talk about relations with the Ceraph Order, though."

"I understand, Ceraph. Thank you."

"Come on. Let's go." Shaide says to Nyu and Amari.

The three of them rush up the spire to their waiting frigate. As they climb, they observe entire companies of Alastair soldiers boarding other vessels and preparing for war.

Shaide watches the soldiers, realizing quickly how serious the situation really is. "Hey, look, Amari…"

She shakes her head "Shaide. I'm coming with you. That's final."

Shaide wants to argue for a moment, but he sees the determined look on her face. He knows that look, and it means her mind is made up.

"You need me to keep you alive, after all." She smiles.

Nyu walks ahead of them "Come on, let's go already!"

Shaide and Amari look in each other's eyes a moment longer, and he feels some kind of understanding pass between them. They always promised to save the world together. He can't very well ask her to stay behind now.

"Okay. Let's go."

"Teehee. I win again." Amari giggles.

"Bite me."

The three of them rush to board their frigate, their shipmates looking at them in confusion. "What's going on?"

Shaide looks over his shoulder as they head for the bridge "Prepare to cast off! We have emergency orders!"

They powerwalk out of the hanger and up the corridor to the bridge, where they find Shipmaster Corolas listening to communications on the comm panel. "Ceraphs! What's going on? There is a lot of activity out there."

"Yorlan. I have emergency orders for you. We depart for Hell's Doorstep immediately. Full battle-ready conditions."

          A.S.GUINN

Corolas looks confused for a moment. "Shaide? What's happening?"

"Get us underway, and I'll explain." Shaide says urgently.

Corolas nods slowly, not fully understanding, but realizing the seriousness of the situation if Shaide is saying this. "Navigator. Plot our course straight to Hell's Doorstep outpost, and have the engine room prepare for intercept speed."

"Understood."

"Now Shaide. What is happening?"

Shaide walks over to Corolas and lowers his voice. "Admiral Harris had the guts to request our assistance. Hell's Doorstep has apparently fallen under attack by a literal army of unknown origin. It's not looking good for them"

"Haven't they been under attack by hordes of corrupted for weeks?" Corolas asks.

Shaide shakes his head meaningfully "Not like this. According to the Admiral, we're talking about a literal, uniformed army. We'll find out more when we get there."

Shipmaster Corolas turns to the navigator "Okay. Disengage from the spire and depart as soon as we are able."

"Sir!"

Corolas triggers the ship's alarms that order all personnel to prepare for combat. "Shaide. Even at engine overload, we're still nearly three hours away."

Shaide locks eyes "We'll do the best we can."

Corolas nods "I understand."

A few short minutes later, the engines of the COV *Last Beacon* thunder to life in full overload, and the frigate turns to the south, accelerating at maximum speed towards Hell's Doorstep.

*   *   *

The battle has been raging for over five hours now. Reno is exhausted, injured, and losing hope, but he pushes himself to continue fighting beyond his limits. Mindless thralls have joined the fray, and they are even more dangerous than the soldiers in many ways. The mindless ferocity of their attacks makes them impossible to predict. In the chaos of battle, Reno has long since lost track of Celeste.

The Alastair forces have been driven back almost to the fortress, and the remaining fighters are giving everything they have to keep the army at bay, fighting what feels like a losing battle to protect the fortress.

"GRAAHH!" Reno stabs his sword through the breastplate of an enemy soldier and channels his spiritual power into it. A blossom of ice explodes from his chest as he roars in pain, blood splattering Reno as he pulls his sword clear. With a violent swing, he spins around and cuts down a thrall in midair as it leaps at him.

He leans on his sword for a moment, trying to catch his breath as wounded men and women, friend and foe, lie around him. He hears a sickening sound, and turns to look south.

Behind a new wave of approaching soldiers, a new problem arises. Dozens if not hundreds of lobos have joined the enemy pack, and he can hear the howling and roaring. Wyverns are in the sky overhead, and the Navy turns their guns and opens fire again on the new airborne threat. But this is not the worst thing on the horizon.

A.S.GUINN

Three full-grown corrupted behemoths leap over the new wave of soldiers to the south, running alongside their smaller lobo companions. Reno grimaces in pain and frustration as he feels certain that this will be the day he dies.

An image of all of his friends passes through his mind. Rayn, Lania, Celeste, Shaide, Amari, and every one of his classmates, both living and dead, appear before his eyes, and he feels a renewed sense of determination. He will not allow himself to give up until the breath leaves his body.

Three enemy soldiers spot him and charge his position. Reno deflects a spear with his shield and skillfully thrusts his sword into a second enemy's neck. He then catches a sword against his armor with his arm and headbutts the assailant, rocking him back and breaking his grip on the sword. He spins hard, and mortally wounds both the spearman and the swordsman.

Then he feels the rumbling in the ground and looks up. The biggest behemoth sprints right past all of the Alastair and corrupted forces on all fours, and runs headfirst into the reinforced fortress wall. The men manning the wall all fall to their knees as the behemoth shakes the entire fortress.

The cruiser overhead turns its railgun on the behemoth and charges of. Right as it fires, however, a wyvern kamikaze flies into the rail. The entire railgun detonates INSIDE the cruiser, and a chain of explosions rock through the center of the ship.

Reno watches in horror as the cruiser explodes inside and starts to list. It drifts into its neighboring destroyer half its size, and destroys the engines on its port side. Both the cruiser and the destroyer spew flames and smoke as they drift to the ground. A frigate that was too below the cruiser gets crushed from above as the larger vessel falls on top of it. All three vessels plummet to the ground from several thousand feet in the air, and three massive fireballs erupt on impact.

A massive cloud of dust fills the air and the shockwave from the crashed vessels brings even Reno to his knees. All of the hope he felt moments ago is now gone.

As if nothing had happened, the behemoth runs back in a circle and slams into the same spot in the wall a second time. Then it repeats and does it a third, and a fourth time. The artillery crews on the wall try their hardest to bring down the beast as the forces in the field are overrun by the new wave of soldiers.

Reno closes his eyes for a moment, praying to Eden and every other deity worshipped on this world. He opens his eyes, and with a massive battle cry, sprints for the behemoth attacking the wall.

With an earth-shaking crash, the behemoth smashes through the wall of the fortress, and the gathering soldiers begin streaming through the breach. Around the fortress, Reno hears two additional identical crashes as the other behemoths crash through the wall, letting enemy soldiers into the fortress.

Reno charges into the line of soldiers streaming into the base "YOU! WILL! NOT! CROSS! THIS! LINE! WHILE! I! STILL! BREATHE!" Reno screams, punctuating every word with a vicious attack. Reno faces numerous enemies alone, but for some reason, he isn't afraid anymore. All of the medics and support mages had retreated into the base, including Lania, and he will gladly give his life to protect them all.

"FOR ALASTAIR!" Reno screams, charging into the midst of them. He turns too slowly, and sees a war hammer coming at him, too late to block.

SHING

In slow motion, a white-haired blur impales the hammer-wielding soldier with a silver halberd from above, dropping him to the ground as she seamlessly pulls her weapon and drives back their opponents with a wide swing.

"RENO!" Celeste yells, covered in blood "LET'S MAKE THIS AN ENDING WORTH REMEMBERING, BUDDY!"

"YOU KNOW IT!" He yells back.

Conscious of the behemoth directly in front of them, the pair fights their way through the hole in the wall themselves, and turns to stop the tide for as long as they can. Behind them, the forces still within the base fight with everything they have, resolved to fight right up until the end.

"MOVE!" Celeste screams, grabbing Reno and yanking him out of the way. The massive clawed paw of the behemoth comes down right where Reno had been standing, crushing a half dozen enemy soldiers with it.

"That paw is the size of a dropship!" Reno yells. He throws himself flat to the ground as a huge cross-swing misses him by inches. He sees now why standard operating procedure for behemoth is capital ship artillery.

He lifts his head and looks around. The Alastair forces are fighting with all of their might, but it looks like hell's doorstep is going to fall.

Reno breathes heavily as it begins to rain. The storm clouds rolled in from nowhere, and lightning arcs across the sky. Through the lightning, Reno sees the outline of a lone ship overhead. He squints his eyes, and then opens them wide.

In the sky overhead, a lone frigate thunders to a stop as the hanger doors open. Several dropships stream out of the vessel as three young adults walk to the edge of the deck.

Through the rain, three lights appear high in the sky. Purple, burning orange, and yellow. Lightning seems to spit from the newly formed glyphs in the sky, and the three young newcomers sprint off the edge of the deck.

Skydiving through the rain and lightning, Shaide spies the base below from behind his characteristic skull mask. They have been completely overrun. The scream of the thunderbird and the phoenix pierce the sky as Rho and Theta drop from the clouds, Theta carrying Tao in its claws. The three angels streak past their masters and drop Tao on the ground, where he sprints at the Behemoth nearest Reno and lifts it off of the ground with the force of its impact. Streams of shadow energy bombard the behemoth at the Shadow Cat refuses to let get, distracting it from the battle.

Rho and Theta streak over the incoming army and hit it with a massive combined attack, releasing an enormous fire and lightning storm that decimates a number of the enemy forces while leaving the handful of surviving Alastair fighters unharmed.

Rho and Theta streak back to the fortress, catching Shaide, Amari, and Nyu just before they hit the ground, breaking their fall as they land gracefully in the middle of the fortress.

　　　　A.S.GUINN

"Rho! Go hold back the enemy outside the base."

"Theta! You too!"

As Shaide, Amari, and Nyu stand backs to each other looking outward, the flying angels streak outside the base to throttle the flow of enemies coming inside. The handful of dropships from the *Last Beacon* deposit a few dozen fresh Ceraph Order soldiers onto the battlefield where they join the Alastair defenders. This still looks like a losing battle, though.

"We have to take out those behemoths!" Shaide yells. "As long as those things are there, the battle is meaningless!"

Nearby Alastair soldiers spot Shaide and seem to take heart.

"It's the Grim Reaper!"

"The Ceraph's Angel of Death!"

"We can win this now!"

The Alastair soldiers begin their counterattack with renewed vigor, the sight of the legendary hero of Lone Ridge giving them their second wind. They begin viciously fighting the invading soldiers with a newfound determination, cutting through the enemy without mercy.

Shaide turns to the behemoth, and he spots Reno on the ground. "Come on! Let's take this thing out!"

Reno watches as the man in the reaper mask sprints past him and lunges at the behemoth, still being attacked by Tao. Shaide leaps through the air and plunges his sword hilt deep in the gigantic beast's neck. He grabs onto the stab wound and thrusts his sword repeatedly in the thing's neck, filling the air with blood.

The behemoth is not going down that easily however, and with a huge whip of its enormous head, it throws both Shaide and Tao off of him. Amari raises her staff and bombards the great beast with a shower of ice shards that explode on impact, dealing a lot of surface damage. The behemoth is so massive however that the damage it is inflicting is only superficial and isn't having any real impact.

Reno sees the behemoth raise its paw for a swing "SHAIDE GET DOWN!"

As Shaide turns his head, Reno leaps up and gets between them. The massive paw slams into both Reno and Shaide, sending them flying through the air. They both hit some debris with a pair of loud crunches, and they tumble to the ground.

Shaide groans and climbs to his feet, and his eyes find Reno. His best friend is lying on the ground motionless, and Shaide cannot tell if he is breathing or not. He watches Amari backflip in the air to dodge a second swing, and Nyu taking turns with Tao attacking from whichever side the beast isn't looking.

He closes his eyes and focuses all of his power, and he mentally calls out *"Rho! I need you! Let's take this thing down!"*

He channels all of the energy he can muster into his muscles. He had always been warned that this was a terrible idea. Using spiritual energy in this manner is effective, but it is hell on your body. Nevertheless, this is an emergency that demands it.

With all of the energy channeled into his legs, Shaide takes several sprinting steps forward and leaps at the behemoth with superhuman speed. His body glows white hot with lightning energy as he slams into the behemoth in a blur. As his blade drives deep into the side of its head, the force of the impact knocks the behemoth on its side.

"RHO NOW! EVERYTHING YOU'VE GOT!" Shaide screams, his very muscles and bones feeling as if they were on fire.

Rho flies straight up into the air, and at the peak of his arc, he falls back and dives straight towards the behemoth, its body arcing with spiritual power as it reaches supersonic speeds.

"GET DOWN!"

Amari and Nyu dive to the ground as Rho slams into the behemoth at over one-thousand miles per hour and self-destructs, hitting the behemoth with every bit of energy it had. Lightning explodes outward as everything nearby is either knocked down or flash-fried.

CHAPTER 14

THE FALL OF HELL'S DOORSTEP

Rho hits the behemoth with the force of a bomb. With Shaide acting as a conduit, Rho discharges its entire aura into the behemoth all at once. The behemoth roars in pain and rage as trillions of amps of electricity course through its body, destroying it at the cellular level. With a last massive roar, the electricity subsides, and the beast moves no more.

Amari raises her head and looks desperately for Shaide, her eyes stinging from the light of Rho's attack. As she blinks the black spots out of her vision, she sees that Shaide is remarkably still standing atop the fallen behemoth, its body disintegrating into a black haze like any other fallen corrupted.

Shaide pulls his sword free with a groan and stumbles off of the behemoth before falling flat on the ground.

"SHAIDE!" Amari yells, running over to him. She rolls him face-up and lays him across her lap "Oh god, please tell me you're okay…"

Shaide groans and reaches up, touching her cheek. "I'm okay, I think. God, everything hurts…"

Amari seems on the verge of tears "You are absolutely insane. You know that?"

Shaide manages a weak grin "I know. But would I be me if I wasn't?"

Amari chuckles weakly in response.

Shaide forces himself to his feet in spite of the pain. "Come on. We're not nearly done here."

Someone begins clapping nearby. A man walks around the behemoth, looking amused. "Bravo, young man. Bravo. Taking out a behemoth in what was essentially solo combat, and surviving the effect of what you just did? Very impressive. VERY impressive indeed. I'm afraid your bravery ends here, however."

Shaide raises his sword as Amari raises her staff. "Who are you?" Shaide asks, watching the man carefully.

"I am called Regal, and I am a humble servant of Belial here on a mission important to my master. But you already knew that, didn't you? And, of course, you know why I am here."

The woman Shaide narrows his eyes.

"Give me the woman, Grim Reaper, and I will withdraw my forces and leave the base be for now. You and your friends will be able to withdraw and live to fight another day. There is no need for more bloodshed."

Amari takes a fighting stance. Out of the corner of his eye, Shaide can see Nyu carefully creeping behind the man. Shaide tries to keep him distracted. "Why do you want her? What is so important about her?"

Regal smiles a smile completely devoid of any humor. "She can lead us to something very important to our cause, and even get it for us. She means more to us than this pathetic fortress."

Nyu leaps at the Fallen, but he spins around and blasts her with some kind of energy, sending her flying away.

Shaide leaps forward and swings his sword, but the Fallen counters quickly, and Shaide stares the man in the face, swords locked together.

"I see you do not plan to cooperate. Disappointing, but not unexpected." With a heavy and powerful swing, he breaks loose and knocks Shaide back. In spite of the pain, Shaide manages a backflip to get out of range of the follow up attack.

With charged energy, Shaide swings his blade across and then down, sending a pair of energy arcs flying through the air. Regal deflects them both and leaps forward. Shaide was prepared, however, and he kicks out, catching the man in the face and sending him back.

Regal roars in anger, realizing this fight will not be as easy as he had expected. "I see you were not given the name Grim Reaper for nothing. You ARE powerful. But not as powerful as you think."

Shaide readies a battle stance again as Regal closes his eyes, channeling a massive amount of spiritual energy. At the same time, a glowing red glyph appears on the ground in front of him. Shaide takes a few steps back in alarm. The man seems to be channeling impossible levels of energy and compressing them, almost as if…

"Oh no. GET DOWN!" Shaide yells. Amari drops to the ground as Shaide braces with his aura.

A moment later, Regal screams, and a massive shockwave explodes from him with a blinding red light. Shaide braces as his aura flares and absorbs the brunt of the blast. When the light clears, Shaide is standing in a moderate crater, an entire massive section of the wall behind Regal blown to pieces.

Shaide looks around frantically, and his eyes find Amari climbing to her feet. Then his eyes fall on something else.

Where the glyph has been now stands what looks like a bipedal lobster in ancient warrior armor with massive claws.

"Cancer! Destroy him!"

Seemingly out of nowhere, however, a ball of fire streaks across the battlefield. Theta grabs onto the daemon and carries him beyond the wall to battle him.

Shaide nods to Amari, inwardly thanking her for the save. "It's just you and me, Fallen. You're not taking the woman."

"And who is going to stop me? You?!"

Shaide and Regal lunge at each other, dueling with their blades with growing speed and ferocity. Shaide swings low at his feet, and Regal simply jumps over it, then Shaide swings across and he leans back to dodge it. Regal counterattacks with several powerful swings which Shaide manages to deflect with his own blade. Shaide takes a step back, and the ground explodes beneath him, blowing him off his feet. Regal counters with a series of non-elemental blasts of an unknown dark energy, knocking Shaide up into the air.

"SHAIDE NO!" Amari screams, running forward.

A large blast detonates right above the airborne Shaide, slamming him hard into the ground. As he hits the rocks, the wind is knocked out of him as an alarming amount of blood erupts from his mouth. He doesn't move…

Amari leaps through the air and hits Regal with her staff like a hammer, knocking him to the ground. She spins it around to bring it down on him, but he rolls out of the way. He looks with alarm at where the staff hit, a two-foot crater left in the rocky ground.

He leaps to his feet and attacks her with a snarl, and she expertly deflects the blade with her staff. A sudden thrust leaves a deep cut across the side of her face, and a quick direction change knocks her staff from her hands.

Rather than being beaten, she switches to hand-to-hand combat and delivers several rapid kicks to his chest and face before punching him to the throat, and then following up with a wide crescent kick across the face that knocks him to the ground. Without missing a beat, she fluidly picks up her staff and swings it around knocking his sword from his hand. With the final move in her sequence, she brings the staff down on his chest like a hammer, knocking the wind from him and forcing him to cough up a significant amount of blood to rival Shaide.

Seemingly on cue, a massive fireball blasts the daemon back through the wall and into the fortress. Cancer rolls past Amari and Regal from the force of the blast and rolls back to its feet.

   A.S.GUINN

ETERNAL KNIGHTS OF EDEN II

Overhead, the sound of additional warships arriving fills the air as an entire fleet from Iron Veil arrives to the battlefield. Dozens of dropships carrying hundreds of reinforcements stream from the fleet overhead, including an especially large deployment from a heavy assault carrier. A handful of the reinforcements are deployed within the walls of the fortress, while the bulk of them land outside the walls, forming a protective perimeter around the damaged portions of the fortress.

Dozens of gunships deploy from the carrier as well, and they rain fire down on the advancing forces outside the walls. The blinding flash of a railgun makes another of the behemoths simply cease to exist, and an artillery barrage from a pair of destroyers finishes off the third.

"You've lost, Regal!" Amari yells angrily "Surrender!"

"NEVER! DO IT, CANCER!"

Amari turns her head, and the giant lobster-crab looking daemon glows with a blinding light. Amari's eyes open wide, and she jumps on top of Shaide, deploying the strongest barrier she can manage.

*　　*　　*

Shipmaster Yorlan Corolas looks down as the reinforcement fleet arrives and rains hell on the enemy forces. With so many friendly forces mixed in, there is little he can do to assist the battle from up here, so he parked the frigate a short distance away where he could observe in case of emergency.

Down below, however, the reinforcement fleet is parked low to the ground, delivering close fire support to the reinforcements and driving off the enemy. In a short time, it looks as if the battle has turned around completely, although the cost appears to be astronomical.

Through the forward viewport he sees a strange blinding light near the edge of the fortress. His eyes open wide as an even more blinding flash fills the entirety of the forward viewport.

"INCOMING!" One of the bridge crew yells.

The entire frigate shakes violently as a deep subsonic thrum rumbles through the entirety of the ship. Corolas falls to the deck as the ship bucks and kicks beneath him. This seems to continue for nearly thirty seconds before the shockwave subsides.

"Status report!" Corolas coughs "What the hell just…happened…"

The entire bridge crew climbs to their feet, looking out the forward viewport. No none can believe their eyes. Through the forward viewport, where Hell's Doorstep stood, a fiery mushroom cloud fills their view.

Over two-thirds of the reinforcing ships were caught in the blast, and they are all crashing to the ground around the fortress. The surviving ships are heavily damaged and seem to be crippled at the moment. The fortress itself is still completely obscured by dust and debris, assuming anything remains.

"Oh my god…" Corolas breathes.

*   *   *

As the waves of energy and destruction crash around Amari and Shaide, Theta streaks from the sky to give them additional protection. Amari screams and cries out as she desperately shields the wounded

A.S.GUINN

Shaide, her barrier beginning to fail as the heat licks her face. Just when she begins to feel as if it will never end, the shockwave subsides, and a deafening silence fills her ears.

The barrier fails and Theta dispels. Amari looks all around her, coughing in the dust. Regal is gone, whether he fled or died she does not know. She looks down and checks Shaide and sees to her relief that he is still breathing.

Nearby, Nyu stumbles to her feet, clutching her ribs. With some quick thinking, Tao had grabbed Reno and leapt to Nyu, using his body to shield them from the blast.

"AMA-*Cough* AMARI! SHAIDE!" Nyu calls out.

"OVER HERE!" Amari cries. She turns to Shaide and begins channeling her healing magic. She is dangerously low on aura, but she uses everything she has to try and stabilize him.

Nyu limps over, dragging Reno. "What the hell was that?!" She asks with a cough, her eyes showing the telltale stare indicative of shock.

Amari shakes her head and whispers "The daemon self-destructed. That much energy exploding at once…"

"Shaide, is he-"

Amari shakes her head, tears running down her face. "He's okay, I think. His lifeforce is still strong."

"Good." Nyu mutters, lying Reno down next to Shaide "Good…"

Shaide weakly opens his eyes "Reno…is he okay?"

Nyu checks Reno's pulse. She feels a faint beat and sighs "Yeah, he's alive. He just seems to be knocked out."

The dust is so heavy, they cannot see a thing around them. Amari focuses all of her attention on Shaide, trying to heal his internal injuries. Her healing magic allows her to sense the condition of anyone she is healing, and while she said he was okay, Shaide's injuries are severe.

"Hello!? Is anyone out there!?" A familiar voice echoes across the ruins.

"OVER HERE!" Amari yells, coughing heavily.

After a moment Celeste emerges from the dust. She is heavily bruised and bleeding, but she seems to be okay. "What the hell happened?!"

Amari shakes her head and focuses again on Shaide. Her aura dwindles as she feels like she may pass out soon, but she continues, nonetheless.

Celeste kneels down "Are they-"

"They're alive." Nyu responds. "They just got the worst of it."

The rain begins again, dampening the dust in the air and slowly dispersing it. As an hour, or possibly even two passes, the fortress slowly comes back into view around them. At some point Amari's aura gives out, and she struggles to maintain consciousness while she holds Shaide's head in her lap.

"Oh my god…" Celeste whispers.

Shaide pushes himself gingerly to a sitting position, supported by Amari, and they look around the fortress and battlefield.

The remains of the fortress slowly come into view as the dust clears. They are all stunned by what they see. The south wall of the fortress where they had been fighting was just… gone. Literally thousands of bodies littered the battlefield, ranging from disintegrating corrupted forces and beasts to their own comrades. Here and there, motion could be observed across the battlefield, and all was silent except for the occasional moans of survivors.

Amari grabs her chest and whispers with a haunted look in her eyes "So much death…"

Celeste looks around, her eyes blank "I've never seen anything like this before."

Amari notices the command building, which appeared to include the infirmary judging from the sign, was still somewhat intact. "Come on, let's get inside."

Amari struggles to her feet, and she and Shaide support each other. Nyu and Celeste pick up Reno between them and drag him across the disaster area. It takes them nearly ten minutes to reach the command building, and several men are standing by the door observing the destruction with shock.

They notice the approaching survivors and yell out "Come on, in here!" They run out and help the injured Ceraphs and soldiers, carrying them into the building to a makeshift triage center in the officer's mess hall.

They help ease them onto cots as medics and nurses work through the surviving wounded, prioritizing them by severity of injury.

"AMARI!" Lania runs over, covered in dust, and jumps on her. Her eyes then fall on Reno, and a look of shock crosses her face.

"He's okay, Lania." Nyu says "I think he's just knocked out. He got hit by a behemoth."

"By a...behemoth? Good god..." She lets go of Amari and kneels next to Reno, channeling her healing magic while assessing his condition. After a moment she smiles weakly in relief.

"Hey! You! Don't go out there!"

A young woman with flawless features and pure white hair walks slowly towards Shaide and Amari. A doctor wearing the name badge Vorzech follows along behind her as she walks up to them.

"Can I help you?" Amari asks uncertainly.

"Child of Eden..." She says, pointing at Shaide.

Vorzech looks between the unknown woman and Shaide, and comprehension dawns on her face. "You WERE looking for the Ceraphs..."

Shaide turns his head "Are you the one they told us about? The one who stumbled in with no memory?"

She nods slowly.

Doctor Vorzech looks at them "What on earth happened out there?"

Amari explains, her eyes locked to the ground "A Fallen was leading the attack. When it looked like he was going to lose, he made his daemon do some kind of self-destruction, and the result is what you see outside..."

"My god..." Vorzech whispers "Is everyone here okay?"

"Can you look at my bo- I mean my squad mate, Reno, please?" Lania says weakly.

Doctor Vorzech nods and walks around to him, checking him over. After a moment, she stands up straight, looking satisfied. "He's going to be fine. He appears to have suffered a moderate head injury, but it isn't life threatening."

"Thank you, doctor…" Lania shifts her healing focus to Reno's head.

"Ceraphs? Are you okay?"

Shaide, Amari, and Nyu exchange glances. Shaide raises his head "I think we're okay. Just worn out and bruised. Nothing serious."

Amari leans over and whispers "Are you sure you're okay?"

Shaide smiles weakly at her "I'm fine. Don't worry about me."

Dr. Vorzech looks at the young woman "Please, missy, you need to stay in my office. You can speak to them later, I promise. Right now, though, they're hurt, and they need to rest. Okay?"

The young woman gives Dr Vorzech a pained look before finally nodding. She walks slowly away back to wherever she had come from, and the doctor bows "I'm sorry. She's been very difficult to control. Her lack of memory makes her extremely curious."

"We're here because of her." Amari says in a low voice. "The Grand Priestess of Eden gave us this mission herself. We will need to speak with her later."

Doctor Vorzech nods in response "Hopefully you'll have better luck with her than we have. I don't know how she knew you were here. She sensed the attack coming before it happened as well."

"Weird girl." Nyu remarks.

"Indeed." Vorzech replies "We know nothing about her other than that she is looking for a 'Child of Eden', so yeah. Weird indeed."

A voice calls across the makeshift triage "Doctor Vorzech!"

She looks around "If you'll excuse me, Ceraphs." She heads off to meet the nurse who called her.

Reno opens his eyes and says groggily "What happened?"

"Reno!" Lania hugs him around the neck before regaining her composure with an embarrassed look on her face "I'm sorry, I'm just glad to see you're okay."

Reno turns his head "Shaide?"

"I'm okay." He replies weakly.

Reno looks around, taking note of his surroundings. "So, what happened? Last thing I remember is that behemoth hitting Shaide and me."

Nyu makes a sour face "Shaide saved the day, like usual. He killed the behemoth with Rho, but it seems like he weakened himself in the process. It turned out a Fallen was leading this attack, which explains why it was so organized. He turned up in person and summoned a daemon and… uhh… Amari? I kinda got knocked out. What happened next?"

Amari is red faced, a little embarrassed for some reason. "Shaide was weakened from the behemoth, and he was knocked out by the Fallen. Some guy named Regal. I don't know how I managed it, but I beat him and took him down about the time the reinforcements showed up. However, he was a sore loser, and had his daemon, some crustacean-looking thing named Cancer, kind of self-destruct, taking almost the entire fortress with it." Amari looks at the ground. "So much death… I've never seen anything so horrible…"

Shaide reaches up and rubs her back "There was nothing you could have done, Amari. Don't blame yourself."

"I know…" She says in a low voice "But I've never seen so much death before… I feel… I don't know…"

Reno's eyes open wide, shocked "What… How many died?"

Celeste speaks from above his head in a flat voice, making him jump "No idea, but out of the thousands of personnel, including our reinforcements, the number of people moving out there is less than those who aren't…"

Reno lays flat and stares at the ceiling "Oh my god…"

Over the course of the next few hours, more and more injured soldiers are brought into the makeshift triage. Before long, they have to find additional locations to treat the wounded as the mess hall is packed to capacity.

Shaide is unable to rest from the noise, so he loses himself in thought. At some point, Amari falls asleep and slumps across Shaide. In spite of his injuries, her warm weight is rather comforting. He once again finds himself wondering about his feelings for her, and whether it would really be so bad if he were to tell her…

In spite of the severe losses, Shaide finds himself feeling grateful for one very particular thing. In spite of the odds, all of his friends managed to survive the battle. They are bruised, battered, and exhausted, but they are all alive.

His thoughts stray to the men and women of Hell's Doorstep. So many lives lost, all in such a short time. He had been with the Ceraphs for around four years now, so he was accustomed to seeing death on a regular basis, but this was beyond anything he had witnessed before. Certainly it was beyond anything he had ever been a part of.

Around him he could hear the groans of pain from his fellow warriors, and he felt a pang that had nothing to do with his own injuries. He had witnessed them removing numerous soldiers who had succumbed to their injuries, and every time he felt a sense of guilt that he has survived when they did not.

At one time in his life, he was set to be a soldier of Alastair just like these men and women around him. He may very well have been stationed here when this occurred. Had he not been a Ceraph, with the aid of an Angel and the increased vitality that came with it, would he be amongst those who fell in battle today?

At some point, Shaide drifts off to sleep as well, exhaustion outweighing the sounds all around him.

*   *   *

Over the course of the next twelve hours, the face of the triage center changes somewhat. Soldiers who were not critically injured were moved to another location, and some even went back out to help look through the rubble. Countless more perished from their injuries, and many others suffered life-altering injuries such as paralysis or amputation.

The worst injuries, however, were psychological.

Many if not most of the survivors were in complete shock, or even denial over what had just occurred. Thousands of deaths before their eyes, many of them friends or close acquaintances, left a feeling of hollowness and loss in them all. Soldiers are trained to handle serious adversity, but with death on this scale, even their training could have never prepared them.

　　　　

Shaide jerks awake as someone stands over him and puts a hand on his shoulder. He opens his eyes and looks up to see the face of his godfather and aunt looking down on them, bittersweet smiles across their faces.

"Hey kid. How are you feeling?" Aton asks in a low voice.

"Dad! Lucy!" Shaide says in surprise. He slowly sits up as Amari puts a hand on his shoulder and pushes slightly to stop him. He reaches up and gently grabs her hand, removing it so he can sit up. "Really, Amari. I'm okay."

She keeps her hand in his for a moment longer before pulling it away as she watches him. His recuperative abilities are really quite amazing, but with the beating he took, even he could not recover so quickly.

"How bad is it?" Shaide asks nervously, afraid of the answer.

Aton looks down grimly "The Alastair forces have seen a total eighty five percent casualty rate, and even the Ceraph forces you brought with you saw sixty percent casualties."

Shaide lies back down and closes his eyes, feeling a pang of guilt and helplessness.

Aton seems to understand what his godson is feeling. "Shaide, this was not your fault. We are dealing with forces here that we do not understand. Even had you known what that daemon was going to do, there was nothing you could have done to stop it."

"That's exactly what I can't stand." Shaide says bitterly, eyes opening and staring at the ceiling. "All of this training, all of this power, and it is still not enough to stop something like this? What are we good for if we can't save everyone?"

Lucy kneels down and puts a hand on his head, speaking gently. "That is the nature of war, Shaide. We may not ever speak of it, but that is what this is. War. You've never really lost before, but this is what it's like. You do everything you can, but you're still just one man. At the end of the day, all you can do is what you can do. Lick your wounds, come home alive, and go on to fight another day. That is all you can really do."

Shaide frowns and looks over and asks a rather important question. "Where did you guys come from?"

Aton and Lucy exchange glances for some reason, and Aton responds "We were dealing with a situation to the east when our cruiser got the call. By the time we got it, however, it seems the fighting was over."

Shaide narrows an eye suspiciously "Do you know why we're here, then?"

Aton nods "We received a coded message from the Citadel on our way over here. Armstrong asked u to lend you our support."

Shaide nods and sits up, swinging his legs out of the cot.

"Shaide, no!" Amari says urgently, trying to push him down again "You're not ready to move yet!"

Shaide gently brushes her hand off before catching sight of someone standing nearby. The same girl from before.

She sees him sitting up and slowly walks over to him. "I'm glad to see you are okay, son of Eden."

"Oh crap!" Aton exclaims, jumping and clutching his chest. He regains his composure and speaks more calmly. "Young lady? Can we help you?"

      A.S.GUINN

She shakes her head slowly and points at Shaide "No, but he can."

Everyone present, barring Reno, watches the young woman curiously.

"You've said something similar before. Child of Eden." Shaide says slowly, wincing slightly as his ribs shift. "We're all servants of Eden, so why am I special?"

She shakes her head "No, they are servants of Eden. You are a child of Eden. Your aura feels…familiar. Comforting. Like hers."

"Like hers?" Aton asks curiously.

She nods, her eyes locked on Shaide "The one who sent me. You feel like her."

Shaide and his companions all exchange a series of befuddled glances. This girl isn't making much sense.

"Why do you need me?" Shaide asks.

She shrugs "When I awoke in that cave, I felt an aura, and a voice inside my head said to 'Bring me the child of Eden.', so I set out to find you."

"Who needs him? And why?" Amari asks, seeming rather defensive.

The girl just shakes her head "I've told you all I know. Will you come with me?"

Shaide contemplates her words for a moment before responding. "Yes. Once I am able to travel, take me to this place. I want to see what is so important."

"Shaide, maybe we should talk about this before-" Lucy begins, but Shaide interrupts her.

"I have orders from the Grand Priestess herself." Shaide says quietly "There is no debating. Whatever this is, it is so important that Eden has taken personal notice."

"I'm afraid I can't just let you leave with her." A male voice says.

Celeste looks up and jumps to her feet "General Warsaw, Sir!"

"At ease, troops. You did well." He returns her salute and surveys the party. The general appears worse for wear. He was bandaged fairly heavily and walking with a limp, but he was still walking around on his own, checking on his men.

"With respect, why not, sir?" Shaide asks, irritation creeping into his voice.

The general kneels to Shaide's level as a sign of respect for their efforts. "I have nothing but gratitude for your efforts. Without you, I have no doubt that we would all have perished here. I cannot, however, just let you leave with the only clue as to why this is happening."

Aton ad Lucy both look at Shaide with concern, afraid that he might get angry with the general. To his credit however, he remains calm and collected.

"General Warsaw, I appreciate what you are trying to say." Shaide replies quietly "However, it is my belief that if this woman stays here. We will all die anyway. That Fallen, Regal, said himself that he was looking for her. As long as she is here, the attacks will continue. If you let us take her with us, the enemy will follow, and your remaining men will have a chance of survival."

All eyes turn slowly to Warsaw, waiting to see his response. This doesn't go unnoticed, and he makes eye contact with every Ceraph and soldier present.

"With respect, General…" Nyu speaks up unexpectedly "My companion speaks the truth. I have fought the corrupted in my homeland, and I have seen their ferocity here. If she remains, you will all die, and it will accomplish nothing. If she comes with us, the we still have a chance for answers, and you have a chance to live on."

The general sighs and looks up at someone "Dr. Vorzech!"

"Sir?" The woman looks up from several rows away. She says something to a nurse before coming over to meet them. "Young lady, didn't I ask you to stay in my office?"

"Doctor, don't worry about that right now." The general says "I need your opinion on a matter."

"General?" She says in surprise.

Warsaw looks around at the Ceraphs around him and explains "These Ceraphs wish to take this young lady and let her show them what she thinks is so important. What are your thoughts on this? You've spent the most time with her, after all."

Dr Vorzech looks at the Ceraphs and back to the young lady, contemplating the situation. She finally says "Miss, are you certain that these are the people you were supposed to meet?"

She shakes her head and points at Shaide. "Not people, doctor. Him."

Vorzech lowers her head and sighs "And are you absolutely certain that this young man is the one you are supposed to see?"

She just nods without a word.

Vorzech looks up at Warsaw and states simply "There is nothing more I can do for her. If these Ceraphs or… this Ceraph… can help her find her memories, then I see no reason to keep her here. In fact, given how the enemy attacks seem connected to her, it may be best to let her go, and lead them away."

General Warsaw looks around one last time at the expectant eyes upon him, and he finally sighs and relents. "Although I am the General in charge of this base, I am no fool. I know that a good leader listens to counsel when it is given. If you all feel so strongly about this, then I will heed your advice. Ceraphs? She is in your hands now. As soon as you are well, you should depart."

Shaide nods respectfully "Thank you, General."

CHAPTER 15

DEADLANDS

"Come to me, child. Come to me." A voice whispers to Shaide. He finds himself walking out in a vast wasteland alone. The ground is cracked earth, dried and dead from centuries f desolation. The sky overhead, although it is daytime, is heavily obscured by some kind of black haze, making it appear as little more than late dusk.

Shaide seems to walk for days, or perhaps it is only minutes, as he feels compelled to continue towards an unknown destination. Eventually, a lone plateau or mountain comes into view through the haze, and what appears to be an opening of some kind lies directly in front of him.

He pauses for a moment and looks around. There seems to be nowhere else to go, so he proceeds into the opening. He examines it for a moment and finds something interesting. This fissure in the rock appears to be recent. The edges are still jagged and sharp, and the rock is not discolored like the rock outside. It can't be more than a couple decades old.

He proceeds down the passage until it opens up, and he finds himself stopping, stunned by what he sees.

The passage has opened up into what appears to be a hallway, clearly deliberately made. Strangely, the hallway seems ancient; thousands of years old or more. It is in remarkably pristine condition, but it still shows signs of age.

He looks around for the source of light dimly illuminating the passage, and he realizes the light is coming from the passage itself. The strange golden script inlaid into deepest black stone is actually glowing, giving off enough light to see his way. There is also a subtle violet glow coming from an unknown source.

Shaide shakes his head and continues down the passage. On the walls, drawings of some kind are on the stone, but the light is not bright enough to see what the depict. He continues until he reaches a great archway, and after a moment's hesitation, he proceeds further through it.

His eyes then fall upon a familiar sight of which he has been dreaming for years. A truly vast cavern, extending beyond his field of vision. A dim golden light emanating from golden decoration laid into the obsidian pillars and obsidian walls lights the cavern in much the same way as the passage behind him.

     A.S.GUINN

ETERNAL KNIGHTS OF EDEN II

His feet carry him forward of their own accord as he approaches the center of the cavern. After several minutes of walking, he reaches a familiar altar in the center of the great space. It is easily a half mile from the entrance, and in fact it could be even farther.

The statue of the horned-headed almost demonic woman stands where it always does, the stone table and altar in front of it. Unlike before when he has dreamed of this place, it is not the purple-skinned woman waiting for him, but a pale skinned, white haired young woman.

She opens her mouth to speak-

*   *   *

Shaide suddenly jerks awake. A pair of pale silver eyes are looking into his own when he opens them, and he jumps, nearly headbutting her from being startled. The unknown woman sits back as Shaide sits up, rubbing his eyes.

"Good lord, don't scare me like that."

She looks down and says simply "I'm sorry."

Shaide and the other Ceraphs are back aboard the *Last Beacon*, resting and recovering before their expedition south. He feels wide awake from the start, so he swings his legs out of his bed and sits up. He's in the ship's small med bay, resting under the eye of the ship's medic. Apparently, he isn't here at the moment.

Shaide gets to his feet and pulls an IV from his arm before looking at the young woman. He asks exasperatedly "What are you doing here? You're supposed to be in the Ceraph quarters where my companions can keep an eye on you."

She just stares at him in that blank way she does, and she replies, "I'm supposed to find you, and take you there."

Shaide sighs and looks out the viewport. It appears to still be nighttime. He figures she must have slipped away while the others were sleeping. His eyes sweep the small med-bay, and he realizes Amari isn't in here. Strange, because he usually can't get away from her. Not that he really tries.

"Hey, I'm going to go for a walk." Shaide says, getting out of bed wearing simple white garments reminiscent of scrubs. As expected, when he walks out into the hallway of the frigate, the woman walks behind him.

"You know?" Shaide thinks aloud "We still don't know what to call you." He turns around to face the young woman "Are you sure you still don't remember anything at all?"

She shakes her head without saying anything.

"Well, we have to call you something." He thinks to himself for a moment. "How about if I call you 'Mystie' for now? Kind of a play on mystery, since that's what you are."

She seems to think for a moment, and then she nods.

With that settled, Shaide turns around and continues down the passageway past a number of compartments that, admittedly, he has no idea what they are for. He has never needed to come back into this part of the ship before. He walks out into the hangar and makes his way to one of the open bay doors, where a moderate breeze blows through the large space.

He looks down at the fortress beneath them. Some time has passed since the disaster, and most of the dust has cleared from the air by now. Shaide's eyes are drawn to the destruction. It looks very different from above. This fortress, which has stood for over two thousand years, now has less than half of its structure remaining. The outer walls are crumbling, the inner structures are little more than dust, and only the command complex stand mostly intact.

Shaide feels a sickening sense, as if he should have done more to prevent such a disaster. He must get stronger, no matter the cost.

His gaze drifts to the south, where the edge of the deadlands is several miles in the distance. He can't actually SEE the deadlands in the early morning darkness, but he knows it is there.

He turns to Mystie "Hey, can you tell me something?"

She looks at him blankly but doesn't respond. He takes it as a yes.

"This place you need to take me to. Where is it?"

She walks up to the edge of the deck, and Shaide tenses up, ready to grab her if she falls. She seems to stare blankly into the distance before she slowly raises a hand, pointing at something far in the distance, due south of the fortress.

Shaide feels a sense of foreboding. "Are you telling me we're actually going into the deadlands?"

She looks blankly "Deadlands?"

"Yes. The area beyond the black haze, where everything is dead and desolate."

She looks blankly at him for a moment, and then nods slowly.

"What is down there that is so important?" Shaide inquires uneasily.

She simply shakes her head "I do not know what awaits you there. Only that she told me to bring you."

Shaide looks out across the land, considering the task before them. Going into the deadlands is essentially a suicide mission. The chances of returning alive are slim at best. The chances of coming back… intact… are even less. His gaze drifts towards the Ceraph quarters, and he makes a decision.

"Wait here, do not move. I will be back shortly." He tells Mystie. She obeys and he makes his way back to the medical bay where he finds his armor and combat gear sitting on a table outside the medic's office. He strips off his patient scrubs and changes carefully into his gear, strapping on the black chain and plates gingerly as he is still sore from the battle.

He puts his sword on his back, and he exits the med-bay, returning to the hangar to find Mystie standing where he left her. He walks over to her and looks towards the Ceraph quarters with a feeling of sadness in his heart.

He must complete this mission at any cost. Eden's priestess gave him this mission personally, and that means that although he does not understand what is happening, this woman is extremely important, and what she has to show him must be as well.

Shaide closes his eyes and says in a low voice "Amari, Dad, Lucy, Reno, Celeste, and Lania… I'm sorry… But I cannot let you needlessly throw away your lives on this. We have lost enough people here, and I could never rest if I lost you as well." His thoughts focus on Amari in particular. "I'm sorry. Goodbye."

He holds out his hand and focuses, a golden glyph appearing in front of him. From the sky, several flashes of lightning and their accompanying thunderclaps reach his ears as a familiar glowing golden eagle drops from the clouds and flares to land in the hanger bay.

Both on the ground below and in the hanger behind him, and number of gazes are drawn to the summoning of Rho.

Shaide looks at Mystie and says "Climb on his back. He won't hurt you."

Rho leans down as Shaide helps her onto his back before climbing on behind her. "Rho. Could you please take us to the edge of the deadlands, as far as you can take us? We have something important to do."

Rho squawks in a low tone before stretching his wings and launching from the hanger bay. Mystie seems remarkably unafraid of this, as if she had flown before. Either that or she was simply very brave.

As Rho streaks across the early morning sky, Shaide give the frigate one last long look as it slowly disappears into the distance.

They are flying somewhere around sixty miles per hour, no particular urgency in their flight. Shaide looks down at the land beneath him and notes the gradually thinning grass and foliage. For a half hour they streak across the southern plains, and near the end Shaide notices a gradually thickening black haze in the hair. Not long after this, Rho enters a slow downward spiral before setting down in the haze, lowering his head for them to disembark.

Shaide slides off of his back and helps Mystie down before turning to pat him on the head. "This may be the last time we see each other, old friend. You cannot help me down here, I'm afraid. If you return to the mountain before I can see you again, then I want you to know that it has been an honor to fight by your side."

Rho lets out a low, sad squawk before turning into yellow light and adding away.

Shaide sighs and turns around to face Mystie. "We're here in the deadlands. I'm afraid we have to walk from here. Do you know where to go?"

Her eyes are blank again, even more so than usual. She slowly raises a hand and points to what is presumably south.

Shaide nods "Good. Take me there."

She looks him in the eyes and nods slowly before departing on foot. Shaide draws his sword and straps on his buckler, ready for a fight at any moment, following a short distance behind her so he can watch for danger. He pulls his skull mask down across his face and sets his mind on the mission ahead.

*   *   *

The following morning, Amari wakes up at dawn. She stretches and yawns loudly before getting to her feet and summoning her clothes. In a flash of glowing blue, her daily outfit materializes. She walks out of her own bunk and looks at Shaide's empty bunk with a sour look on her face. The medic kicked her out of the med-bay last night, stating that he couldn't have her in there overnight. She tried to argue but she was unsuccessful.

Instead she is heading to the med-bay first thing this morning. She starts to head for the door and pauses, backpedaling to Shaide's bunk and looking in. That strange girl was supposed to be sleeping in here. Did she slip off again?

She pokes her head into Nyu's bunk and whispers "Nyu? Hey, Nyu?"

Nyu just grumbles and waves her off, rolling back over in her sleep.

Amari rolls her eyes and sighs. She heads out of the Ceraph quarters and walks through the hanger on her way to the aft section of the ship. The hanger is not nearly as lively as normal. Most of the shipboard crew is down in the fortress below, helping with recovery efforts. It feels unusually lonely now.

She reaches rear corridor and is confronted by the ship's medic.

"Miss Tamiel? Have you seen Shaide?" He says rather accusingly "He isn't in the med-bay where I left him, and his gear is missing."

Amari freezes, her eyes wide. "Shaide is missing?!"

One of the crewmen behind her stops and speaks up "Shaide left early this morning. I thought he told you."

Amari spins around and stares at the crewman, whom she recognizes as one of the hanger supervisors with rising panic in her chest "What did you say?"

"He left early this morning, a few hours ago." He replies, looking surprised. "He summoned his angel, and then he and that strange pale girl flew off."

Amari's eyes open wide with indignation and anger "And you didn't think to tell anyone!?"

"Ma'am, with respect, he is a Ceraph like you. It is not my place to be nosy with what he does. I assumed he had a task or mission to complete."

Amari grinds her teeth in frustration but inwardly admits he has a point. "Did you at least see which way he went?"

The crewman nods "Of course. That bird of his glows like a freakin beacon. They flew virtually due south, and as far as I could tell, they didn't change direction while they were in view."

Amari feels numb for a moment, and everything seems to go silent around her as the panic rises. Not only did he leave her behind, but he went off on his own when he was still recovering from his injuries.

The panic gets even worse when she realizes where he has gone. Rho is very bright. If he kept flying south until they were out of view, then that means...

"Are you telling me he went into the deadlands!?" She says in a high-pitched voice "Alone!?"

The crewman looks very uneasy seeing Amari in a state of panic like this. She is usually very composed. "Umm, yes ma'am. I suppose that is where he appeared to be heading."

Without another word, Amari takes off running across the hanger. She nearly crashes into the door as she flies into the 2nd Ceraph quarters, yelling at the top of her lungs "ATON! LUCY! GET UP! GET UP NOW!"

A loud thud comes from Lucy's bunk as she crashes to the floor, and Aton skids out of his own bunk looking alarmed. "Amari? What's wrong? What's happening?"

Amari dashes into her bunk and grabs her combat gear. "Shaide took the girl and left this morning! We have to go after him!"

As Amari dashes for the door, Aton yells at her "Amari, hang on! AMARI WAIT!"

Amari comes to a stop and turns around "What is it? We don't have time!"

Aton walks over and puts a hand on her shoulder "Just… Slow down for a second. Tell me what happened."

Amari tries to slow her breathing as she explains "Shaide wasn't in the med-bay, and the hanger supervisor said he saw him leave with the girl a few hours ago overnight. The got onto Rho and flew straight south, into the deadlands."

Aton's eyes open wide in shock "Why would he leave without us?"

Lucy leans against her doorframe, her eyes closed "If he went into the deadlands, then you already know why he went alone, bro."

Aton slowly nods, understanding.

Amari looks at her, not understanding "I don't it. We're supposed to do everything together. Why would he leave me- us here?"

Lucy looks at her almost with pity. "As well as you know Shaide, you already know the answer to that. He feels so much guilt over failing to stop the daemon from destroying the fortress and killing so many people, he can't stand the thought of taking the person he cares about most on what essentially amounts to a suicide mission."

"Person he cares about… most?" Amari says, a little slow on the uptake.

Aton lowers his head, looking up at her. "You, Amari. You are the single most important person in the world to him. From the time I took him from your home eight years ago, I guarantee he has thought about you and missed you every day. I believe that while he is happy to fight alongside you and save the world with you, he would give anything to keep you safe. Especially with how… unstable he is right now; I don't think he can stand the thought of taking you down there."

Amari's eyes open wide in shock and terror "So we're just going to let him go alone!?"

"No, we are not." Lucy says firmly, summoning her own armor. "The thing is, Shaide is our family, and we protect that which we care about as well."

Aton nods. "We're going."

"Where are we going?" Nyu's voice comes from the doorway. All three of them turn and look to see the Nekomata standing in the doorway, her ears flat against her head and her tail swishing in agitation. In their rush, they had almost forgotten about her sleeping across the hallway.

Aton looks up at her "Shaide left this morning with the young woman. We're going after him."

Nyu tilts her head back and sighs "It's a good thing he's hot, or I would never put up with this much crap."

"So, will you help us?" He asks.

Nyu looks at him in amusement "Of course I will. You know me. Life would be too boring without him around."

"How will we find him though?" Lucy asks uneasily.

Aton looks at Amari "You said the crewman saw him fly south, right?"

"Exactly due south, yeah."

Aton thinks "And the soldiers who found the girl said she came from due south."

"I get it." Lucy says, slamming her fist into her hand. "If we go due south as well, we should find him."

"Don't forget about me." Nyu says "As long as we can get close to his path, I can sniff him out."

Amari looks at Nyu with a bright expression, tears glistening in the corners of her eyes. Nyuralisiania, I have never been so happy to see you as I am right now."

Nyu walks over and puts a hand on her shoulder and whispers quietly "Come on, Amari. We may have our differences, but we both care a great deal for Shaide. I will do whatever it takes to help him, same as you."

Amari nods and mutters back "For once, I am glad for that." She raises her voice "So, are we going or not?"

Aton nods "Indeed. We leave as soon as we are ready."

"I'm set."

"Me too!"

Aton looks a little taken aback. He expected at least a FEW minutes. "Alright then. Off we go."

"Come on, Amari." Lucy winks at her "Let's go save your boyfriend."

She is very surprised when Amari doesn't retort like normally does, but then she sees the pink on her cheeks and realizes what's going on. The young woman's crush isn't just a crush anymore. Amidst the slight panic she herself feels, she also feels a slight touch of pride. Their young proteges are growing up

"Now's not the time for that, Lucy." Aton says exasperatedly "Come on. Let's go."

*   *   *

A short time later, the four of them are riding a dropship down to the plains below. Unfortunately, Amari is the only one of them with a flying Angel, so they have to go down and hump it on foot.

The four of them disembark the dropship and look around. They couldn't go nearly as far south in a dropship without risking a crash, so they'll have to play catch-up big time. Nevertheless, they check their compasses and head due south at a rapid pace.

"Hey! Where are you going without us?"

The quartet freezes and turns around to find Reno, Lania, and Celeste all standing there, fully geared and looking expectant.

Nyu looks amused. "Reno? What are you guys doing here?"

"We heard that Rho was seen heading south, so we thought we should follow. We ARE supposed to be helping you after all."

The four Ceraphs exchange glances "About that..."

Aton quickly and succinctly explains the situation, and all three exorcists look stunned. Reno says quietly "That prick... He seriously just left all of you behind? All of us?"

Several heads nod sadly.

Reno tightens his gear belt. "Come on, then. We have no time to lose."

Aton gives the Exorcists a very serious look. "You do understand what we are doing, right? We are going into the deadlands itself. The corruption is strong, and stronger as we go south. This is most likely a one-way trip for all of us."

Lucy nods "The corruption is going to get into our bodies. Those of us with angels have a slight resistance to it, but even we are unlikely to come out unscathed. Are you really prepared to go knowing that you are almost certainly not coming back? And even if you DO come back, you will almost certainly not be the same?"

Reno, Lania, and Celeste all quietly exchange glances. To everyone's surprise, it is the usually meek Lania that speaks up first. "Shaide is our friend. He has pulled our butts out of the fire more times than I can count. He has always been there when we really needed him. I am tired of him always being the one to help us. It's our turn to help him now. We're going."

Reno and Celeste both give Lania extremely surprised and impressed looks. The girl may look like a kid, but she has a fire in her.

Amari speaks up, her patience finally breaking "Okay, glad to have you. Now, can we please get going? The longer we stand here, the further behind we are falling!"

Six pairs of eyes turn to her, and Aton nods. "Alright Ceraphs and soldiers. Time to move. Let's go.

The party of seven heads south at a jog, determined to make up as much time as possible. Amari in particular is determined to find him at any cost.

*   *   *

Shaide kicks a charging corrupted drake in the snout before backflipping, kicking it under the chin, and then driving his sword through the bottom of its head. He channels his aura and detonates an ice bloom INSIDE, tearing the great lizard's head apart. With a great thud, the beast falls flat to the ground.

Out of breath but out of danger for now, Shaide pulls the sword and wipes the blade, turning to look for Mystie. "Hey, are you okay?"

She stands up from behind a rock and nods.

Shaide walks up to her and pats her on the shoulder. "Good. I'm kind of screwed if something happens to you, after all."

Curiously, she doesn't seem to tire. Just like her odd tendency to never sleep, her body seems quite durable as well.

Shaide waves her on "Shall we continue?"

They've been walking for two days. Trying to save as much time as possible, Shaide pushed himself to go all night without sleep or rest, but now as the sky begins to darken on the second day, he feels himself reaching his limit. His movements are beginning to become slower and more sluggish. In spite of this, he is determined to continue as long as he can.

The deadlands are true to their name. What was once supposedly a vast and enormous land lush and teeming with life is now little more than a desert. The ground is dry and cracked. What little vegetation lives is not of the beautiful variety. Red cacti, thorny brush, and the occasional patches of brown jagged grass are the only things breaking up the sand, dirt and rocks decorating the terrain.

He has, however, made some interesting discoveries in his time here. The corrupted beasts are plenty in number, as expected, but given the lack of available sustenance, Shaide is beginning to believe that the fully corrupted beasts have no real need of food. The number of creatures he has seen, and killed, has been far too disproportionate to the amount of food he has seen.

As they pass a particularly large boulder, one that protrudes fifteen feet from the ground at an angle, Mystie turns around and speaks "We should rest here for the night."

Shaide is taken aback. She doesn't appear to be tired at all. In fact, aside from being dirty, she looks just as fresh as when they left. "Are you finally getting tired?"

"No, but I can sense your fatigue." She says simply "I am supposed to bring to that place, but I cannot do that if I lose you from exhaustion."

Shaide raises his eyebrows, but he inwardly admits that she has a point. He probably won't last much longer.

"Lie down. I'll watch."

Shaide narrows an eye at the odd way she said that, but he complies. He dispels his blade and lies back on the ground, feeling a dull pain in his lower back from exhaustion. After a few minutes, however, he feels everything relax, and before long he drifts off to sleep.

*   *   *

Nyu is on the ground on all fours, sniffing the ground and the air. Reno find it slightly comical the see her acting like an animal, but then Lania catches him watching Nyu and glares at him, causing him to look down in shame.

"Well, we're catching up." Nyu says. "We're catching him slowly, but we are catching up. Actually, I think they slept here just last night."

Amari looks up at the large rock sticking out of the ground and nods. This IS the kind of place Shaide would pick to rest. They have a wall to their back and shelter overhead, so it is a viable place to rest in this hostile wasteland.

Aton looks around "To be honest, we probably need to rest soon as well. We're catching up, but we've been going for over two days without rest. Some of us-" He looks at the tired Reno and Lania "can't keep up this pace forever. We're no good to him if we drop once we find him."

Amari starts to protest, but she sees the exhaustion on Reno and Lania's faces. Even Aton, Lucy, and Celeste are showing signs of fatigue, and Nyu is breathing a little heavily. She has to admit, she is feeling some exhaustion herself.

Aton looks at her expectantly. He is slightly afraid of her reaction. She has been extremely short tempered on this trip so far, after all.

"Okay, let's rest here." She replies unexpectedly. Everyone gives her a look of shock. "What!? I'm not completely unreasonable…"

Reno averts his gaze "Well…"

     A.S.GUINN

"Reno…" Lania reproaches him.

Amari looks down, feeling a little ashamed of herself.

"It's okay, Amari." Celeste consoles her "We all know how much he means to you. He is important to all of us. We know you just want to help him as soon as possible. Don't worry about it."

Lania nods "Yeah, we get it. Trust us."

Reno glowers at them a bit, but he keeps it to himself.

Lania sits down against the rock wall and leans back. "Hey Reno, come here."

Reno walks over to her and looks confused "What's up?"

She pats her lap and whispers "Lay down."

Reno looks a little taken aback, but pleased. He unbuckles his cuirass and lies down, laying his head in her lap. She leans back but rubs his shoulders affectionately as they rest.

Amari's gaze finds them, and an unpleasant look falls across her face. Not for the reason you would expect, however. She is not angry that they are relaxing, but rather she feels somewhat jealous. Her increasing affection for Shaide has left her longing for closeness from time to time, and seeing her friends have what she doesn't makes her heart ache. She shakes her head and leans back against the rock, trying to cast it from her thoughts. With a start, she realizes that she is so accustomed to being around Shaide all the time, it just feels completely wrong for him to not be here now.

Lucy smiles slightly as she observes this little internal struggle. The woman may act like a shallow perverted hussy, but she is very attuned to people's emotions and body language, and it does not escape her notice that Amari is feeling particularly lonely now.

She would offer her company, but she is certain that Amari is only lonely for one person, and her attempts to comfort her would likely accomplish little. She goes and leans back against the rock by Amari and remains silent.

The rest of the party finds a place to rest as they try and prepare to resume their pursuit. Aton, Nyu, and Celeste are not as tired as the others, but even they need their rest, so all seven companions are soon fast asleep.

*   *   *

Shaide and Mystie are approaching the end of their journey. Shaide, for his part, is feeling an odd sense of déjà vu. The path they now walk seems disturbingly familiar to him. Like something out of a dream. Mystie picks up the pace slightly, and Shaide follows her as a massive dark shape emerges into view ahead of him. As they reach what now appears to be a large, lone plateau, Shaide freezes in his tracks.

He sees the fissure in the rock ahead of him, and he realizes this IS the place in his dreams. He slowly walks forward and touches the edge of the fissure as Mystie watches him expectantly. Indeed, the outside stone looks ancient, but the stone inside the fissure looks far younger and more recent. He turns to look at Mystie.

She nods and walks forward into the fissure. With little choice but to follow, he proceeds inside behind her.

Just as in his dream, the fissure opens into a large hallway made of black stone with glowing golden inlay. He follows Mystie further into this strange place, until the hallway opens into the enormous cavern.

Mystie leads him into the open space, the eerie silence creeping Shaide out. It is so quiet that he can hear his own heartbeat, yet his footsteps are strangely muffled.

"Mystie. Hey, Mystie!" Shaide urgently whispers to her.

She appears to be in some kind of trance, however, as she does not respond to him. She simply walks inexorably forward as if some unknown force now compelled her to continue walking.

Soon, they reach the familiar altar. Now that Shaide sees it in person, he realizes that it looks like an angel's altar, but far more ornate and detailed. He looks closely at the being depicted by the statue. She looks both beautiful and terrifying at the same time. Shaide carefully avoids getting too close to the altar, knowing that however unlikely, it would end very badly for him if he were to accidentally activate the altar in his state of exhaustion.

Curiously, the angel does not resemble any of the angels he has heard of before. He has heard of more than a few humanoid, or at least hominid, angels before, but this particular one does not ring any memories.

Mystie suddenly stands up straight, as if she is listening intently to something.

"Mystie? Is everything okay?"

She turns to look at him, a mile-long stare in her eyes. "Gaia, the Archangel of Death, greets you Shaide Darkmoon, and welcomes you home."

CHAPTER 16

GAIA

Shaide stares at the girl for a moment. "Excuse me?

She doesn't respond, and she maintains that blank stare.

"Mystie? What the hell are you talking about?"

*Clap*Clap*Clap*Clap*

The slow clapping of someone echoes across the vast chamber. Shaide spins around and feels his heart drop. An unpleasantly familiar face approaches him across the chamber, with a second unfamiliar face accompanying him.

Regal speaks out gleefully. "Never did I dream that you would lead us directly to this place. We thought that we would have to launch another assault on your decrepit base, but then we saw you leaving with her and realized we could simply let you lead us here!"

The unknown man with him seems a bit more cautious and intelligent. He observes Shaide carefully, assessing what is in front of him. "Regal, you are a fool. You talk far too much. Have I mentioned that before?"

Regal shoots him a glare "Lucien? Who are you to lecture me on talking too much? When you get started you won't shut up, even in the middle of killing someone!"

Lucien starts a deep chuckle that escalates into a terrifying and sadistic cackle. Shaide feels chills in his very bones as this second man's laugh echoes through the cavern. Not being a sensory type, Shaide cannot be sure, but he feels as if this second man, Lucien, is far more powerful than Regal. They just barely managed to drive off Regal before, so Shaide is certain if he tried to take them both, he would lose for sure.

Stalling for time as he tries to come up with a plan, Shaide cautiously asks "What is so important about this place? Why were you looking for it?"

Regal barks a single laugh "You mean you followed her here, and yet you have no idea why? That is hilarious! That's why you Ceraphs are going to lose this war. You blindly follow your orders and yet you don't even know why you are doing it!"

Shade narrows his eyes. How did they know he was here under orders? Granted, why else would he be here, but still…

"This is the chamber of an Archangel!" Regal exclaims gleefully "By taking control of this one, single altar, we destroy any chance you have of possibly destroying our lord and father, Belial!"

Shaide's blood runs cold. They must be referring to the prophecy. That would certainly explain why they could never find the Archangels. If one of them is in the deadlands, it would be hidden from them.

"Mystie, I'm sorry." Shaide mutters "I will try to hold them off, but you have to run. Get out of here. Find the others, and make sure they get a message to the Citadel. Do you understand me?"

Mystie just stands there blankly, not reacting at all. After a moment, she slowly turns around and places her hand on the table at the altar. A strange, echoing voice says "No. You will not fight the today. You are mine, child of Eden, and I will have you."

The ground begins to shake as a deep subsonic rumble rattles every bone in his body. The ground seems to lurch back and forth as both Shaide and the two Fallen drop to their knees.

Regal yells out "What is happening!?"

Lucien responds in an oddly pleased cackle "The bitch is summoning the Archangel! This is perfect!"

Shaide looks up at Mystie and bellows at the top of his voice "MYSTIE! RUN NOW!"

She doesn't hear him. Her entire body envelops in an intense violet light as a circle of interlocking violet glyphs rises around both him and her and begins spinning around them. Sensing movement, Shaide sees Lucien and Regal scramble to their feet and take off running for the edge of the chamber. Another light casts everything into a dark shadow, and the circle of glyphs expands outward rapidly. Shaide forces himself to his feet in spite of the quaking and turns to face the young woman as a column of burning light erupts into the ceiling of the cavern, and a massive explosion ensues…

*　　*　　*

The seven allied pursuers increase their pace to a jog. Less than an hour ago, Nyu detected an additional pair of scents that appeared to be pursuing Shaide and the young woman. The urgency increased as they were closing in rapidly, certain they had almost caught them.

All seven of them skid to a stop as the ground begins to quake beneath their feet, bringing all of them to their knees.

"What the hell is this?!"

Amari looks up and points at the shadow of some kind of geological formation at the edge of the haze. "It's coming from there!"

Without warning, an ultra-intense beam of violet shoots into the air, and the roof of the plateau explodes sending chunks of rock the size of capital ships hurling through the air. Amari, Aton, and Lania all react instinctively, throwing up kinetic magical barriers to shield them from debris as chunks of rock slam into the ground all around them.

As the largest chunks subside, Amari drops her barrier. "Come on! We have to get in there!"

Reno scrambles to his feet and takes Lania by the hand "What's going on!"

"That's an Angel summoning! Not one I've ever seen before, either!" Aton yells!

The seven of them sprint and weave through the falling debris, heading for a large fissure that opens in front of them. Amari looks up and notices the strange violet glyphs blinking randomly in the sky, and bolts of purple lightning arc in the storm clouds forming

A.S.GUINN　　　　　　373

rapidly overhead. She shakes her head clear and sprints headlong into the cavern…

*   *   *

Shaide ducks as the cavern ceiling explodes above him. He watches in shock as enormous chunks of rock fly away, and violent swirling storm clouds whirl overhead. Purple lightning arcs across the sky as the column of light burns through the clouds, causing a small rift in the center as the storm swirls around it. Shaide watches for the angel from above, but then his gaze is drawn to what WAS Mystie.

The light that is now her body begins to change form. The petite young woman who stood there grows to over six feet in height, and wings seems to sprout from her back as spiral hors grow from her head, and a long, thick tail grows from her backside. Shaide watches in horror as she settles to the ground, and the light fades.

Standing in front of him is the very being from his nightmares. A feminine figure, standing even taller than him, with black feathered wings, violet skin with the same glyphs as the sky burned into her skin, black curled horns growing from her skull, and that long dragon-like tail. Her body is sheathed in black armor that he is almost certain is dragon-skin, and then there are her eyes… Those yellow, glowing eyes.

Something is wrong with her appearance, however. Her features are distorted, as if someone had sculpted her, but was not particularly skilled with details.

In fact, she looks corrupted.

ETERNAL KNIGHTS OF EDEN II

Shaide raises his buckler and sword in front of him, ready for what is likely to be the last fight of his life. "Why have you brought me here?"

Gaia looks down at him, hovering a foot from the ground, her armored boots pointing at the ground. She speaks in a deep voice that matches the distortion of her appearance as she says "Welcome home, child of Eden. I was so distraught when I found you had been taken, but I knew you would return to me someday… Now come. Greet me in the traditional fashion of the angels, and I shall make sure you never leave me again!"

Seven swords made entirely of violet light form a vertical circle around her as she lunges forward at Shaide. Shaide reacts by backflipping and deftly deflecting the blades whirling through the air as she directs them at him without touching them.

Shaide tries to counter by lunging at her, but he is thrown backwards as the blades of light seem to teleport in front of her and repel his attack. Shaide, still weakened from the recent battle at Hell's Doorstep, has the wind knocked from him as he hits the ground hard, flat on his back. His eyes stare into the sky for a moment before catching movement. He quickly rolls to the side as seven blades of light bury themselves in the ground where he was just a split second before.

With no time to rest, Shaide throws himself to his feet and attempts to channel his spirit. When he goes to hurl arcs of lightning at Gaia, however, his sword sparks weakly and the energy fizzles out.

With a sinking feeling he realizes that the deep corruption of the deadlands has invaded his body and is now suppressing his ability to wield his spirit.

With his physical body weakened, and his spiritual ability suppressed, Shaide drops to a knee and closes his eyes. He has failed. He spends his last moments thinking about those he left behind, and he pictures Amari in his mind to say goodbye to her one last time.

"SHAIDE GOD DAMNIT! GET UP AND FIGHT!"

Shaide's eyes snap open and he spins his head around to see seven of his friends sprinting up to the barrier.

"We have company!" Lucien cackles "It seems we will get to have some fun after all!"

Shaide suddenly feels a renewed sense of vigor as his friends sprint in to help him, even if they are trapped outside of the barrier. He feels a strange sense, as if his spiritual and physical energy are both recharging themselves. He can't let them fight those Fallen alone, so he has to finish this fight quickly, at any cost.

Shaide sees movement and raises his buckler and sword in time to stop seven bladed of light from smashing down on him. He grits his teeth and leers at Gaia. "I'm afraid I can't let you have me just yet!"

With an unexpected surge of strength, Shaide throws the swords clear and lashes out with a powerful straight kick, hitting Gaia in the gut and cracking her armor beneath him.

When he makes contact, he feels a strange feeling. It's as if some of her power surged into him when he made contact. He brings his sword around and hits the armor again, and this time a powerful blast of lightning slams into her, sending her back a few feet. Shaide licks his lips and rushes forward again, feeling for a moment that he just might be able to do this…

BOOOM!

A bright flash of purple light explodes and Shaide feels as if a helicar hits him, hurling him several hundred feet across the cavern. He slams into the ground hard as he skids and spins uncontrollably across the ground.

Outside of the barrier, Amari cartwheels and narrowly dodges a blast of fire. She hurls a volley of ice shards at one of the Fallen before screaming at him "SHAIDE GET UP! YOU CAN'T DIE HERE! GET UP NOW!"

The sound of her voice invigorates him once again, and he climbs to his feet just in time to see Gaia's next attack. Multiple orbs of violet light form in the air around her, and Shaide feels a sense of foreboding. He takes off at a dead sprint as the orbs suddenly flare, and then burning beams of pure energy strike the ground here he stood. The beams intensify and follow him as he runs with all of his power, and new beams strike the ground ahead of him, forcing him to leap and weave through them. White-molten rock sprays the air where the beams strike, and pools of lava remain everywhere the beams strike.

Shaide is certain that a single hit means death.

As this though crosses his mind, a different beam strikes the ground, directly in front of him. The concussive overpressure blast throws him a hundred feet into the air as he hears a scream beneath him. He is certain that he feels his internal organs rupturing from the impact as he arcs back towards the ground.

In spite of the pain he feels, he manages to detonate a blast of fire beside him, flattening his trajectory so he hits the ground at an angle. In spite of this, he still hits the ground with enough force to fracture the rock, and he yelps in pain as he is certain his left shoulder is dislocated.

He tumbles across the ground and comes to a stop, his ragged breath shaking as he cries out in pain. He sees a purple glyph glowing above him as Gaia prepares to burn him to ash, and a single thought crosses his mind.

Amari! I cannot die here. Not now.

With the most effort Shaide has ever exerted in his life, Shaide roars aloud and channels his lightning magic through his own body, throwing himself clear with all of his might as the ground explodes where he lay a moment before.

Shaide kids across the ground and miraculously manages to end up on his feet. His gaze falls upon the corrupted Gaia as she streaks across the cavern towards him.

This has to be the single most powerful Angel I have ever laid my eyes on. If this is truly an Archangel, then I have to beat her at absolutely any cost. With her on our side, we could actually turn the tide against these damn corrupted. But, how do you beat something this powerful?

In spite of his battered and broken body, Shaide forces himself into a fighting stance to meet the oncoming Gaia, but something distracts him, directly in his field of view just outside of the barrier a mere hundred feet away.

Aton duels Regal sword-to-sword as Lucien blasts Amari away from him. Aton knocks Regal's sword from his hand and kicks him in the face, sending him flat on his back. Aton stands over him and raises his sword as Shaide tries to call out a warning to what comes from behind him…

"DAD LOOK OUT!"

Time seems to slow to a crawl as Shaide watches in horror as Lucien drives two swords through his godfather's back. Even from this distance, Shaide can see his eyes bulge in shock as the jagged blades sink hilt deep into him. The blood seems to hang in the air as Lucien kicks Aton in the back, dislodging the blades from him as he hits the ground, motionless.

A feeling of overwhelming rage blinds him. All sense goes out the window as a sudden massive surge of energy wells up inside him.

"NOOOOOO!"

As Gaia's blades of energy make contact with Shaide, a tremendous surge of energy equal to her own explodes from him, throwing the overwhelmingly powerful Archangel away from him as if she were a mere ragdoll.

*   *   *

The fight between the Fallen and the allies is intense. Aton, Reno, and Lania duel Regal while Amari, Lucy, Celeste, and Nyu all battle with Lucien.

A.S.GUINN

The two Fallen duck and dodge their attacks with inhuman speed, augmented by their corruption. Meanwhile the Ceraphs and soldiers do their best to overpower their enemy as Shaide's battle with the Archangel rages on in the middle of the cavern.

Reno cries out in pain suddenly as Regal lands a glancing slash on his cheek.

"Reno!" Lania cries out.

Regal lunges past Aton and hits Reno in the head with the pommel of his sword, sending him to the ground motionless.

Lania screams and hits him with a blast of pure lightning, causing him to retreat backwards.

Lucien meanwhile ducks under Celeste's halberd and strikes the ground beneath her, launching her into the ceiling of the hallway, she hits the ground flat on her bag and struggles to move.

Nyu lunges in with her twin daggers, abandoning her partisan in favor of the quicker weapons. She moves in low, slashing rapidly until Lucien catches her blades in the jagged edge of his own twin swords. He grins and cackles maniacally as he strikes her in the face with his armored knee, and then kicks her in the face a second time, sending her flying unconscious across the hallway.

Lucy lunges forward with her longsword as Amari acrobatically duels him with her staff. Lucien, however, seems to just be playing with them, as he smiles and makes exaggerated expressions while effortlessly blocking and dodging their attacks.

Regal aims a blast of fire at Aton, but as Aton braces himself, Regal changes its trajectory mid-flight, making it strike Lania instead.

ETERNAL KNIGHTS OF EDEN II

Lania manages a barrier just in time, but the blast still knocks her headfirst into the wall, sending her slumping to the floor, unconscious.

"Lania! Kid!" Lucy yells, distracted. Lucien kicks her straight to the gut, knocking the wind out of her and sending her to the ground.0

Amari resumes dueling with Lucien with all of her might, Aton and herself being the only two still standing. This Lucien, this Fallen… He is not normal. He is far too powerful. She finds an opening to hit him, but then the air explodes in front of her, knocking her down and knocking the breath out of her as well.

She looks up in horror, expecting him to finish her off, but Lucien instead spins around and lunges at Aton. She tries to cry a warning, but she cannot breathe. She hears a familiar voice scream as Lucien drives twin jagged blades into Aton's back, and then a second scream… She had never heard such a horrible sound come from Shaide before as he watches his godfather fall before his eyes.

A sudden overpressure wave hits them all, coming from within the barrier. Lucien is blown clean off of his feet, and even Amari slides along the ground a little on her back as she shields her eyes and turns her gaze to Shaide. What she sees is beyond terrifying.

Shaide is glowing, enveloped by a series of golden glyphs that look alarmingly like Rho's summoning glyphs. Pure white energy is swirling on the ground around him, carving out the rock beneath his feet as every bit of exposed flesh glows white as well.

His foe, Gaia, floats back to her feet and seems completely dumbfounded herself as the glowing white light envelops Shaide's entire being and begins to take another form.

Amari watches in shock as wings of light grow from his back, and his body seems to bulk and increase slightly in size. In the confusion, Lucien grabs Regal and retreats to the entrance of the cavern as Amari is powerless to stop them.

Amari has to close her eyes as the light from Shaide becomes blinding, and then fades. When she opens her eyes, she cannot believe what they see.

Where Shaide once stood is a glowing white being that looks like a semi-hominid dragon of purest white. The leathery wings are pristine and more elegant than one would expect, and he slender white tail looks both beautiful and terrible at the same time. Amari thought that Shaide was summoning Rho's power, but this… This is something else.

Shaide rockets forward with inhuman speed as he reengages Gaia. As she counterattacks, her violet swords slash violently at Shaide, but they are deflected by some kind of light barrier that pops into existence where they strike. Shaide's sword is now glowing white and larger in size, and he strikes Gaia with several impossibly fast heavy slashes, causing purple energy to fountain where he hits.

Gaia retaliates with a blast of violet energy so powerful that Amari feels it from even this far away. Shaide is thrown backwards and skids along the ground directly towards her, and she braces herself as he skids to a stop just inside the barrier. He doesn't immediately move, and Amari fears the worst. She can see his white scaly exterior cracked from the force of that blast.

She summons all of her will and cries out "Shaide! You have to get up! You have to fight!"

     A.S.GUINN

Shaide twitches as her voice reaches him. Gaia rockets at him, violet blades spinning in the air for a finishing attack.

In a flash, Shaide jumps to his feet and dives INSIDE OF the blades attack radius, making Gaia overshoot as his clawed hand find's her throat and clamps down. He leaps into the air, rocketing straight upward as Gaia flails, not expecting this level of power.

Shaide carries her a thousand feet into the air, and then glows with a blinding energy before rocketing straight down. A sonic boom erupts just before impact as he breaks supersonic, and then the world seems to explode as he drives Gaia into the ground at over seven-hundred-and-fifty miles per hour. The energy he had collected in the jump explodes outward with searing intensity, and Amari clamps her eyes shut as the intensity of the blast sears her flesh slightly.

As the dust settles, Amari peers through her singes fingers and sees Shaide standing over something in a large crater, pinning it to the ground. Suddenly, a purple foot kicks upward, knocking Shaide away from her, and Gaia flips out of the impact point, landing on her feet.

No way! Amari thinks in shock. *How could ANYTHING survive that.*

Gaia's blades form a vertical circle in front of her and begin spinning like a wheel. An ultra-intense ball of pure spiritual energy forms inside of the circle, rapidly intensifying as a supersonic scream fills the air.

Opposite of her, the dragon-like Shaide forms a ball of pure white energy in front of him, spinning and compressing it in a similar manner to Gaia.

Amari realizes this is the deciding moment in the fight, and with all of her remaining energy and will, she summons a barrier to cover her and her friends.

Just as she puts her barrier up, Shaide hurls himself across the cavern and slams his energy sphere into Gaia's. Amari closes her eyes as the world resolves into deafening roar and blinding light.

Amari cries in exertion as her barrier flares, struggling to absorb the shockwave even from this far away, until just moments later (that feels like a lifetime to her) The blast wave subsides, and her raised arm collapses. She opens her eyes to see what happened, and sees in horror as a purple figure is still standing while Shaide appears to be on his knees.

Amari has no power or energy remaining, and she watches in horror as Gaia slowly drifts over to Shaide.

*   *   *

Shaide's blinding rage seems to subside as he struggles to even move. He is on his knees, and he feels…different. As if he isn't quite in his own body. His senses seem impossibly sharp as he can feel everything around him.

He also feels as if his entire body is broken.

He looks up and sees Gaia approaching him. He tenses up, but he is unable to move. He just watches as she approaches and comes to a stop in front of him. He looks up at her defiantly as she just floats there. Then she does something completely unexpected.

She smiles gently and extends a hand to him.

He looks up and notices that she seems different somehow. Her features aren't distorted anymore, and she looks somehow less

A.S.GUINN

scary. Shaide wonders, did he somehow purge the corruption from her?

She nods at her extended hand, indicating he should take it. As he reaches up and places his hand on her, she says in a much softer voice than before "Welcome back, son of Eden. And… Thank you."

Shaide's entire body feels as if being electrocuted as Gaia's essence surges into him. He feels every single nerve and spiritual fiber in his body burning as more energy than he has ever felt in his life surges into him at once.

He screams in earnest as pain far greater than anything he has ever felt wracks his body, feeling as if his very atoms were on fire. For a few seconds that feel like an eternity, Gaia and an unknown power merge with Shaide, becoming a part of his being forever.

And then it is over.

Without realizing it, Shaide had reverted back to his human state. He slowly climbs to his feet and begins limping over to where Aton lay on the ground. Amari sits up and crawls over to meet him as Shaide takes the last few steps at a run, and drops to his knees beside his godfather.

"Dad! Dad, no!" Shaide gently rolls Aton over to see his eyes on him.

Aton coughs and smiles gently "You did good, kid…"

Nearby, Lucy struggles to her feet, blood pouring from a wound on her head. She limps over to them and whisper "Aton… Bro, no…"

Aton shakes his head weakly as his sister, godson, and Amari look over him in shock, not sure what to do.

"It's okay Lucy, Shaide…" He whispers, barely able to make a sound. "It's okay…"

Tears run from Shaide's eyes as he cries weakly "Dad… No…"

He reaches up a hand to touch his godson's face, a weak smile on his own "It's okay, Shaide… Thank you… for…"

His eyes lose focus as he falls limp, is hand falling from his godson's face.

"DAD NO!" Shaide cries out again.

Lucy's head drops as she cries silently. Amari scoots over next to Shaide and manages to put her arms around his neck and pull his head to her shoulder. He puts his own arms around her as he cries.

"It's okay, Shaide, let it out." She says, tears running from her own eyes. "Come on, let it out. I'm here, Shaide. I'm here."

Lucy lays across her brother's lifeless body as the only sounds remaining in the cavern are the sounds of sobbing.

Reno, Celeste, Lania, and Nyu all lie scattered about, unconscious but relatively unharmed. Amari lays Shaide's head on her chest as she comforts him, her grief at Aton's death mingled with a great feeling of relief that Shaide survived his battle.

Her gaze falls upon the battlefield left behind by Shaide…

The center of the cavern inside of where the barrier stood is completely destroyed. The floor is nothing but a crater of rock and glass. She is certain That this cavern was flat when they arrived, but now it is unrecognizable. She feels a sense of disbelief mingled with her other feelings. What in the hell IS Shaide?

*　　*　　*

Reno rubs his head as someone seems to be touching him. He gingerly opens his eyes and sees Lania bandaging his various wounds. She has a number of bandages as well, but she seems okay.

"Hey, how are you feeling?" He asks her.

Lania looks up at him, but there is no smile on her face. She seems… Sad.

"What happened?" He asks her cautiously.

She turns and points gingerly over her shoulder, wincing slightly "Aton…"

Reno's gaze slowly rises, and what he sees horrifies him. Some distance away, Shaide, Amari, and Lucy are all sitting on the ground, and Shaide's head is lying on Amari's shoulder. On the ground in front of them lies Aton, covered in blood and unmoving.

Reno breathes "It can't be…"

Lania nods and whispers, dabbing a cut on Reno's face "That other Fallen, Lucien killed him. Shaide went berserk and apparently destroyed the angel after that, but it was too late. They couldn't help him."

Reno looks up in horror. He had come to see Aton as this invincible hero. Shaide had always gone on about his godfather as this immortal superhero. To see it end like this…

"Shaide?" Reno asks gingerly

Lania shakes her head "He hasn't said a word since I woke up."

Reno's gaze pans across the cavern and he sees Celeste leaning back on the ground, one knee raised as she looks on, her expression unreadable. Nyu is sitting cross-legged near Shaide, looking unsure of what to do or say.

"I'd give them some time." Lania says quietly as she finishes tending Reno's wounds. She sets her pack aside and lays her head across his lap and scooting closer to him, catching him by surprise. Nevertheless, he strokes her hair and tries to process what happened. What the hell happened after he was knocked out?

Shaide slowly gets to his feet.

"Shaide?" Amari says quietly.

He looks down at his godfather and says in a dull, flat voice "We should get back to the fortress before…"

His eyes sudden lose focus, and he begins to fall forward. Amari springs to her feet and catches him. "Shaide? Shaide!" Her head darts around frantically as Lucy jumps to her feet too. "LANIA, HELP!"

Lania springs up off of Reno's lap and runs over. Reno, Nyu, and Celeste slowly get to their feet, looking extremely concerned as well.

Amari and Lucy ease Shaide to the ground, and Amari cries out "Shaide! Shaide, what's wrong!"

Lania checks Shaide over, but she can't find any major wounds. She turns on her sensory magic and observes his aura, and her eyes go wide as dinner plates with shock.

Amari grabs her shoulder and shakes her, panicking. "What's wrong with him? Lania! What's wrong!?"

Lania is stunned for a moment. She has never actually seen this in person before. "His… His aura is almost at absolute zero. I can't believe he maintained consciousness as long as he did."

Lucy looks at her, fear spreading across her face "Absolute Zero? But if you hit Absolute Zero…"

"ALMOST zero." Lania corrects her "He must have used nearly everything he had in the fight with that Archangel. He probably only stayed awake as long as he did from adrenaline."

Amari holds Shaide's head in her lap as she looks up "Will he be okay?"

"We should get him back to the fortress." Lania shrugs "He needs rest."

Lucy sighs, feeling some relief that at least Shaide will be okay.

Lania frowns and continues "We need to get out of here as soon as possible. The less time we spend in the corruption the better. I'm worried it might hinder aura regeneration too."

Lucy looks around, clutching her ribs "That's all good and well, Lania, but I don't know if we will be ABLE to make the journey anytime soon."

Amari looks at Shaide, unconscious in her lap "I can't take everyone, but I COULD try and summon Theta, and fly Shaide back to the *Beacon*."

Reno looks around "Hey…Wait a minute."

All conscious gazes turn to him.

"Where is the girl? The one who led Shaide here?"

Everyone looks around, looking for any sign of her. The only person who would know is unconscious at the moment.

"I think she's gone." Lucy says quietly "I wonder if that Angel… well, anyway. I'm more concerned about us than I am about her right now. We've sacrificed enough for her."

Nyu looks at her in shock, finally speaking up. "Lucy? I've never heard you talk like that before…"

Lucy looks down at her brother, and then at Shaide. "No, maybe not, but I've had enough of this. Let's just get out of here."

Amari focuses hard, straining her dwindling aura reserves. Miraculously, a moment later the summoning glyph for theta appears, and the phoenix streaks down from the sky to land in front of them.

Amari reaches up and strokes him. "I'm sorry, I know this place is hell for you, but I need your help."

Theta squawks softly and bows his head. They strap Shaide and Aton to Theta's back, and Amari climbs on with them. "I'll get them back safely. Don't take too long." She tells her friends. After a running start, Theta manages to get airborne, and carries his passengers north.

The five remaining watch wistfully for a moment, before Reno finally speaks up and says, "We should be going too."

The five of them quietly walk down the long hallway and through the open passageway which they find mercifully intact in spite of the excitement. A time later, they emerge back into the open air, and begin making their way north.

CHAPTER 17

SALT ON THE WOUND

Amari rides on the back of Theta across the Deadlands streaking back towards Hell's Doorstep. She is exhausting a great deal of effort maintaining her connection with Theta over the Deadlands, as the corruption rising from the land strains her spiritual connection. Nevertheless, her determination prevails, and before long she can see the edge of the Deadlands where Alastair begins.

She looks down below at the hellish terrain and takes it all in. Although heavily obscured by the infectious haze, she can see the desolation. The land is flat, dead, and cracked as far as the eye can see except for a single large lake that is surprisingly full of water. In spite of her stress with an injured Shaide and a fallen Aton riding with her, she can't help but appreciate the eerie beauty of the land.

She turns and looks at Shaide with a soft expression on her face. He is truly an amazing man. His determination is greater than anyone she had ever met before. She puts a hand on his forehead with a slight smile.

"Mmm… Amari…" He mumbles groggily.

Amari starts slightly, not expecting him to react to her. She smiles again and watches him for a moment.

Then a memory crosses her mind: Shaide transforming into that strange white hominid dragon. The sheer amount of power coming off of him was so great that it was emitting a visible aura around him. When he transformed, he became powerful enough to take on that violet angel as if he was her equal. What exactly IS he? That power wasn't human or Miteran…

As Theta starts to descend, Amari turns to face forward and immediately realizes something is very, very wrong.

The warships that so recently dotted the sky are now smoldering wrecks on the ground, and the fortress of Hell's Doorstep is nothing but dust and ash. As Theta enters a slow descending spiral, Amari looks around for any sign of life, but there is no movement whatsoever.

As she gets lower to the ground, she notices something strange. Some of the warships crashed on the ground aren't of a design she has ever seen before. They are deep black in color, their hulls made of sharp angles and heavy metal not found in any Alastair, Eritan, or Dorim warship in her memory. What the hell happened here?

ETERNAL KNIGHTS OF EDEN II

With a start, she sees a familiar design and feels a pit deep in her stomach. The hull of a frigate that appears to be of Ceraph design. She has Theta circle closer to the vessel and her heart plummets.

A single intact panel reads: COV *Last Beacon.* Their own warship has been destroyed.

She steers Theta towards the ruins of the base and comes in for a soft landing. Her energy nearly expended, she slides off of Theta's back just before he squawks and disappears in a flash of light.

Shaide and Aton hit the ground with a slight thud as their ride disappears, and Amari drops to her knees from exhaustion. She breathes heavily for a few minutes as she tries to recover herself enough to move. Once she catches her breath, she crawls over to Shaide's side to check on him.

He is still breathing, but his aura doesn't seem to have recovered at all. She forces herself to her feet and looks around for any sign of movement, but there is nothing. The fortress has been completely destroyed and, curiously, there are no people in sight, living or dead. She limps to the command building where they had been keeping the wounded, but then she realizes it has been crushed beneath a cruiser-sized vessel of that unfamiliar design.

She feels despair set into the depths of her soul as she realizes that there must be no one left alive. She limps back to where Shaide lies on the ground and sits down with him, a sense of panic setting in as she has no idea what to do or how to help him.

Fatigue overwhelms her, and she feels dizzy as she lays Shaide's head in her lap, before she lies back and passes out.

*   *   *

Some hours later, Amari regains consciousness. The sky is dark overhead, and the air is cooler than before. She looks at the sky for a moment feeling disoriented before she feels the warm weight in her lap. She sits up and sees Shaide, still unconscious, and remembers what had transpired.

Thunder echoes across the land, and Amari sees lightning flash in the distance. It appears that a thunderstorm is coming in. She looks towards the crushed command center and makes a decision. She pushes herself to her feet and with a grunt, she picks Shaide up in her arms. She struggles, as Shaide weighs nearly two hundred pounds, but she is determined to get him shelter from the incoming rain.

She slowly struggles across the ruined fortress until she reaches the building itself. Upon closer inspection, the first floor appears to be intact, although the upper floors have been destroyed by the weight of the fallen vessel. She carries Shaide inside and finds, thankfully, that the cots and stretchers remain in place. What disturbs her is the complete lack of anyone, alive or dead, anywhere to be found.

She sets Shaide down a cot and drops to her knees, exhausted from carrying him this far. Her work is not done yet, however, and she makes a second trip to drag Aton's body into the building as well. After both round trips, she leans back against Shaide's cot and closes her eyes to catch her breath.

Once she recovers, she gets back to her feet and heads for the actual infirmary from where she saw Dr. Vorzech frequenting during the battle's aftermath. Once again, she is deeply disturbed by the complete and total lack of any human presence. She finds a key lying on the doctor's desk and uses it to unlock a medicine cabinet. She searches through the stocks looking for certain medicines that she knew from her schooling in Erita would help the body regenerate spiritual energy. She was pleased to find a significant amount of said medicine in stock, and hurries back to Shaide's side.

She carefully puts an appropriate dose in his mouth and tips some water down his throat, massaging his throat to encourage him to swallow. Once he does, she sits down on the bunk next to his and just stares, at a complete loss for what to do next. She was desperately hoping to find help for him when she arrived here, but finding the complete destruction of the base, she is now on her own, and she has no idea what to do.

Curiously, even though she knows that the decimated fleet outside and the complete absence of all life is extremely alarming, she finds herself unable to worry about anything but Shaide's well-being. She shakes her head and puts her hands on him, channeling what aura she can spare to him.

*   *   *

Several days later, Celeste, Lania, Reno, Lucy, and Nyu all limp out of the deadlands into the clear air of Alastair. Nyu feels a sense of relief when they cross the border, and she stretches her arms with a wide yawn.

Lania too is especially relieved when the exit the corruption into the clearer air of Alastair. As a natural sensory type, the oppressive corruption weighs heavily on her senses, and the clear air is particularly relieving for her.

Reno walks up beside her and asks, "Hey, are you okay?"

Lania looks up at him affectionately with her wide brown eyes and replies "Yeah, I feel a lot better now that we are free of that hell."

Lucy has not said a single word since leaving the cavern. She looks straight forward as she continues towards the fort, not paying any attention to what transpires around her.

They have all recovered somewhat from their beating in the cavern, but their movements are still somewhat slow and sluggish. They did not rush their return, taking their time to traverse the deadlands drawing as little attention as possible. As a result, over five days have elapsed since the events of Gaia's Sanctum. For the next several hours they continue walking north towards the fort, but after some time, Lania begins to feel troubled.

"What's wrong?" Reno asks her, noticing the troubled look on her face.

She looks around slowly, her eyes lit up green as she uses her scanning magic. "Reno, something is wrong."

Celeste walks closer "What do you mean?"

"The aura here is cold. Dead." She says, looking into the distance towards where the fort should soon come into sight. "It feels like… Something terrible has happened."

Nyu frowns "Well, there WAS a massive catastrophic battle recently, to be fair."

"No, worse than that." Lania says, shaking her head. "There was life in the air after that, even though so many had died. I'm not sensing ANY life energy at all, though. I should be able to sense it by now."

ETERNAL KNIGHTS OF EDEN II

Celeste and Reno exchange troubled looks, and the former says "Try not to worry too much, Lania. This place has been, well, pure hell for a while now. I wouldn't be surprised if everything felt off."

"You think so?" Lania asks skeptically. "Then where are all the warships?"

All five sets of eyes look north, and everyone's eyes open wide. They SHOULD be able to see the fleet by now.

Less than an hour later, their fears are confirmed as the hull of a destroyed Alastair destroyer comes into view. They all exchange glances, and the rush to the top of the hill obscuring their view.

When they reach the top, they all are frozen stiff in shock. The landscape in front of them is dotted with the hulls of dozens of destroyed warships, and not a single ship can be seen in the air.

Reno's eyes are drawn to a ship near their position. "What is THAT?"

Lucy walks up next to him and follows his gaze to the black, angular warship about the size of a destroyer. She stares for a moment, and then speaks for the first time in days. Her voice is scratchy and hoarse as she says "That warship does not belong to Alastair OR the Ceraph Order, nor does it belong to Dorim, Pandora, or Erita. That warship is…something else."

"What the hell happened here?" Celeste asks in shock, walking up with an expression appropriate to being hit over the head with something heavy.

Nyu raises a finger and points at a crashed frigate with a familiar design "I… think that was our warship. The *Last Beacon*."

The five of them cautiously make their way through the battlefield towards the destroyed fortress. The complete and utter silence is nerve-wracking. The only sound is the occasional whistle of the wind, the crackle of still-burning debris, and their own footsteps.

"Lania, do you see anyone?" Reno asks timidly

She pours her magical power into her sensory magic, cranking it up to its highest level. She carefully pans across the battlefield before shaking her head. "No. No survivors. Curiously, I don't detect any sign on bodies either. It's like they're all just… gone."

"Let's just head for the fortress." Celeste suggests, "We should be able to meet up with Amari and Shaide there. Perhaps any survivors are holed up there."

Reno still feels nervous. SOMETHING is wrong here. He turns to Nyu "Hey, Nyu? Can YOU detect anyone out there?"

Everyone watches as Nyu carefully sniffs the air. Her eyes open wide as she slowly meets Reno's gaze and shakes her head. "That's strange. There are no scents out there at all, aside from our own. Lania's right. It's like everyone is just gone."

Without any leads, the party continues onward to the fort. Within the hour, they are crossing the outer debris wall and heading for the command center; the only structure still remotely intact, aside from the unknown warship sitting on top of it.

Nyu sniffs the air. "They're inside."

"Good." Reno says with relief.

The party of five proceeds into the command center and meets with shock once again. A week ago, this room was packed with casualties. Now, however, there are still cots everywhere, but the wounded are all gone.

"This is getting beyond weird." Celeste mutters uncomfortably.

They carefully work their way towards the infirmary and ease open the door. Inside, they find Amari sitting beside a bed holding Shaide, a fluid IV running to his arm. She appears to be sleeping.

Nyu holds out an arm to stop the others and eases over to Amari.

She whispers gently "Hey, wake up."

Nyu ducks fast as Amari yells out and swings at her. "WHOA HEY! SAME TEAM! SAME TEAM!"

Amari stares at her in shock, breathing heavily from sudden adrenaline. After a moment she catches her breath and asks, "When did you all get here?!"

Nyu puts a hand on her shoulder and smiles. "We just got here."

Lucy walks over and kneels beside Shaide, looking concerned. Reno, Celeste, and Lania all gather around as well now that Amari is awake.

"So, how is Shaide doing?" Lucy asks quietly, her voice a little hoarse from lack of use over the past few days.

Amari shakes her head, looking at him with concern. "I was hoping you could tell me. He just won't wake up, and it feels like his aura is barely flickering,"

The others look at Lania, and she activates her sensory skills yet again. Her eyes widen in surprise as a troubled look crosses her face.

"What is it?" Amari asks, looking concerned at her reaction.

Lania shakes her head, eyes locked on Shaide. "His aura hasn't recovered at all since the cavern. In addition, he's showing early signs of corruption everywhere. Nothing drastic, but it's there."

"Corruption?" Amari repeats slowly, a horrified look on her face.

Lucy explains quietly, making them jump. "Our spiritual force, our aura, allows us to resist the corruption for a time. The stronger our aura, the stronger our resistance. The weaker our aura, the less resistant. His spiritual energy has been so low for days, it must have seeped in and infected him."

"Could it be preventing him from recovering?" Reno asks with concern.

Lucy nods, staring at her brother's godson. "It is possible."

"What do we do?" Amari asks, slight panic in her voice.

Lucy shakes her head "You know most of what I do, Amari. There is nothing we can do. Either his body with purge the corruption on his own, or it won't. All we can do is wait."

The room sits in silence for a few minutes as everyone contemplates Lucy's words. Given what Shaide accomplished back in the cavern, he is the strongest of the group with Aton gone. Unfortunately, he is also out of commission.

"Not to sound like I'm not concerned about Shaide, but, what about us?" Celeste asks nervously. "Are we infected with corruption? We were out there for a long time."

Lania carefully looks everyone over and shrugs "Everyone here, except Amari for some reason, shows traces of corruption in our bodies, but it's minimal. It should straighten itself out with time."

Celeste lets out a sigh of relief, and even Reno admits to himself he shared her concern. He just didn't want to say anything.

Nyu asks the question burning at the back of everyone's minds. "So, what the hell happened here? Where the hell did everyone go?"

Amari snaps out of her reverie and responds "I have absolutely no idea, I'm sorry. Everything was like this when I got here."

Reno's gaze lingers on his best friend for a few moments before he clears his throat and straightens up. "We need to start working on getting back north. Staying here won't do any good. Does anyone have any ideas?"

The room is silent again for a good moment before Lania makes a suggestion. "It's possible that there is an intact dropship in the fort somewhere."

"No, I already looked." Amari replies, "The hanger was smashed by that weird warship above us. Nothing intact in there."

Celeste looks out the window, somehow miraculously intact. "Maybe onboard one of those crashed ships? I find it hard to believe that with the sheer number of crashed ships that there wouldn't be at least ONE intact gunship or dropship."

"Good suggestion." Reno says, impressed by her cool headedness. "Everyone should get some rest, and then we can start scouring the wreckage for anything we can use. If we're lucky, we might find a ride."

Lania mumbles "Hey, Reno? That's a brilliant idea but… Can anyone here fly a dropship?"

"Shaide could." Amari says dejectedly "But…yeah…"

Lucy raises a hand "I can too. I'm no expert by any means, but I should be able to fly us at least to the nearest town."

"Assuming nothing has happened to it." Celeste mutters.

Reno nods his approval and raises his voice slightly. "Okay, everyone should get some rest, and then we can start the search."

Everyone just mumbles before finding someplace comfortable.

Reno checks his bag. They're out of rations. He sighs and leans back against the wall.

"Hey, Amari?" Lucy says quietly.

"Hmm?"

"Where is my brother? I want to see him." Lucy asks quietly.

Amari points at the door. "He's in the next office over. I put him under a heavy freezing enchantment to preserve him."

"Thank you." Lucy gets back to her feet and proceeds out of the med bay to visit her brother's remains.

Amari leans back and relaxes, watching Shaide as she thinks back to better times.

*　　*　　*

 A.S.GUINN

ETERNAL KNIGHTS OF EDEN II

Reno jerks awake from the chair he was napping in and looks around. Lania is asleep on the cot beside him. The infirmary was short on beds, so Reno just slept in the chair beside Lania. He looks at his girlfriend with a slight smile, noting how cute she looks while sleeping. He then feels his stomach rumble.

"Crap, I'm hungry…"

He notices that everyone else is still asleep, so he quietly gets to his feet and leaves the med bay, heading for the nearest supply storage area and praying it survived. He was stationed here for a short time, so he knows the layout of the base.

He comes to a locked door and frowns, pulling out his sword and busting it open. The ceiling has caved in on the back half of the supply room, but to his relief, the food is stored near the entrance. He finds a massive stockpile of dried rations and, although not the most delicious things in the world, he grabs a crate and loads it with an assortment of different foods and heads back to the med bay.

When he re-enters the room, Celeste jerks awake and looks at him and mumbles sleepily, "What's that?"

Reno raises it for a moment before setting it down. "Preserved food. We used up our rations, so I found more."

"I'm fine eating preserved food and living rough," Celeste groans, heading over to get some dried meat. "but I would kill for a hot meal right now."

Reno nods "Yeah, honestly, me too."

Over the course of the next half hour, the remaining members of their group slowly wake up.

After eating a quiet breakfast, Reno stands up "Okay we need to head out and start searching for a way to get…well…somewhere. Lucy, Nyu, and Celeste? I think the four of us should go while Amari and Lania remain here."

Amari doesn't argue about remaining behind with Shaide. Reno notes that she is holding his hand while he is unconscious. They have to get help very fast. Being unconscious, he hasn't had anything but fluids for over a week now. He won't survive forever like this.

"Why do I have to stay here?" Lania asks, looking hurt.

Reno gives her a soft look as he explains "You're the only other medic here. I need you to look after Shaide for me. Can you do that, please? For me?"

Lania sighs explosively, but she looks at him affectionately. "It's a good thing I like you. Yeah, I can do that for you."

Celeste rolls her eyes "For Eden's sake, you're going to make me sick."

Nyu chuckles quietly.

The four of them gather their gear and weapons, and then head out through the command building and out into the fortress grounds. Reno looks around at the shattered remains of his most recent deployment and lowers his head for a moment. Once called Hell's Doorstep due to its proximity to the deadlands, the landscape now looks like something straight out of hell itself.

"Come on. We should move." Reno says quietly, leading them out across the ruins and out onto the landscape beyond the walls. His first target is the carrier ARV *Hive of Fire* He's choosing this vessel first not only because it is a carrier-class warship with plenty of smaller ships aboard, but also because it is the closest ship not completely disintegrated.

Celeste taps Reno on the shoulder and whispers, "By the way, when did you get so take-charge? You're usually more of a go-with-the-flow kind of guy."

Reno shrugs "Everyone else seems just sort of lost and confused. Someone had to, and I'm not just going to stand around while my best friend is dying."

"Hey, I'm not complaining." Celeste says with a slight grin. "I'm just surprised. That's all that I'm saying."

As they approach the carrier, Lucy nods her approval. "Carrier. Good idea. With the number of ships aboard, the odds of finding one intact are much higher."

The hanger bay is gratefully fairly close to the ground. Nyu summons Tau and rides him as he leaps into the hanger bay, then she throws down a rope for the others to climb aboard.

Reno comes up last behind Celeste and Lucy, and then looks around the hanger bay. His heart sinks almost immediately.

Nyu lowers her head "Well, I guess it was too much to hope anything survived. This thing looks like it hit pretty hard, and most of the ships were probably airborne for... whatever happened out there."

The hanger bay is nearly empty. Only a half dozen dropships remain, and none of them are in one piece. They go ahead and investigate the dropships anyway, just in case one is at least barely operable, but no such luck.

As they disappointedly climb back out of the hanger bay and drop to the ground, Reno looks off to the south. Deep black storm clouds are building in the distance, and Reno's gaze lingers on them for a moment.

"Hey, leader. Come on. Where do we go next?" Celeste asks, looking nervously at the building storms as well.

For several hours they go from intact ship to intact ship, looking for absolutely anything they can use, but luck doesn't seem to be in their favor. They comb through cruisers, destroyers, and even small frigates hoping SOMETHING survived, but alas, most of the smaller ships are crashed along the landscape, and it is clear that most of the smaller transports were in use during whatever happened to cause all of this.

Nyu points ahead at the Ceraph frigate they are now heading towards as the sun sets on the horizon. She comments "It's the *Last Beacon*. That's our ship."

The hull is shredded and scattered, but the superstructure appears miraculously intact. Reno nods and says "Come on. This is the last one for today. Let's give it a shot."

When they get close, they can see that the ship took extremely heavy fire. Burn marks from magicore cannon rounds are all over what's left of the ship, but the frame is in surprisingly good condition. It even still appears to have trace amounts of power left as he can see light flickering in the shadows.

Unfortunately, getting to the hanger won't be easy. The hanger deck is twenty feet above them.

"It looks like we'll have to make our way there through the corridors." Celeste remarks, pointing at a hull breach at ground level.

"Got it!" Celeste yells, climbing down.

Lucy looks around as all of the instruments come to life. "Okay. Let's just hope the engines work.

As Celeste reenters the troop bay, Lucy sends power to the turbines. With a slight screaming sound, the six turbines on the outside of the dropship spin to life.

"Okay, cut us loose and I can take us back to the fort."

Celeste and Reno exchange nods and head out into the hanger. They break loose the chains holding the dropship to the deck before climbing back on board.

"Are we good?" Lucy asks.

Reno nods "Yeah, we're clear. Let's get back to the others."

With the pull of a lever, the screaming of the dropship engines intensifies drastically, and the dropship hovers off of the deck. Lucy nervously flies the vehicle out of the hanger bay and heads back towards the fortress.

Celeste sits down in response to the bucking deck beneath her: Lucy is not a particularly skilled pilot. "You know? This is definitely the roughest ride I've ever had on a dropship."

Reno chuckles "Even that time we crashed in the mountains?"

"I wasn't there for that." Celeste replies with an annoyed look.

Reno thinks to himself for a moment before replying "I guess you weren't. You've been with us for so long, I forget you weren't with us from the beginning."

"Nice..." Celeste rolls her eyes.

Reno looks off to the south again. The dark clouds have grown huge in the past few hours, and Reno is feeling concerned.

"Lucy, we should get back to the fort asap."

A voice echoes from the cockpit "I'm working on it. I said I knew how to fly these. I didn't say I was good."

Reno frowns as he looks south "What is that?"

Celeste looks out the back with him. Her vision is better than his, and her eyes open wide "It looks like… A cruiser? It's not one of ours though."

Reno looks across the battlefield for a moment, thinking. A huge battle occurred here, all of their warships are down, and there are a number of unidentified warships as well. Suddenly it clicks.

"Lucy! We have to get them and get out of here now!"

*   *   *

"They've been gone for a while. Do you think they'll find anything?" Lania asks Amari.

Amari changes the IV bottle on Shaide's bed before giving a response "I hope so. If they can't find something, we may all be on borrowed time.

Lania nods, looking determined. "Well, I believe in Reno. He's a little lazy and laid back at times, but he comes through for you when you need him."

Amari wrestles with some awkward feelings. She finally gathers up some courage and asks, "Lania? How DID you and Reno get together? I mean, I know I was kind of there, but still. You were friends, and now you're together. How did that happen exactly?"

Lania looks at Amari, and then at Shaide, before she smiles slightly. "I don't really know exactly. I think I had a crush on him for a while, but it just happened, and it felt right. I don't think either of us really planned it."

Amari has a bit of a sour look on her face. "Oh. I see."

Lania can't hold back a chuckle. "You know, I'm pretty certain that Shaide would NOT say no to you, no matter what you asked of him. The guy has been by your side pretty much ever since you two reunited, right?"

Amari turns bright red and looks surprised "I umm…well… yeah. More like I've been by his side. I'm not sure he needs me nearly as much as I need him. He is so strong he's taken on enemies that seem impossible and can even beat them alone. But me… I don't like to admit it, but I don't feel right if I'm not with him."

Lania looks at him on the bed and shakes her head "Sweetheart, I don't think this boy would even still be alive if you weren't there looking out for him. Look at the number of times I can remember you having to look after him after a fight."

Amari looks up at her "Do you really think that?"

"I do. Don't worry about it-" She's cut off by the sound of turbines outside. "They're back! And they found something!"

Reno comes rushing through the med bay door suddenly "Come on. We have to leave now. We have a huge problem.

CHAPTER 18

ANGELS FALL

Reno carries Shaide outside at a run with Amari and Lania hot on his heels. To the south, a single warship appears to be flying towards them.

"We have to get out of here now!" Reno yells, running on board the dropship.

Lania runs on board the dropship, and Amari pauses at the back hatch, looking south in confusion.

"Amari come on! We have to go!"

Amari climbs back on board the dropship as Lucy goes to liftoff.

Reno lays Shaide down on the floor and secures him as best he can. He looks to the cockpit and yells "Lucy! Let's go! Now!"

"I'm having a problem here!" She yells as the engines whine and sputter but won't engage.

"Come on! Come on, come on, come on!"

Lucy turns and yells over her shoulder "Hey, asshole? Yelling at me ISN'T HELPING!"

Reno looks out the troop bay as Lucy struggles to get the dropship airborne. "Damn. Too late!"

The large black warship decelerates as it lets a number of dropships loose from its hanger bay, as well as something else. The warship itself is huge. Somewhere between the size of a cruiser and a small carrier. The exterior is made from some shiny black metal with sharp angles, and the ship looks to be extremely heavily armored.

"Lucy! Keep working on it!" Reno runs out of the troop bay with Lania, Celeste, and Nyu right behind him.

Amari looks hesitantly at Shaide for a moment, and then she follows the others out.

The dropships land some distance away from them and open their rear doors. Immediately, hordes of almost zombie-like thralls rush out of the troop bays, spitting and snarling as they charge at the five defenders of the dropship.

Reno pulls his sword and roars a battle-cry, charging headlong into the oncoming horde. Celeste and Nyu follow right behind him as Amari raises her staff and hurls barrages of fireballs at the incoming horde to limit their approach. Lania crosses her hands and holds them straight out, channeling her aura as she quietly chants a series of spiritual enchantments to boost her allies speed, strength, and magic power.

Behind the horde, a black winged Daemon reminiscent of a devil lands and allows a familiar man to dismount. Regal dismounts behind Lucien and summons Cancer beside him, but they hang back for some reason.

The thralls throw themselves into the wall of fire that Amari is trying to maintain, burning themselves to ash but continuing on as if rabid.

Nyu is projects a purple glyph as she yells back "Amari! Summon Theta!"

A deep black shadow cat emerges from the circle with a roar, and proceeds to violently tear into the oncoming horde.

Amari grimaces. She was hoping to preserve her aura, but they are at a severe disadvantage at the moment. She raises her hand and a familiar orange glyph appears above her hand, and mirrors in the sky above.

With more effort than she is used to, Theta the Phoenix screams a battle screech as he divebombs from the clouds and lets loose a tremendous ball of flame that incinerates a good portion of the incoming horde, and even manages to burn a dropship as it lifts off.

"Yeah!" Reno yells as he swings violently and cleaves a thrall in half.

Celeste hits, slashes, and impales thrall after thrall in an elegant dance of death. She yells at Reno "Hey! Have you noticed!?"

Reno grits his teeth and yells back "Yeah! I have!"

Many of the attacking thralls are wearing tattered Alastair Royal Army and Navy uniforms. Reno feels a sick feeling in his gut when he realizes that he is fighting his former comrades.

Nyu ducks and weaves, electing to use daggers in close quarters like this as she yells "I think we know what happened to all of the troops who were here!"

A sword suddenly comes out of nowhere and grazes Reno's face, leaving a shallow cut across his cheeks and the bridge of his nose. He reels back in pain and lashes out, sword hitting another sword.

A newcomer snarls at him as they lock swords. "I was sure that would get you. You're faster than you look, fatso!"

Reno stomp kicks the man back as he simultaneously hits a thrall with his armored elbow "Don't call me fat, asshole!"

Blade-on-blade echoes nearby and Celeste yells "RENO! WE'VE GOT-"

"I BLOODY KNOW ALREADY! JUST FIGHT!" Reno screams in frustration, charging the swordsman with his own blade. They cross blades several times as Reno takes heavy wide swings. Normally this is easy to counter, but because of Reno's strength, he recovers much faster than most. In spite of this, his foe almost seems to be just playing with him.

The winged daemon watches Theta performing a number of strafing runs to hinder the horde of thralls, and then it suddenly lifts off and tackles Theta out of the air. They tumble to the ground inside of the horde, and Theta launches back into the air, hitting the daemon with a stream of fire. The daemon deflects the fire with some kind of barrier, and then counters with a stream of focused dark energy. Theta launches itself upward to dodge the attack and breathes a second stream of flame. The daemon seems to be enveloped by the fire this time, but then a stream of focused dark energy splits the flame and lands a direct hit on the phoenix.

Theta screeches as it disintegrates into a starburst of orange aura.

"THETA NO! DAMNIT!" Amari raises her staff and starts waving it in a slow circle, gathering and focusing light-blue magical aura into a tight ball the ball grows and grows to the size of a person's head. As the Daemon turns to face Amari, she screams in rage and hurls the ball at it with blinding speed.

The ball strikes the daemon and erupts in a deafening chain of explosions, spikes of ice erupting in a matching chain all throughout the daemon's body as it roars in rage. It drops to the ground and takes a knee, but somehow it doesn't disappear from existence.

In the back of the enemy formation, cancer seems to be gathering energy for some kind of attack, and Amari recognizes this with a start.

"We've got to stop that thing right now!" She screams.

*   *   *

Shaide's eyes open suddenly. He hears the sound of the battle outside and feels a sense of disorientation. His senses seem almost supercharged, and he can feel the mass of thralls outside, as well at the enemy Fallen and the daemons.

He sits up and feels something restraining him. He unfastens the belts holding him in place and gets to his feet. He notices Lucy in the cockpit struggling to get the dropship fired up, and with a pang he remembers Aton falling in battle. He closes his eyes, trying to contain his rage as he steps out of the troop bay and onto the battlefield.

As soon as he steps off, the dropship suddenly screams to life. Shaide ignores this and proceeds forward onto the battlefield, his eyes on Lucien at the back of the horde.

Amari turns her head and looks shocked "Shaide!? What the hell!? You're okay!"

Shaide looks at her and nods. He sees Cancer at the back, charging its self-destruction attack, and he braces his leg. He feels his spiritual aura surging to levels beyond anything he has ever felt before, and bright violet lines appear on his skin, crisscrossing all over him.

Amari backflip-kicks a thrall and smashes another's head with her staff as she yells "Shaide! What are you doing!"

Reno turns to see Shaide as well and almost goes into shock.

"GAME OVER!" Lucien's voice cackles across the field. Cancer's glow intensifies suddenly, and Amari braces herself for the explosion.

Whoosh…*TING*

In a streak of violet, Shaide suddenly disappears. At the exact same moment, a hole appears in the chest of the giant crab-like cancer, and with an earsplitting screech, the daemon vanishes.

At the same moment, Shaide reappears behind the creature as Lucien turns his head to see what happened.

Regal turns to look at the exact same moment, and before either of them can react, Shaide vanishes again. Lucien manages to block the nearly instantaneous attack, but a spray of bright crimson erupts from Regal as a deep gouge appears in his chest and shock crosses his face.

Shaide comes to a stop, and his gaze reaches the second daemon.

Lucien screams "Zodiac! Destroy him!"

Before the daemon can reply, however, Shaide disappears a third time, and reappears near Amari. Without any sign what happened, the daemon Zodiac roars a scream as it dispels from the battlefield.

Amari looks at Shaide in shock as he stabs his sword into the ground, and a powerful wave of violet energy erupts outward, enveloping everything aside from his allies, and clearing half of the battlefield in one go.

"Shaide? Is that really you?" She asks uncertainly. His aura feels different. Not unfriendly, but it definitely feels different.

Shaide lifts his skull mask and smiles surprisingly gently "Yes, it's me. Don't worry."

"I WAS worried. Worried sick! You've been unconscious for a week!"

As Lucien looks on in shock, trying to regain his composure as he sorts out what just happened, Shade sighs and lowers his gaze "I see. That explains a lot."

Amari looks at him with great concern on her face. "Are you okay?"

Shaide nods "For now. I need you to listen to me very carefully Amari."

Her eyes open wide as she listens to him.

"I need you and the others to get back on that dropship. Get out of here and warn the Citadel about what is coming."

Amari reaches out and puts a hand on his chest piece "I don't understand. What about you?"

Shaide turns his head and looks at Lucien. "I can buy you time. Besides, I have a score to settle."

"No way!" Amari yells. "I'm not letting you do that!"

"Amari please…" Shaide says sadly "The corruption has gotten into my body. I can feel it. There is no way we are all getting out of here, and I can give you the best chance."

A sudden streak of black, and Shaide turns just in time to block Lucien's twin swords as he attacks.

"You beat the archangel." Lucien cackles, his face inches from Shaide's as they strain against each other. "Impressive, VERY impressive. But I am afraid that now I cannot let you leave here. Now that you have seen what we are doing, we cannot allow ANY of you to leave."

Shaide strikes him in the ribs with his knee and pushes him back.

"GO!" He yells at Amari.

Amari disobeys and runs in, determined to work together with Shaide to take down the man who killed Aton.

Lucien cackles as he ducks and weaves, blocks and dodges, unable to land a single blow on Shaide himself, but likewise preventing either of them from landing a blow as well. Shaide slowly gets angrier and angrier as the violet lines on his skin grow slowly brighter.

Reno struggles against the remaining thralls as one gets him by the leg and takes him to the ground.

"SON OF A-" He yells as they pile on top of him.

Shaide suddenly explodes in a violent repulsive force, knocking both Lucien and Amari away from him.

"GAIA!"

A violet glyph circle appears on the ground around Shaide, and the familiar violet Archangel rises from the ground. At the same time, Tau is overcome by numbers and fades from existence.

Nyu screams "We need help!"

Immediately understanding Shaide's wishes, or perhaps this simply being her default move, Gaia throws her hands in a wide circle, assuming a t-pose, and a mammoth shockwave of violet energy erupts from her in a broad circle, expanding outward leaving all of Shaide's friends unharmed, but consuming the thralls, Formers, and Fallen, blowing them away and making them simply cease to exist.

All except for Lucien, who survives the wave and tumbles to his feet a short distance away.

Then something new happens.

With a roar of rage, a swirling black circle of pure dark energy forms around Lucien, and a black shadow takes over his body as he begins to change shape.

"Even that didn't kill him?" Shaide whispers in disbelief.

Gaia speaks unexpectedly. "Bahamut, he is a legacy of Belial. He isn't human!"

Shaide watches for a moment as the shape of black leathery wings erupt from Lucien's back, and a black dragon-like tail grows from his tailbone.

As Reno, Nyu, and Celeste run over, covered in minor to moderate wounds but still standing, Shaide realizes what he has to do, while he still can.

He puts his hands on Amari's shoulders and looks into her eyes as he says gently "There's something I need to tell you, and I think this will be my last chance."

Amari's eyes widen "Shaide! Now isn't really the time for-"

Shaide puts his hand behind her neck and pulls her face to his, planting his lips firmly on hers. All of the fight goes out of her all at once as Shaide gives her the thing she has wanted more than anything else for some time now. For a moment, everything around them seems to fade away as her mind goes blank from the first kiss she has ever had, from the man she loves more than anything.

As he breaks away, she looks at him with tears in her eyes, both of happiness and sadness.

"Amari, for as long as I've known you, I've loved you. I do love you, more than anything. I wish things could be different."

"What do you mean?" Amari asks. Suddenly her eyes bulge as Shaide chops her in the neck, rendering her unconscious.

Shaide closes his eyes "But this is goodbye... I'm sorry..."

"What did you just do!?" Reno yells as he, Celeste, Lania, and Nyu all run up to him.

Shaide holds up a limp Amari and hands her to Reno. "She's your responsibility now, brother. Get her out of here and get her to safety. I'm not letting these monsters take anyone else from me."

Reno takes her in his arms and looks at Shaide in shock "What the hell are you planning to do?!"

A swirl of pure white energy appears at Shaide's feet as he grabs Reno by the hand and looks him in the eyes. "You are the best friend I have ever had. I will never forget what you have done for me. Now take the girls and get out of here. Warn the Ceraphs, and make sure to punch Armstrong for me."

Reno squeezes his best friend's hand in return, tears running down his own face. "I will, Shaide."

"What's happening?" Nyu asks, confused.

Reno turns and runs for the ship "We have to go! NOW!"

Lania follows him, looking back at Shaide in confusion. Celeste and Nyu take off behind them, looking back at Shaide, not entirely understanding what is happening.

"Goodbye, friends. Thank you for everything."

As they board the dropship, Shaide turns to face the mutating Lucien.

Gaia hovers next to him and asks "Master Bahamut. Are you certain about this?"

Shaide gives her a funny look when she calls him Bahamut a second time, but he nods "Yes. It's the only way to ensure my friends are able to escape, so shut up and do it."

"As you wish, Master Bahamut." Gaia holds out her hands towards Shaide, and he herself turns into a brilliant violet light. The light swirling around Shaide intensifies, and a white glow overtakes his body, just like in the cavern.

He roars in pain as his body begins to change form. He grows in height as he sprouts a set of white wings that are both leathery and feathered. His head changes shape and takes on a strange cross between the face of a dragon and the face of a man. A white scaly tail grows from his tailbone as he takes on an incomplete mirror of Lucien across the fortress grounds.

Lucy turns around as everyone boards the dropship. "What in the hell is going on out there!?"

Reno yells, tears running down his face "Just get us the hell out of here!"

Lucy doesn't notice the missing passenger, and she throws the power into full and launches off of the battlefield.

Gaia's violet light streams into Shaide and becomes a part of him as the light dims, revealing his almost god-like white form. His glowing golden eyes open as Lucien launches some kind of energy blast at the dropship. In the blink of an eye, Shaide intercepts and deflects the attack.

"DAMN YOU CHILD OF EDEN! DO YOU REALIZE WHAT YOU ARE DOING!?" Lucien screams at him.

Shaide screams back "YOU KILLED MY GODFATHER! I DON'T CARE!"

In the blink of an eye, Shaide slams into Lucien, and the dragon-like and demon-like beings exchange a violent series of blows. Even with his power-up, it is taking everything Shaide has to keep up with the fully transformed Lucien.

"DON'T YOU GET IT?! YOU ARE A CHILD OF THE DEIFACTS! YOU COULD BE A GOD!" Lucien drags Shaide along the ground by his throat.

Shaide retorts, kicking Lucien off of him and blasting him with lightning "I AM THE CHILD OF LODRICK AND JUVIA

DARKMOON! AND YOU BASTARDS HAVE TAKEN EVERYTHING FROM ME!"

Lucien throws himself backwards and screams in rage "IF YOU WON'T GET OUT OF MY WAY, THEN I WILL JUST KILL ALL OF YOU!"

Lucien stands up legs and arms apart like an X as swirling black negative energy forms in front of him in a tightly winding ball. In his new form, Shaide can sense this ball contains more energy than anything he has ever seen in his life. If Lucien uses that…

"NOW DIE!"

The ball erupts in a violent stream of energy. Shaide throws up a barrier of light just in time, containing the blast as it continues to drill into him. The barrier flares and gleams, repelling the overwhelming attack if only just.

Shaide screams in agony and effort as he struggles to maintain the barrier. There is only one thing left he can do to save his friends. He begins channeling every scrap of energy in his body and soul, feeding on both Gaia and Rho's energy as well, focusing it all into a single point in the center of his body.

As the barrier begins to falter, Shaide closes his eyes and thinks of Amari one last time and says to himself. "Amari, I am so sorry I could not keep my promise. I love you." He pauses as the barrier falls and Lucien's attack slams into him.

"Goodbye."

*   *   *

The drop roars away at maximum throttle as Reno screams at Lucy to go faster, and she in turn screams that she is going as fast as she can.

Amari's eyes open and she sits up. She looks around in confusion for a moment before asking "Where is Shaide?"

No one answers her, their eyes on the ground.

"WHERE IS SHAIDE?"

Lania watching the energy fluctuations out the back of the dropship, just slowly point back towards the fortress.

Amari walks forward, not understanding. She hears a voice inside her head say one word.

"Goodbye."

In that moment, a blinding flash of light consumes the fortress. Everything around it seems to go black as everyone aboard the dropship screams.

A dome of vapor a half mile across appears instantly around the fortress, and as it clears, a gargantuan mushroom shaped cloud of fire and dust rises from where the fortress once stood.

Amari drops to her knees in complete shock as she feels Shaide's lifeforce disappear in the blink of an eye, the connection she has felt with him ever since joining the Ceraphs.

"Shaide?" She says blankly, before screaming "SHAIDE!"

A monster shockwave can be seen racing along the ground, rapidly catching up with the dropship. Reno closes his eyes in honor of his fallen friend for a moment, and the screams "LUCY! GO GO GO GO GO GO GO!"

Lucy looks over her shoulder as she flies with everything at maximum power "Come on, come on, come on! Crap crap crap crap crap… WE'RE NOT GOING TO MAKE IT."

The shockwave is nearly to the ship.

"BRACE FOR IMPACT! EVERYONE HOLD ON! EVERYONE JUST HOLD ON!"

*   *   *

Silence echoes across the land as the dust settles in the aftermath of the doomsday-level explosion consumed the remains of Hell's Doorstep and everything around it.

Lucien, back in his human form, shakes his head as he rises from the dust over a mile from where he fought with Shaide. He looks at the massive glass crater where he stood only a short time ago, and then closes his eyes.

"I really did not want to kill you. Father would have loved to have you join us, but instead you chose to defend these damn mud-monkeys." Lucien sighs and shakes his head. "A damn shame."

The heavy cruiser he had accompany him, the *Principle of Domination,* was nothing more than vapor now. He laments the loss of Regal, but in the end, he was only a Fallen. He can be replaced.

Lucien raises his hand and re-summons Zodiac to the ruins of the battlefield. "Come on. Our job here is done. Let's go home."

He climbs on Zodiac's back and sets off to the south back to where Borealis waits on his report.

Across the ruins of the battlefield, a single object survives the blast. A black sword, made of Termer craftsmanship out of a hybrid metal of ebony and obsidian, sticks vertically out of the ground unscratched and unblemished where its master once stood.

Shaide gave everything, but his friends escaped, and Ceraph could not hope for a finer end.

     A.S.GUINN

CHAPTER 19

IN MEMORIAM

A short time later, Lucy sets the dropship down in the recently rebuilt town of Lone Ridge: the town they saved from a dragon attack only a few short months ago. To the survivors of Hell's Doorstep, it seemed so long ago…

Amari remains in her seat, staring blankly at the floor. She hasn't moved or uttered a single word since they witnessed the complete destruction of the fortress, and Shaide along with it.

Reno feels numb himself, the loss of his best friend not quite feeling real yet. The army contingent at Lone Ridge gathers around the dropship curiously, sensing something amiss, but he doesn't immediately register their presence.

Sergeant Luna Wyatt approaches the back of the dropship to meet them "Ceraphs, Exorcists. It is a pleasant surprise to see you again. What brings you here?"

Celeste puts a hand on her older sister's shoulder and shakes her head "Now isn't the time, sis. Let them grieve. I'll tell you everything in private."

Sergeant Wyatt would normally not tolerate her sister's tone, but she senses the absolute seriousness in her voice, and she accompanies her as she walks away. "What happened, Celeste?"

Celeste gives her a pain-stricken look as she replies. "Hell's Doorstep has fallen, and…" She takes a deep breath and closes her eyes "We lost two very good friends there. The Ceraphs Atondier Norvus and Shaide Darkmoon…"

Sergeant Wyatt stops in her tracks, stunned "Shaide Darkmoon? The Reaper?"

Celeste nods, still not meeting her sister's gaze. "Yes, the very same."

Sergeant Wyatt looks completely shocked as she takes in what Celeste just told her. She slowly nods as she processes what she just heard. "I will make sure he is remembered."

Celeste nods "Leave them be for now. Amari, Lucy, and Reno in particular are taking it really hard."

Sergeant Wyatt nods "Very well. Now, what about Hell's Doorstep?"

Celeste explains to her sister the events that transpired as they walk away from the landing platform.

　　　　　　　A.S.GUINN

Back at the dropship, Lania walks Reno out of the dropship as he is only half-aware of his surroundings. "Sir? We've been through the worst kind of ordeal. Is there somewhere quiet we can go and rest?"

The soldier nods "Right this way, ma'am."

Lucy sits in the pilot's seat of the dropship and just stares out the viewport, trying to process the loss of both her twin brother, and the boy she'd helped raise since he was a child. She feels as if she has lost everything, and she isn't quite sure if it is even real yet.

"Come on, Amari, out we go. You need to be somewhere private. Not here." Nyu, her face streaked with tears herself, coaxes Amari out of her seat and slowly leads her down the ramp and follows Lania and Reno.

Not too long after, Lucy walks down the ramp and follows her fellows.

*   *   *

Several hours later, Amari, Celeste, Lania, Lucy, Nyu, and Reno all sit in the infirmary of the Lone Ridge Alastair Royal Military outpost after having their wounds treated. Amari has still not said a word since Shaide fell, and it seems unlikely that she will speak again anytime soon.

Celeste enters the infirmary, walks over to Amari, kneels down, and pulls her into a hug. "I am so sorry, Amari. I know nothing I can say will ease the pain, but I am so sorry for what you've lost. I heard what he said right before… it happened. I'm so sorry…"

Amari says only one thing, her eyes locked ahead as tears run down her face. "I never even had the chance to tell him I loved him too…"

Celeste squeezes her one again and leaves her alone, knowing she needs time to grieve. She looks around the room and observes Reno leaning on Lania's shoulder, Nyu staring out the window, and Lucy drinking from a bottle that she strongly suspects is alcohol.

"Reno. Lania. I know that now isn't the time, but we have new orders."

Reno looks up at her and shakes his head "I won't take orders from Alastair anymore. Their pissing fight with the Ceraphs cost my best friend and Aton their lives. I'm joining the Ceraphs."

Lania nods "Me too. After seeing how little lives really matter to the higher ups, I can't go back. Not now."

Celeste has an odd bitter grin on her face as she replies "I thought you might say that. I told my sister the very same thing. She yelled at me for a minute, but then she dropped it, saying she understands."

Reno forces himself to focus as he asks, "What do we do now?"

Celeste shrugs "I honestly don't know. I say we take some time. Cope with…everything that has happened."

"No, we can't do that." Lucy says, setting down the bottle and getting to her feet, surprisingly steady. "I need to take time to grieve as well, but we don't have that luxury. They gave their lives so we could continue fighting and protecting this world, and we have to warn the order what's coming."

"What's coming?" Reno asks, confused.

Celeste shakes her head "You're really not that bright sometimes. The corrupted have warships. Judging from the unique design and our annihilated fleet, they have a fleet of their own. War is coming."

Reno shudders "So it's too much to hope that we won't lose anyone else?"

Lania hugs Reno tightly "Let's just make sure we both make it."

"Let's make sure all of us make it." Reno corrects her.

"Agreed." Says Celeste.

Amari simply stares at nothing, reliving her last moment with him in her mind over and over, grieving over her loss, and that she never even got to tell him she loved him too, or even tell him goodbye…

*   *   *

Admiral Harris stands aboard the bridge of the flagship dreadnaught ARV *Vengeance of Temenos* as he overlooks the landscape of south Alastair from twenty-thousand feet. He is very troubled by recent events and has the entire remaining Iron Veil fleet at full combat alert.

"Admiral, I have a report."

Adm. Harris walks over to the communication station and leans over. "Let's hear it, warrant officer."

The female communications officer looks at her CO with a pained look. "Admiral, we have lost contact with the scouting flotilla sent to investigate Hell's Doorstep. They are now a full twenty-four hours overdue for check in. Captain Jaeger is presuming them lost and requests further orders, Admiral."

Harris clenches his fists. It has been over a week since they lost contact with all three of their border fortresses. The Ceraphs he allowed to pass have also gone silent, and he is beginning to fear the worst. They have sent two wolfpack flotillas of frigates to investigate, but both wolfpacks have fallen silent as well, creating a very high level of tension in the command structure.

"Orders, Admiral?" The comm officer asks uncertainly, but he does not immediately respond.

The Admiral walks to the forward viewport and looks across the landscape once again. Something is happening at the capital. He has requested additional support from the home fleet, but every time he does, he is told that by order of Queen Ilium, they cannot send any reinforcements. What does the capital know that he doesn't?

The comm officer suddenly jumps to her feet "Admiral Harris, Sir! We have a report coming in from Lone Ridge! You will want to hear this, sir!"

Commander Lane rebukes the comm officer "Warrant Officer Jarvis, watch your attitude when you-" The Admiral waves him down.

"Jarvis. Put it on."

She nods and connects the comm speaker for the bridge to hear.

"Admiral Harris, this is Sergeant Luna Wyatt, acting commanding officer of the 41st Exorcist Corps. I am declaring emergency code Black Dusk. Hell's Doorstep has fallen, and all hands are lost, and it appears that an unknown fleet is responsible for the

 A.S.GUINN

destruction. We have recovered the surviving Ceraphs who were sent on a classified mission and, if their story is true, we will need every scrap of backup we can scrape together. I say again, I am enacting emergency code Black Dusk. Please respond immediately. We are in desperate need of assistance."

The bridge is deathly silent as all eyes turn to the Admiral as he stares at the comm station deep in thought.

"Sir, Black Dusk, isn't that-?"

Commander Lane answers "Yes. Black Dusk is the code indicating a mass-corruption level threat. It is a code that is only to be used if war is imminent."

The Admiral continues in deep thought, debating his next course of action.

The commander walks over to him and stands at attention. "Sir? We need orders."

The admiral snaps out of his reverie and nods, a determined look on his face. "Commander. Give the order. We are taking the fifth fleet to Lone Ridge in force. I want to know what those Ceraphs found down there, and I don't believe Corallina is going to help us. Order the Seventh fleet to remain here at maximum alert, and close down the pass completely. No one in, and no one out."

"Understood, sir!" The commander moves to the comm station and has Jarvis pull hail the fifth fleet.

The Admiral addresses the bridge in a clear voice. "Men and women of the Alastair Royal Navy. Something is happening that threatens the lives of our comrades and fellow countrymen, and I intend to find out what it is and put a stop to it. If the reports are true, something is moving in the shadows that possesses the capability to down an entire fleet and destroy one of our most well-equipped fortresses. I will not lie to you, there is a chance we will not all make it through this crisis alive. However, we are sons and daughters of Alastair. Protectors of Queen Ilium and servants of the god Eden. As long as threats exist to our families and our way of life, we will not allow these threats to continue. We are Alastair!"

The men and women aboard the bridge stand up and shout "SIR!", the nervous atmosphere of a moment before disappearing almost entirely. They are ready.

"Should we send a message to the Capital?" Commander Lane asks.

The Admiral shakes his head "No. I fear our communication security may be compromised. If something IS happening down there, I don't want them to risk knowing we are coming."

"Understood."

The Admiral turns and resumes his watch as his fleet prepares to move out. "I'll be damned if anyone will threaten my nation while I am in charge."

*   *   *

Sergeant Wyatt leans back in her chair as she waits for a response from Iron Veil. "Why aren't they answering? It's been hours…"

Reno stands beside her as he fidgets restlessly himself. His grief and rage have him itching for action, but so far, he has been trapped here in Lone Ridge unable to do a thing.

Nyu walks into the command center with Celeste, and they make their way to Reno.

"How is Amari doing?" He asks with concern.

Celeste shakes her head, looking more depressed than he has ever seen her. "She still isn't speaking, and she refuses to eat or drink too. She just stares out that window."

"Give her time." Reno says, not quite believing his own words. "Shaide was my best friend, so I kind of know how she feels. Ceraph or not, you don't bounce back from this that easily."

Nyu lowers her head and looks up at him with a serious expression not usually seen on her face. "And what about you? How are YOU doing?"

Reno turns around and hides his face as anger crosses his usually kind features. "I'm doing okay. I don't have time for grief right now."

"Oh really?" Nyu leans around him and looks up at his face. "Because you know, I can literally smell the anger and grief on you, and you smell almost as grief stricken as her."

Reno's eyes tear up as he hears her words, and he quietly responds "Of course I'm angry, and of course it hurts, but I can't let that control me right now. If I do, and I do something stupid, then his sacrifice will be for nothing."

"Right..." Nyu mutters, looking slightly ashamed.

Celeste puts a hand on Nyu's arm "Hey, come on. We should leave him alone for now. Let's go check on the others."

Nyu puts a hand on Reno's shoulder and nods "You know where we are if you need us."

Reno stands next to Sergeant Wyatt in the command center for several hours. As night begins to fall, Reno closes his eyes and turns to leave.

The comm panel comes to life *"Lone Ridge outpost, this is the ARV* Tower Rampart. *We have multiple contacts coming in fast. Attempting to contact."*

Reno runs over to the comm panel as Wyatt picks up the microphone "ARV *Tower Rampart*, this is Sergeant Wyatt. Understood."

"Patching them through."

A vaguely familiar voice comes across the comm panel. *"Lone Ridge command, this is Admiral Harris, currently commanding the Alastair fifth fleet. We are arriving to provide your requested support. If those Ceraphs are there, I would very much like to speak with them as soon as I arrive."*

Sergeant Wyatt scrambles to reply "Yes, Admiral. Thank you very much. Things are looking bad. We will be ready for you when you arrive!"

"Thank you, Lone Ridge. Admiral Harris out."

Sergeant Wyatt looks up at Reno. "I know you're technically refusing orders, but I need you to do me a favor, Coltide."

Reno already knows what she is going to ask "Not a problem, Sarge. I'll let them know."

Reno turns and jogs out of the command center.

*   *   *

ETERNAL KNIGHTS OF EDEN II

Amari looks wistfully out the window, lost in memories of a time that now seems so far away. She remembers the day she first met Shaide, and the gravity of what she felt upon meeting him.

Lodrick Darkmoon shakes hands with Koraru Tamiel outside of their Erita mansion. "Koraru, thank you so much for agreeing to look after him for us. There was no one in the capital who could do so."

Juvia smiles and nods "Also, we thought it would be good for him to experience another culture. Help him avoid the racism becoming far too common these days."

Koraru Tamiel smiles a rare smile in the presence of his friends "It is not a problem at all. Our little Amari has little in the way of friends, so having someone to play with her might be very good for her. Come on out, Amari. Stop being timid."

Amari leans out from behind her mother and sees a ten-year-old Mitera boy looking at her. With some encouragement from her mother, she steps out and says shyly "Hi, I'm Amari."

The boy bows politely and replies "I'm Shaide. It's a pleasure to meet you."

Amari notices his gaze lingering on her hair, and she puffs up rather defensively "What's wrong? Does something about me look funny to you?"

Her elder sister, Anika, watches the exchange with an amused expression.

Shaide, undeterred, shakes his head and smiles "No, I was just thinking that I like your hair. It's very pretty. I've never seen anything like it before!"

Koraru and Aria exchange amused glances. He could just be being polite in front of them, but he seems sincere.

"Yeah, and I bet... Wait, what did you say?" Amari is taken aback as she realizes what he said.

Shaide walks forward and touches it for a moment, an earnest expression on his face. "I said it's very pretty. I've never seen anyone with hair quite like it."

She blinks in surprise, feeling a sense of elation and joy rising in her for the first time in a long time. She grabs him by the hand "Come on, let me show you around the house!"

Shaide looks over his shoulder in amusement "Bye mom! Bye dad!"

Looking back on it now, Amari realizes she may have been falling in love with him from their very first meeting. The first boy she had ever met that not only wasn't bothered by her unusual appearance, but rather seemed to embrace it. If she had only realized it sooner, and told him how she felt, would he maybe still be alive? Would things have happened differently?

Lania leans over and hugs Amari gingerly around the shoulders "Come on, you've got to eat something, or at least drink. You can't just give up and waste away here."

Lucy stares into the bottom of her bottle, mourning the end of her liquor in addition to her grief.

Moments later, however, Reno suddenly bursts into the room. "The fifth fleet is arriving. Admiral Harris will be down to speak with us soon."

Amari finally seems to return to Eden. She gets to her feet, surprising everyone in the room. She feels a sense of determination now that she knows what she wants to do.

"Amari? Are you sure you're okay?"

Amari struggles to find her voice, and it cracks slightly as she speaks. "It hurts… God it hurts more than anything I have ever felt, but I don't think he would want this."

Celeste, Lania, Lucy, Nyu, and Reno all watch her, listening intently.

She continues, a tear running down one cheek. "I want nothing more than to lay down and just give up, and just sleep until it's over. But I can't. I want to find the ones responsible for what happened to Shaide and make them pay for what they took from me."

Amari's aura begins to burn a bright magenta around her as her anger and grief become visible.

"But Amari, Shaide took them out with in that final moment. Nothing could have survived that."

Amari shakes her head and continues as her aura calms down. "No. Even if they are dead, someone is pulling the strings. I want to find the cause of all of this and end it. For good. Once I have made them pay for him, then I can rest."

Reno feels a sense of inspiration behind her words. It's a tall order, but he agrees with every word she says. He walks over and stands in front of her, a proud expression on his face.

"Amari, never have I heard truer words in my life. I'm with you."

Lania walks over and takes Reno's hand "If you go, I'm going too. Shaide was my friend as well."

Celeste puts a hand on both Reno and Amari's shoulders "Impossible odds? Avenging our friend? Blood and death lining the road ahead? Count me in."

"I'm not letting you have all of the bloody revenge." Nyu purrs. "I'm coming too."

Lucy looks at her bottle for a moment and tosses it aside. "I'm in as well. I won't be able to sleep until the bastards that took my family have paid."

Amari looks taken aback at the unexpected level of support she is receiving. "This is not going to be a pleasant campaign. We're talking about flushing out the root of the corruption and taking the fight to it. This is a suicide mission, and I'm not expecting to come out of this in one piece."

Reno looks at Amari with a serious, almost pitying look on his face. "Amari, we were all close to him, and we are all friends. If you want to do this, we are doing it together. Shaide would never let us rest if we let you die alone. With all of us, we just might succeed."

Amari looks at her friends, feeling hope at the edge of her grief for the first time in days. She looks at the loyal, loving faces standing around her, and she nods. "Alright. They started it. Let's finish this fight."

Continue the adventure in
ETERNAL KNIGHTS OF EDEN III: ARISE

 A.S.GUINN